TELLAFROG TWO

TORIN MACRATH

TORIN MACRATH

I would like to dedicate this series to all of my family and friends. Without them and all of the lessons, both good and bad, my wonder at the world would not be what it is. A very special thanks to my beautiful wife, who quite literally, took what I wrote and made it into something we could share. It was no small feat, as I had never written before and neither of us had any experience with editing, formatting, copyrights, etc. Thanks, shorty, I love you three much!

CONTENTS

PROLOGUE

I n my previous work, I detailed the beginning of my en-
tanglement with parts of our shared history and world
that I, Raileanu Tellafrog, a man born into the magical
world, did not know before the events explained in that
volume. The origins of magic were explained; indeed, the
facts laid bare by those events showed an older world
than we knew had forged magic by methods still unclear
to me, and perhaps by even more ancient civilizations
before that. Most startling of all was that magic was created by ordinary peoples, by a form of technology that
we may be heading towards again in our lifetime. Beings
described long ago, the High Elves, now relegated to our
shelves of mythical tomes, were not only among us, but
their continued vigilance was necessary for the survival
of us all, magical and ordinary alike.

The process of my becoming involved in these events
was at a high cost; both my parents had been killed by
an ancient relic, or more correctly, by those in our world

seeking those artifacts to hold sway over the whole of mankind. Many more died surrounding that one brief encounter with one of these Orbs, and having lost all but one of the people I cared deeply for, I agreed to assist - if by casual observance only - the guardians who seek these ancient tools. Before I could return home to Texas, I would have to attend the funeral of a brave soldier in the truest sense of the word. Not a wandering soul that found himself in the service of a nation in exchange for a hot meal and some discipline. No, a true soldier knows almost from the earliest stage that their duty to God, to the world, their very design, is to place themselves between the ruthless and the helpless, their bone and blood be the shield that protects the innocent. That was my friend, Arterous Metternich, whose funeral I must attend before I can leave Austria for home. For Texas.

CHAPTER ONE

T he meeting between Arterous Metternich's father and mother and me was to take place at a small country estate just east of Vienna, the morning before his funeral. Monika Binder, my newly announced fiancée, helped me with the tailor, so my attire was well-suited to the status of his family and the seriousness of the appointment. Being born and raised in Texas, I have spent most of my time in wild places of the earth seeking to understand the intricate links and balances of the natural world and the connection to what we refer to as 'magical'. Therefore, I was at a significant disadvantage in matters of the Royal Court. Monika was familiar with the customs, and I was so grateful for her help. I was very nervous. Arterous's assignment to be my personal protection was the cause of his passing. His funeral would be the first time I had met them, and the occasion was awful.

Monika ensured that I was dressed as a formal member of the royal family's court, with the appropriate regalia for the titles of Advisor to the Counsellor and Professor, titles bestowed upon me before Arterous and me went to Texas by Klement Metternich, Counsel to the Emperor of Austria. No title or position protected my father, mother, Bandos, Father Callious, or Arterous, nor the Digger family. They all fell to the designs of an ancient artifact, the hands of aggrieved Comanches, and an assassin sent by a dark witch. Arterous's parents know this, and so the formal attire felt heavy and pointless to me. I honestly couldn't describe the uniform, its cords, or medals. I thought it was a formality and the proper way to show respect to them and express my appreciation for Arterous's sacrifice. My mind was focused on ignoring the regalia and on meeting the parents of my friend, who died in the wilds, having sworn to protect me.

While Monika was making sure the uniform was correct and adjusting the plumage on the headwear, a butler of Klement's house knocked on the thick oak door frame to the room.

"Sir, madam, the carriage has arrived," he said.

"Thank you, we will be right down," I said, walking away from the fastidious Monika. "You know I am expected to meet them alone for this, my dear. I am grateful you have agreed to travel with me, you're my only family now, and I don't want to be without you a minute longer than I must."

"I will be with you every chance the world allows, darling." She smiled and reached around my waist to attach the saber belt, buckling it in the front.

"I am NOT wearing this helmet thing in the carriage." I took it off, looking at it in disbelief. "It looks like a rooster nailed to the bottom of a cooking pot."

"You ARE wearing it in the carriage, at least until we leave the city boundary," she said firmly. "That is the Metternich carriage, and you are in an official position now. And you will have to run a comb through that hair before you go in to meet them. You can say all the argumentative things you want to me, it will not change the outcome of the ceremonial procedure of this day," she said, stuffing a coarse-toothed comb into her handbag.

She may have a point. My hair was dark brown, full but not thick, and was all about the same length, falling just to the edge of my shoulders. Plus, the trip would be about an hour on dirt roads, so it would likely be unruly and dusty by the time we arrived. Fiddling with it now seemed pointless, but if it made her feel better, that was fine.

"Let's go downstairs now, we need to arrive before midday, they have further funeral details to make before it begins this afternoon," she said, picking up her parasol and handbag.

We went down the back staircase from the third-floor room to the ground floor, through the formal reception hall, to the foyer, and out the front doors of the Metternich's home. I usually spend a few minutes whenever I walk through their home, taking time to appreciate the craftsmanship of every fixture, noticing something new each time. Today, however, I was so uncomfortable in the uniform, nervous about the impending meeting of

Arterous's parents, and concerned about seeing such a heroic man laid to rest that I only knew for a short time. I recall not looking at anything other than where I was walking, and trying not to mark anything with the flared end of the ceremonial saber scabbard on the way out the front doors.

Once out front, under the rounded, aged green copper plate walkway cover, the butler opened the door to the open-top carriage, and I held Monika's hand as she stepped up and into the seat. I boarded, and as the butler closed the door, he leaned in closer to me and whispered, "Raileanu, sir, it will be alright, no need to be nervous. Arterous's parents are excellent, gentile folk, and were here the day after he left for Texas to assist you. They were very proud of his volunteering to be of service to you." His name escaped me, but the look in his eye was quite serious, and he meant every word. "Being Prussian aristocrats, both are well satisfied that he fell in combat defending the helpless. Did you know they are descendants of the Hospitallers? They only want to hear the details of his valor in his last moments. You have nothing to fear. Also, your hat is under the seat." He gave me a little smile and a wink.

"Thank you, sir." I reached my hand out to shake his hand, which he complied with. "I will see you tonight."

The driver looked back to confirm we were ready, and then looked forward and used the leads to usher the horses off. The shoes of the horses began their click-clacking down the brick road, to the end of the block, and then turned right, heading to the main road leading east out of town.

The morning began with low wisps of bright white clouds slowly wandering through the sky, temporarily cool, as the sun was already warming the atmosphere, and the heat from the road surface and buildings was rising. It was the first days of September now, so enjoying the warmth of the day on the ride over was a good idea, as the north winds would begin in a few weeks. I had been injured in an event when I was twelve that left me with no magical abilities whatsoever. I gained a heightened sense of smell and hearing. It was all twenty-three years ago now, and I have learned only to use it when needed. However, with the knowledge that I would soon be leaving Austria, I couldn't help but try to remember every scent and sound. Passing vendors on the road and shopkeepers setting up their tables of wares lined both sides of the path as we neared the city's unpaved area, showcasing the harvest and products they made in and around Vienna, with several musicians filling the warm air with music from their handcrafted violins and cellos. That reminded me of the lady I met upon arriving via Runewheel just two days ago.

"Monika, do you know Haizek Moon?" I asked her when she had finished enjoying the music of the last artist on our way out.

"Yes, she was a music instructor. She was gifted to master any music, song, instrument, or writing of the acoustical powers in magic." I looked at her, pushed my chin up, and was impressed. She smiled back. "She has invented over a dozen new instruments, and it is rumored that a visit she once had with Benjamin Franklin at a gala in Paris led him to create the glass armonica."

"What's a glass harmonica? Why would someone put a glass instrument in their mouth?" I asked, confused at the fragility of glass being used in a person's mouth. During more than one expedition abroad, the fragility of glass vials and jars and the like was always too apparent. Roads that seemed smooth and well-maintained to me had revealed the lack in my packaging skills and materials all too often, so I was eager to make the fearful connection between glass and one's mouth.

Helpless to control laughter at my ignorance, Monika tried at least twice to stop giggling at me before finally composing herself. "Armonica. Not, harmonica. It's a device like a lathe, a spinning wooden rod to which glass, um, bowls are affixed horizontally." She motioned her hands apart, in a wide "C" shape. "Wetting one's hands, fingers are allowed to rub against the spinning glasses of different sizes, creating quite a heavenly sound." She giggled again when she finished, her cheeks red with a broad smile under the shade of the sun parasol she had wisely brought along.

"Oh, I understand. Well, do try to protect me from myself today, and don't hesitate to smile like that at my expense again. I love it when you smile."

The carriage had moved to the dusty, dry roadway now, and the vendors and merchants had disappeared; now, only the occasional farmer was selling vegetables and fruits from oxcarts. The yellowing grasses along the roadside, brittle and dry from the summer, loosed tiny fragments that swirled and swept across the path with small gusts of sun-heated ground, circulating and mixing with downdrafts from the alpine passes. Once we entered a section of the road shaded by firs and pines, I took off my helmet and set it beside me, then reached under the seat to put on my hat.

"You know, as silly as you think that helmet looks, your hat from Texas looks even more ridiculous to anyone who happens to notice it. Just be forewarned. They will not assume you, or anyone of stature in this whole nation, would wear that. And you will NOT be wearing that within a mile of the Metternich's estate," she said, and meant it. I continued to look off to my side of the carriage, not ignoring her directive, but not conceding it either. Besides, the sun had nearly cooked my head in that steel pot.

The trip alternated between woods and lush meadows with the last flowering colors of summer, to switchgrass and cattails next to streams, the sound of the horses and carriage wheels steady, save for the occasional mortared stone bridges over little rivers. It took just over an hour, according to the pocket watch Klement had given me just a month ago. When we emerged from the final wood and crossed into the broad valley of planted barley surrounding the Metternich manor, I hid my hat under the seat and put on the helmet. The wind kept gusting from behind, faster than the carriage moved forward, blowing the plumage into my face, but I was a trooper and ignored it.

The road surface also changed from dirt to sand with a layer of fine gravel on top, a foot above ground level. From this point on, the road was dead straight, leading to the guardhouse at the perimeter of the estate. It was a small slat-sided cottage, really, with thatched roofing, and painted bright white with red trim. A long beam painted bright white, as well, with a little hinged leg about two-thirds of the way down its length, measured from the beam's pivot point post. A wooden box, located at the end by the shack, acted as a counterweight, filled with rock, no doubt. The guards, all in full uniform, recognized the driver and carriage and stood at attention as we passed by, raising the beam so we could proceed, our carriage slowing to a walking pace. Past that guardhouse, the grounds were lovely, with tall green grasses punctuated by occasional terraces, each level lined with manicured trees. The manor came into view now, passing the last of the gardening features to reveal a concave, white-washed stone house, four stories high. The dozens of windows were all wood-framed, painted black, with a dark grey slate roof at a steep angle. Small, squat, arched windows inside the roofline peeked out across the whole width of the structure. At its center was a five-story, rounded tower entrance, with Gothic stone pillars extending thirty feet toward us, topped with massive oak beams that supported the roof and sheltered those entering the estate. The roadway we were on ended at a circular path, where the driver turned right, led under the entrance canopy, and stopped so we could disembark.

A butler was waiting, with two porters, at attention. The butler wore a black tuxedo with a black bow tie and a fluted white shirt; the porters wore grey uniforms with black embroidered braiding on the chests and black buttons. Their small caps matched the uniforms, and their low European boots were spit-shined. When the carriage had stopped, the butler came forward and opened my door first, and I exited, walking around the back of the carriage to Monika's door. I insisted on opening it and helped her out with her free hand. Once on the ground, she closed her parasol and set it in the carriage. She would send a porter for it later if needed. I retook her hand, and the carriage proceeded around the circular drive and went to the stable house on the far north of the estate, judging by my finely-tuned nose. Upon entering the main foyer, the butler whispered to one of his assistants, who went off to a room to our left.

"Sir, may I take your helmet?" the butler asked.

"Please, thank you." I handed him the ridiculous headwear, secretly hoping it would get lost.

"Lord Dietrick Metternich and Lady Jona Metternich will receive you in the parlor now. Follow me," he said smartly, and turned rigidly to the right and proceeded across the foyer at a quickstep.

The foyer featured beautiful Italian marble floors, patterned in white and blue with veins of gold running through them. It passed through the pure white marble fluted columns on either side of the archway into the next room, supporting a single wooden beam adorned with deep-cut floral patterns and cherubim that was at least twelve feet long and eighteen inches high. The marble floor ended in an arc into that room, where highly polished wood floors filled the rest, with thick red carpets with gold edging laid where the seating area was, which we were approaching. Brown leather couches with bright brass tacking and feet made to look like eagle claws clutching orbs surrounded a central table, next to a massive fireplace. Mr. and Mrs. Metternich stood to greet us.

"Lord, I present Professor Tellafrog and Miss Binder," the butler said, setting my helmet on the table beside me, dangit.

Dietrick, dressed in his full regalia for the funeral, was impressive. He was at least six and a half feet in height, so a good three or four inches taller than I was. He had well-cared-for hair, blonde with some greying visible in his thick, downturned mustache. Jona was appropriately in all black, with above-the-elbow gloves, and prepared with bunned blonde hair and a somber expression. Her eyes showed both acceptance and nobility, but a longing desire to know the details only I could convey.

The butler returned with a small tray of coffee and tea, and associated condiments. The second tray he set down was an assortment of cheeses, with long, slender forks —one for each of us. The cheeses were Roquefort, Emmentaler, and a hard cheddar I was unfamiliar with. I actually love cheese with black coffee, but I didn't know anyone else might. Perhaps Arterous's mother was an empath of some sort, or a gracious hostess who asked Klement what I might enjoy.

"Please, both of you, sit. I have many things we must discuss, and time is short." His speech was very heavily accented. Dietrick gestured to the two-person couch, and we sat; then they did, too, all of us sitting straight-backed and rigid. The fit of this uniform I had to wear made it nearly impossible to sit in any way other than erect with my shoulders back. I had to sit to the far left, so that the saber could hang beside the seating. I was still nervous, and the saber rattling in the scabbard betrayed my jitters. Monika reached over and put her hand on mine, and gave me a comforting smile. She had known the whole Metternich family for some time. So I trusted her effort to calm me.

"Thank you, sir, madam, for allowing me to visit, um, allowing us to visit you at this time." Dietrick held up his hand, stopping me from continuing. He motioned over his shoulder to a man in the distance, whom I overlooked upon entering the room. This must be his translator, I thought.

"Raileanu, please. Do not be nervous. Our family is sworn to God to defend the helpless. We know roughly how he died. Please tell us what you found at the site of his death, as much for our knowledge as for you to begin the healing process. I also request that Monika stay. There is no need for her to be excluded from this," he smiled at me and was sincere. "This man will listen to the discussion. I understand enough English now that I want to hear it. If I misunderstand any details, he can explain them. Proceed," he motioned with a broad sweep of his hand.

"Sir, a terrible storm passed over my home where we all were, headed towards a Spanish Mission with a single Priest in poor health in residence." I had to stop and clear my throat, recalling the images in my mind of the massive tornado. I looked at Dietrick to make sure he wanted me to continue, that he was keeping up. He nodded at me to continue. "It was quite near dark, and I cannot dislocate, but I was concerned about the safety of that solitary Priest, Father Callious, all alone. Arterous did not hesitate and agreed to travel there and verify if the Priest was safe or in distress." I took a deep, unsteady breath. Did they know about the nature of the relationship with the Comanches? I decided to keep telling everything as best I could.

"I can piece together what happened by the evidence I found the following day upon arriving, the condition of the mission on a previous visit, and the letter the Priest wrote in his final moments." Mr. Metternich looked to his interpreter, who whispered something, probably guessing what word or phrase had confused him. Then he nodded and refocused on me. So, I kept checking with the interpreter and Dietrick as I spoke. "Shortly after arriving to check on the Priest, the compound was overrun by Comanche warriors. The Comanche had actually taken the brunt of that terrible storm. It's called a tornado. The truth is, those storms are so powerful that this entire estate could be struck by one and have every stick of structure thrown into the mountains of this valley in mere minutes." I paused and looked at all three of them to make sure they knew how serious it had been before I continued. "The Comanche were in a heavily wooded grove sheltering from the storm when all but a dozen were killed by the tornado. Probably fifty or sixty of them - men, women, and children - died when the tornado twisted that whole grove of trees into a single tightly-wound knot.

Mr. Metternich began stroking his chin and the bottom of his moustache as he looked down, trying to imagine the forces at work in such an event. Jona Metternich held her gloved hand to her mouth, imagining whole families being wrenched in such a way. I continued. "They felt the influence of magic had caused the tornado, maybe even directed it to them, and went to the mission to exact revenge. Arterous and Father Callious were trapped in a basement. Arterous's wand was found outside the heavy door, and the Comanche had broken it. He was hit through the arm and the liver by arrows before making a final stand at the bottom of a narrow stairwell under the church, protecting the Priest. Were it not for his valiant stand, Father Callious couldn't have had time to explain in a letter the source of my father's illness."

"I see. Mmmm. I accept this gift you have given us, knowledge of our son's passing in bravery." Dietrick looked at Jona, who had let several tears spill forth during the explanation, but had regained full strength and dignity by the time I also looked at her.

She nodded as well, saying, "Thank you, Raileanu. God bless you." She paused for a moment, breathed deeply through her nose, chin up, and looked at Dietrick, communicating something —I suppose they needed to tell me.

"Yes, you're right, my dear." Dietrick started. "About the funeral. I do not believe you will be able to attend. 'That woman,' Runetta, has already made certain she is to be in attendance through her connections with the royal family. There is nothing I can do to keep her from it, but rest assured, no movement of this woman will go unnoticed by our security services, both ordinary and magical. Were either of you to be here for this, I'm afraid it would only tempt her to taunt you further. I hope you understand." Monika and I looked at each other, more confused than hurt, really. "I am pleased our son spent his last days with someone of good, hearty character like you. We are both grateful he did not fall on some remote battlefield with thousands of others, and we could never find him, nor know how he fell. Thank you again. I will have the driver return you to Klement's house in Vienna. Thank you." Dietrick stood, as did Jona, and I shook Dietrick's hand, bowing as I did. Then Jona held out her gloved hand; I took it and bowed as well. I took Monika by the hand, and the butler led us back out front, where we waited for the carriage to arrive.

"I'm sorry that we cannot attend," Monika said, acknowledging my disappointment.

"Me too. I know that we would be a distraction, and that's not what I wanted to be. As long as his parents are satisfied, I will be as well."

Only a moment longer, and the carriage came about, and we boarded, both a bit disheartened. Unfortunately, the butler had not lost my helmet during our short visit, nor had he missed that I had left it on the table. After I had boarded, he handed it back to me. I gave him a nod instead of a thank you.

Dietrick and Jona came to the front steps and waved to us, both smiling and appearing grateful for the news of Arterous and his deeds. One day, with no crowds of mourners, I could return and say goodbye in my own way.

After the carriage had traveled out of sight, Dietrick turned to Jona, alone now on the front steps of their home, and gave her a serious look.

"Dietrick, what is it?" she wondered.

"The Emperor has ordered me to discover what it was that Runetta Lynchos was after, and what she and her order may already possess connected to it. This violates our directives about allowing the ordinary access to any part of the magical world. Someone in his circle has clearly influenced him to believe that whatever this is, it can bring him power. He doesn't know it is of magical origin, but it is something I have been ordered to do. What I do know is that man, Tellafrog, and Monika Binder have no more understanding of what it is beyond an object that led to the deaths of nearly everyone who came near it. I know my brother has some idea of what it is, and I will speak with him after the funeral today," he let out a heavy sigh after telling her.

"I, too, will keep an attentive ear today. No doubt that woman will try to offer humble condolences, which everyone expects from her, given her forced presence at this service. It will be alright, darling." Jona reassured him.

17

They returned to the house, arm in arm, and prepared for the somber events still to come to them that day. Laying brave Arterous to rest.

CHAPTER TWO

I can detail to you now information I have collected over these many years in service with the Sentinels that I did not know during the events of this story. At appropriate times in the course of these retellings, I will give you relevant information, such as now regarding the Dwarves.

Fourteen thousand years ago, give or take, when changes to the people of the earth were made possible through the artifacts and tools of CIGI (Crystalline Integrated General Intelligence), many forms and creatures we regard as magical or mythical sprang forth—some by intentional design, some by chance, some as unintended consequences for users. Many of the nations of the world at that time were very advanced in their CIGI tools, while others had primitive versions, and some had none. One such nation, small and with poor systems and an inadequate understanding of its true potential, felt the need to collect rare minerals from its land that were difficult to mine, process, and refine. They were, in fact, poisonous to anyone even near them in an unrefined state; a normal person could only be in the vicinity of these minerals and would have all their bodily systems fail most horribly in a matter of days. This country took its poorest, least educated segments of the population and used their CIGI to alter the very essence of those subjects, making them twice as strong, live twice as long, never question their masters, be impervious to injury that would cripple a human, and be immune to the effects of the rare minerals they sought. They had named themselves the Kirin Mante. The people responsible for the alterations to the Kirin Mante, having satisfied themselves that their creations were perfect for the task they had in mind, sent over five thousand of them into deep mines and then even deeper into natural crevices to harvest the mineral. The mineral was unique in that it radiated a dangerous field of energy; its emissions could not only alter gravity, but the energy itself exerted a gravitational field twice that of other matter of the same mass. When focused and refined into specific waveforms, it allowed tremendous amounts of work or travel, for nothing more than the energy needed to concentrate its radiation. Named for the lady who discovered it some years before in another nation, the mineral was known for two hundred years before the Calamity as Bendra-17, the seventeenth recorded discovery by this remarkable scientist. Fearing the enhanced abilities of the Kirin Mante, however, they made certain that they could not leave the mines, sealing the shafts behind them, opening the great stone slab only for trams to lift the rare material out of the mine vertically.

Over the next hundred years, the miners, whom we now call the Dwarves, built vast networks of tunnels and cities for themselves as their numbers grew, dutifully sending the one material up that they were meant to. The flaw in the masters' plan was the few directives they had been given. So, as their numbers reached twenty thousand, and they had found many wonders that met their needs deep in the earth, they decided to keep all of those discoveries to themselves. They discovered vast oceans of fresh water in caverns. They learned to harness the very magma of the earth to power their cities and grow their own food.

It was about two hundred years that the world wrestled with the good and evil of the CIGI and CISI before the Calamity. In that time, the nation that created the race of Dwarves had even discovered a man-made replacement for the mineral they were initially sent to mine, and stopped opening the lid to the mine altogether. This did not concern the Dwarves, as they had created their own civilization during that time and were very contented with it.

The few places the High Elves know of to reach the Dwarves nowadays are but mere chasms in the most formidable mountain ranges, impossible to access for ordinary people, even at the time of my writing. At the same time as the Dwarves had busied themselves with their new home, the High Elves were created by their own hand. They intended to amass knowledge of everything, and they could see and hear anything they chose to examine, as if from above. When the Calamity occurred, they had recorded the openings leading to the Dwarves, but lost their omnipresent ability to observe from above. It was through these openings that the Dwarves brought in fresh air, collected animals and seeds to domesticate. The Earth's surface was significantly altered during the Calamity. The land that created the Dwarves, for example, is actually several hundred feet below the sea now. For a time, about 7-14,000 years ago, the Dwarves had impenetrable fortresses near these openings where they would trade with the world above. All of those are destroyed now, either by the Dwarves themselves or warring factions of ordinary humans.

The Dwarves alone understand every aspect of the physical earth we live on. Every rock, liquid, mineral, gemstone, and, yes, the dangerous material they were created to mine for. Their entire knowledge base is restricted to themselves, and they do not share it even with the High Elves. Their only collaboration concerns the dangers of the previous world's use of CIGI and the need to prevent it at all costs.

****

A thousand feet below the crag where Hochosterwitz Castle is currently perched in Lower Austria, in a vast cavern carved fourteen thousand years ago, stands the solid stone mirror image of that impressive fortress. The cavern itself was created in the second age, in the last two hundred years before the Calamity, by the Dwarves as one of their refuges. Only a dozen places on earth have such places that can be accessible even to the magical, as the Dwarves retreated from the insanity that ensued on the surface in the last two hundred years before the war and asteroid strike the High Elves Corfus and Kleet had described in my previous work.

The remainder of the Dwarves, like the High Elves, stay isolated, enhancing their kingdoms below the ground and scarcely take notice of the rabble of surface-dwelling humans, and that remnant of humans - ordinary and magical - knew little of them. Interactions with them increased only after about five thousand years, or 9,000 BC. Now, only the High Elves know the locations on the earth where contact with the Dwarves is possible. The fortress in that cavern had been abandoned by the Dwarves, who chose to move further away from the surface in the last four thousand years.

The castle stood on a central stone hill of the cavern. It was carved from solid diorite, giving it a sparkling, dark grey appearance. Standing over a hundred and fifty feet high, it had a single entrance by foot. Around the dome it sat on, filling the whole cavern, was a lake of spring water a hundred feet deep. The cavern was sealed off from the outside world, meaning only those who can dislocate and know of its location can gain access, apart from the Dwarves themselves. Even Elves do not understand how the Dwarves move about in the earth, but their own movements are, to themselves, so infinitely superior that they never bothered to ask the Dwarves how they do it. Bright blue light fills the cavern, the glowmoss coating the entire roof, creating a duplicate image of the castle on the perfectly still waters surrounding it.

In the 400s AD, a witch was held as a prisoner on a stone spire on the surface, within a small wooden fort. For crimes of a vile nature, she was sentenced to death. A wizard was party to her capture and had cast a dome of protection over her, preventing her from escaping. She attempted to dislocate out of the fort, but the only un-protected means of dislocation was down. Facing death by fire, she went the only way she could, straight down, and found the abandoned Dwarvish castle deep below. After exploring it and seeing it abandoned, she left, but not before she noted its location in a book inherited by Runetta Lynchos's family. The connection with that family and this place is evident to anyone with knowledge of both, as the one on the surface today was a replica of the one the Dwarves created below. Since the 900s, they have used the secret underground castle for meetings and for imprisoning enemies.

In a secret room of Lynchos Castle, known only to Runetta now, as the women of her family assumed own-ership upon its discovery, lies a stone slab platform four feet by eight feet and a foot thick, supported by pillared stone legs. Lying on the slab was what looked like a suit of full plate metal armor illuminated by the bright emana-tion from the tip of Runetta's wand, standing on its own at the head of the table. Slinking around the table, her right hand dragging across the form's surface, Runetta has tried to unlock the mysteries of this metal man, but, like her ancestors before her, she has had no success. Its helmet is more akin to a smooth, featureless mask. The hands are segmented like a human hand, and the joints of the arm and leg are the same as a human's. The metal skin is half white, half strange colors and patterns. Almost as if it were damaged, or unfinished. Metal workings behind the segments of plate, so fine they resemble hairs, the remains of an unknown skill that none can reproduce. At the foot of the slab was what looked like half a large, broken crystal ball. It was, in fact, an Orb, like the one found recently in Texas, but broken and powerless.

"I will find the secret, my dear, to breathe life into you again." Runetta leaned over the head and gave it a gentle kiss on the blank faceplate. "For now, however, I must attend a 'friends' funeral. Don't go anywhere." She picked up her wand, flicked it off, and dislocated.

****

Monika and I arrived back at Klement's home in Vienna around mid-afternoon. We both went straight upstairs to change into more comfortable clothing and met in the formal parlor about half an hour later. We would spend the afternoon discussing our plans for the near future, as we would have to announce a wedding date before long. We agreed that at the Christmas gatherings here, we would set a date to announce. We decided to avoid having the ceremony at my family's home in Texas because most of the guests would be coming from Europe, and Barthow would be the only one traveling from Texas. Additionally, the fewer people who know about the 'ol homestead's location, the better. We had agreed to compile fieldwork into books and to overwinter in privacy in Texas. Monika suggested we travel to one of her family's estates near Vienna rather than to Hungary, and announce our engagement in person. While there, we would find a suitable location for the wedding, for the spring of the following year, 1837. Monika suggested that at the end of those discussions, we visit the magical merchant square near the Hofburg this evening. Apparently, the wisdom of Barthow back in Texas had reached the cutting edge of outfitting here, as hawks were all the rage here now for exchanging correspondence, well, except those with an inclination towards falcons. The fare and its vendors would only be in town for a few more days and would not return until the end of December. We should each select a hawk. If we were successful, we would free our owls tonight, which is always a happy occasion for all involved, owls especially. They enjoy being helpful to our world, but every single one ever recorded has put on a special celebratory display, like a roller pigeon, when released from service. Much like the feeling of honor and relief a soldier feels when their term of duty is completed successfully.

We dined with the security staff, and Wenzel, assigned to our security by Klement himself, offered to take us to the square afterward. It was only a short six blocks northwest, and we agreed to walk in the last days of summer, to take in the beginning of the autumn colors' emergence that had recently begun in town. Wenzel also informed us that the materials I had collected over the summer were already being transferred to my home, now known as Circle R Ranch, even though it was just a homestead, and not technically a ranch. Apparently, everyone here assumed that everyone in Texas owned a ranch of a thousand acres, and I had no heart to explain how small and humble it really was. Barthow had agreed to give them entrance, and Wenzel would verify once it was complete. Barthow had arrived while we were at Dietrick Metternich's estate earlier, and given a portrait to Klement he had done in San Antonio after the meeting with the High Elves Kleet and Corfus. It now hangs in Klement's gallery of his private study, cementing the alliance to find the artifacts and secret them away from the magical and ordinary worlds, with the help of the High Elves.

Monika and I went to our separate rooms and changed into more casual attire suitable for a long walk in the city, trying to remain inconspicuous at the same time. We rejoined Wenzel in the foyer of the home and began our walk to the square together. Wenzel suggested he walk ahead of us to survey the path for any concerns, as was his duty, as Klement himself had prescribed. By this time of day, the carriage and cart traffic was rather heavy, and the noise allowed Monika and me to carry on a private conversation that even Wenzel couldn't hear.

"What do you think about a winter wedding, if my family is agreeable to it?" she asked with a playful, hopeful smile.

"My dear, if the parties around us are all in agreement, we would be walking to the church right now. In fact, I suggest you send a letter by hawk tonight, providing there are any for sale, informing your family of the impending announcement of good news upon our arrival." I said without pause or breaking forward gaze. Monika gripped my arm tightly and was ear-to-ear with smiles. We were both in our thirties now, and that did not dampen her excitement to induce several skips in her step, which I matched.

The foot traffic increased as we neared the Ferdinand Bridge, and dissipated after crossing it, and we came to the corner of Tabor Strasse and Hafner Grasse. Just to the right side of the alleyway between the streets was the double-wide, slightly crooked, and mortared round stone archway that was about six feet deep, and to anyone ordinary, appeared to be bricked up. Intentionally, the darkness of the deep doorway allowed those with magical blood, and those they escorted with physical touch, to enter through the illusion of bricks into the market square for the wares we were seeking. Wenzel waited to the side of the entrance, checking his pocket watch to the casual observer, but actually watching for anyone checking our movements.

The doorway actually concealed a larger space than the small storage space the ordinary world assumed was in the vestibule. Inside the open square were every variety of merchants, vendors, restaurants, clockmakers, and rare-animal shops one could imagine. Hostels, two grand magical hotels, sausage makers, and even two breweries had storefronts facing the square's center, while smaller vendors had little wagon shops filling the square's open area.

"The animal shop is this way," Wenzel said, indicating to the left, allowing Monika and me to go in front now, so that we might enjoy the shopping trip at our own pace. The aromas from the first chocolatier drew us in, and I recall this shop from a visit a year ago. Once inside the bullseye glass-paned front entrance, I realized the sheer number of offerings was far greater than on my previous visit. Clearly, the owner's international travel had broadened her horizons, as selections from Chile, Arabia, and Hong Kong were front and center. Pure coca leaf extract chocolate from Chile, Arabica finely ground coffee bean white chocolate from Arabia, and green tea chocolate from the Orient, each tickling my tuned nose in ways unfamiliar before.

"Oh, Raileanu, Monika! So nice to see you again!" It was the shop's owner, Darsy Kolz. It had been at least two years since I first met her, yet she had no trouble recognizing either of us. "Oh my! And arm in arm I see," throwing up a cagey smile, cocking her head to one side.

"Indeed, Madam Kolz. Our engagement is formalized," I explained, "and if you would permit us, I would like to invite you to cater our desserts for the spring wedding here in Austria." I had intentionally steered us to the shop to ask that very question. Monika, open-mouthed, then smiling, punched my arm.

Perhaps having always consumed too much of her own products and full of spritely energies, Darsy jumped up and down, clapping and squeaking for a whole minute before she stopped and threw both hands on the glass counter of chocolate beans of every variety and said,

"This is the first occasion of any sort anyone has ever asked me to cater for! I am so excited! AAAAAAH!" She put her hands on her face and yelled out with her mouth wide open. The other dozen patrons then stopped what they were doing and looked at Darsy and us with blank stares. Maybe I should have asked to speak with her in private, without drawing attention. Hindsight and all that. Oh well. I looked at Wenzel, who was by the front-door displays, pretending to sample wares while staring me down, shaking his head in disgust.

"Raileanu, I have to thank you soooo much for alerting me to the myriad of candies you have encountered on your travels. I had no idea. The mystique of their process-es and ingredients has been so popular that I have not been able to keep them in stock. Several of the sorceress-es I met traveling to the places you described have sent their eldest child to operate their own carts with unique offerings in the square here! I was even able to teach them some of my recipes in exchange, and they are selling them in great quantities. I can't thank you enough. I had never traveled outside the German-speaking countries before, and I should have. Thank you." Darsy said without pausing for a breath, it seemed.

"Uh, you're welcome, I suppose," I said. In truth, I just commented on one kind I had tried in a small village near Puma Punku in Chile. "I am glad it has broadened your horizons. Will it be all right to send you the formal invitation to the shop here?"

"Yes! I have this whole building now!" Darsy indicated by waving her arms around and up into the air. "The shop is on the first and second floors, the kitchen is on the third floor, and I have an apartment on the fourth. The basement is all storage for ingredients," she said excitedly.

"Excellent, we are so happy for you, Darsy," Monika said. She truly was. Monika is the one who brought me here the first time and was happy to see someone so passionate about something and doing so well at it. "We have a few things we need to buy in the square. We look forward to seeing you again soon."

"Oh, here then, take these for your walk. They are yak milk cheese wands with a crunchy chocolate coating. Guaranteed not to melt, and stay cool inside for a whole day! It's my newest thing!" Darsy reached into a small wooden chest on the countertop and handed us three.

"Why three?" I asked.

"Wenzel is one of Klement Metternich's guards. You are obviously here in his home; ergo, he is with you. Remember, chocolate is good for the mind." She gave us a smile and a wink and went to attend to other customers.

I looked at Wenzel, who again was shaking his head at me in disapproval. We walked to the door, and I asked him, "What did I do?"

"Nothing, sir. I am amazed at how many people in my city know a nonmagical botanist from Texas, that's all." Wenzel joked.

"Surprises both of us, I think," I replied, and handed him his yak milk wand.

We exited the shop and turned left, as I planned to make the whole square first, then mingle amongst the carts and wagons in the center. Monika and I looked at the chocolate wand, smiled nervously, and then I took a bite. Monika watched to see if it was actually any good. Some of Darsy's ideas were just plain silly, but most were surprisingly delicious. The chocolate was indeed crunchy, and none fell to the ground, and the yak milk cheese was so sweet and rich that it reminded me more of iced cream. It was magnificent! So rich and sweet, I could only take a nibble every few minutes to bear it. Monika could manage a bit more sweet than I, and hers was gone by the end of the side we were walking. As we passed the wand store in the corner, I saw in the reflection of the glass ahead that Wenzel was already finished with his, nodding wide-eyed at it.

The window display of the wand store had something that caught Monika's eye. She stopped suddenly, fully releasing my arm, and was transfixed on the display. It looked to me like a spriggy white oak branch with wooden rings on it, different woods and colors, all with prices that I couldn't dream of affording, so I was really hoping she wasn't going to ask for one as a gift or wedding band.

"What is it, Monika?" I asked with hope in my heart.

"Wenzel, come here. Have you seen these before?" She pointed at the ring display.

"No ma'am. What are those?" He asked.

"Raileanu, Runetta was wearing one of these the first time I met her. It is a type of wandmaker's wood that has been crafted into a ring and allows some use of magical focus without a wand. I'm not sure the power or range of them, but it was the only one I knew of until now." Monika said.

"Well, it is a shop, they are for sale, I will inquire within and find out," Wenzel said plainly. "Continue, I won't be long."

Many of these ancient buildings on the square were timber-and-batten with stonework features and looked very similar to each other. Being in the corner, the wand shop's front entrance was rounded, wood-framed glass, painted soot black, and had suffered subsidence over the millennia, crooked in places as the height increased. We saw that, although the front was just a ten-foot-wide archway, it opened into a larger, wedge-shaped interior. Neither of us had been in before, as I did not need a wand, and Monika had been gifted one by her deceased husband of unmatched quality and personalized power. She had the one from her childhood at home, in case she ever needed a spare. We continued, turning right and going along the row of shops across from where we had entered.

This housed the clothiers, some of whom were renowned throughout Europe for over two thousand years. The oldest, most respected, was in a five-story structure of solid white granite blocks cut and set by magic to absolute precision. The entire front of the first story of the store was made of blocks depicting the formalwear, uniforms, dresses, gowns, and cobblery for royal families they had created. A single solid glass door with a crystal push knob set into it sat dead center of the facade. Just as I was trying to walk past it, Monika forcefully turned me toward the door, which magically opened. Before I could politely protest, we were in a place I had no business or desire to be.

Perfectly white marble, polished like glass, made the floors; mahogany sheets, hand-rubbed with mink oil, glowing intensely, covered every inch of the walls. The finish on these made it appear three-dimensional. Creating these sheets that can cover hundreds of feet in a single seamless layer of rare wood is one possessed only by magical peoples, they literally guide an angled cut into the wood with a thirty-foot long damascus blade to the depth of a quarter of an inch, then rotate the trunk of the tree across the blade, creating a single unbroken sheet, as long as the trunk is thick. As a child, I watched some men in the Amazon work to perfect the technique. Small divider stands filled the center of the space, each made of planks of a wood equally rare, most of which looked to be a thousand years old or more. These were presumably where fittings took place. Samples of fabric were in small cubby boxes, floor-to-ceiling, along the back wall. The wall to the right held all the glass pegs showing ties, cravats, cummerbunds, cordage, and, nearer the front, shoes, boots, and ceremonial sabers.

"Monika, what are we doing here?" a statement, not a question.

"You will be fitted for proper attire to attend a wedding. Our wedding, sir." Her statement in reply, obviously.

"I see," is all I could say realistically. "I agree to be measured and select style, color, and material, but that's all. And I get to pick the hat."

"Absolutely not. You will wear a top hat like a gentle-man," she pointed her finger at me, and since I would wear my own hat at home anytime I wished, this I would grant her.

"For this occasion, my dear, I agree to your terms," I said, and to the tailor we proceeded.

Sparing you the lengthy details, I can report that my lovely fiancée picked for me a light grey tailed jacket, black silk top hat, white tuxedo shirt with high collar and bowtie, white vest with gold filigree embroidery and buttons, light grey slacks, gold embroidered side strip-ing, and black patent leather half-boots. Measurements taken, materials chosen, and an hour later, we exited the shop with the order placed. Waiting outside was Wenzel, enjoying an apple, leaning against the next shop.

"Where is the wildlife storekeeper?" I asked him.

"On this next side, sir. Care to give a preview of the groom's attire?" he asked.

"No, no one is to speak of it until after the date is an-nounced and people begin planning the ceremony. That's an order. Don't even speak of this being the store we are using. Clear?" Monika told him. He nodded, obviously not the type for gossip anyway, which would be a poor quality for a personal bodyguard.

Once on the final side of the square, we came across an outfitter for foreign travels, and I wanted to go in for a visit. It was an older shop, with hunter green paint and a heavy iron sign hanging from an ornate curling rod above the door. It read "Travelers Tools". The door was open, and the smell of a leather-working shop and hemp canvas drifted to me. Inside were very old counters and shelves made of yew and ash. A service counter stretched from wall to wall, with glass-fronted cabinets beneath. Mountain-climbing gear and ropes occupied a small area in the far corner, which seemed curious to me in a store exclusively for people who can appear anywhere they want or ride a broom to any height they wish. Perhaps some aristocrats have taken up the challenge. Tents of every size, material, and color adorned the center of the store, along with stoves and seasoned cast-iron cooking sets. Folding chairs with heavy canvas seats were displayed next to them.

The central floorspace was lined with baseboard-to-ceiling shelving, with hundreds of small houses, cottages, tents, bungalows, mansions, castles, and even small fortresses, in perfect scale and detail, from a few inches to a couple of feet in width and height. To the unfamiliar eye, they appear to be toys. However, they are actual structures that are shrunk down to a portable size, which magicians can pack up and take with them, and then, with a single wave of the wand, restore to their original size. Wealthy magical folk are the only ones who can afford the most magnificent ones, as the cost is higher than an actual structure, as a skilled craftsman must enchant every single block and stick of furniture before it can work. The tents are much more reasonable, and after years of hauling actual tents around the globe for my work, I really wish I could use them.

"Hey, are you okay?" Monika asked. She had come over and noticed me daydreaming at the displays.

"Yes, using one of these would be so much more efficient for my field work, that's all. I was imagining what it would be like to use them," I said, not having realized how long I had stared at them.

"You do realize you aren't alone anymore. We can use these as long as I am with you in OUR travels," she said, smiling at me when I looked to her.

"It hadn't occurred to me, no. Sharing life with you is going to be transformative in so many ways I can't even know yet. I love you," I said, hugging her tightly.

"I will wait at the front. We do need to get to the animal shop, don't be long. We will pick our equipment together before next year's excursions," she squeezed my hand tight before letting go, and watched me as she walked away to the front.

Boots with metal side cleats were on display behind the counter, presumably for climbing trees, while whole-foot cleats for ice or snow travel were next to the snow shoes and winter parkas used by the Norse and Icelandic explorers. Wicker sets of baskets sat between the tent and portable home displays, some for picnicking, some similar to the ones I had used for sample collection, and even copper wire fish traps were among them. I was happy to have found this store, as I didn't remember it from my last visit to the square. It was at the Christmas Festival, probably around eight o'clock in the evening; perhaps it was closed that day. I would remember it for my next foray in the Austrian area, indeed.

Monika was not really interested in the store and was happy when I headed to the front to leave, anxious to get to the pet shop. So we didn't waste any time and went straight there. Several street performers were gathered outside its door, juggling torches, jumping through displacement rings, appearing through another of the large rings flung high into the air, only to emerge through a third, standing with arms upraised, all to the applause of children.

I had to refrain from going into the aged cheese shop, because that surely would have delayed us even more. I had always loved artisan cheeses from the nations I traveled to, and after I gained more acute senses, the specific processes and bacterial cultures intrigued me to no end.

Several doors further, across from the crystal figurine dealer, we found the shop. This, too, was one I had not been in before. As I recall, the owner was quite elderly and only opened the shop for customers on written request. The last time I was here, it was poorly maintained, the paint on the framing had all gone, a few small panes of glass were broken, and the sign hung by one ring. This time, it was all freshly painted, and all the glass had been replaced, save the one with the hand-etched name on the door. "Wiggles & Squiggles." The door was open, and several people were inside, petting, tickling, and coddling the critters inside. None of the creatures sold here were caged, and the policy was that only animals that bind to a witch or wizard were authorized for sale.

Snakes, lizards, birds, land jellyfish, desert squids, there are so many animals here I hadn't seen before. The shelves and cabinetry were all brand new white pine, and the lighting was provided by white rope lights, which I had only seen once before in Constantinople, looped around the entire top of the store. The new, large brass register sat on the counter, along with books about rare animal care. Behind the counter was a young lady who, after finishing with a customer buying an operatic finch, smiled and looked at Monika and me.

"Welcome to Wiggles and Squiggles. I am Regina Colter. What can I help you with today?" She stood about 5'6" tall, with gentle, curling blonde hair and dark blue eyes. Wearing a felt hunter green frock with long pointed collars, with her sleeve cuffs rolled up, wearing a custom black cotton apron with pockets covering the whole front full of scissors, combs, and treats of all kinds. She wore a matching green felt hat with folds, adorned with a green peacock eye feather. Just as I was about to reply, the eye of the feather blinked at me, distracting me.

"It's a new charm I am trying, animating the bounty of God's world to make everyone happy," she said.

"Interesting, I like it," I said, looking back at her. "My fiancée and I are hoping that you have some hawks we can select from. Both our owls have reached the age of release, and, being from Texas, we normally use hawks. I understand they are quite popular now, but they are a necessity for us."

"Of course. The demand for the free hawks that choose to work with us has gone up dramatically, and the truth is, many of the ones we have sold over the last year have returned to us. The owners apparently purchased them only to impress other aristocrats, and after a couple of months of being useless, they just returned here. So the costs are not that dramatic as they were just a few months ago. May I have your names, to speak to them and see who will volunteer?" Regina asked, smiling and looking back and forth between us.

"I am Raileanu Tellafrog. This is my fiancée, Monika Binder." I said with my arm around her.

"Soon to be Monika Tellafrog!" She exclaimed. I gave her a little kiss, and Regina returned the smile and went through a door in the back. I heard her ask the group of hawks about helping Monika and me, then probably a dozen mild screeches and squeaks from them. Their conversation continued for probably five minutes, then the little door opened, and Regina came back out to the counter.

"They want to know if you, sir," pointing to me, "are the Tellafrog from Texas who knows Barthow. I told them you were from Texas, and they wanted me to clarify."

"I am. Barthow is a friend of the family." I said.

"They also want to know if you will be staying in Europe or if you will be traveling abroad," she asked us.

"I will be here for another month or two, then I will overwinter in Texas. We will hopefully be back in Europe in the spring for our wedding. We haven't set a date yet, but yes, travel is in store for them." I said.

"There are three who are willing to meet you and who desire to travel. The rest have family groups in central Europe and do not wish to leave them yet. Would you like to meet them?" Regina asked.

"Please." We both nodded.

"Trafalgar, Odious, Morgan, would you come out front, please?" Regina opened the door for them. One after the other came out and lit on the counter. One was considerably larger than the other two, that one on our left. It was about two feet high, with a bark-colored back, wings, and head feathers, and a variegated off-white and black underside.

"This one," pointing to the larger one, "is a Northern Goshawk. His name is Odious." The bird bowed its head momentarily, then looked straight at us again.

"This second one and the third are Eurasian Sparrowhawks. The middle one here is a female named Morgan. The one on the end is her male sibling, Trafalgar. Don't be concerned about separating them; they argue all the time and would prefer to be assigned to different families. Not uncommon for predatory birds, actually." Regina said.

"Actually, the Northern Goshawk is about the size of our red-tailed hawks, or even the black hawks back home. I think the larger one would be more suited to working in Texas, if he agrees." I postulated.

"Birds of all kinds are somewhat telepathic. There seems to be no distance that hinders it, actually. Odious agrees; he knows the dangers, the climate, and the responsibilities. He would be pleased to take part in letting McCort retire." Regina relayed, as she pet his neck.

"Is Morgan agreeable with working there from time to time?" Monika asked.

Regina looked at her, and Morgan nodded. "She is happy not to have Austrian mountain winters if that helps," she said, smiling. "If you can pay and take them with you today, I can make you a housing and a helmet for both in just a few moments."

"Yes, indeed," I said, reaching for my wallet inside my vest pocket.

"I'll be right back. Trafalgar, would you like to mingle with the nice people in the square for a while?" She had the other two hop onto her forearm, and Trafalgar flew out the open front door with a little squeal. She went into the back, closing the door behind her.

I wandered about the store for a few minutes while we waited. One thing I didn't find was orox dung, or emerald worms. Quite a few Komodo dragons were walking about the store, arranging and restocking things. Knowing what I do about them, they may be interns. While very methodical and helpful to the magical world, they prefer much warmer climates. Aside from some large actual dragons, they are the only other ones who can speak in human tongues. Some families have walking monitor lizards that serve them on estates, but usually not in Europe. Regina came back with both birds—one on each shoulder—and two small cigar-sized boxes, each with the hawk's name, setting them on the counter.

"Mr. Tellafrog, we are ready when you are," she said loud enough for us to hear, so we went back to the counter.

"Regina, I notice you don't have emerald worms or orox dung. Would you sell them here? If I were to know where to find some?" I asked

"Well, the only shop I know of that has orox dung is the Tea Times store on the outskirts of town, and as for emerald worms, yes, I would love to stock them here. I haven't had a source since I bought the store almost a year ago. Do you have any?" Regina wondered, head cocked to one side.

"I do know where to find both, and would be happy to share that information with you, provided you can guarantee it is harvested in the most honorable way to the location," I said.

"Of course, that proviso you outlined gets you the friends and family discount here anytime you are in town. How about fifty Guldens for the two hawks and care boxes?" she said.

"My heavens, dear, that's a quarter of what it probably should be. Are you sure that keeps you in business?" I asked, in shock, about the price.

"If I can have emerald worms here, even one batch, I can probably replicate their habitat downstairs and never have to collect them again. And well, orox dung, what that's going for, goodness, half a pound a year would keep the doors open! That's totally worth it," she said excitedly.

Satisfied with the arrangement, I gave her the payment in Guldens and scribbled the location near the scree falls by Lake Königssee, where I had found both the items in question earlier in the year.

"That'll be our secret, I promise," Regina said. "Good luck to both of you, and congratulations on your engagement!"

"Thank you, good luck with the store as well, Regina," I said, both of us letting the hawks mount our arms as we turned to walk out of the store. As soon as we got outside, Monika whispered where they should meet us later, and we let them flutter off into the sky.

"All done shopping?" Wenzel asked, leaning on the wall, waiting outside for us.

"Yes, let's get back to the house and say our goodbyes to our owls," Monika said, as we picked up the pace to the exit of the square.

We proceeded on the same path back to the Metternich home, with the afternoon sun on the backs of our necks now. This time, Wenzel stayed a full hundred feet or so behind us, watching everything. Just after the turn onto the row of houses where we were heading, Wenzel was right behind us and walked past us. "There is a man following us; he was watching when we left the square, and has been watching you intently. Keep going, don't look around," and he kept walking past us, then, using our bodies as cover, he dislocated.

We had another three hundred feet or so to go, and we saw the guards come out from under the covered entrance of the Metternich's house, and run towards us. We stopped and stepped to the left up against the stone walls of a row house, letting the guards run past us, presumably to the stranger. We looked as they went by, but saw no one, and they stopped, looking all around. I guess Wenzel went into the house and alerted them. We just went straight to the house at a quicker pace until we reached the doors, which were held open by the butler and another guard, and we closed them behind us. Then let the other two guards in who were out of breath.

Wenzel then touched my shoulder from behind, startling me a bit. When we turned to him, he was a bit calmer than I expected.

"Not to worry. I spoke with the man in question, and he is a magical Jesuit Priest who was sent to speak with you at your convenience. I told him tomorrow is currently unscheduled, and he will arrive around ten o'clock in the morning to meet with you." Wenzel reported.

"Well done, sir, thank you," I said. "Should it be alright for us to go onto the rooftop to release our owls from service?"

"Yes, yes, all is well. I will have the stairwell to the roof unlocked right away." Wenzel waved to one of the other security guards, who went straight up the main staircase to do that.

"I'll meet you up there in a few minutes. I need to freshen up and collect my owl." Monika said.

"Alright, I will see you there, dear," I said.

I went straight up and called McCort, who came in through the window and sat at the table next to me. I dug around in my suitcase, finding the last can of emerald worms I had. I gave him the last two I had, and he gobbled them down, rubbing his head against my chest. While I can't speak to him through my mind, he has been able to hear my thoughts since the day we picked each other out in Boston's Dark Market the week before I set out for school. It was that week alone that we could speak to each other, as it was only a few days at sea when the accident occurred that cost me my magic. He has never failed me, never let me down, nor failed to comfort me when it was just us abroad. He knows his faithful service has earned him honor, and apparently, my kind care for him and my appreciation of him have been widely discussed in bird circles. The birds of Wiggles and Squiggles knew of me and seemed eager to pick up the standard held by McCort. I thought, and tried to make sure he heard, that I truly loved him and hoped he would visit me often. He cooed with his beak up and then rubbed me again, as close to a hug as he could manage.

"Are you ready?" I asked him, who bobbed his head up and down. He hopped onto my shoulder, and I went outside my room, to the staircase at the back of the house, and up to the fourth floor. At the end of the hall, the door to the stairwell leading to the rooftop gantry was open. It was an iron lattice walkway that ran the entire perimeter of the inside slope of the roof, meant for servicing slate shingling and chimney work. We were not visible to anyone else there, except for the windows facing the small interior courtyard of the Metternich home. Waiting on the weathervane were our hawks, who came over to the little wrought iron table and chairs on our right. I walked over to it and took a chair to wait for Monika, setting McCort on the table. McCort immediately began conversing in bird tongue to Odious. As sad as this is for me, I know how proud McCort is. Birds who willingly serve us experience a peace and comfort that virtually doubles their lifespans. In fact, they don't age at all from the time they join us until they leave. He will undoubtedly go on to have a family and tell his offspring tales of our adventures. It didn't stop me from tearing up a few times while sitting there alone with him and Odious. Morgan joined us after a few minutes, and all three seemed to get on quite joyfully. I really wish I could hear everything that was being said.

"Ah, good, they've made it alright," Monika said, coming out the door onto the roof with me. Changed into a white long-sleeve heavy cotton blouse, with lacing untied at the neck, and navy blue riding pants and boots. She always felt more comfortable and relaxed dressed like this, her dark, honey brown hair loosely waving down across her shoulders. Her full physical description —I'm sorry —remains entirely mine. If interested, readers are welcome to visit our portrait in the Imperial Museum in Vienna, painted just before our wedding. Barring that, you must know that I remain smitten with this woman to this day —now in my mid-eighties, I can safely say I will forever.

After each said our tearful thanks and expressed our love to the noble companions, we sat side by side, holding hands, and, with a wave of her wand, Monika released them from service. Each owl nuzzled the hawks in turn, then spread their great wings, and leaped up into the air, flying straight up to a hundred feet, then tucked their wings and tumbled down to ten feet above our heads before throwing their wings out again and gliding away over the city. When they'd gone out of sight, we looked back at the table, and both our hawks had their wings spread wide, backs to us, having also watched the display.

They tucked their wings back as it finished, and began 'talking' to each other again in little clicks and coos. I honestly wished Momma and Daddy could have seen this, but at the same time, I was glad Barthow handled it for me back home. I was distraught enough as it was; releasing mother and father's owls would have been too hard when I was there.

We spent the rest of the evening discussing how to word the letter to her parents. When we agreed to be intentionally unclear about the potential wedding date, Monika penned the letter. She sent it off with Morgan, sharing the location with her in a few moments of silence between them. She also said that we had intended to be at their home in a couple of days. We heard the sound of several carriages stopping out front in the last hour of daylight and rightly assumed it was Klement, Laverne, and the children. We went downstairs to greet them, and everyone was quite stoic, as expected. The butler said dinner would be ready in about an hour.

During dinner, Wenzel informed Klement about the Priest who had sought to speak with me. Klement agreed to allow it to be in the house the following morning. Klement also told us that Runetta had attended, feigning sorrow and heartache at Arterous's passing. Arterous's parents did not even look her in the eye, however, and she did not linger after the service. Nor did she offer any behavior at the service worthy of note. She spoke with no one else, sat with no person of note, and left immediately afterward.

The next morning, Monika's hawk, Morgan, was back already and had returned with a letter from her parents. They were having a family gathering during the timeframe we mentioned and were about to send her the invitation for it when they received the good news. They promised to keep the news secret and allow us to announce it in person. We ate breakfast together in the foyer of my room near the little window overlooking the courtyard. Afterward, I dressed a bit more formally for the meeting with the Jesuit Priest.

Just after ten o'clock in the morning, he arrived at the front doors and was brought into the parlor where I was waiting.

"Good morning, sir. I am Father Walton Zeiss. Thank you for your time. And thank Mister Metternich for me as well for welcoming me into his home," he began.

He was tall, gaunt, with olive skin and thick, dark, straight hair. His floor-length robe was tight on him and perhaps needed letting out. His rosary was well-worn and probably needed re-stringing before long. He sat in the chair across from me, straight back, and on the edge of the seat.

"So, Father Zeiss, what would you like to discuss with me?" I got right to it. I was actually preoccupied with planning the trip to Monika's family estate, hoping this time actually to have a portion of it on a train.

"You have been in contact with Kleet and Corfus recently. I know this because I am the Priest in charge of training those of us in the calling to be men of God who are also born with magical blood. Do not fear, this knowledge is not shared with any other part of the church. We are our own separate branch that answers only to the Pope. The Pope is only authorized to ask us about matters that overlap the worlds of sorcery and ordinary, and by design, we are not bound to answer, given to our own imperatives," he said rather hurriedly.

"So you are a part of the church, but not bound to the Holy Father in all things?" I was confused, but as a protestant, that probably wouldn't surprise him.

"I know what the High Elves have told you; that is good. Let me explain how my order came to be," he let out a heavy sigh. "In the first hundred or so years after Jesus, many magical people came to believe and became followers of Jesus. The early church was very accepting of them, and their gifts were seen as tools God had given to help the people of the world, as Jesus commanded. For a time, they served alongside ordinary members, using magic to heal who they could, to feed who they could, and so on. When more and more ordinary people looked to the magical peoples and what they provided, they ignored the credit and praise the magic gave to God. These people came to demand more and more from them, and cursed God for not giving the same gifts to more who believed in Him. They were ordered to stop using ALL magic for ANY reason." His hands, inactive until now, rose from his knees and made a flat-handed swipe through the air.

The butler came and delivered lemonade and iced water with lime to the table in the room, and Father Zeiss paused until he had left and closed the door behind him.

After taking a long drink and another, he set the glass down and continued.

"Those of us who are magical are only allowed in the Priesthood if we vow never to use, or even reveal our gifts to other Priests. We are cloistered in our own conclaves and are charged to minister to the magical world, each other, and record histories concerning our kind in relation to the church. The Pope can call upon us to answer or investigate events to determine if magic played a part, but we cannot use magic to help or answer him. It is truly forbidden for us, because it takes away from the glory of God, even though we know the truth. "

"What truth is that?" I asked.

"Our work in the last eighteen hundred years. Each time scrolls, manuscripts, books, stone carvings, or anything undocumented come into the church's possession, we are charged with unraveling their mysteries, cataloging them, and working with magical leadership to keep them secret. The truth we know, the church that is, is the same thing that the High Elves know. Human civilization is tens of thousands of years older than commonly known. Most leaders of the world's wizardkind suspect it, but work with us to store all of that knowledge in the Vatican. The reason is simple. Things classified as dark sorcery and those who seek to use it are far more powerful and affect far more of the world than the machinations of the world's most evil ordinary folk. The source of magic itself is simply the remainder of man's own handiwork from before the Calamity, fourteen thousand eight hundred years ago. Their ability to change and manipulate the smallest pieces of life, consciousness, physical forms, and forces is greater than we can imagine. Their influence reached into the stars and deep into the earth, and they could control every mind on the earth. It shaped ancient places by forcing stone, water, fire, and even light to bend to its will. It is all from the mind and hand of ordinary men. It was the cause of their downfall. Their reliance on it, their desires for fleshly power and control, shaped every part of their mind, and they didn't just ignore the disaster coming at us from the heavens; their complacency actually made surviving the event far, far worse. It did, however, give the High Elves the ability to exist with all knowledge, for dragons to slumber for a thousand years at a time, and for the Dwarves to have lived over fifteen thousand years, unaffected by troubles on the surface. The High Elves chose to embrace knowledge and logic like none other, sacrificing reproduction and empathy. None of these beings, or even what we call magic itself, is the work of the hand of God. Yet, we are all beings created by Him, loved by Him, and have souls crafted by Him. Despite the advanced nature of these sciences, there is little difference between magic and us mastering iron into steel. Steel could have been seen in 900 BC as magic, or 'of the gods', but it is simply a science we have mastered that our ancestors did not. The church decided in 180 AD that all people of magical origin deserve the forgiveness of Christ, just as any other human. When we collected and studied the Library of Alexandria, it confirmed this, and the order I serve was founded and given autonomy. Our mission is the same as yours. Find and isolate the Relics and Artifacts, including writing and other knowledge. However, in light of recent events concerning you and your family, we feel it is imperative to formally align with you and prevent mankind from discovering and attempting to use these items to accelerate its progress toward the same fate as before. I am here, telling you all of this, so that you know you can find sanctuary, even use as a repository, any church that bears the symbol of this specific Celtic cross."

He then handed me a small bronze amulet, a two-inch-tall Celtic cross with an interwoven pattern on its surface. The circle between the post and arms also had the crosshatch pattern. A black leather cord was attached through a loop hole at the top, indicating it was to be worn around the neck.

"The second reason for my visit is to warn you. These threats of ancient artifacts are grave, indeed. However, the forces that threaten one's soul are also at work. They strive for the fall of man as well. Men drive towards it, marveling at their own invention, while the evil spirits that have beset mankind from the garden also have existed from the beginning and know of the power in these discoveries as well. They will seek to influence those who hunt or use them. They will enter ones whose will is lessened by those devices. Stories in the last several thousand years of creatures wrought with nightmares are not stories. We believe some are actual creatures, either forced into those forms by the tools we speak of, or ones that have lain dormant from the age before, found and awoken by agents of evil. Demons can inhabit the works of man and influence their use, just as they possess the bodies of people. Several of us have, by special order of the Pope, been asked to use our magic for the first time in over a thousand years, to dislocate an artifact, to push a demon out of a person, manipulating the space between spaces and the energies within. Our workload is growing, pointing to the same concern Kleet and Corfus had."

Father Zeiss paused, obviously seeing that my brain was having trouble keeping up with all this new information. He quietly sat back in the chair, casually drinking his lemonade.

"So, monsters and demons. Right? And your order is becoming more active, using magic against them? What happens when you must do it in the presence of the ordinary?" I asked.

"Yes, essentially. Some are possessed people, some are leftovers from that previous age, awakened by accidental disturbance, or on purpose by those seeking these powers. Occasionally, we are tasked with dealing with it when the witnesses are in a remote area and have been quick to come to their local church seeking help. When immediate action to save lives and souls is required, a member of our order can do what is needed, and then the action is attributed to 'miracle status' and allowed to stand as is. Sometimes, what the ordinary perceive as 'magic' is, in fact, relayed to us by the High Elves as demonic forces. In those cases, we dispatch an exorcist, allowing them to dislocate to the area immediately."

Now I needed a few long drinks to help swallow all of this. It made sense; at no time had I ever heard a sorcerer assume their supremacy by magic alone, but personal hubris. My soul is God's property, and I have done my best to protect it as such.

"I just wanted to meet you, and Corfus had described the circumstances of your father's passing, and your family's rare acceptance of the ministry into magical prisons. He explained how Arterous fell defending a Priest. The work you and Barthow did to help stabilize the events, with no knowledge or direction guiding you. Beware going forward, that the trials you may find yourself facing might not be old technologies of man, but trials of the spirit, and you are not alone in it." Father Zeiss finished with a tone of comfort; the tightness exerted around his face during this discussion now relaxed and softened.

"I am grateful, sir, and will indeed be on guard," I said, genuinely grateful. Not for the new set of circumstances, but knowing after having lost so much of the ones I counted on for support, we were even less alone than I thought.

I thought for a few minutes and decided I needed to know something. "So, Father Zeiss, the High Elves, the Dwarves, all of them acknowledge God?"

"Yes, in fact, the High Elves were the ones who gave the descendants of Noah some of the original texts which had been preserved for them to continue. They felt the original works belonged with the descendants of those who wrote them. As they put it to me, they could find no logical science to deny intelligent design," he explained. "In some instances in history, the High Elves have been mistaken for the Watchers." He paused, awaiting the expected response from me.

"Watchers?" I asked, unsure of the definition he was referencing.

"Yes, here," Father Zeiss reached into a pocket and pulled out a small pamphlet-sized booklet and handed it to me. I took it and read the cover, "Book of Enoch," and the smaller print below it read, "Book of Giants."

"What's this?" It is an ancient writing included in several canons worldwide, including those of the Eastern Orthodox and Ethiopian Orthodox churches. It details many events and beings that are still relevant, no less a part of the bible than any other book traditionally included. The Watchers are the fallen angels, and are briefly mentioned in Genesis as the cause for the Flood." I looked up to him from the little book in amazement, as it was the first time I had heard about it. He continued, "They are here, they are responsible for possessions, for corruptions, and every diabolical event that persuades men and women of any kind to follow evildoing." He sat back in the chair, crossed his arms, and exhaled heavily, pausing. Then he looked up again and held his right index finger to his mouth briefly. "They are actively colluding with ones like Dolphus Tangleweed, in ways we can sense but not predict."

"Yes, but as I have said to those who want to discuss such things with me, I tell them that God is not afraid of our questions. Many are not able to hear, even those with ears. So, the ancient traditions of the far east, India,

China, places like that, how do their traditions relate to the stories you and the High Elves have spelled out?"

"From what they have told me, some areas of the earth's surface looked much different then; land masses have changed, and where the ocean lies is different. In the Orient — China and Japan — and in some parts of South America, those places had advanced technologies and were affected by asteroid fragments, but not as much by the discharge of the weapons men used against each other. Much of the advanced tools and 'powers', if you will, that they had before the Calamity were still functional for several hundred years after. That was some thirteen thousand years ago. Those who wielded them were able to do, know, and act in ways the survivors saw as godlike. Many of the texts from those times, and tales of their teaching and influence, have passed down in colorful myth. Some similar accounts of these technologies, seen by many and recorded, date back as recently as three hundred years; one such case occurred in the 1500s in Nuremberg, Germany, if I recall correctly. Thousands saw incredible lights and shapes in the skies, and some described it as a battle. That event was a situation similar to the one you had in Texas. A CIGI was found intact, along with several sky vessels it could operate. When they were discovered, they were all activated by the mere presence of a human. That poor soul died of shock just seeing them leave the little cave he found them in."

"I think I understand. In the future, then, I will need to be aware of the workings of the Spirit, of demons, or the fallen angels, in addition to the handiwork of man from the previous age, yes?" I wanted to be sure that was the task for me.

"Yes. There are several books held in the Vatican that explain events in more detail than the canon currently employs. Some offer events that are excluded altogether. What I can tell you is that all these creatures that are living beings are crafted with a soul by the hand of God. Be mindful of their souls, as none are exempt from God's love. Some have been lost for so long, either by their own doing or what was done to them, that they have abandoned hope of reconciliation. There is hope for all. However, I heard that you had access to a goblinwerked monocle in Texas when you were looking for the cause of your father's illness." Father Zeiss began shuffling through the pockets of his brown robe and pouches on his rope belt.

"Yes, Arterous had it as I could not use it, because my magic is gone," I told him, which he should have already known. "It was lost, however, when Arterous was overcome in the attack at the mission."

"Yes, well, I have something for you. It, too, was made by the goblins, the ones who work inside the Vatican, but for our people. It is different from the one Arterous had in that you can use it, but it is also honed and refined from layers of lead crystal, sapphire, quartz, and coppered glass to show the tiniest trace of ancient technologies, so it would have shown you what the other one missed." Father Zeiss handed me a jeweler's loupe with a silver cover. It was small, but probably better suited with its convex lensing for looking at tiny things.

"Thank you. I am not sure I ever want to be in a situation where I need to use it. I don't know what I would have done with it before, with no information on a subject I never knew existed." I said.

"Professor Templeton would have relayed it to us; we would have been able to intervene sooner, I think. Also, the hex jars that your mother was wise enough to use on your father, we used this very loupe on those and confirmed it. We know it works."

"I honestly don't know what to say. In a matter of a couple weeks, I have lost my parents, actually met High Elves, had a good friend die, seen a massive tornado that went on to kill most of a Comanche tribe, seen an assassin kill a shapeshifter medicine man and my mother, saw the effects of unhinged aggression, learned of ancient human technology that lies in wait to strike us, been told of a pre-historic civilization whose hubris nearly killed every living thing on the planet, and also proposed to my fiancée. I think what I really need is some time away to consider all these things and what part I play in them." I went ahead and let it all out to this Priest, which was uncharacteristic of my usually stoic attitude. I had really had my fill of these things, and almost told him I wasn't interested in 'helping' anymore, as my 'help' hadn't amounted to much in my eyes.

"I do understand. Really, I do. I thought it best, since you had already been drawn into these things, that you proceed with all the knowledge and tools possible. Even if you choose a completely normal life and refuse to pursue these things, it is still better to know about them, as the people and events of the world may not be done with you. Telling you that everything is under control would be a lie," he said, leaning back in his chair. "Not one person who knows of these things would dare question your resolve to stay removed."

"Well, Father, I thank you for this gift, and for the trust in these matters. Honestly, I intend to visit Monika's parents, announce our engagement to them, return home to finish my work on this latest book, and hopefully in the spring, have a wedding and teach a course or two." I said frankly, then I stood to thank him again, hoping to usher him on his way.

Father Zeiss stood, grinning widely, and reached to shake my hand, and I did as well. Aside from further involvement in these matters, I was actually relieved that the spiritual world had fighters against this menace as well.

We walked to the front door, where the doorman opened it, and the Priest left. I went upstairs and found Monika in Klement's study, speaking to a portrait of her parents. I sat down to wait for her, and several times she turned, smiling and looking at me, clearly talking about me. After about ten minutes, they finished, and she came over to see me.

"They received the letter, and were not fooled by the vagueness I tried to introduce into it. They guessed straight away that we were engaged, but promised to keep it quiet until we arrive," she said excitedly.

"I intend on leaving tomorrow, and allowing a carriage ride of a few days to help me reflect on things and relax."

"What did that Priest want?" she asked.

"Well, dear, it seems there is another component to the wider world we have entered that is also willing to help. The Holy Roman Church has a sect of magical Priests who are also interested in the spiritual aspects influencing the people who seek these artifacts. He gave me this as well." I pulled out the loupe and handed it to her.

Monika took it, opened it, and began looking at things through it. "Oh, I see, this can detect magic, like the one Arterous had."

"Well, yes, it can see traces of magic, but also traces that Arterous's monocle couldn't, like the sickness that my father had. Also, I can use it, where the one Arterous had was useless to me. He gave me this as well," I pulled the little cross up and showed her. "Any church with this symbol should have a Priest who is familiar with things like we dealt with."

She held it in her hand and then said, "Well, it's good to know the fate of all souls is held in high regard by the church. I guess I understand the separation."

"Don't worry, I'll tell you everything on the trip. For now, let's get something to eat in the servants' hall. Klement and everyone else will probably return late tonight, and we won't see them until morning." So we did.

CHAPTER THREE

D ietrick Metternich sat in his study at almost midnight, waiting for someone to arrive. The family, guests, and attendants had all finished the duties of Arterous's funeral, put everything away, and the family had finished dinner together. Dietrick was torn: the Emperor of Austria had ordered him to find out what caused the events in Texas; his own brother, Klement, had suggested he feign ignorance, and he had just buried his son over the matter. How should he try to find out? The Imperial family knew that the magical and the ordinary must stay separated, but surely his majesty had some knowledge that it may not be related to magic at all. If that's true, then it isn't a disservice to the world his family exists in to at least try and find out what it really was. He felt he owed the royal family his dutiful loyalty, and also he owed it to his son's sacrifice. Thus, he had summoned a man recommended to him directly by the

Commandant of the Imperial Secret Services. His name was Jon Roqueford.

A knock echoed through the room, and Dietrick said, "Enter!" loudly. He sat behind his desk, hands clasped with elbows on the writing pad. The door opened, and a large man, smartly dressed as a noble gentleman, with a dark grey suit, a bowler hat, and a black cane, appeared. The cane was a sword cane, no doubt, with a silver handle, the pommel carved as an eagle's head.

"Jon Roqueford, sir, at your service," he said in a low, gravelly voice, bowing his head slightly, removing his hat at the same time. He had dark brown hair, streaked with grey at the temples.

"Please, Mr. Roqueford, take a seat," Dietrick said, motioning to the chair in front of the desk. "As you know, the Emperor has asked you to assist me in understanding the nature of what occurred in Texas to my son."

"We can begin with what you already know, sir. If you don't mind, that is, I know this was a difficult day for your family." Roqueford said, looking around the room gathering details, and saying words expected at a time like this, but clearly not with meaning.

Dietrick could already tell that this man was suited to the job, saying whatever pleasantries a person might want to hear and being polite enough to be aware of the circumstances, but not inclined to offer them in private life.

"My son volunteered to join a friend of the family on a trip to a dangerous territory in the Americas to visit his ill father. During that expedition, a violent storm passed through the region, and my son went to check on the welfare of a solitary Priest in a nearby mission. Indigenous persons ambushed him, and they were both killed by them." Dietrick didn't want to volunteer information to an ordinary person, even of this man's stature. "He fought a greater force from a defensible position until he was overwhelmed."

"This 'friend' of the family. This was the Mister Tellafrog?" He grumbled, now removing a small notepad and pencil from his jacket, and writing.

"Yes, he has been a longtime friend of my brother, Klement. He was just named a Professor At Large, specializing in flora and fauna." Dietrick said.

"And where was Mr. Tellafrog when your son was killed?" He said clearly as he scribbled in his little book.

"Over ten miles away, at his family's farm. His father had just passed, and he stayed with his elderly mother."

"You don't feel that it was foolish for Arterous to go to a dangerous place alone, I mean to say, shouldn't Mr. Tellafrog have gone with him?" Still not looking up, he kept writing.

"Absolutely not, Arterous was a strong and dangerous fighter himself, Mr. Tellafrog, not so much. Besides, with the number of attackers being as many as a dozen, and they came upon the old walled Spanish mission and had them trapped in a basement, I suspect even five or six men would have been cornered and killed. If it weren't for Mr. Tellafrog, the facts about this event would be lost, as would the full evidence that showed selfless dedication to the protection of the helpless. I could not be prouder of my son." Dietrick stated proudly.

"You know why I was referred to assist you, sir. We were tasked with learning about a device that is rumored to be involved. Surely you can see the interest. If there is a dangerous, unknown tool that exists anywhere in the world, it will be of interest to any powerful nation. We can agree that if such a thing were to exist, it should be the Austrian Empire that owns or disproves such a thing, correct?" When he finished saying this, Jon looked up to see Dietrick's response.

"Absolutely, in fact, I think the only person alive who knows such a thing is the woman who ordered an associate of hers to Texas, killing at least two people, looking for the same thing we are. That assassin was himself killed in the process. The woman who sent him was Runetta Lynchos. She was here today, in fact. The nerve of that woman, coming to my son's funeral." Dietrick said, huffing and twisting his head at her name in disgust. Then, it occurred to him that while she was well known in magical circles, he might not know her.

"An assassin, you say. Mmmm. I don't think there is any way I can do anything about a murder or two in American Territories, and I am not familiar with that name, but I can check our files at the office. I was instructed not to include anyone from our office, so I have no assistants on research at the central file facility. That seems a good place to start, though, especially if she is in the area now. Was there no name of this assassin that anyone knew or heard?" He didn't look up and kept writing notes.

"No, no name, I'm afraid, and his remains are interred in Texas somewhere. You can imagine I want to know more about this as well."

"Thank you for your time, sir. I know it has been a long day for you." Jon stood, finished his writing, closed the notepad, put it in his pocket, then reached into his vest pocket and pulled out a small card with writing on it. He handed it to Dietrick. "This has my name and two addresses where I maintain offices—one in Vienna and one in Budapest. The post can be sent to either office, and those offices should know where to find me if you have any new information. I will start with this, Ms. Lynchos, in the morning. Thank you again, sir." He put his hat on, gave a short bow, and walked to the door.

The next morning, at Klement's home, everyone gathered in the main hall for breakfast. After enjoying the meal and having the pastries brought in, I decided I wanted to know about the funeral.

"Sir, how was Arterous's funeral?" I asked Klement. He thought as he ate some of his sweetbread, looking right at me. When he finished, he looked at Laverne, who was very attentive to him after my question, and she set her fork down, touched her face with her napkin, and hustled the children out, excusing them.

"I'm happy to say that it was befitting a hero of the Empire. I am unhappy to report that Runetta was there, and that the Emperor has ordered Dietrick to seek out whatever caused the problems you had in Texas. I suspect word reached the security services that some new tool or breakthrough was involved. They don't suspect magic, and definitely not this new wrinkle we have stumbled into." He set his fork down and leaned back in his chair, dabbing his moustache with a napkin. "No, I feel more like they suspect an illness, like perhaps the Black Death, and are being cautious. Dietrick asked me about it, and regardless of the barriers between worlds, I urged him not to mention anything of the Orb and the involvement of the High Elves. I am not pleased with this, but I do understand it. We cannot allow the great houses of Europe to begin a search of the world for powers they cannot wield. I suggested Dietrick point this investigator towards Runetta. Hopefully, this will satisfy all parties."

"What can I do to help with this, sir?" I still felt somewhat responsible, even though no rational person could look at all I had suffered through and say I was to blame at all.

"I suggest you and Monika leave today for her parents. This investigator, Jon Roqueford, is aware of the engagement. Proceeding as you are both living normally for persons living through tragedy and starting a new chapter of your lives." He then nodded at his own statement, as we all often do. "I am already having your materials, specimens, and samples you collected earlier this year sent to your estate in Texas. They should all be there in a week or less. They have already met Barthow and been shown the way in. Separation of us all, I think, is the best policy for now."

"I understand, we will depart today," I said.

"Yes, I spoke with my parents last night, and they have sent a carriage which should be here this afternoon," Monika informed all of us.

"Very good, please let me know if there is anything else that occurs regarding the recent happenings," Klement said.

"Thank you, sir, for your hospitality, my friend." I smiled at Klement with all honesty. "I think we should go pack." I stood and held out my hand for Monika.

"Yes, thank you very much for everything, Klement," she said as we went to our rooms.

Texas

Barthow Corden had been back in Texas for only a day when a new problem arose in his area of concern, essentially central Texas. He was in charge of everything from the piney woods of East Texas, north of San Antonio, and west to the great escarpment, and most of the time, he stayed a hundred miles south of the Red River. There were three other Rangers who patrolled the towns along the Red River, and these days, there was a great deal of work to do there. Barthow had been in Fort Worth, checking out some new arrivals from Europe who had come by wagon train after coming south on the Mississippi River from Tennessee. The sheriff was called out to deal with some Indians who had wandered in, and he made them stay outside town. A trapper in the saloon where Barthow was at the time, who spoke several Indian dialects, said they were going on about giant monsters. That was enough for Barthow to check on. There are many, what ordinary folk call monsters, which are in fact considered under the protection of the magical world. He finished his drink, making sure he was unnoticed, showing no interest in that story, and that it was already dark outside. That gave him much more latitude to visit with the Indians.

He behaved as though he had one too many drinks, because trail townfolk ignore drunks as a general rule. He untied his horse, clumsily climbed into the saddle, and set his horse to a slow walk north of town to look for them. Being September now, the nights were cooling off, stars were out, and it had rained earlier. The main street was a wide trough of mud and horse droppings, with the aroma still hanging in the air. Just a quarter of a mile north of the last buildings, Barthow could see two teepees on the left side of the trail, with a fire in front of them. The skins that made up the outside of the teepees were buffalo. That was strange, honestly, most of the tribes this far south didn't have access to buffalo, let alone enough to cover whole teepees. Barthow also noticed that the adults sitting around the fire were wearing elk-hide clothing. Whoever they were, they weren't from tribes in Texas, and they didn't belong here. They could be refugees, but who they were and what trouble they'd come into would have to wait until he got closer to ask about it.

There were two women and four men sitting on logs around the fire, and they stood as he approached. The dark would allow him to speak using his wand inconspicuously, he hoped at least. Barthow tied his horse to a mesquite tree branch and approached the group cautiously. He held his right hand as if he was holding the back of his neck, trying to speak 'hello' in Apache, Comanche, Navajo, and finally, some commonality in phrases. He pointed to a large rock, gesturing if it was alright to

69

sit with them, and they agreed. He then rested his chin on his right hand, and he would have to switch from neck to ear with his wand in his sleeve, but without it, he wouldn't learn much.

"So, where are you all from?" Barthow tried to begin.

They gestured north, and he asked what tribe they were from. They explained they were Piaute, from northwestern territory. They had come into the narrow strip at the top of the Texas Territory, which existed at the time, because we were technically the closest nation—the Republic of Texas—that could help. Barthow asked politely what it was they needed help with, and they whispered amongst themselves, and Barthow couldn't hear it very well. After a few minutes, they turned to him and were asking something he couldn't understand, even with the wand.

So he asked them, "What is it you were trying to get away from when you came here?" Then they were clearer, asking whether he had any authority and whether they would just be run off again if they told the truth. "Well, I'm like a sheriff for a whole region of Texas, and I wasn't going to run you off at all, just wanted to know if y'all needed help."

They proceeded to tell him that they were the last of a tribe that had been run out of their land by giant hairy cannibals. They wanted to exchange whatever wealth they had left from their entire tribe to have these beasts killed so they could return home. They had suffered much at the hands of the Comanche on their travel here and had suffered at the hands of at least four distinctly different Comanche bands. They had lost over twenty of their troupe, unable even to bury them properly, as they were carried off. They had little left to barter with, and lacking means, the sheriff mistook them for vagrant troublemakers. Being scrawny, tired, and essentially unarmed, save a few knives, the sheriff did the Christian thing and allowed them to camp *outside* town, dogeared with specific threats of annihilation if they so much as set a foot inside the boundaries.

"Well, fellas, I can send some people with a couple of you, if you're willing, to guide them to the area. It won't cost you anything, because it is their job. It will take them a couple of days to get here, and Barthow assured them he would talk with the local sheriff and make sure they were alright to stay a few more days. They discussed amongst themselves for a moment and agreed to wait. Barthow stood, shook all their hands, and went to get back on his horse, and went back into town to find the sheriff and talk with him. He had decided to tell the sheriff that these were his guides he had hired, and they'd be on their way as soon as the rest of his party arrived. Once he had done that, as the sheriff was still in the saloon, he went to his room on the third floor of the hotel, opened the window, and whistled for his hawk. Then he sat at the little table by the bed, and wrote a letter for the two Rangers who were on leave near Waco, and tied it to the hawk's leg, and sent him off. In the cool of the night, he could probably reach them by morning. They were instructed to head straight up to Fort Worth on horseback, with supplies for two weeks of ordinary travel, and wait

71

for him. The few magical Rangers of the Republic of Texas were encouraged to ride as ordinary people, because their ability to interact and gather helpful information is limited when they dislocate everywhere. Barthow had to get back to Raileanu's homestead, make sure his home was in good shape, and let the last delivery of Raileanu's trunks of materials be allowed in. In the morning, he would dislocate there, as time was now tighter than it had been earlier in the evening.

His hawk screeched and tapped the glass, waking Barthow, who shot straight up and swiveled his head about as is good practice for a frontiersman. That motion, not for the first time, had strained a muscle in his neck, and he grabbed at it, moaning and upset that he wasn't as young as he once was. Throwing his legs off the bed, he went to the window and checked to see if anyone was in the street below, looking at this bird behaving strangely. The few people out and about before the sun cracked the edge of the horizon were busy watching their steps and minding their own business. So he opened the window and let the messenger in, shutting it behind him. Rubbing the sleep from his eyes, he noticed there was a message on each leg. When the crust and grime had been cleared away, and he opened his eyes wide and shut them several times in quick succession, he untied the notes and sat back on the poorly packed mattress atop the rope bed, the frames and ropes creaking under his weight.

One was from his Rangers, confirming they were set to leave this morning to meet his Piutes, and the other from his boss. The one from his boss said that the young man in Patterson, NJ, was pleased to have done business with them on the order earlier in the year for 100 of his new revolvers, thanking Barthow profusely for giving him the courage to press on with his designs. Mistakenly, the young man, Samuel Colt, had believed that he was engaging with the Texas Rangers as an organization, not the order Barthow had paid for in gold coins, and the address for delivery was the Magical Ranger's office in Bexar. Barthow had told me some years later that it was probably good that that shipment had come to the Magical office at this time, because it would be a few years before the Texas Rangers were an effective and dangerous foe for the outlaws of the territory. Had they received them this early, their numbers would have been given out or sold at high profit to surveyors and the like, and most of the firearms in 1836-1839 would have fallen into the hands of the Comanche, which would have been horrible for everyone involved.

Barthow had been following the trail of magical crimes that stretched from Santa Fe to Baltimore at the beginning of 1836. He caught and delivered this hombre to prison in the Eastern US District of Magic when he decided to take a week to look at the 'civilized' world back east, visiting the large cities and taking in what was new. It was that fateful trip that he came across Samuel Colt, when he happened to hear five shots fired in quick succession, and he decided to investigate. Maybe it was a crackshot kid or traveling exhibition shooter. The Republic of Texas, ordinary not magical, could use someone who could ride and shoot, and the influx of new blood from the rest of the world in this century of wide-eyed dreamers, people with grand plans, or those who just brought ideas from the Old World that were unwelcome, was enormous. One trait of any good ranger, compared to tight-laced, stiff-necked military men, was that they readily admitted they didn't know everything, and were eager to learn. So, Barthow found Colt working on his design, and right before he entered the field where the firing had been, five more shots rang out just like before. Stepping into view of the event, he saw the cylinder, the swap to another pre-loaded one, and again five shots were loosed. Barthow was sold without even speaking to him. But the meeting took place, the order was issued, payment was happily dispensed, and that is how the Patterson Colts and the longer carbines entered the territory in good numbers and began working their way into the hands of those who needed them most. Well, when Barthow and his boss decided on the tactics and survivability of the new Texas Ranger companies, they went from rag-tag to Congressionally authorized, using men who were capable and qualified.

Vienna

Jon Roqueford slept only five hours after he met with Dietrick Metternich. He was bothered by the lack of details, and that a woman had been attending Arterous's funeral, who had essentially been named in dastardly goings on. He hadn't been forthcoming; he had heard that name in recent weeks, but that report was as vague as the one he had heard the night before. Two of his guards reported that a woman fitting that description had been menacing a guest at the Imperial Gardens just a week prior, right here in Vienna. He rose at five o'clock in the morning, according to his pocket watch, giving it a couple of winds as he sat up, stretched, and began dressing for the day. He would stay in his office, going through files to see what else he could discover about this woman. Runetta Lynchos. Neither name seemed familiar, and he was certain every person of note in Vienna he could recall the name of. He left his home, locking the door, at five-thirty, still dark outside. It was only four blocks across three streets to his office. It was a plain brick building, attached to a grey, stone-and-mortar building, but its entrance was in the alley behind, through a locked wrought-iron gate. From the street out front, it looked like an extension of the stone building, but that's the way the security service liked it - anonymous.

Once inside, and the door securely locked, he lit a lamp, got the small potbelly stove on the first floor going, and set his water kettle on it. He would go to the second and third floors where all the files were locked in windowless rooms, and set to it. He would have at least a couple of hours before his personal secretary arrived, then he would have more help.

It was indeed two hours before he heard the door downstairs being unlocked, and, astute as he was, his secretary called out to see if anyone was there, only to find the stove was on and the kettle was hot.

"I'm on the third floor, Stephan!" Jon called out.

"I will be right up, sir!" Stephan responded.

The sound of quick steps echoed up the narrow staircase and landings until he reached the third floor, also carrying a lamp.

"Up early, sir?" Stephan asked.

"Yes, I am looking for whatever I can find in our records of a Runetta Lynchos. I have been at it for two hours and can't seem to find anything." Jon responded.

"Sir, is that not the name we received in the report from the Imperial -" Jon cut him off.

"Gardens, yes, it is. However, short of that report and her description, I don't have anything else on her. I tell you what, with my lack of sleep and early start, I am going to the bakery down the street for some fresh air. Please keep looking. I have been through this whole side of the third floor." Jon motioned to the row of cabinets in front of him.

"Yes, sir." Stephan went straight to the other side and started looking.

Jon took his lantern and went back downstairs, out, and back onto the street, hands in pockets, thinking intently. In a few minutes, he came to the cafe, sat, and ordered a pastry and coffee when the waitress came. She returned with both cream and sugar as he liked, and she also brought him a broadsheet to read. He pretended to look it over for a couple of minutes, but then just laid it down and pushed it away, as he wasn't retaining any of it, preoccupied with the events surrounding his assignment.

After checking his watch and seeing a whole hour had passed, he gave it a wind and decided to head back to his office. The coffee had pepped him up a bit, and perhaps

Stephan had found something useful. A man of perception and logic, Jon had spent his younger years dashing any sensations of premonition or precognition. Still, as he rounded the last corner to his office, he was overwhelmed with the feeling someone was watching him. So after he took a couple of steps past the corner, he went back to it and peeked around at an oblique angle, carefully observing each person he saw as he slowly leaned around it. On the opposite side of the street, looking into a store window, he saw a man in a gray tweed long coat, with a black scarf and a tatty burgundy top hat. None of those things were common on the streets of Vienna. Jon watched him for about two minutes and saw the man actually watching the corner in the window's reflection. He went quickly to the alley, through the gate, and into the office, locking the door as always behind himself.

"Stephan! Come here!" Jon shouted. He heard the hurried footsteps approaching, and Jon gave him a quick description of the man and sent him off to follow him. If he had found anything in the files, he usually left them on Jon's desk, so he went there and found nothing. Taking Stephan's lamp, he went back upstairs and decided to start on the second floor this time. He had another strange feeling, as though he already knew nothing would be in the files. So after 30 minutes, he abandoned it and went to sit at his desk, waiting for Stephan to return. It was about noon when the rain began to grow louder, and Jon heard the door unlock and open. Stephan walked into his office, soaked to the bone.

"Well, what of our friend?" Jon asked.

"Sir, I followed him until the last ten minutes. He never did anything out of the ordinary, really, just walking and window shopping, I suppose. He never went into any of the shops, however." Stephan was shaking himself off and put his jacket on the hook nearest the stove, then added wood to it.

"The windows he stopped at. Were they angled windows, or facing the street?" Jon asked.

Stephan thought for a minute and then realized they were all angled. "Yes, sir, they were all at an angle or rounded display windows. Why do you ask that?"

"Because he wasn't window shopping, son. He was using them to watch you. It's alright, it's not something I ever taught you. You are a file clerk, and an excellent one indeed. Not to worry. But now we know he is a person interested in us, that's not an indication of any concern right now." Jon thought for a moment or two, then asked, "Did you come across anything in the files before I sent you out?"

"No, sir, not a thing," Stephan responded.

"Alright, I would like you to make a report on our friend and send it to our field agents. The last thing we need is a troublemaker being nosy about where our office is."

"Yes, sir. I will do that first, then get back on the search through the files for our other person of interest." Stephan said.

"I am going to make a few house calls. If you find anything, please leave it on my desk. And Stephan, take my spare high collar slicker and umbrella when you leave, so you don't look the same, and that man doesn't spot you." Jon said, grabbing his spare umbrella, as he headed out into the rain. He heard Stephan lock up behind him.

Jon had a long walk ahead. He was going to visit a friend he had known for over 20 years. Along the way during his investigations, he had come across this man who ran a rare musical instruments shop, really more of a museum, as he would buy them, but wasn't sure he'd ever sold any. If Jon had discovered thieves or smugglers with rare musical instruments, the higher authorities would often just discard them or give them away as gifts. Over the years, he had seen things he thought might be priceless destroyed by drunken antics in a pub, and it saddened him. One night, twenty years ago, this man had watched from the back of the room as junior detectives broke a lyre and witnessed how upset Jon was. After the lads had left for the night, this man came over, explained his work preserving those things, and offered to pay him secretly for any Jon helped save. Jon had been to his shop once before, nearly ten years ago, but since then, they had just corresponded and exchanged packages in dead drops to avoid trouble for either of them. Perhaps, after all Jon had done, he might know people outside polite society, and this time he might help Jon. It was probably two miles on the other side of the center of Vienna, in the driving rain. Perhaps best, the rain would make it difficult for him to be followed.

The shop was in a triangle-shaped building on the edge of a row of homes and shops: four stories high, with all exterior glass framed in black-painted wood. Only the six feet of his building that was attached to the rest of the block was stone, large white limestone. The front door was a single-wide, nine-pane panel of walnut-and-glass with a brass French-style handle. The sign in the window said "CLOSED," but it was never turned to "OPEN." There was a knotted rope running through the door frame on a brass arm, the other end of which was connected to a bell. Jon knew that to get this man to answer, he could only try ringing the bell, so ring it he did. In between polite pauses, Jon looked all around and saw no one on the streets in the afternoon downpour. After the third ring, he heard shuffling in the room just inside.

"Who's there! We are CLOSED!" the voice said, as if just awakened.

"Mason Stringfellow, it is Jon Roqueford. May I come in?" It was worth a try.

"Jon, yes, yes, let me..." he fumbled with the door and its locks. Sounded like three internal locks with no outside key slot or barrel. After a minute, the door swung open. "Come in, please."

Jon stepped in the doorway, shook off the umbrella and his overcoat, and came on in, and Mason shut the door, locking it again. Jon looked around the shop, seeing dozens of cabinets and shelves that were new, with instruments and things he couldn't identify. Most of the shelving around was original to the building, pine, now handled and rubbed smooth over time, with each one having hand-fitted dovetail construction.

"My goodness, Jon, what brings you here after all this time, and in such weather?" Mason asked.

"Actually, I was hoping after all the antiquities I have helped rescue, this time you might help me with something," Jon said squarely, never being one for meaningless jabber.

"Really? What help could I possibly be?" Mason asked, still waking up and rubbing his head.

"There have been several reports coming in of disturbing things related to a lady, perhaps of some means, for whom I have no records or knowledge. Her name is Runetta Lynchos. Have you ever heard that name?" Jon sat on the edge of a low counter at the back of the shop, crossing his arms and still dripping on the floor.

"No. Neither name. Seems out of place for Austrian family names....Or older than most. I may have some records I can look through here. Sometimes when I am looking for or selling antiques, I take notes on such things. Interested parties, possible owners of rare items, things of that nature." Mason said, then let a long yawn go, which he covered with a fist, his eyes squeezed tightly shut. "Would you like to come into the back office and get some tea? I need some tea," and he turned and lifted the hinged countertop by his register and went through a narrow mirrored door, leaving both open. So Jon followed.

There was a lounge chair next to the fireplace with a pillow and a couple of thin blankets, and the fire was just coals. Clearly, he had been asleep for some time before Jon woke him. Scattered around the room were open and stacked, ancient books and scrolls with drawings of music and related instruments. Dozens of custom crates with packing straw were littered about, each one no doubt made for a specific type of instrument, by their unusual shape. Mason set the kettle on its hook and rotated it over the coals, then added five or six sticks of small firewood to get it going again. He sat down at his desk and motioned for Jon to take the chair in front of it.

"I will have to get my notebooks out for the last few years and go through them. It's times like this that I seriously consider hiring an assistant." Mason said, again rubbing his head.

Jon looked around and noticed that several large instruments he had personally helped recover were in the office when he last visited, and, looking at the crates, decided to ask how business was.

"Whatever happened to that old cello we saved a while back? I don't see it in here." Jon said.

"Oh, indeed, I have packed many of the more con-temporary items up and shipped them to Florence, where I was given a large display area for them so that they can be appreciated and admired, but not sold. I still have more than a dozen around here. I need to get them parceled up and sent off before winter." Mason said. "The pass south into Italy will be far too difficult in less than a month, and I refuse to send any of them by sea."

"I see. Do you think that if you don't come across a name before your time is too valuable, you might make a few inquiries to the gentry that help us save these examples of refined humanity?" Jon was intent on using every tool he thought of without burning any bridges.

"Of course, I will send word to you in one week of whatever I uncover." The kettle began to boil, so Mason went and poured two cups, pressed the tea, added two small spoons of sugar to each, and handed Jon his.

The two sat and enjoyed the tea in peace, and after ten minutes, the rain outside stopped. There were only two hours left until dark, so Jon thanked Mason for the tea and his time and decided to head back before it might rain again. Mason saw him out and relocked the door behind him. It would take Jon a bit longer to get home than it did to get here. Everyone was hurrying around in the break of the rain, and it was the end of the day for everyone as well.

Jon returned home, unaware that anyone was observing or following him, and was actually more tired than he should have been after a day of paperwork and a short visit. Regardless, he did have some Roma tomato plants and some dill plants that needed attention before bed. Nine o'clock came, and found Jon in bed, already asleep.

Mason hadn't been honest with Jon. After he had left, he pulled several files showing that three years earlier, he had sold Runetta several fake crystal balls. She, according to his notes, was interested in any crystal ball, in any condition, and wanted the first right of refusal for anything similar he came across, and always paid handsomely. For that reason, he didn't tell Jon, because Mason was dead set against anyone collecting those things, for any reason. The ones he sold her were glass ones he personally watched a glassmaker in Milan produce. He only agreed to sell them to Runetta after she spotted them in the shop window; he knew they were fake, and he wanted to keep some information on this woman. That being the only information Mason had, and how irrelevant it would have been for Jon, he didn't feel any guilt about the fib. The file notes showed an address where a note should be sent to contact her, and that he might pass that along to help.

One of the benefits of compiling these works after years of perspective and dot connecting is that Mason was not a normal person. He was completely non-magical; he was an entirely normal human, save for one thing. He is what we would call immortal; however, like any individual we average people assign that title to, it's not true. They can, and have been, in my lifetime, killed. No, not immortal, but he had been alive as long as the High Elves. He had been one of the few people who had volunteered for emerging technologies and their effects on auto-repairing devices being put in their bodies. From that day, he had not aged a single day. His hair did not gray any further, and his joints and skin remained strong and healthy. This technology continually repaired his mind, blood, and organs. The purveyors of these experiments had, rightly, assumed that the brain had the capacity to learn and retain infinite amounts of memory.

Mason was a graduate student in the last hundred years before The Calamity, studying musical history. The scientists who perfected this technology were the ones who pointed that skill at themselves and became the High Elves. In fact, if Mason ever came across one, they would recognize each other, as neither's memory had dimmed at all in the last fifteen thousand years. His collection and wealth had been built after surviving the Calamity by providing musical instruments and teaching the survivors for 20 years before moving to another town. As lifespans had increased in the last hundred years or so for ordinary people, he had settled on every 50 years between moves. He spent the remainder of the day scouring his records for additional information, perhaps some would prove helpful to his friend, without revealing too much else.

CHAPTER FOUR

PORTUGAL

In 1717, construction began on a massive royal residence, library, friary, and basilica in Portugal, all made primarily of Lioz stone. The vast wealth of Columbian gold and diamonds pouring in over the last hundred years has funded this massive construction for King John V. It is of importance because during the planning, the mother of Runetta, who it is rumored to have been involved in some way with the arranging of the marriage of John V and Maria Anna of Austria, was granted a private library to be built as part of the main library. Still, once it had been filled with books, the workers were instructed to block off the only entrance; in fact, there was no doorway ever framed for it. It was an open wall that was blocked in, as the interior facing the open square was finished. It was only fifty-two feet wide, as deep as the friary wing, and four stories tall. The family, the architect, and the monks did not concern themselves with the strangeness of the request, as the generous donation of funds was ample, and royal families are peculiar in many ways. The name of this palace is the Royal Building of Mafra, and Countess Lynchos approaches it now through the vast surrounding hunting grounds by carriage. No magical people are living or working here, and she has business with the librarian, not just her private space.

Approaching the front, she looked with amusement at the enormous structure, well enormous for ordinary men, six hundred feet or more square, three stories tall, in a square, with four story square towers at the front corners, a five story square bell tower on each side of the main entrance, which had a roman style triangular roof atop two rows of five columns, in a way resembling the balcony of St Peter's Basilica. On either side of the main facade were two large church towers, about 200 feet high, containing many bells rung for important occasions, their carillons echoing. The dome of the central basilica was visible as one approached, but once there, only the spire rising from its peak was visible. She was always amusing herself at the great lengths men go to for some sense of permanence, or importance, all out of vanity; she had come to think. All things pass away, and the untold toil and suffering that went into creating such a thing, regardless of its beauty and permanence, that much she enjoyed. In fact, the order of monks that had maintained the monastery and library had been evicted a few years earlier, another sign of the impermanence of good intentions. Some groundskeepers, staff, and a few soldiers remain, as the grand palace is used for little more than a hunting lodge anymore.

Over a thousand deaths had been recorded during its construction, and as all vain and self-important people always do, she took comfort in the idea that thousands, one day, would die for her. I am guessing she took comfort; she surely had no concern for anyone but herself and her imagined power, and I have come to think people such as this measure, secretly, their success in both how many foes fell to them and how many 'common' folk died in their service. In my opinion, this is why all human designs without the moral core God gave us always fail. The greater the reach or 'power' of the person with a sinkhole where their heart should be, the greater the suffering around them.

Before the carriage had halted, and the doorman could come out for this uninvited guest, Runetta had strode out of the little door, letting it slam into the side, nose high in the air, and walked quickly past the doorman, into the lobby and began her long walk - which she despised doing for the sake of 'lesser' peoples - through the building, to the left, and then a right turn down the long wing to the library. Never once did she look or react to the servants, trying politely to get her name or intention, to no avail. She passed rare paintings from Italy and France, the most fantastic handcrafted furniture in Europe, and incredible tapestries, as well as animal heads hung along her path. She never moved her eyes from her target, and after a few minutes, the servants gave up and just stayed a room behind her progress, in case she shouted for service. None of the royal family was in the house today, and she wasn't a burglar, so they let her be.

Arriving at the olivewood doors, she threw them open, with no regard for damage to surrounding walls, and shouted, "Librarian! Where are you, fool?" After the church's purview over the library ended a few years earlier, Runetta had continued her family's support of the structure and the library, as her mother had, to keep that treasure of documents safe and under their control. The man she was looking for was born to magical parents but possessed no gifts. He was always sickly and frail, prone to prolonged coughing fits and fevers at least twice a year. The prospects for such people are grim, unless they can thrive in the ordinary world, as they are of little use to the world gifted by magic. I often wondered if Runetta and her ilk knew the true source of magic, if it would make her more insane, or gentle her down a bit with the ruthless way she dealt with people in her employ.

As she rounded one of the many bookshelves, evenly spaced to allow ample light and air to help preserve the books, she heard the raspy hacking and dry, fuzzy coughing of her target, emptying his lungs uncontrollably each time. The kind of cough that made others want to cough or clear their throat as well.

"Fool, come here!" She shouted. "Right now! Do not make me walk another moment!"

"Countess Lynchos! So nice -" coughing, two full bouts of it, "so nice to see you," the man said. He was wearing a brown tweed jacket and pants, a buttoned vest, a natural wool sweater with a long neck curling up under his chin, and shabby little brown leather shoes, all scuffed and with dirt around the soles, probably from walking around the grounds and carelessly bringing that into the library. He had a ridiculous stocking cap on, and his eyes looked twice as large as they should have behind his magnifying spectacles. The hat was on because he was completely bald, even though he was no more than forty years of age. His name was Pedro Arkput, and he owed Countess Lynchos everything for this job, as no one else in Europe would employ him for his continual illnesses. His mind was very sharp, and he had a memory that astounded Runetta, even though she would never tell him that. In the couple of years that she had him working there, he had memorized the names and locations of every book, numbering more than 35,000. Neither of them knew it, but his tenure wouldn't be long, as the royal family would be gone in a few years, and he would have to move on. He had become very good at befriending the grey long-eared and serotine bats, whom the monks had initially begun supporting decades before, for their ability to keep moths and other book-damaging insects from feasting on the library.

"I have a job for you. I need you to research the lineage of the Tellafrogs, in any language variant, and the Binder family, originally from Hungary. I expect to have a comprehensive report on their families in one week. I will return, and want it in my hand when I do," she said sharply, looking around, never at him, then turned, hand on hip, and walked away, not caring to hear a response at all.

Once out of sight of Mr. Arkput, and before the house-keepers were in view, she dislocated into her private wing of the library. This is where her chained servants watched 'The Book' in her possession. After the vault was completed, she brought in her own magical craftsmen and soundproofed the entire space, then had the walls lined with cork so that even the irritating sounds of others were dampened when work was being done in there. She had such disdain for these indentured servants that she only referred to them as 'The Lookers'. Their job was to remain chained to the oaken table with cuffs and links of enchanted bronze, watching the book, and immediately inscribing what they saw into a standard copy that would be examined only by her. Clothed only in rags, and chamber pots fitted under their chairs with holes in the seats, side by side, one slept while the other watched. They were pale as the pages they stared into, only a few strands of long red hair left on their scalps, their skin almost translucent and thin from malnourishment, having only passing light once a day through an arrow slit horizontally built into the outer wall, next to the floor above, about nine feet off the floor. Charms emptied the waste pots once a day, and a pitcher of water between them was also filled. Each had a wooden bowl and a wooden spoon, which were filled with oat gruel twice a day. They were little more than skeletons and were bound for life to this task. Their parents were granted the privilege of caretaking Runetta's family cottage in the far northern woods of East Prussia, in exchange for their twins, at the age of twelve, neither of whom had magic. They had determined that their sacrifice was worth it, since their parents were relatively poor, had no claim to land of any kind, and, before the twins' departure, had been given a child by God who was healthy and possessed magic.

"Lookers! Pay attention! Have any inscriptions been made in the book in the last two weeks?" she demanded.

"Countess, only two entries, about 100 words total... but..." the looker on the left, who was awake, trailed off when speaking.

"But! But what, you fool?" she screeched at him.

"Look, my liege, it is indecipherable. We don't know what language this is." The frail looker leaned away and pointed to the ledger they wrote in.

Runetta lunged at the table, shoving the looker into his brother, knocking the chair over in the process. She glared, boiling with rage. The looker knew what was happening, so he just lay there with the chamber pot filth all over his backside as it tipped over with the chair. Runetta began shaking with fury. She slammed her hands flat on the table, looking up at the wall of ledgers, filled with writing from ages past. This had never happened before. The languages of the world have been set, more or less, for a thousand years after the Calamity, and now some coded cipher was being used. She pulled her wand, took a few steps back, before the slow march of the soiled waste on the floor reached her perfect footwear. She flicked her wand at the looker, whose chair, his behind, pot, and mess were all righted. She sheathed her wand, then went over to the large bound book with new symbols, and waved her hand over it, the one with her family's new wandwood ring. A few small, bright flashes appeared over it, and she stepped back. Both the lookers were again face down, doing their job, fearful of her wrath now.

"Keep doing what you're doing—every symbol, every word, everything. Everything is fine. Keep doing your work." Runetta said, calming herself, not for the looker's sake, but for her own. She thought for a moment about leaving in the same ordinary manner as she came, but in her anger, she just dislocated back to her home, carriage disappearing from the stable as well, with no concern for a fuss that might cause. Caring for others' opinions wasn't really something Runetta did well. In fact, leaving a trail of confusion, heartache, sorrow, and awe is what she enjoys somewhere on earth, every day.

Texas

Barthow had been sleeping late into the morning after arriving in Beaumont late and felt lucky there was even a room for him to stay in. The night before, he only stopped at the bar downstairs for a single shot of whiskey before lugging his gear upstairs and falling, face-first on the bed. He was awakened by severe jostling, as if someone had a hold of his whole body, trying to wake him. He had his right hand tucked under his head and pillow, and whipped it down instinctively to his pistol, and at the same time, still lying face down, looked to his right with one eye to see where to aim. He saw his acquaintance Corfus across the room. Although wearing completely native garb, Barthow could tell it was him because, regardless of clothing, his white hair and seven feet of height made it difficult to miss if you knew someone who fit that frame. He was sitting, and his long, straight white hair must have been tucked down the back of his shirt, because it was difficult to see any of it between the large hat, large trail kerchief around his neck, and coat collar.

"Barthow, be calm. I need to speak with you. Are you awake enough to converse?" Corfus asked.

"I dunno what converse is, but I'm awake." He said, his voice muffled in the pillow. He sat up, holstering his pistol, and then rubbing his eyes. "Yeah, okay, what's the trouble now?"

"You have two deputies who are going to help some Utes having trouble with reported giants. Please handle it, as it is a group of large giants, some of the last survivors of the Calamity in the New World. They cannot be allowed to live, but at the same time, these aren't to be handled the same way the artifacts are." Corfus said.

"We come across them once and again. We'd been destroying evidence of 'em when they cause trouble, anyway." Barthow said, then letting a few big coughs loose, probably from his copious use of pipe and whiskey.

Corfus began speaking, "They were fully created beings. They were made by men in the previous age, from nothing. They have no human soul. The first ones were made for heavy labor, construction, and soldiers. They could do simple tasks, and were bound by - again - what you call magic, to those who created them. With a built-in desire to serve and be loyal to their masters, along with a powerful instinct to survive." Barthow sat up, having finished his face-rubbing and eye-blinking. He was pretty attentive now, as these history lessons the High Elves had recently started bestowing on us were very interesting, even to Barthow, who usually cared only about where the problem was and what was required of him. Corfus knew he was paying attention now, so he continued. "When the world that had made them collapsed, they were no longer cared for and became feral. Much like domestic pigs remain fixed in state, but if they are released into the wild, they return to their undomesticated state, their longer hair and tusks will return."

"So these things were everywhere?" Barthow asked.

"Yes, there were probably a hundred thousand of them, some on every continent, but that was pre-catastrophe. Within a hundred years of the collapse, fewer than a thousand were here in the Americas."

"Well, buddy, I know there were some of them red-headed ones up 'round Maryland, my great grandparents actually fought a whole clan of them on Psutie Island, killing about twenty, as the story goes, back in the 1590s. Heck, wasn't a generation later, and the ordinary folk were huntin' n' killin' us. Pretty ungrateful, but that's how my folks ended up here." Barthow explained. "So you know anything about the ones a'plaugin' these Utes?"

"Yes, there is a large family group in their territory, maybe twelve to sixteen of them. Once feral, as these have been for fourteen thousand years, isolated in the northwest of America, and deprived of food sources, they will feed on any meat, humans included." Corfus told Barthow.

"Well, I can just head up 'ere and take care of them, and get rid of the evidence, if it helps." Barthow had kicked off his boots sometime in the night, and so he reached around on the ground under the bed and started pulling them on.

"Yes, there is nothing that can be gained by finding these creatures, but they will continue to hunt and kill innocent people, so we must act. However, because it helps our cause when ordinary people find proof that undermines their fixed narrative, please leave the bodies in the cave they inhabit. One day, it will assist us in preparing people for the things of the world they must be ready for." Corfus spoke in such an emotionless monotone voice, Barthow nearly nodded back asleep a few times, and Corfus cleared his throat, indicating he didn't have time for silliness.

"Sorry, I just need to know where to go. I'll head straight there, boss."

"It is north of the gap between Big Slough and the Humboldt River, in the Nevada Territory, in those hills, you will find the cave they inhabit. Send your other two rangers with the Utes to return, and let them find their remains. Ask the rangers in secret for specific descriptions and numbers of them, and where they roam for food, so you can complete this task before they return. Also, let us know if you hear of any other giants in the course of your future work, Barthow." Corfus stood and disappeared.

"Well, guess as busy as I am, I'm glad he doesn't waste time." Barthow stretched his arms up and let out a groan as he did. Gathering up the few belongings he had in the room, he glanced out the window at the rain, then decided to have a good breakfast before leaving. He opened the window and let out a whistle for his hawk to come, so he could send word to the two gents going to escort the Utes back north. The few people out in the street were hurrying from one sheltered boardwalk to the next, trying to stay out of the muddy mire that flowed down the path that used to be Main Street. Holding both their coat collars and hats, heads down, watching their steps as they went, nobody would see the bird enter his room.

Barthow sat on the little stool provided with the table in his room, pulled his case of writing materials from the saddlebag, and set them out on the table. He laid out clear instructions for gathering information of note from the Utes and for not destroying evidence of the giants, while simultaneously not leaving them in plain sight. He waited for it to dry, found a patch of deerskin to protect the note for the long flight, and gave it a read before looking out the window to see if his carrier had arrived yet; he had, resting on the window ledge. It was preening and shaking water off, politely, where it wouldn't get inside the room. He wasn't concerned with the weather affecting the message, after all, what good is magic ink if it runs in a little rain shower? When the bird finished grooming, it squealed and came over to the desk, extending its left leg to receive the message. "Now look here, ol' buddy, once you find them fellers, you just come back here and wait on me. I shouldn't be too long." Once the message was ready and appropriately tied with a leather strap, Barthow gave him a good petting on his head and back and sent him off. Now to that plate of steak and eggs, grabbing his hat, and seating it in the correct indentation of head and hair, he went downstairs to a fine breakfast.

Austria

Runetta may be impetuous, especially when angered, and her uncle had warned her that it would be the undoing of the family's work - their secret quest to gather, understand, and use artifacts to allow the supreme creatures of earth, the magical, to rule uncontested. She despised him for all he had done to her and for the costs of dealing with him, even today as an independent adult. It had been two years since she had seen him, face to face, so to speak, but it seemed after this latest development, she could think of no other option. When she left Portugal, carriage and all in broad daylight, she reappeared in Prague, in her private townhome, the location of which she shared with no other living soul, save her wayward half-sister. She had spent the remainder of the night she arrived going through her library of runes and codes of the past, of glyphs and symbology, all with no profit. The codes she witnessed entering the book were new, and her chance of deciphering them was very low. She knew that when she brought this news to her uncle, he would rightly blame it on her recent, dramatic, and overt activities. Between now and then, she would think of some retorts that would shut his ancient, foolish mouth. She wandered about in her lavish rooms, muttering insults and sharp-witted stabs, practicing her verbal attacks on Dolphus. The first thing she would do with the power they sought would be to kill him, but she would need the power of these devices to assist her with a few details before that glorious event.

What Runetta did not know was that while word had not reached Dietrick from Portugal, the appearance of her carriage, and her walking about in her home in Prague without either passing by the front of the house or entering the front door, was noticed by Dietrick's investigator. To this day, the name of his investigator remains unknown. I have seen the record made in the years since. He had been alerted, by official notice, less than a week ago, to monitor any movements in and out of that house. The nature of the records shows the investigator, hence also Dietrick Metternich, knew it belonged to Runetta Lynchos. In that time, the investigator noticed no movement, no deliveries, no butler, no porters, no wood or coal deliveries, no guests, not even a light in the house. In the early afternoon, on the day she arrived, he saw her open the windows on the second and third floors and walk around inside. Still, he witnessed no speaking or other interaction that would indicate anyone else in the residence. He reported, but his sources, not all of whom were named, made clear that the house had been empty for more than a month before her arrival.

I have walked that street in Prague in the years since, and across the street is a barber shop proudly displaying a sign that reads, "Open since 1726." If I had to wager, the source was working in the barber shop at the time. A person in that position sees everyone in the neighborhood, knows them well, and can keep a close eye on the view right out the front window, as Runetta's door was directly across from it.

Word was immediately sent to Dietrick, and only three days later, he was also made aware of her presence at the library in Portugal, her confusing behavior, and the disappearance of her and her whole carriage, horses, and all. Dietrick, well aware of the magical world, as his brother was in that community, decided to write to him with his findings as well. That message departed Dietrick's estate the next morning. He also sent word to the contact who had asked him to look into the events that led to his son's death, advising them that Runetta Lynchos was directly responsible and behaving peculiarly, requiring more attention. Dietrick requested two more investigators, one to begin observing the Lynchos' forestry operation, as it was known to ordinary peoples. They supplied rare, old-growth lumber for the great houses, palaces, hunting lodges, cathedrals, and carpentry artwork throughout the civilized world, from their vast stretches of old forests in the center of all Europe.

Dietrick knew now that this did involve dangerous witches and warlocks; it was the only way she could have travelled from Portugal to Prague in a day, and his caution about involving the two worlds inclined him against providing too much information, too quickly. He sent word for Jon Roqueford to come to him and share what, if anything, he had uncovered.

*****

Approaching the Binder's home, I became unsettled and nervous, recalling how her mother had dismissed me outright as a suitor on our first meeting at the ball, what seemed like a decade before. She was correct, for the right reasons. I was not magical; I was nothing more than a field researcher travelling around, living in hotels and tents, and my father was a territorial magical prison warden. She spotted my rough hands, sun-browned skin, and discomfort in social situations from across the whole ballroom. As so often happens in life, when I found myself completely out of place, God had me right where he wanted me. I caught sight of Monika from over a hundred feet away, and it wasn't the impeccably fitted silk ballgown she wore; I honestly couldn't tell you what color it was. I saw her, all of her, her spirit, her aura, the very luminescence of her glowing skin, her sharp and intelligent eyes, burled-hazel and brown, like two lit suns over the gentle hills of her cheeks and flawless smile. Her smile was wide, energetic, and effortless, driven by her genuine care for others. Radiant long brown and chestnut hair up, but allowed to dangle onto her left shoulder. I only give those details because after I saw her, her mother watched me marvel at each detail, only being drawn from one feature's brilliance by the majesty of the next. She watched carefully, waiting to see her daughter's reaction, and, in an instant, upon seeing her react in a similar, uncontrollable way, she set to work. Before Monika even made her way politely to her mother to inquire about me, she had already determined it couldn't work.

"What is it, what are your eyes doing so far off in the distance?" Monika startled me out of my befuddlement.

"Is your family ready for this, uh, for me, us, to um..." I tried.

A long blank stare is all I got for a moment, then she said, "It is no longer up to them." She wrapped her arm around mine, squeezing it tightly, like an overboard passenger to a life preserver, the light in her eyes beaming, and calming me. "Besides, it is already spread from the family home throughout the whole countryside, I'm sure," she finished with a smile.

"Oh God, are you serious?" I asked, since that kind of thing won't help my panic, which was becoming real at this point.

"We will know if you're mobbed when we arrive," she said, reaching over to kiss me on the cheek.

It didn't help; I was nearly petrified now at what might be happening. I really didn't want to deal with hostility from her family in any way after burying my parents so recently, nor did I want her to choose me if they felt that way, which I was sure she would. I took a deep breath, hoping secretly that I wasn't going pale. The carriage came upon the maintained road surface as the track left the woods and entered the open fields, where the approach to the front of the estate was tall, grassy hay. In the next week or two, they might go from green to brown and be ready for harvesting. The tops waved in the breeze much like the surface of a green alpine lake, bordered not by land but by a lovely new three-rail fencing that must have been whitewashed earlier in the summer, as it still looked fresh. The closest open areas to the house were bound in with holly shrubs and were full of lavender.

There were beautiful maples, all the same size and shape, with some of the leaves already turning yellow. The house was a long, four-story, yellowed limestone block building with a dark grey slate roof and black-painted trim. Trellis let climbing roses cover the gaps between all the windows, and they were all sparsely blooming, but shimmering red in the sunlight.

I seemed to calm a bit as we approached, and looked at Monika, who was smiling in a very mysterious way, looking at the front of the home, weaving her head side to side around the posts of the door to get the best view out of the little windows, occasionally glancing back at me as we drew close. Her excited actions were not helping me maintain my calm, and I took a few more deep breaths as the carriage stopped in front of the door.

"Here, darling, wear your own hat, especially if it helps. I mean it. You are dashing in it, and I love it." She handed me my green-brown mushroom stetson hat and took the silly bowler off I had been wearing for some time for her sake. I took it and gave her a little kiss of thanks as I put it on and adjusted it properly.

No one I could see was outside as of yet, so I waited for the carriage to stop rocking forward and back before grasping the door handle, opening it wide, and stepping out. I straightened my vest and jacket before walking around to the house side and letting Monika out.

I approached her side and put my hand on the handle when I finally heard the front door open and some movement. I decided to remain straight-backed and focused on Monika and her safe exit, extending my left hand for her to grasp and using my left foot to draw the carriage steps forward from underneath. After all, I am a man and built to concentrate on only one thing at a time. She poked her head out, fully illuminating her breathtaking face in the full sun, took my hand, and began to step out. She was watching, what I thought was the butler, behind me, and suddenly broke into an explosive smile, covering her mouth with her free hand, and finished disembarking. I shut the door and turned around to retake her hand, for my own support this time, only to see the display that caused her amusement.

There before us was her entire family filling the wide stone porch at the top of the few steps to the front door! Her parents, her three sisters, their husbands, her eleven nieces and nephews, and the entire house staff, all lined up smiling, half or so crying, all promptly burst into applause! As so often in life, the fears I had were replaced with a whole new set. Being naturally solitary and private, I stiffen up again, hoping to be worthy of all this excitement and be what they all hoped I could be for Monika. It was clear they all adored her and had wanted her happiness for years; it felt warm and welcoming. I smiled, and, starting with the front row of excited, restless little ones, they descended the stairs in waves, hugging and then hugging us again. Two of the little boys wanted to see my hat, so I obliged, and they ran off into the lavender bushes with it. I'll get that back later. The brothers-in-law came and greeted me with a good handshake, saying they were delighted to meet me.

Comforted by the unexpected familial warmth and welcome, I became more at ease with each passing moment. A problem that has plagued me over my years is being uncomfortable with large groups and meeting new people, especially if there was an expectation for me to be personable. Paradoxically, everyone always told me what a good person I was to be around in the same circumstances. All of this crowded my mind while this was going on to the point that I couldn't remember any of the countless families' names. That didn't help my unease either. Finally, Monika corralled all of the family except her parents into the front doors, leaving us alone. With her trademark sideways smile, she shut the doors for just the three of us to have some peace and quiet.

"Sir, Madam, thank you for receiving us on such short notice for an announcement." I reached my hand to her father to shake, leaving my left hand behind my back, hoping it would be alright.

He had his left hand behind his back, and his right thumb hanging loosely from his jacket buttons, but jerkily removed it and reached for mine with a broad smile, almost as wide as his long, waxed, and pointed moustache. He had a friendly smile, thin but full dark blonde hair, and dark blue eyes. His expression was actually very friendly and encouraging, and his grip and handshake were vigorous and enthusiastic.

"Viktor Binder. Great, great pleasure to meet you, Raileanu. I know my daughter, and she truly adores you, sir. I learned years ago to trust her, and I can tell I have no reason to stop trusting her. Hmm Hmm!" he said. Thank

God, I could not even remotely recall my fiancée's father's name. Ugh. "And this is my wife, Mariana." He released my hand and motioned towards her, then stood erect again, both hands behind his back.

Mariana extended her elbow-length, gloved right hand, fingers together, and I took it in my hand for a moment, bowing a slight bow, praying I was behaving correctly. None of this etiquette was taught on the little farm where I was raised in central Texas. She smiled, and it was apparent that her features were given to Monika and Monika's practical nature from her father. "Shall we go inside? I understand there is an announcement of some importance today." Mariana said, trying to contain her excited smile, turning and taking Viktor's arm, walking through the doors, which apparently had not been closed as I thought. Once her parents turned, I looked at the door, and there were at least four sets of heads peeking through the cracked-open gap, who burst into giggles and let it open all the way as they ran away. Maybe one of those rascals had my hat, I thought, as I followed Monika's parents into their home.

CHAPTER FIVE

O ne of the rarer trees that grew around the hollow that Dolphus Tangleweed called home was the Bloodthorn. It never grew taller than forty feet; its trunk, at three years of age, was usually four to five feet in diameter, and its canopy could be as wide as sixty feet by then. Every inch of the trunk and limbs was covered in three-inch thorns, a quarter of an inch in diameter each, with a tiny hole in the beveled end. Any animal unlucky enough to brush against it would experience the sharp draw of a vacuum for just a moment, but long enough for the tree to draw a copious volume of blood for such a slight prick. The wound would cause festering and dizziness for as much as a week. The leaves were broad and shaped like a three-lobed water oak. They were not carnivorous, nor is it known why they seem hungry for the fluids of living animals. When cut down, which is difficult, the grain is as hard as old-growth post oak, and the traces of each encounter with blood are recorded in the rings by a vertical stripe that goes from the thorn into its roots. I mention this species and its specifics because of the vast numbers around his small cottage. The way in is absolutely impossible for ordinary people and animals; they grow too thickly, and no doubt managed by magic for that very purpose. Mr. Tangleweed loved the tree for its emotionless protection of his sanctuary, for its merciless taking of intruders' blood. Some nights, when the weather suited it, he would sit outside, eyes closed, just listening to the vast thousand acres filled with those trees around him for any sound of unfortunate creatures mauled by them.

Runetta knows his affinity for these trees and intentionally arrives at the time of the evening when he relaxes outside to watch the dying of the sun, at the edge of the land where a ring of the bloodthorn stands guard. She doesn't even draw her wand, just choosing to use her ring today because she knows how her uncle hates the blasphemy of the ring over the wand. Waving her ringed hand from side to side as she walks carelessly, breaking the trees apart, crashing and cracking out of her way. She knows that magic can heal damaged living things; they cannot repair ones totally severed from life, as a tree from its roots. When Dolphus heard this rending, he gritted his teeth, knowing it was Runetta. As the light fell from the sun passing away, the ring on Runetta's finger let her whole hand grow into a glowing orb, and now Dolphus could see it.

Dolphus seethed with fury as she approached. Those trees were one of the few living things he identified with, and he felt foolish for a moment letting someone like Runetta sense it, but he restrained his movements and rage until she was closer. He wanted her to be filled with gleeful smugness at her wreckage and see her face before he acted. She was getting closer, only a few dozen yards now...

Mr. Tangleweed was a hundred and forty-four years old now, and while the powers of magic that brought him physically this far in life had begun to fade, the power of the mind, as in most magical people, had grown to its zenith. He had once stood six feet four inches tall, with almost comically broad shoulders, and a powerful stance and presence in any room. The length of his arms and legs meant that while he never grew bulbous muscle groups, the strength of length alone meant he could overpower any opponent who came within arm's reach. His hair, once a prideful mane of thick and shiny black hair, had degraded into a tangled mass of filthy grey. His hands were also once quite large, but the tendons and musculature had shriveled, and his joints were just painful, knobby talons now. They cause more mayhem than productive work these days, clumsily dragging and catching on things, dropping cherished valuables without warning. Hours on end spent staring into the hundreds of crystal balls about his place had worn his face into a sagging, leathery mess. But no person alive could fail to notice the fierce, wise, and angry eyes that had never lost focus or detail perception. There he sat and waited for his niece to come closer, hunched over the globe, dimly glowing before him, under a black sackcloth robe pieced together to warm his large frame, still wearing the same hunter green suit he had first come to this place forty years earlier. The wear showed its neglect in this place.

Runetta strolled into the clearing, pretending not to have a care in the world, almost as if it were a gift to the old man before her that she even visited him. But it was not a courtesy visit; he had summoned her, and she knew she had no choice but to return when called. Dolphus kept staring at the ball, showing no sign to her that he noticed her ridiculous entrance display, building energy inside his old bones until the last second, like winding a mainspring until the mechanism was so tight it was about to fail.

When Runetta was young, she used her wand one day to take three of her uncle's favorite crystal balls into the front yard and destroy them in a way she thought was beautiful. She levitated them high up, maybe a hundred feet, one at a time, then caused them to explode into a billion glittering shards. By the time he made it out front to see what was happening, they were all gone, the last of the particles falling all around him. He ran to her, snatched her by the throat, lifted her a foot off the ground, and glared into her eyes, choking the life from her. He saw the pain and fear of the event, studying it intently, looking for her worst fears to appear. It was the feeling of cold as blood stopped circulating, but the nerves continued to transmit information to the brain. That sensation caused her the most fear: the cold. Getting the information he needed, he threw her to the ground, ripped her wand from her hand, and snapped it in half, throwing both pieces in the firepit near the table he used for keeping warm while remote viewing outside. It was the loss of her wand that day that drove Runetta to develop the rings she now sells throughout Europe. And another reason Dolphus hated the wand rings.

He, and he alone, also knew that with the use of the wand rings, with silver, copper, or copper-nickel wound centers, a greater number of what they called ordinary people would gain powers as well. He felt sure that knowledge would die with him before long, as the Lynchos and Glauer families would never allow it in the hands of the ordinary.

When Runetta reached the midpoint of the open area around Dolphus's home, she fell into a trap designed and used only for her. The ground was an illusion that she might have spotted if she weren't so busy looking down her own nose at the horizon and strutting around like a fool. It swallowed her up to the neck, immediately encasing her in a gelatinous goo that Dolphus made sure was zero degrees Fahrenheit. Only her head remained above the trap. Now he sprang up, and like an artificially animated skeleton puppet, he made it to her faster than she had seen him move in years. He crouched down to one knee and looked in her eye, waiting until the shock and anger passed, and he saw the same fear he had seen in her eyes when she was a child. She would be more docile then, but this time she would not be in danger of death. Dolphus pointed his wand at the ground near her right side, forcing Runetta's right hand to move just above the surface. He grabbed the ring on her finger, once firmly in his knobby grasp, her hand whipped back into the freezing mire. He didn't even look at the ring; he just flung it over his shoulder, landing it among the coals of the fire. She watched it, but shivering and teeth chattering, didn't actually care about the ring. Dolphus then poked the tip of his wand hard into the top of her scalp, twisting and turning it until she felt the skin tear and blood begin to seep.

"I told you to get that illness for me. I told YOU to get it for ME! Not one of your idiotic minions. I told you WHERE to get it, WHO to get it from." Dolphus yelled at her, spittle showering her face, then jumped to his feet, turning his back to her. "I do not stare into the void for a hundred years so that a petulant child whom I raised and gifted powers none other possesses, to strut around toying with ancillary peoples! The first Orb to show itself, AND ITS POWERS TO OTHERS, in two hundred years! Now, my dear, because of YOU!" he fell back to his knees this time, placing the wand between her nose and left eye. "Now the High Elves know we are looking for the Orbs and have changed the writing in the book to a code we don't have," he sneered at her, hating her arrogance. "There is only one way for the magical peoples of the world to rule over all, my dear. Only I know it, and for it to work, we need one Orb. Just one." Dolphus went back to his little table by the fire and sat down. "That's not all I have seen. Those involved from Texas are now shielded from my view. As is the Imperial family in Austria. I do not doubt that the other great houses in Europe will follow suit soon enough. They, the ordinary people, are also now seeking covertly the same things we are, my dear. Those people, for reasons I refuse to share with you, because of your obvious foolishness, selfishness, vanity - pick one, must not ever find one, my dear." He went back to staring into the crystal ball on the rickety old table. Flicking his wand at her without looking, she was thrown from the pit high into the air and away from the entire forest, landing about twenty miles away safely in a haystack.

*****

After a lively and very long lunch with the assembled family, with children taking turns using my hat pretending to be cowboys, using their hands like little finger guns, and running around the table shouting and playing, I looked at Monika, who was quite ready to stand before them all and make our announcement. So I stood, took her hand, pulled her chair out for her, and we walked to the center of the table so as few people as possible had to turn around, and said, "Ladies and gentlemen, could we have your attention?"

The adults all turned in anticipation, shushing the children, each member of the gathered family grabbing whichever child was nearest them by the arm and getting them collected and settled.

"I would like to ask permission from all of you to ask Monika to be my bride," I said nervously, for some reason. I was going to do it regardless, but I did want her family to approve of her choice. Her father stood, setting the little boy he held down as he did. "I not only approve, sir, but I also request that it be held here at this very house in the spring, at a date which suits you both!" Rounds of "here here!" spread around the table, men shouting and the ladies raising their glasses to us, again, some with heavy streams of tears cascading down their cheeks. I glanced at Monika, who was fully blushing now.

"In that case, we would like to announce to you all our engagement to be married in the spring," I said nervously, Monika hanging on my left arm now, smiling and bouncing up and down a bit. She had kept her ring in her pocket, apparently, and I had not even noticed, being concerned about everything else. She put it in my hand, behind my back, out of sight of everyone else. I took it and closed my hand around it. She released my arm and turned towards me. I put the ring in my right hand behind my back, knowing what the plan was now, and then turned to her, knelt, and looked at my beautiful lady.

"Monika Binder, will you be my wife in the eyes of God, my partner in all of life, for as long as I have life to give you?" Steadily and firmly, now I spoke, in steadfast resolve because I genuinely mean every word of it.

"YES! Yes, I will! None other could be my husband!" she said, tears falling from her eyes to her hands now. So I took her hand, revealed the ring, and put the magically crafted, pure-copper ring, woven with silver and orichalcum and set with a Louisiana fire opal, on her delicate ring finger.

The whole room erupted into cries of Hungarian victory, words I don't know, and applause, which the children really enjoyed, clapping so hard it must have hurt, yelling along with the rest of them. I held tightly to her hand, stood, and gave her a gentle kiss on her cheek, turning to the assembled crowd, who were still clapping.

They came in a large gaggle around us, slapping me on the back, shaking my hand, little ones tugging at my pants for handshakes, the ladies all gathered around Monika, who was showing the ring to them, explaining its history. I had left Austria for Texas to be with my mother, tending to my father's illness, the cause of all the changes in my life as it turned out. My father and I were suckers for interesting rocks, naturally occurring metals, crystals, or ores. He had collected some raw copper around our little family homestead and left it in a pile on the table before he became ill. I sent it to Klement while I was at home, intending to make it into a ring for the engagement I planned to propose to Monika on my return. With the grim circumstances I encountered, and having lost both parents in the first stage of my struggles in the new wider world, Klement had it ready when I arrived, and had used it to propose immediately upon my return from Texas.

Her father congratulated me heartily, shaking my hand for an extended time, commenting that the ring was magnificent, and asking if I knew Mrs. Binder's ring was also orichalcum with a violet diamond. I admitted that I had not seen it, and she then showed it to me, remarking on how coincidental it was that I had chosen such a similar composition. I assured her it must be fate, as I did not know of their fondness for the ancient metallurgical curiosity.

"It's said that Atlantis itself had vast stores of orichalcum." Mrs. Binder remarked. "I have always loved its unique color, almost different in every light, from gold to green, bright silver, and tints of copper. I must say, I have never seen a Louisiana Fire Opal before; it's beautiful."

"It was, in fact, collected by my father during his time at Wormwell prison. The rock and earth excavated during its construction were still on site, deposited amongst the iron ore slabs that line the perimeter of our homestead. Father would scour them in his free time, always amazed at the treasures held deep in the earth. Once he found the few opals, he used magic of some sort, I'm sorry I can't recall, to locate where the gem-bearing strata may extend to. He saw it went deep underground, undulating closer and further from the surface, stretching all the way into Louisiana, where it was closest to the surface. He knew that when ordinary folk stumbled across them, it would be in that state, so that's why he called it 'Louisiana Fire Opal'. He had one wish that he was never able to achieve, but it really was more of a wish than a goal. He had wanted to visit the Pale Dwarves, which are difficult to reach and have an entrance to the surface world at the southern end of the Rocky Mountains, the massive mountain range in the western United States. He would have loved to study ores and gemstones with them for a while."

"We are so sorry, Raileanu, about your parents." Her demeanor fell to a state of consolation, as did her shoulders and eyes. "Truly a tragedy how they came to meet their end. Awful. We are so proud to welcome you into our family," she said, her hand resting on my shoulder.

Not wanting to dwell on that subject any longer, I said, "I have not seen a violet diamond before; it is stunning, ma'am." I said, "The properties of light diffraction in well-ground diamonds are legendary."

"Ahh, the secret is that at its core is a purple garnet; the polishing is done so the angles radiate proportionally around the geometric shapes of the garnet itself. That is where the distinct color comes from." She said, smiling.

"I see. Impressive indeed." Again, I find myself nearly out of public comfort with all the attention and caring huddles of Monika's family. I just smiled politely and couldn't think of anything else to say.

"When do you think that you can return, Son?" Viktor said, emphasis on the 'son', stretching his smile to meet his moustache again. "From your scholarly work retreat back home in Texas?"

"Spring, as we said. I have literally not had a moment to think of the work I crated up the last day I was here, literally a whole summer's worth at Lake Königssee. I can't say a specific date, as I feel Monika and Mrs. Binder will have more say than I do. I will need her help to collate and put into book form the year's work, since the commission I received from Klement Metternich requires the first volume to be ready before next year's term begins at school. We should be able to achieve that mark, but just." All of that was true, barring more interference from diabolical actors.

"Well, son, we are very, very excited for the wedding, for meeting you, and extremely sorry to hear about your parents and the dark events surrounding your time at home. Nefarious actors seem to be at work when we least expect them, I'm afraid. I hope you know that you aren't alone anymore, everyone here is dedicated to each other, and now to you, sir." I could tell he genuinely meant it.

"Thank you, I shall try to live up to your expectations, sir," I said, shaking his hand again briefly before he patted my shoulder and went back to the table.

We stayed inside for the rest of the day, visiting ancestral portraits, explaining family members and the history of their family, having an extensive tour of the whole house, including Monika and me being shown to our adjoining rooms, in which the connecting door was keyed. I locked it and handed it to her father before returning my hands to my back and continuing the tour. None of us minded being inside, because despite the passing clouds, it was hot and still outside.

After a meal that was the largest set table of food and settings I had seen since my time in school, they brought out a bottle of Ramisco, which I had never seen or heard of. Her father explained that it comes from a region of Portugal with particular soil and weather conditions, and that its grapes are grown only in that vineyard, which is very expensive.

"I can say that this bottle has only been opened before to celebrate the engagement of my four daughters. I vowed upon its initial opening that it would be its only authorized use. Since this will be the fifth time it has been opened, I must say there is only enough for the assembled adults here to enjoy a small glass, then it will be gone. I can think of no greater use for it." He went around the table, pouring just an inch or so into each glass, then finishing it off, trying to make each one as equal as he could.

"To my Monika and Raileanu! May their lives be long, happy, and productive in the eyes of God!" He shouted loud enough for the gardeners to hear outside, proud of the occasion. A chorus of "CHEERS!" circled the table, as we all sampled the rare vintage. Stout and very red, dry, with a surprisingly sweet finish. Very good indeed.

Monika and I met outside our rooms at probably nine o'clock in the evening, where she returned my hat to me, as the kids had fallen asleep playing with it. I embraced her, absorbing as much of her smell, her soul, all of her as I could, cupping her cheeks gently and kissing her goodnight. We went to our separate rooms, and I could see under the door connecting our rooms that her light was out in less than ten minutes. It had been a very long day, and despite any of my earlier concerns, her family was fantastic. Not long and I too was asleep.

Chapter Six

Texas

B arthow Corden was adept at many things in the wilderness. Time, trial and error, interacting with those native to the land, and, of course, being stuck in pickles, forced the necessity for the invention of things and procedures that didn't exist before. He had tried to pass along as many of these skills as he could to the new fellas involved in rangerin' from time to time, but it seemed that most of them felt it was a waste of time. They felt that, with the railroads heading further west and technological innovations emerging from England and returning east, the time for trailcraft was limited. Therefore, he had decided to keep one of those skills learned when he was south of Matamoras with the locals there, quite secret indeed. People who dismiss their past, for whatever reason, are not suited to powerful knowledge. He had learned a process by which a magical person, or even sometimes ordinary ones, could expand their mind far outside their bodies, and travel to places great distances away. They could observe, investigate, listen to conversations, and move in and out of places regardless of physical protections. There are magical means to prevent this, but most places in the world don't have them, and even if you encountered them, that alone was a good sign that something important was there.

He had a vial of ayahuasca potion and two whole dried pantherina mushrooms with him most of the time. He learned that if he took a one-inch piece of the pantherina and ground it up in dried deer urine, rubbed that on his forehead and eyelids, then took a sip of the ayahuasca and sat calmly, he could push his mind outside of his body, and go to a specific place, any place, he wanted.

Barthow went north of town, turned west along a creek, and down a cattle trail until he was sure he was going to be alone for a couple of hours. Anyone coming this close to town would stay on the main road, as there were plenty of affordable accommodations this time of year. The larger parties and anyone moving herds would also have to remain on the much wider path. Even rascally bandits would stay clear of the tight brush and cottonwoods that lined the creek for a couple of hundred yards, and the deeply gouged hills to the east of the wide trail would be much better for ambushing travellers.

He tied the horse up next to the Neches River, cast some protection charms around the site, which was fifty yards off the trail, and set up his tent with a few waves of his wand. Once inside, he sat in front of his fire pit and got out a deep steel bowl that would have been incredibly heavy if he were an ordinary person. When everything was set up, he prepared the pantherina, applied it, took his sip of ayahuasca, and settled in to project his mind to the Nevada Territory to try to find the giants.

As he drew in his consciousness from every corner of his body, and then let it drift out the front of his head, he rose into the sky. He could see the grasslands bordering the squiggly, muddy brown Neches River split a few times and wander off to the northeast. The pines on the flatlands looked like very dark green grass at this height, and he moved northwest over thickets and little creeks, and the further he went in this direction, the browner and flatter the land became. He drifted over Fort Worth at incredible speed, and the only feature he could make out at this point was the Red River, then the Canadian River. He could now make out the snowy peaks in the Rocky Mountains ahead, and when he could see the Grand Lake, he turned his attention west. Once the Humboldt River was visible, he descended his point of view, closing in on the base of the mountains. Here he paused, maybe ten thousand feet in the air, trying to concentrate on the images of giants he had seen before, to 'feel' if he was close to where they were. Straining with thought, he could feel their void of intelligence was west, further west from here. Yes, there is a single rise of craggy brown rock extending some hundreds of feet above the sandy ridges just south and east of the next extensive range of mountain peaks. That's where they are. Barthow slid around the east side and went to the very northern end of the ridge and found a large entrance, maybe fifteen feet wide and twenty feet high, which was hidden from the sloped ground below by several large boulders directly in front of it. At the mouth of the cave were, in fact, eight giants, all quite hairy all over, with buffalo hide clothes draped on them, working around a fire. There were pieces of many animals that had been consumed tossed around the perimeter of the open area, and yes, there were, in fact, human skulls and bones among them.

Barthow went past them, into the cave, which was very, very large. It was a fissure that descended at a steep angle, with a flat floor at the bottom. Inside were twenty, no, thirty more of them, only three of them were little ones, and honestly, at their age, it was hard to tell the sex of them. They were curled up under animal skins. Even this early in September, the weather was already quite cold, and flurries were lazily drifting through the skies, gathering in gaps between the cold stone spires of this outcropping. There was no fire deep inside the cave, probably because there were no trees of any size in the landscape. The giants Barthow had dealt with in the past were more likely to steal wood from human-built structures. Deadfall wood was scarce here, and he suspected the giants had raided and attacked anyone in the surrounding area and retreated to this cave in hopes of wintering there. He decided it would be best to find a nearby source of wood, if possible, and wait until most of them went further into the cave in the night, then close the entrance with rock and wood, setting it on fire to smother those inside. He would have to be careful, as they were terrified of fire out of their control, but if it were mainly stones, the giants could easily move a one to two-ton stone with no problem.

Barthow withdrew his mind from the tower of stone, down the slope which, upon being closer to the ground, he could see was a whole half mile long, a steep slope of sand and small rocks. This would be helpful information: if he found himself on foot on the slope side of the tall stones blocking the view of the entrance, he would be as likely to fall down it as to retreat safely. He pulled his mind towards the Humboldt River, moving north and south along its banks, looking for a trail or bridgehead, or even a ford where a ferry crossing might be, and was hoping to find discarded lumber there that might be used to construct a fire of sufficient size and intensity that could serve his grim purpose. After a few minutes, he found a pile of railroad-sized ties, perhaps offloaded in hopes of using them later to make a crane platform for unloading cargo off barges. He could see no signs of work in that area, habitation of native peoples, nor of pioneers. Maybe it had been offloaded in an effort to raise the waterline of an overloaded barge. The rainfall in the Texas territory had been relatively slight this year, but he had no way of knowing the conditions this far north and west. He had never been on the west side of the Rocky Mountains. The closest he had come was the prisoner transfer from Wormwell to Schism, which was in a narrow gap between peaks in the San Juan mountains. That location looked much like what Barthow imagined Switzerland might be. There was a colony of goblins that lived there, and it was also the only place that Barthow knew of, where any contact with American Pale Dwarves was possible.

Sliding his mind through a narrow funnel-like slipstream back into his own body, he was back in his little tent along the river's bank, a few miles north of Beaumont. The effects of the potion and salve would linger for a couple more hours, and the distance west meant he had probably eight full hours before he needed to go. He would pack everything up and dislocate there with his full complement of supplies and his horse. Better to be ready for an extended stay than be in a very remote place with no support, planning to fight a whole horde of giants. Even if he could handle this nest of them tonight, the poor Utes wouldn't be able to make the trek back over the mountains to their home before the snows filled the passes. He would have to set up a place where they would be safe for the winter on the east side of the mountains as well. First things first. Let these effects wear off, and rest up.

Vienna

Haizek Moon was up early in the morning, dark enough that she had to light lamps on the whole first floor. She glanced out the front window of her house, and while the sun was not up yet, the warm glow of it in the east heralded its arrival soon enough. She was expecting a guest this morning, at sunrise, someone she didn't want to miss a moment with. The years had passed, with them as close as they dared be. Too many of their friends and families over the thousands of years the two of them had walked the earth had met their end at the hands of those who sought their secrets. Once, in the 1100s, they had cohabited for a few years in Prague. It was a mistake, as travelling wealthy patrons of the musical arts had recognized them, in a moment of shock, as the man in question was in his seventies, but recalled seeing them at a musical performance when he was only eight years old. That man, whose name Haizek couldn't remember, as they'd never been formally introduced, knew that they hadn't aged in more than six decades. Both of them had to leave that very night. It was physically and practically easier for Haizek, being magical. But for Mason Stringfellow, he had to abandon so very much of his collection, which he was able to recover some of, but not all.

That was not the only heartbreak for them both in the 1100s. Their extended love and cohabitation had resulted in her pregnancy, which both thought impossible. For the first time in 13,000 years, they had been together more than a few times over the course of a few years. It may seem odd to us, with such short lifespans, but after as long as they had been alive, and both suspected their physical changes of the previous age prevented childbirth, like those they knew now as the High Elves. But in 1140, after they left Prague, Haizek was indeed with child. They fled to Rudloe Manor in England and stayed there until she gave birth. The owner at the time was abroad and allowed them to stay permanently, as he was magical and knew Haizek. She delivered two children that long night, a boy and a girl. They were blessed to have a familiar magical midwife, for both were born with green skin. To this day, none can explain why. With the midwife sworn to secrecy, they raised the children in the tunnels and chambers below Rudloe Manor, protecting them from both the magical and the ordinary worlds. Neither Mason nor Haizek fit neatly into the world's versions of right or wrong, natural or unnatural. More heartbreak lay ahead, as they learned in only a few years that neither of their beloved offspring was magical, nor what is referred to as immortal, like their parents. Later, they would learn that the High Elves called the offspring they had "A Spalding" and the reasons for it. In time, they agreed that, because of their own lack of aging and one being fully gifted with magic, the children's only hope of a normal life would be in the ordinary world.

Both of them had lived a hundred and fifty lifetimes already. Losing those closest to them was something they had done far too many times, but this hurt worst of all. They settled on a small village called Woolpit, and after careful consideration, they delivered them to the town, and it was the first time either had been outside their underground refuge. Over the years, they watched closely and found both lived as happily and ordinarily as possible. I only mention it here to show the internal strength and resolve my two friends have had over the millennia, and so you can understand their role later.

Haizek went to the kitchen and prepared coffee and tea, as Mason's taste seems to vary wildly from visit to visit. Cream, sugar, honey, and a small bowl of blueberries filled out the tray. She made some croissants as well and drizzled honey on top. He had better knock on that door soon, she thought, as the food was causing her tummy to rumble in a very unladylike manner.

She was looking forward to their visit; it was only a few times a year that they allowed themselves to be together. There was another task due for the day as well, the soon-to-be-Tellafrogs were heading back to Texas today, mid-morning, and because I couldn't travel by dislocation, we would need the Runewheel in the basement. No sooner than she had placed her hand on a croissant with the intent to devour it, than there was a knock at the door. She walked quickly to the front door, unlatched it, and let him in quickly. Mason stepped to the threshold, turned, and surveyed the streets around in the dark, and saw nothing of note, and no one in sight either, so he went in and shut the door, latching it behind them.

"Hello, Mason," Haizek said, walking away toward the kitchen with her back to him.

"That smells so good, Haizek. You are so much better at hosting our meetings than I am." Mason said.

"I know, eating dried cakes and leftovers in your dank storeroom is not my idea of hosting a dear friend." She pulled out his chair at the little round table, then seated herself across the table.

"I had a visit from Jon Roqueford the other day. He has been asked to look into what happened with the Tellafrogs." Mason took a bite of the steaming croissant. "Mmmm, that's very good!"

"Does he know that it is all to do with magic?" Haizek said, taking her own bite, finally.

"No, he does not know of any of that. After Mr. Metternich lost Arterous, I guess the crown felt he would be agreeable to looking for the cause. He does know Runetta has to do with it; he's looking for her." Mason set the pastry down on the plate, which was white china with a beautiful blueberry leafy pattern. He took the small, matching cup, poured himself some coffee, and added a couple of spoonfuls of the raw brown sugar, stirring without touching the sides of the cup.

"I think, with what I'm seeing, we are getting close to the time where the ordinary people will lose interest in those like us, and in the magical world at all," Haizek said. "They are becoming more and more self-absorbed in their technology again..." she trailed off.

"Just like last time." Mason finished for her, without looking at her. "Do you remember the last hundred or so years before the collapse, the Kobol?"

"Yes, the slender ones that volunteered to go exploring the asteroid belt, Mars, and Uranus?" She looked confused as to why he would be bringing it up.

"I was reading some stories about space and the worlds that might be beyond our own. Fictional works, and mostly ridiculous, but I swear, sometimes the things that people 'imagine' are strangely mimetic to what you and I have seen already. You would think that after the thousands of years we, and the High Elves, have been around, we could explain why themes and images keep looping back into consciousness again and again. That piece I read explained how the Kobol looked, slender, grey, large heads and eyes, all of it." Mason fidgeted in his chair. He would rest his hand on the table, holding his cup. Not a few seconds later, he would release the cup to wave both hands next to his head, being more expressive than Haizek had seen him in years. It was a bit off-putting to her, and she began to worry he might be sensing events to come that they should both be concerned about. Furrowing her brow in an uncharacteristic way for her, he paused long enough to lean back a bit in his chair and calm down his rant a bit. He softened his expression, almost as an apology. Making her worry is the last thing he wanted to do. "It's either that or some of the Kobol have been returning, and have been seen by some. I just don't know. It makes me nervous. I know that the path from near decimation to technological prowess is unstoppable, but..." Mason stopped and let out a long sigh.

"It does seem to be speeding up, doesn't it?" she concurred. "Trains, steam machines, electrical discoveries, you're probably right. I don't know how to help them avoid what went wrong before. From what Monika told me of the High Elves, there are only around a hundred of them left. They are just trying to keep the relics out of everyone's hands. If they knew a way to steer it to a better path, don't you think they would?"

"I really don't know. I guess they have some hope, or they would have all gone already. If there's even a hundred here still, maybe they have a plan and are following it. Especially if they're reaching out to the likes of us, I mean, you and I know, and the Elves, that there is no such thing as magic, but those like Runetta, I imagine, she would use as many ordinary people as she could to get her hands on what she *thinks* is power. If you and I are right, there's less than two or three hundred years before we are at peak technical ability again. It could be so good for everyone, it just never is."

Haizek reached across the table and took his hand. "The thirst for knowledge is in every one of us. I cannot believe that God intends for it to end in catastrophe again."

"Do you remember when we were apart, before the fall of the last age, and I was in central Africa? When I was learning how to make their instruments by hand?" Haizek nodded and pulled her hand back to cover her mouth, suddenly trying not to cry. "Those in the neighboring villages came to attack, and we were all overwhelmed by the ferocity of the fighters. The dozen or so of us who weren't killed outright were lined up, and they were going to cut our heads off one at a time. I bowed my head and prayed for God to do with me as He willed and to comfort you. With no way to tell you, you knew. Somehow, you knew. It was the first time you dislocated to an unknown location. You came, in a flash of light, sheathed in light and brilliance, like an angel; you were there. You blinded everyone there, and grabbed me, and dislocated right back to our home," he said.

"I remember. I think of it now and again," she answered, with some tears falling now across her hand.

"God has a plan for all of us. Even me, and I believe that plan is for me to use my gifts to make musical instruments and collect them when I can, and to be forever connected to you, to love you, without end. For fourteen thousand one hundred years, I have survived with no special power like you have. Promise me that if we see the end coming, as it did before, we will give up this charade of hiding for the sake of the world, and be together until the end. That you will come to me as you did then." Mason said with seriousness.

"I promise." She squeezed his hand and pulled her arm back to her cup of tea, reclining against the back of the chair, her eyes down. "I had even thought about leaving Europe altogether," Haizek looked at Mason again, "we could go to America, and stay together there as a couple," she proffered.

"Whenever you decide it is safe, I am ready. I have always been ready." He said.

A knock came to the door, just as they both had paused to consider the discussion and how it might work, fleeing to America to be together. They had both taken another bite of the pastries and decided to wait and see if the knock came again.

"You weren't expecting anyone, were you?" Mason asked.

"No, I don't know who it could be this early," she replied.

She stood and went to answer the door, looking back at Mason, who had moved his chair to see down the hall to the door.

"Who is it?" Haizek asked.

"It is Jon Roqueford. Are you able to receive a guest, ma'am?"

"Yes, I suppose, let me get the door latch." She fumbled with it and opened the door for him. "Please, come in."

He stepped inside, removed his hat, and moved to one side so she could close the door. "I had asked the shopkeeper near Mason Stringfellow's shop if he knew where I might find him, and he said he might have come here to discuss antique horns or trumpets or something. Is he here?"

By now, Mason had begun walking down the hall towards them, and seeing Jon, he greeted him. "Jon, how are you?"

"Fine, fine. I wanted to ask if you had any information on the whereabouts of that Runetta Lynchos woman. My superior is asking for a report, and I haven't heard back from you yet. That's all."

"I didn't have anything that would help, no. There isn't much hope of my hearing from her, short of an estate sale having something she might be interested in." Mason said, shaking his head and looking down, disappointed he didn't have anything more. Then he paused, had a thought that might help, considered whether it might lead to anything dangerous, and decided it didn't. To Jon, an experienced investigator, Mason's face showed deep consideration. "Actually, I did remember something she said once. She said she had a private book collection somewhere in Portugal. It was in passing, I think she was trying to impress someone else in our proximity, but she didn't say where, actually, as I recall."

"Mmmm. Interesting." Jon pulled out his little notepad and jotted it down, then flipped it shut. He knew full well about the place in Portugal; this was just excellent confirmation.

"Ma'am, you don't know this lady at all, do you?" Jon asked, looking at her with the piercing eyes of an investigator, watching for any tells a person might give off. It was a habit he had, irrespective of the person in question.

"No, I have never met, nor heard of her before now."

"Good, stay clear of her if you do." Jon pointed his finger at Haizek, then turned back towards the front door. "Trouble seems to follow her, that's my advice. She is mysterious and quite well-traveled. Nobody seems to profit from her acquaintance."

"I will do just that, sir," Haizek said reassuringly, her hands clasped in front of her. "I don't need anyone like that in my acquaintance."

"Thank you both for seeing me. Have a good day," Jon said, refitting his hat and walking out the door, closing it behind him.

After an appropriately long pause to ensure they heard him walk away, they locked the door and went to the kitchen again, taking their seats and resuming the delicious breakfast.

"When are Raileanu and Monika coming again?"

"Actually, " she leaned back and turned her head, and looked at the mantle clock in the front room, "just about any time now."

"Probably best they weren't here, he would really like to get their views on Runetta, and they might let magical references slip in their anger toward him." Mason paused and glanced back into the front room over his left shoulder, realizing that he had seen something when he arrived that he had failed to account for, and reseen it when speaking with Jon. "Is that a camera obscura in your front room?"

"Yes, I am going to get a silver nitrate camera quite soon. I have been using it to draw landscapes around the school grounds lately, then when I return home, I paint them with watercolors. I love doing it," she said.

"Well, at the risk of overstaying my welcome, I should get going before they arrive. I would very much like to see your paintings next time I am over, if you will allow it." Morgan stood, and Haizek stood to meet him, and they held each other's hands. "Until next time, my love." Mason pulled her gently closer and kissed her right cheek, holding her left cheek with his right hand. "Together until the end," she said. He smiled and left, reminding her to lock the door, with eyebrows raised, making a turning motion with his hand.

*****

Runetta had earned the diabolical treatment at the hands of her uncle. She knew that, but their interests aligned. She wanted the power to rule over all, him most of all. He was correct that the secrets the ancient artifacts held were the key to achieving that goal. Dolphus knew his only disciple was also his only hope of finding any of the Orbs. Mistreating her, as he had discovered, was the only way he knew to motivate her. Indeed, there was the risk of her turning that power on him, but any magical person of noble lineage ruling the world would suit him fine. He knew the world of the ordinary was developing tools and machinery, not seen in thousands of years, that would allow them to increase in numbers and improve their health. Given enough time, magical people would not be on the fringes of the world, but would be so insignificant that they could fade into irrelevance. It was Dolphus's mission in life to ensure the supremacy of the magical world. Suppose the world of magical people were going to ignore him and his warnings. In that case, it might even become suitable for him to aid the ordinary world in bringing about their collapse by helping them develop tools of destruction that they would undoubtedly use on each other.

He had used Runetta, to her delight, to sow discord and anger between the great dynasties in Europe. He had even seen one occasion where she had covertly cast charms on three young men in one evening at a formal occasion in Paris, causing them to strip their clothes off and settle their differences in traditional Greek wrestling, to the shock and horror of all in attendance. It was literally the last time he laughed out loud. The aftermath was, of course, the royal courts assigning the persons of magical heritage in their service to seal all sites noted for public gatherings against charms or hexes of any kind. No one knew it was Runetta who had done it, but Dolphus watched the small image in his crystal ball with glee, centering on the grim faces gnashing their teeth of the patriarchs, trying to will their heir to win the ridiculous spectacle.

Sitting on that haystack, in the complete darkness of the inky black cloud-woven night sky, she watched the fog gently billow around the ground, thinking. There was one person who would know how to read that cipher, one who hadn't attracted much attention from her, yet. Professor Magnus Templeton. She decided to go to her home in Prague, and view him in her own seeing stone, and choose a time to take him. This time, she would be more careful and less reckless. If she could get the key to the code, perhaps even his copy of the book, all would be made right again. In a wink of her green eye, she was back in her house in her divining room.

She selected her favorite black silk viewing shawl, made to her specifications, woven thick so that no light from outside can penetrate once she is seated at the table, but very lightweight. She learned the technique as a young girl, when, at night, after a torturous day serving Dolphus, she would pull her covers over her head and watch her only window to the rest of the world. She sat, adjusting comfortably at her special table. It was about four feet in diameter, topped with a thick pillow across the whole surface, save the circular stand about one foot from where she sat. The crystal ball sat there, just in easy reach, with her elbows and forearms resting nicely on the pillowed top. She reached back to her shoulders and pulled the long shawl over her head and over the ball. Now, the only light and sound was emanating from the crystal, energized and focused by her magic touch.

A spiked glow began in the center, and Runetta now imagined the Professor, forming his image in her mind. The light grew as it honed in on where he was. She could tell it was taking her to his location in real time. Sometimes, this was good, as when she saw Monika some years before, it could show her things from the past or future, and it was sometimes hard to know exactly what she was seeing, forcing her to watch for extended periods. These visions were sharp and immediate; this 'homing in' action meant it was real time, which is what she wanted. She recognized the room in the image, and the view moved up to the floor above, then to the second floor, and there he was - in bed and asleep. She knew the place was the house's basement in London, where she had intercepted Raileanu on his return trip from Texas the month before. She knew she could arrive there, cast a sleep spell on the Professor, and then take him anywhere she wanted. But where to take him? To Dolphus, or to her secret underground castle? No. Not there. He would be able to find it then.

Since the trouble in Texas, Professor Magnus Templeton had busied himself with several tasks after each day of work at the school. The days of preparation for the next term were shorter than when students are present. He began collecting all the lore regarding the High Elves into a single section at the school's library. It was one of the most prestigious libraries of the magical world at that time. Several codices of the actual Library of Alexandria resided there, and they were at the cost of many lives of the witches and wizards who strove to protect them.

One of them did have very early accounts of its activities, teaching simple survival skills after drastic changes to the world nearly 70,000 years ago. However, that book was written three thousand years ago and was therefore always treated as fiction. Two books were from the Indian subcontinent, one from Tibet, and the Elves themselves reportedly penned two others in Scandinavia. Some of the earliest runes used there were recorded in that tome.

He had also worked to develop a rotating key using an ancient Persian calendar system as a guide, for which the Mayan symbols would then be mirrored in the new correspondences in the book. Without the agreed start year and both works, no one else would be able to use the book again. He had spent the last two days at the townhouse in London, ensuring that the markings on the runewheel there didn't have any correlation to the symbols they had chosen.

This morning, his work completed, he was going to meet Raileanu and Monika at Haizek Moon's house before they left. He gathered his things and said goodbye to the housekeeper, who lives there and maintains the house for visiting professors. He picked up his bag full of books, put his hand on his trunk, and closed his eyes, dislocating to Vienna, showing up in Haizek's back garden. The likelihood of being spotted there was far less at about nine o'clock in the morning, Vienna time. The inspector Jon Roqueford had just left, and Mason Stringfellow was standing just a few yards from the front door, having purchased a broadsheet, and was leaning against the wall of an adjoining building. Mason didn't know it, but Jon had done the same thing and was around the opposite side of Haizek's building. She occupied the pointed end of a block of buildings that was at the apex of three converging streets. Jon and Mason had taken up opposite sides of that, oblivious to the other's location.

Only a moment later than the Professor had left, Runetta arrived in the basement of the house in London, where the Runewheel was. She drew her wand and began moving silently up the stairs, hoping to catch the Professor unaware. At the top of the stairs, the door stood open an inch or so, so she peeked through. She saw a woman in a long, light-blue dress with a long white cotton apron tied at the back, her grey hair in a bun, working in the kitchen. She couldn't see anyone else. Just then, the lady she saw said, "I hope he made it alright, he was not giving himself much time really…" She was cut off mid-thought by Runetta, who had slinked up behind her and had her wand in her left hand at her throat, and her right hand, with her wooden wand ring, against the lady's right cheek. She was completely immobilized, and her mind was being scoured now by Runetta for the Professor's movements.

Moving backwards from the current moment, Runetta saw her clearing dishes from the table, then coming down the stairs, having left the Professor's bedroom, gathering his water basin and cup. Hmmm. Before that, he had been speaking to her. Ah ha, he was going to meet the lovely Monika and Raileanu in… in…Vienna. With her eyes closed, a broad, open-mouth smile spread across her face as her head tilted back. The house she saw in the housekeeper's mind, though, she remembered seeing it, but not exactly where. It was east and north of the cathedral; she recognized the junction of the two streets and the triangle-shaped front and stonework... Runetta decided to begin at the cathedral and walk there; by this hour, there would be significant foot traffic in that area. Excellent. She pulled her wand and hand from the housekeeper's head, along with any knowledge of her visit, and the blank gap of time would not be anything but a ragweed-induced fuzzy head moment.

Runetta was immediately in the eastern alcove of the cathedral's exterior. She glanced around, and no one seemed to be paying attention to her or her arrival. She would stand out with her fine clothing, but few would give her a second look, as the 'commoners' would recognize her as nobility of some sort on first impression, and not dare look again. So she strode out, turning left along the open plaza, heading to the east until she could orient herself to the building she was seeking. Taking the Professor directly to Dolphus was her plan now, as he could extract all information from him at his pleasure. As long as the disappearance was unexplained, no one would know what happened, and have no chance of tracing it back to her or Dolphus.

Yes, this street is the one that leads to the building she saw, so she turns left again, dodging horse droppings in the roadway, but using her mere presence and tall frame to force little people to walk around her. With fewer than a hundred paces, she could see the building from her vision. She let the diabolical smile creep again to the edges of her face; she was close now.

She strode from the left side of the street across the convergence of the three roads right to the front door step of Haizek's home. She did not notice Mason sitting fifty feet or so on that same side of the house that she had approached from. He was sitting on a bench, still reading. However, the same elegance and wealth Runetta exuded, which she counted on people not giving her a second glance, is precisely what made Mason look again, and he knew immediately that it was her. He panicked, having no magical power, no weapons of any kind, no authority, so he threw down the paper, stood, and began towards the front of the house, hoping to either save Haizek or find Jon Roqueford, but surveying the road as far as he could see, he didn't see Jon. He would have to go to the front of the house, maybe in front of another person, she would not act rashly. So running, he got to the front and saw her still on the doorstep waiting. He retreated, out of her view, took a few deep breaths to calm down, and hopefully appeared calm and pleasant. The ability to detect fear, nervousness, concealed intent, anything like that was a well-known skill of the diabolical. So then he walked around and went straight to the front steps, looking down to watch his step and not trip. When he looked up, Haizek was at the door with it open, and plainly terrified. So Mason walked straight up to the two of them, both turning to look at him, both surprised.

"Why, Mason Stringfellow, what a nice surprise!" Runetta remarked. "Are you here to see me?"

"Actually, it is a happy chance that I find you here, Runetta. I have a business meeting with Haizek this morning."

"Mmm, business, you say...What business is that, may I ask?" she said suggestively, smiling and looking back at Haizek.

"She is a music teacher. I deal in rare instruments..."

"Oh. You mean business. I thought you meant *business*." Again, looking in a sultry way at both of us, fishing for a connection she might use against them. Mason was sure.

"No, I'm afraid, Runetta, actual business."

"Shame indeed. I'm sure your business is, well, magical - shall we say?"

"What brings you here, Runetta?" Haizek asked pointedly.

"I was actually interested in an academic matter myself. I checked at the school, and they said that Professor Templeton might be here today."

Haizek noticed Runetta fumbling with something in her pocket briefly before extracting only her hand. She knew Runetta had used her wand for something. She didn't have to wait long to find out what. The sky went from a few wispy clouds on a bright morning to heavy, dark, rolling clouds unravelling across the whole city, and low rumbling thunder drawing closer. She was indeed devious. She had used magic to bring rain, and the inevitable following request.

"Oh my, it seems to be about to rain, might I come inside?" Runetta said with intent implied.

"Yes, Haizek, let us all go inside together," Mason said, already moving to usher them indoors. Once in, Mason shut the door, while Runetta stood mousily with her hands clasped in front of her, swaying from the waist up like a child might in expectation of something sweet for being cute.

"So, is the Professor here today? I don't recall you answering earlier."

"He is indeed in the parlor. Would you like to see him briefly? I'm afraid we have a whole day lined up making lesson plans using Mason's extensive collection of rare instruments from past ages." Haizek said without even looking at her.

"That is correct. I suppose it would be all right for you to set an appointment for a later date to address whatever might be on your mind, *Runetta*." Mason augmented the name Runetta in hopes the Professor might hear it.

Professor Templeton, advanced in years and having zero knowledge of music or its history, was not only tone deaf but also nearing actual deafness to anything he wasn't in the same room for. But the enhanced pronunciation of Mason, he did hear. He gripped the medallion given to him by Corfus the High Elf and whispered, "Runetta is here. I fear what she might want. I have the works we used to encode the book. Help us." He released the pendant, tucked it back under his shirt collar, just as she sauntered into the room. He had never met her in person and was immediately struck by her elegant beauty. He jumped to his feet, quite spryly for his age, which amused her, the smile increasing her intoxicating presence.

"Did I hear correctly? Could this really be *the Runetta Lynchos*?" he said, trying to use an ingratiating tone to hide his actual nervousness about her presence.

"I am, sir. I can hardly believe I haven't met you before, sir. I am well-traveled, and know the most important men in our world," she mused, holding her right hand out in expectation of a gentleman's proper greeting, looking away. He complied, cradling her hand in his and bowing to it, all the while praying Corfus would immediately show up and help. Then it occurred to him that all of this could be a trap to catch a High Elf; Corfus might not show at all. Now he felt sick. Behind Runetta, he saw Mason and Haizek watching carefully, not sure what to do either.

Runetta turned, looking each of them in the eye for a moment, trying to suggest she wanted privacy with the Professor, but they were paralyzed by her magnetic green gaze and still scared of her intent. No one saw her hand in her pocket again, and therefore did not realize they were actually paralyzed by her now as well. With the spell fully immobilizing them, Runetta walked around behind the Professor, who was also paralyzed by the magic, placed her hand on his shoulder, and vanished with him.

Having been startled by the presence of so many others at the location who knew who she was, regardless of her suave demeanor, Runetta was unsettled but pleased that she had made it out of there with her target. She arrived at the clearing in front of Dolphus's home, this time without a dramatic entrance and the destruction of his cherished trees. She saw he was asleep at his table, obviously having slept through a morning shower or heavy fog, as he was soaking wet and snoring. It was cold there, more so than Vienna had been, and every minute or so, he had an unconscious and violent shivering tremor, still snoring away. She glanced at her prey, the Professor, who had been bowed forward, holding Runetta's hand at Haizek's home, but here, he was in the same position, and it struck her as ridiculous. She let out a giggle that was both cruel and childlike, and like no other. Dolphus recognized it immediately and shook himself awake, blinking wildly to clear the haze of his aged vision, waving his wand aggressively, the tip already glowing red, indicating his intent to harm. He assumed in that split second she had returned to harm him, for his punishment previously inflicted on her. That action, feeble and foolish it seemed to Runetta, also incited a giggle, further angering him. He staggered to his feet, his blanket falling off his shoulders to the chair.

"Damn you, woman! What do you want?" He shouted at her. The spittle that had collected during his sleep shot from the pockets in his drooping, elderly cheeks as he yelled.

"I brought you something. This is the man responsible for the new coding that *The Book* uses. Aren't you proud of me, Uncle?" She stood swaying side to side with her hands behind her back, proud of herself regardless of his feelings.

"What? Who have you brought to this place, you foolish girl!" he said with a dry voice from sleeping, smacking a few times to let him speak more clearly. "Is that the Professor who helped that ordinary fool defeat you in the New World?" He refused to acknowledge the names civilized society gave to the Americas, feebly clinging to the idea that it should have been the sole dominion of the magical world. It was an old idea, polluted by the lies and schemes of angry dark workers of magic for over a thousand years now.

"It is, I will let you two get acquainted." She said, releasing him from his frozen position, but he was still unconscious. He fell into a disheveled pile, face-first in the damp dirt and leaves. Then she dislocated, leaving before he could assign stubbornness or stupidity to her venture. She knew it was foolish to have done this in the view of so many, and refused to let Dolphus pry the details of his acquisition from her.

Dolphus, stiff and old, hobbled over to the Professor, his wand aimed directly at him, ready for any fruitless attempts to escape. He cast his own memory lock on him, washing away any knowledge of where he was, how he came to be there, or who he was dealing with. Another angry wave of his wand, and the Professor's eyesight was taken from him. Permanently. He would not know it for some time, but the eyes glazed over in their sockets, filled with yellow mucus now, and would never work again. "Hmm. That should do, now, let's confine this heretic until after I have had some breakfast." He circled his head several times, with a glow at the end of his wand alternating between green and brown. Roots of his favorite trees would now have to sacrifice themselves for his needs. Their prickly, woody arms ruptured the ground all around the Professor, binding him tightly. As thick as a man's arm, they held him to the ground, and the odor of newly disturbed ancient earth filled the glen. He then made a whipping motion from the thorny cage, to him, and the Professor's wand exited the confinement, landing with a slap in Dolphus's empty hand.

CHAPTER SEVEN

UTE TERRITORY

B arthow had collected the cut lumber he found by the riverbed closer to the cave where the giants were staying. There were no other people within ten miles, at least two hours ago, when he patrolled from within the lowest clouds in the sky, out of sight of any ordinary people who might have been watching the cold, wintry clouds that had rolled in near dusk. Night had fallen now, and he was going to take a closer look at about midnight, so that he could be sure they were all asleep, and also that there were still the same number of them. He was certain that the deed could be done if all were in the cave, or the mouth of it, without difficulty. If even one of them were to come up from behind, while he was occupied with consuming them with fire, it could easily kill him. They will often smash unsuspecting people they come across with their fist in a hammer motion, collapsing the skull and breaking the spine out of their backs. Their strength is nearly incomprehensible to humans. They can rip a two-foot diameter, fifty-foot-high pine tree right from its roots, and swing it with enough force to wipe a two-story frame house from the ground, leaving it in a pile of debris like it was a child knocking a sand castle down. Barthow didn't need to be dealing with that kind of threat out here all alone. Surely they had been driven here to this remote, desolate place from encroaching settlers. Their food sources now were so sparse, hardly any vegetation, and the only meat was elk, deer, and bighorn sheep. All of those are far too fast and elusive for them to be effective at harvesting in sufficient numbers. They looked very lean and hungry. But feeding on humans for any reason is unacceptable. If he were to leave them for settlers to deal with, the word would soon spread. The number of people coming to the region to hunt and gain glory from such an endeavor would bring only the worst sort, creating panic that would further stretch tensions among those seeking a harmonious balance in the region. Using magic of any kind would be unacceptable, either to kill them. Spells that can render that large a beast dead leave marks unexplainable by natural means. A fire, trapping and burning them, however, is simple enough. So he had to do this, reasons be damned, he thought.

The cold north wind swept across the already frozen northlands of Canada, bringing air at a speed that would feel to anyone unprotected like a million icy knives stabbing at them. He was, of course, wrapped tightly in his enchanted clothing and was quite comfortable. The coat was the same one he had worn for almost twenty years.

Sure, it looked almost at the end of its useful life to ordinary people, but magical people's belongings often did. It was so easy to repair, modify, enhance, or adjust physical things that the items are notoriously long-lasting. As he thought about this, he thought back to the small hamlet his family lived in back east. To an ordinary person, it might appear to be a thousand years old, and they might marvel at how it lasted that long, especially in the relatively new cities of the United States. Sure, the grime and soot of an overcrowded town were noticeable, but the buildings themselves were new and, in some ways, exciting to Barthow. Too often in Europe, new constructions are a reflection of a nation's royal ambition, a statement to other ruling dynasties, and a grander version of the one they modeled it on. In this way, much of it was backward-looking. In this new country, the buildings were products of commerce and visions of the future. Perhaps subconsciously, they were in rebellion against the old world, but most of the time Barthow felt they were entirely new creations, necessary to improve the station and circumstances of those involved in the work. In that way, they were not reflecting anything from the past or someone else's work.

Alright, time for another check. Barthow deduced from the moon's glow through the clouds that he had been sitting nearly three hours since dark; it's possible they were all asleep. He gave his horse a "ssshh. I'll be back, buddy." He stood up and took his broom by the wide, curved throat near the end of the handle, and silently lifted slowly up, looking around as he did until he reached the lowest clouds. The moon was north of where he would be on the route, and the clouds were not letting much light through, so he wasn't worried about being lit up by it. He sniffed the air and detected far more carbon than flammable gases from the burning of seasoned wood, meaning the fire should be no more than coals now. Either the ones outside had gone inside and fallen asleep, or were so soundly asleep that they hadn't added more wood to the fire. He was less than a quarter of a mile away now and didn't stop until he was above the very entrance.

The fire had gone to coals, and he couldn't see any of the giants outside of the cave at all. The ring of stones they had assembled for the fire was massive, maybe eight feet across. At this place where the slope of the ground-down mountain changed from solid stone to sloped rock and gravel, there was no dirt or vegetation at all. It seemed to be a sheer stone. This made Barthow happy, because he didn't want what he was going to do to spark a dangerous wildfire. He decided that the top of the standing stone in front of the entrance was large enough for him to land on and stand. He would also basically stay ON his broom, in case he had to flee in a hurry. Closing his eyes, he visualized the pile of beams, as he couldn't actually see them from where he was, and pulled his wand. Pointing it in that direction, he brought the pile to his location, and over his head, and they set them as quietly as he could in the mouth of the cave. It was a narrow opening, maybe six feet across and twelve feet high, so the logs arranged themselves to basically stack lengthwise into the opening, like the bristles of a brush. The weight of them, and having been wedged in tightly, once on fire, would make it impossible for them to be moved.

He set his feet on top of those large flat stone slabs, about forty feet away from the crag opening with the wood sticking out of it. A quick survey of the surroundings to ensure their isolation, and he decided he must go ahead. He cast a cone of intense white-hot fire onto the stack of wood, igniting it, and the pile burst into a massive conflagration. The north wind was pushing much of the fire into the cave, while Barthow's intent focus drove it into the den. As the first plumes of smoke drifted out the top of the opening, Barthow narrowed the cone of fire he was producing at the bottom of the stack. Only a moment later, he could hear the growls and yips from the creatures inside. He hoped the intense fire seething out the back side of the pyre was enough to keep them from trying to push their way out, and so far, the hope was founded. He dared not release the fire he was creating, as any lapse might invoke primordial drives in the beasts to try to exit the furnace. After the first yells, the sound changed to a mournful gurgling howl and became more distant, coming from deeper in the cave.

Not wanting to watch the inferno the whole time, as the heat pulsating off this spectacle was becoming unbearable, he glanced up and around the hillside to see if there was an alternate exit he had not seen in his earlier mental excursion through the cave. The rise that housed this den was a good half mile long, and he was at its base, at the foot of the solid rock protrusion. From this angle, there weren't any plumes he could see. Once he finished, however, he would need to double-check that. This continued for about twenty minutes, as Barthow figured nothing could survive breathing the fiery, hot, poisonous fumes for that long, under any circumstances. He relented on the fountain of fire from his wand, but the opening blocked by tightly packed timber was halfway done burning. He waited a few more minutes to see if there was any sound or movement, but he saw none. He lifted off the rock and pointed his broom up to the crest of the rise, still not seeing any emissions of smoke. He descended to about half the height of the mesa and flew around the right, or west, side, checking the entire area for smoke leaks. The cavern he had seen was downward sloped to a flat floor, and he didn't remember seeing any openings down there large enough for even a young giant to exit, but he had to be sure. Once he reached the south end and satisfied himself that it was clear, he went up the east side back to where he started and lit on the same rock he had started from. This time, he dismounted the broom and sat down on the wide stone slab, laying his broom beside him. With his feet dangling down the side and facing the crevice, he dug around in his pocket looking for his pipe and tobacco pouch. Scraping the bowl as clean as he could, he packed it with a large plug of leaf, settling down for a wait. Sparking a flame with a snap of his fingers, he fired the bowl with a few long puffs, and the light of it lit his face up under the brim of his hat. Now to wait for the fire to burn itself down.

Vienna

In Haizek's home, she and Mason were released from their frozen state as soon as Runetta had left. Both were terrified by what had happened and by what else might come from Runetta's actions. Raileanu and Monika would be here in less than an hour, the Professor can be anywhere in the world, and how can they even explain this to the authorities? Do they need to contact the school? The local police? The magical authority? Just then, a knock at the door shook both of them with a quiver, as they had been sitting almost motionless since it happened.

"Haizek! Are you there? Haizek! Open the door!" They both looked pale and then at each other, wide-eyed. It was Jon Roqueford. The tone of his announcement probably meant he had seen Runetta on the street, then saw her walk in here! How could they tell him what she did, or worse, where she went?? Haizek could mention magical things to their own authorities, but not in front of Mason, for their involvement and relationship were more valuable than the lives of any person, magical or ordinary. He could tell Jon she was here, but not how she left. And neither of them could say what happened to the Professor to Jon, as while an Imperial Investigator working for Arterous's father. Ah, Mason had an idea.

"Haizek," Mason took her by the arm and leaned in, speaking in a low voice, "just tell him that Runetta left through the back courtyard."

"Okay, he might not even ask about her, right?" she asked with her eyebrows raised in hope. Mason shook his head, no. He wanted her to be ready for it. She went to the door and asked, "Who is it?"

"It's Jon Roqueford, ma'am. I am looking for a woman who came in here. Can you open the door, please?"

Haizek's hand shook as she slid the latch to the left and turned the knob. She opened the door and looked at Jon. He was staring straight through her, into the house. "Do you mean Runetta, Runetta Lynchos?"

"I do, that is who I am looking for. I saw her come in, may I?" Jon motioned with his right hand, palm up, towards the partially open door.

"Yes, of course." Haizek held tight to the door's edge and handle as she eased the door open. Jon strode up the two steps and straight through the door several paces into the front room of Haizek's house. He surveyed and catalogued everything he saw. His head was weaving as he stepped to one side and then the other, getting the best views of the interior he could.

"I also saw my friend Mason Stringfellow come in. Where is he?"

"I'm here, Jon." Mason walked in from the kitchen, drying his hands on a cup towel. "What brings you here?"

"Runetta Lynchos. I saw her come in here. Where is she?" Jon now spoke with a tone of certainty, not necessarily politely either.

"Really? Haizek? She was here?" Mason asked her.

"She came in the front, and went straight out the back. I didn't even know who it was. I thought it was a lady trying to get in out of the rain. She walked right through the parlor to the back door that goes into the courtyard of all these row houses. It was the strangest thing." Haizek pointed through the parlor to the back door. Jon looked and saw the wet footprints on the rug there, leading to where she was pointing.

"Mason, you didn't see her?" Jon now demanded in his tone.

"No, I was cleaning up after breakfast in the kitchen. I never heard anything with the racket I was making with the dishes and the rain." Mason stopped with the towel and put his hands on his waist, looking at the wet marks on the floor. "Huh. What would she want?"

"Both of you, stay here, lock the doors behind me, and do NOT let her back in again." Jon held his right hand up, pointing his index finger at both of them, while looking and listening to the direction Runetta was said to have gone. Then he took long, quiet strides following the footsteps, checking left and right for doors that might have led somewhere else.

"Yes, sir!" Mason said, craning his neck as if to make it easier for Jon to hear.

Jon went out the back door, opening and closing it quietly. Mason followed him to the door and slid the latch lock shut, as instructed, and watched him follow the right side of the enclosed courtyard. He reached a corner that Mason didn't remember seeing, a small entrance to a gate going to the street, maybe. Jon rounded the corner and was out of sight. Mason went back to the entrance, and Haizek was standing there, eyes closed, with her pointy finger held up for Mason to know he should wait a moment. He did. Smirking a bit as he waited, he was curious about what she was doing. Her cleverness never failed to impress Mason.

After about two or three minutes, Haizek opened her eyes and lowered her hand. Mason was there with a hot cup of tea for her, seated and waiting. She took the cup from him and sat down. "So, my magic lady, what did you do?"

"I made an opening for him to leave through in the courtyard, and gave him the impression he was following her in the rain. It should last for an hour or so." She sipped the hot tea cautiously as Mason tended to make it hotter than she liked. "The Professor's bags are still here?" she asked, as she set the teacup down, still shaking a bit.

"Yes, I saw them by the back door," Mason said.

"I think I need to get them to Klement Metternich. Immediately." She took another drink, "I think I will have to see you later, Mason."

He finished his cup with a big drink, set it down, leaned over the small table between them, and gave her a gentle kiss on the cheek. He went to the front door, smiled at her, and unlocked the door, as the rain had stopped, at least where they were. He pulled it shut behind him, waited to hear her latch it shut again, and began his walk across town to his house.

Haizek pulled her wand, opened the back door to make sure no one was around, and shrank the Professor's bags down to the size of sugar cubes and put them in her pocket. She went to the angled entrance in the middle of the garden, which to everyone else was a root cellar, but for her and all other magical people who touch the door, it's the tunnel to the Metternich home. She glanced over to the wall where she had made the exit and gate to the courtyard, and with a wink, put it back to normal. Then she went into the tunnel, walking with a profound sense of urgency.

Haizek did not know about the troubles Runetta had been involved with. She was not included in the circle of confidants who were informed of the details regarding the deaths of Raileanu's father and mother. She had spent an entire school year with Professor Magnus Templeton and knew that he was a great man, scholar, and dedicated to preserving and expanding knowledge for all to share. There is no rational or legal reason she could fathom for Runetta paralyzing and absconding with the Professor. She knew Klement Metternich was a very important official in the Austrian government, and a liaison of sorts between the magical and ordinary worlds. He would know what to do. It was, as she knew, his responsibility for the construction, maintenance, and knowledge of the tunnel itself. Klement is the Emperor's entrusted Counsel for all matters related to the magical world, including the Runewheel and the house Haziek lived in. Klement himself must authorize the sale or rental of properties that contain such critical historical pieces of magical history, and Haziek must apply in person for permission to buy the home with a Runewheel. It was the only time they had met before, and it was brief, clinical, and professional. This meeting was going to be none of those things.

Haizek arrived at the door leading into the kitchen storeroom of the Metternich home, and saw there was no handle, latch, or knocker on her side of the heavy iron-banded, hand-hammered, riveted oak door. She knocked as best as she could, but the hardest she could knock resulted only in dull thumps that didn't seem to travel very far. She drew her wand and held it to her ear, and then the other end to the door. Hoping to hear someone moving or talking on the other side, she waited a few more seconds. Amplifying the sounds for her, even the use of the wand didn't reveal anyone around. She cleared her throat, then she repositioned the wand to her cheek.

"Hello! Is anyone there?!" the voice now boomed and surely was audible in the room on the other side. "Hello! It is an emergency!" she switched back to listen again. Haizek was sure she didn't want to be standing this close to the door with a pointy stick near her face if someone threw the door open. She heard some shuffling now and quickly took a step back.

"Who is there?" a man's voice asked.

"It is Haizek Moon. I live at the other end of the tunnel. Something terrible has happened, I must speak with Klement immediately!" She could hear latches sliding and bars moving with some urgency. In no time, the door was swinging open towards her. A startled, earnest-looking man in chef's clothing was pushing the heavy door aside, looking frantically around the tunnel, then up and down her from head to toe.

"Are you alright, Miss Moon?" He asked when his survey was done.

"I am, but I need to come inside. May I?"

"Yes, yes, come in so I can shut the door," he motioned for her to hustle in. She did, and he pulled it shut and set to relocking all the latches. "Go on through the kitchen, then up the stairs, and turn left. The butler should know where Mr. Metternich is exactly."

"Thank you, sir."

"Mr. Swansea. Go ahead, ma'am." When Haizek glanced over her shoulder, she saw there were a couple of large padlocks he was fiddling with to re-lock on the latches.

She went as directed, and sure enough, the butler was coming towards the kitchen, with a distressed look. He approached her, gripped her arm, and looked around her into the kitchen stairwell.

"Miss -" he began.

"Moon, Haizek Moon. I live at the end of the tunnel out the back of the kitchen. I must speak with Mr. Metternich, please," she urged him. He looked at her now, top to bottom, and nodded in agreement. He let go of her arm and proceeded to walk to her right quite quickly.

"Follow me, please," the butler said, barely turning his head to the side as he walked as quickly as dignity would allow.

They went to another set of stairs, and went up to the third floor, down a hall about ten paces or so, and then the butler knocked on the door, leaning to the door with his ear, and then turned the handle and held the door open for Haizek, standing at attention.

"Hello, Ms. Moon," he paused when he glanced up from the desk of papers he was looking at. He saw she was distressed, her eyes darting around the room, standing a bit hunched forward, her hands clasped. "What has happened?" He then held his hand up to Haizek and turned his attention to the butler. "Sir, please bring some tea for our guest." The butler nodded and pulled the door shut without a sound. "Sit down, please. Take a moment if you need to."

Klement stood, walked around the large desk, brought her to a high-back, cushioned chair, and held her hand as she sat down. She had to be careful, not to mention Mason, and be sure to give him as much information as she could to help the professor.

"The Professor. Professor Magnus Templeton was at my house, I presume, to see Raileanu and Monika off. He hadn't been there a moment when a woman came to the door in the rain. I know now she was magical, she made the heavy rain this morning, but I didn't know it then." Her voice began to shake, and as she looked at her hands, they shook too as she lifted them; she set them back flat on her knees, then shifted her weight a couple of times in the chair. After a few deep breaths, she was able to continue. "I let the lady in the house, I thought she just wanted in out of the rain. She saw the professor and went to him, she froze him, and dislocated with him!" She began breathing heavily again, looking up, blinking, and pursing her lips, trying to hold in her emotion. A few seconds later, she had better control over the urge to begin crying. "It was Runetta Lynchos. I only know that because a moment after she left with him, a knock on the door came, and it was Jon Roqueford. He said he was following her, he said her name."

The butler opened the door, and a lady brought in a tea tray and set it on the table between Klement and Haizek. Haizek took the brief interlude to try to compose herself further. She realized she would have to alert the school to what had happened to the professor, and the thought of that was too much. She saw Klement take the opportunity of her discomfort to make her a cup of tea. He paused and handed her a napkin. Haizek decided there was no reason to try to keep her shock and fear in anymore. Clutching the napkin in both hands, she held it to her face, and the stuttering breath and whines were muffled. Klement decided to prepare his own tea, not knowing how she took hers. He stood when he had finished preparing his tea, and stood next to her chair, and put his right arm across her right shoulder.

"Take your time, Haizek. Finding out everything that happened is important; we will not rush it." He patted her a couple of times on the top of the shoulder, then sat back down in his chair. It was not very long, and Haizek had gathered enough composure to lower the napkin from her face. That's when she noticed it was very fine monogrammed silk, and then she felt awful about that, raised it back to her face, and let out another couple of muffled exhales. Her posture collapsed as she lowered it and let her hands fall into her lap.

"I will have to tell the school what has happened, won't I?" She asked Klement, brow wrinkled from her eyebrows pushed up in a sorrowful face.

"We will see. First, how do you take your tea?" He picked up the tongs and reached for the sugar cubes in a fine china bowl, looking to her for direction.

"Two is perfect, thank you, sir."

"Cream as well?"

"Just a dash, please." She began to look around the room, noticing all the portraits and official regalia that showed Klement's position and connection. Haizek looked back at Klement, who was preparing the cup of tea, and saw the bowl of sugar cubes.

"OH, I almost forgot, the professor had set his bags by my back door when he came in. I brought them," she said. He handed her the cup.

"That is good. In fact, it is perhaps the best thing that could have happened, given what has gone on. I can have those taken to his home, and I will also speak with the school and the authorities for you. I don't want you to worry, dear." Klement sat back, infuriatingly calm.

"Sir, I don't see any good here. A distinguished professor has been kidnapped; how can you be so reserved right now?" She let her frustration out in her tone.

"Indeed, regardless of the purposes she may have in mind, he is not only well known, prestigious, and quite skilled, but expected by the Emperor's Staff this very afternoon. I am alarmed, but also somewhat comforted by the earlier statement that Jon Roqueford was looking for her. He is an Imperial Investigator. So if any unpleasant event befalls him, she would no doubt suffer for it."

Haizek nodded in agreement at learning all that. Maybe it would be alright. "Do you want his luggage? I have it here." He nodded as he was sipping his tea. She dug around in her pocket, produced them, and set them on the floor. She pulled her wand and glanced behind her, around the back of the chair, to be sure the door was closed. With a tap on each, they returned to their original size.

"Are you sure you will be okay?" he asked.

"Yes, yes, I suppose so. Do you think I need to worry about her returning to my house?" she asked, then took the last drink of her tea from the cup and set it down.

"I never know what to think regarding that woman. I would perform any further enchantments you can think of on your home. Please be safe, I know that if anything were to happen to you, well, my nephew would be heartbroken." Haizek's face changed from confusion and dismay to honest puzzlement. "He has a bit of a consuming fancy for you, I am afraid, and never spoke of music before your class. He began attending school and your class just last term. So, your safety is in everyone's interest." Klement then finished his tea and replaced his cup on the tray.

Haizek had no response to this. She considered that, as a man of both worlds and having held the position for many years, he must be effective at this work. It shouldn't surprise her that he knew of her work and had a greater awareness of her than she did of him. With all the happenings of the day up to this point, and wary of her betraying connections to Mason to a 'mortal' of any position, her mind was still racing. She couldn't think of his name, past his surname, of course.

"That is so kind. Please tell him I asked after him during our visit. Thank you for putting me at ease over this. Would it be all right if I went home and rested a while?" Haizek set the napkin gently on the table.

"Yes, of course. Please don't worry about the school, I will inform them, and get his belongings to his house straight away. Do you want me to mention it happened at your hou -" she threw up her hand, closed her eyes, and shook her head, no.

"I don't want to think about any of this anymore, if that's alright, sir."

"Of course. Please let me know if anything else occurs to you. I will also deal with Jon Roqueford as well, and reassure him that you were an innocent bystander." Klement stood and held out his hand to help her stand. Then he walked to the door and opened it, sticking his head out and calling for the butler.

"I want to have a security man to walk you back home, through the tunnel. I think it is best that you don't come out of my home, for your own privacy." Klement walked around her and saw the butler coming, and met him. They spoke briefly and quietly, and he went away with purpose. Klement came back to her and walked her down to the kitchen, and waited for the guard. He gave the guard stern, clear instructions: walk her all the way there, check the whole house for her safety, then return. Haizek gave a nervous smile and a little wave to Klement as they set off.

Klement went quickly back to the study, locked the door, sat at the desk, pulled out the silver medallion, and held it tightly in his hand. Quickly and somewhat nervously, he recounted the events, hopefully conveying to Corfus the High Elf the terrible danger of the Professor being in the hands of Runetta. He had held his composure with Haizek the best he could, but it was clear in his own voice that he was quite nervous about this turn of events.

CHAPTER EIGHT

RUNETTA'S CASTLE

R unetta had fallen asleep after depositing the professor with her uncle. She had returned to her underground castle lair, whose location no one knew, and had been awakened by a sound. Still half asleep, trying to both cling to the dream and the world of the awake, she couldn't remember the sound now. Then it came again. A terrible growl and raspy barking from a massive set of lungs. It reverberated in the stone walls several times, and now, not recalling the dream that had been important, she recognized it.

Stretching and never being in a hurry for any living creature, she sat up, congratulating herself for the hundredth time on the design and construction of her lounge bed. It was bright brass tubing, about three inches in diameter, woven with magic, not having a single seam, into a swan-shaped frame. The bedding itself was made from sumptuous arachnid silk and filled with Great Goose down feathers. She had made a point of arriving at the farm where they were raised in Wales on culling day. Nearly eight feet tall, the Great Goose down feathers were as big as a grown man's hand. Once she carefully selected the hundred of them she had paid for, she sat down at an outdoor table and watched as they were caught, killed, and plucked. She enjoyed a nice dinner of their cooked flesh while the down feathers were packed for her.

She sat up and put her feet on the floor, and decided she needed another good stretch and a yawn before throwing aside the white bear pelt she slept under. The air was cold and still, just how she liked it. Her string-strapped black silk sleeper was delightful on her silken mattress bed, and she slid her hands down her thighs as she stood, pushing it down its full length. The room was cylindrical, formed of solid stone polished by the heat of magical energies; the walls reflected her perfectly, regardless of where she was in the room—enjoying the image of herself, as she walked from the bed to the doorway leading into her antechamber. Built into the wall itself were hundreds of tiny nooks. In every single one was a jar, with a heart in it. Every one of them was beating. Some were small, the size of children. Some were large, from giants, beasts, even one that barely fit in the gallon-sized jar. That was the single dragon she had employed, and the four jars near it were alive in Runetta's service for the sole purpose of raising boar to feed the dragon. She put her palms flat on the narrow table, fingers facing away from her, and locked her elbows as she swayed back and forth, surveying the collection.

Again, the barks and roars echoed through the halls of her castle. She let her head fall back in disappointment that she had duties that had to be tended to. Things would be so much easier if I had a servant here, she thought. Ah, but no human she had ever met was worthy of her lair, she considered. Twisting her lips to one side and narrowing her eyes, she pretended to think about that. Had she ever met anyone she wanted here? No. She reached her right hand down and lifted the edge of her sleeper above the edge of her wand handle held in her garter. A swish, and she was clothed in black dyed deer-skin, with a silken cape, and her trademark high-buckled boots, off to work then.

She left her beloved room of servants' hearts, the doors of her lair now responding well to her ring-wand. They would fling open silently but with purpose. Striding from her chamber at the rear of the dual-keep structure to the front entrance of the castle, she approached the portcullis in a few minutes walk. It was solid iron, with hundreds of years of rust caking it. It had never been opened and might shatter if it were ever tried. Right outside on the narrow stone strip that protruded forward in a semicircle was the source of the rumbles that had woken her. When she was close enough to reach out and touch the gate, torches on either side of the exterior wall burst into life, spewing sparks and smoke. Illuminated in the orange flickering light were two hulking, hairy forms that bowed their heads down to her presence.

The two were a mix of light brown and grey fur, each strand nearly a foot long, and as strong as steel. Many magical assassins in her employ have used a braid of only three of their hairs as a garrote with great success. She spoke to them in her mind. "Stand, my lovelies."

They uncurled their hunched forms, the width of their ears now visible, almost as broad as their shoulders. The wide, knobby, short-haired foot-long snout of each lifted with huge canine teeth from their upper jaws, overlapping the lower jaw. When fully erect, they stood ten feet tall, their arms so long their clawed hands were even with their knees. Lastly, their snouts rose parallel with the ground, revealing their eyes. Runetta looked back and forth at them, making sure their gaze, reflecting only ruby red from the torchlight, was submissive to her.

"Hungry, darlings? Of course you are. Here." Runetta turned and walked away from the gate, flicking her wand over her shoulder, and two entire pigs appeared in front of the werewolves, who promptly let blood-curdling snarls out as they dove into their meals. She could hear them biting hard enough to crush their skulls and cracking through the spines. "There we are. Work done. Back to leisure."

Not a year after she discovered the underground castle's location in her mother's inherited documents, she heard at a party about the twin sons of a nobleman in Bavaria who had been attacked by nearly extinct dire wolves and infected. The whole of the ordinary population still felt this was a demonic blood curse. Magical persons knew it was clearly a magical curse. Both were wrong. She offered her services, carefully and compassionately, to scour the world for a cure. Of course, she had no intent of curing them; the potion she gave them made them appear dead. The nobleman's family thanked her for her efforts and asked her to assume care for the corpses, for fear of them returning. She didn't even have to charm them in any way. The potion she had used let them sleep for three days, and when they awoke here, in this place, they would remain sentient werewolves for the forty or fifty years they had left in them. Now in her service, because they knew they weren't welcome anywhere else, and they could never leave this place. Only dislocation can free a person from here. Or bring food. Runetta did make sure they ate in return for protection on the outside of the castle.

Only a few years before I began writing these stories of our personal histories, Corfus explained that the true source of magic - and curses like werewolves, vampires, and indeed what are referred to as zombies - are all a result of emites. In my previous volume, Corfus called them particles for the sake of time and the world's lack of understanding of such things. Emites are tiny machines, as small as a cell of blood, that exist in our bodies, formed from a yet-to-be rediscovered mineral called Bendra-17 and other materials too complex to describe. They do things like extend lifespan, focus ethereal energies (also too difficult to demonstrate), modify living creatures, and allow what we call magic. They were designed and used prolifically in the hundred years before the Calamity, but only by the wealthiest and most powerful people and nations. The technologies used to do this were not always benevolent. Some were forced into specific forms against their will, such as the Dwarves and Goblins (as we call them). Some willingly chose these alterations, following deep desires to become animals.

The original werewolves were soldiers who were given this ability to change at will into these fearsome monsters. Those, Corfus explained, had long been assumed by the High Elves to have passed in the machinations of the Calamity and its aftermath. They believe that in the days after, several of them had been attacked by, wounded, and eaten by the dire wolves in the wilderness. For about 12,500 years, the dire wolves were the only ones who could pass on this trait to wounded victims. No doubt Runetta had planned on trying to extract this mechanism from her captives to use for her own purposes.

It is not untrue that silver can injure them. In fact, a sufficient injury to their heart, using silver weapons, will disrupt the ability of the emites to repair the injured host, as critical injuries to major organs will draw the most attention from the emites. The tiny emite machines require warmth and water of a living host to operate correctly. Significant blood loss, a stopped heart, and large quantities of silver (which disrupt their ability to coordinate and work collaboratively on their host) can kill a werewolf. So, being passed through injuries into the bloodstream, calling it a blood curse isn't far from accurate.

Ute Territory

Barthow jumped down from the tall standing stone outside the cave of the giants. He used his wand to push aside the remnants of the timbers, mostly white ash now barely held together. After they had crumbled into piles on either side of the entrance, the air changed. He could smell what he had done. The burnt hair, smoked flesh, some of them must have tried to get past the burning barricade and died close to the pyre. He pulled his kerchief and tied it around his neck, lifting the doubled front over his nose. Regripping his wand and keeping it pointed lower than he would normally, to face giants, he took the first few steps onto the downward slope he had seen in his vision. Along the right side was the frame of a giant, face down and pointing downhill. The left side of its body was cooked, the hair burnt off, the skin blackened, and in grotesque shiny bubbles from its hand to its thigh. This must have been the one he could smell. It was easily fifteen feet tall. Barthow went quickly past the creature. The creosote and ash were still crackling and falling in small patches, like dried leaves from the ceiling of the cave crunching under his boots. It sent a cold shiver down his spine; he sure hoped they had all died. If even one heard his footsteps approaching the large open part of the cave, they could hurl a rock to kill him. Or jump on him, crushing him before he could react. All he could do was proceed, trying to watch where he was walking to avoid making noise that could cost him the critical seconds he would need if any were still down there.

When he reached about fifty feet down the narrow passage, the light of the remaining fire above was gone.

It was pitch black, and he had no choice. He thought for a moment, recalling the phrase that he could use to enhance his night sight. Then he squeezed the wand and felt the sureness of magical energy passing through his arm and up to his head. Slowly, the path and the edges of the sharp rock lining the walls became clearer. Then the bottom of the slope, which opened into the large cavern, appeared. It all had a green tint, but was now very clear. He couldn't see any others just yet, so he proceeded cautiously down to where it leveled out and stopped there, allowing for more adjustment in his vision.

The sides of the cave were hard to make out; boulders, long tree trunks stripped of branches, leaned diagonally up on the wall in some places. He couldn't make out the far side at all. He decided to stick close to the right side of the cave. At least that would have his back to a wall if he were surprised. Then he couldn't be attacked on all sides. It looked about three hundred feet long in total; the ceiling of this large part wasn't visible at all. The sides were steep, and only a few places were ribbons of a more brittle rock running through the harder stone. Those had places where large stones had fallen out and made little piles on the floor, but not so large that a giant, even an infant, could hide behind. It was completely dark here, and they had worse night vision than even ordinary humans. If he moved carefully and quietly as he could, they wouldn't know he was there.

That was the plan anyway. When Barthow reached halfway through the cavern, he could see a vague outline of a pile at the far end that definitely was not rocks.

It was a pile of giants. Crouching next to the wall and trying to catalog the size and placement of every rock that his movements might disturb, he attempted to scour the opposite side for any sign of them. Or worst of all, a survivor. He could see clearly that the poles leaned up on the far side were not giants, just furs, crates, things that they had collected. So he turned again to the very back, the pile, and continued on. After twenty more feet, he came to something that he had thought a moment before was a rock, but it was the scat of a giant. As he got closer, he could see the skull of a human infant in the droppings. And a hand. Barthow stopped and just squeezed his eyes shut for a minute.

This is why he didn't bring those younger rangers with him. These are some of the last of this kind in the New World. Not many have dealt with them, nor should they have to. Barthow's grandfather and his grandmother's father had dealt with them before; it's the only reason he thought he should do this. If it can be the end of this cursed form of life, then he would see it through. The kids nowadays, and by kids he was thinking of anyone younger than thirty, learn about giants in school. They only teach a two-day block on what they call the 'former' giants of the Americas. Everything else they were taught is of a completely different genus of European, Asian, and African giants. Those are nearly gone as well now, but they were perfectly reasonable, thinking, compassionate, long-lived, generous members of the magical communities. These were never that. Truly, they were no different than twenty-foot-tall, two-legged coyotes. Corfus had told Barthow before he left something about them being created that way on purpose. Why would someone do that? Didn't matter, he had to make sure this was finished, so he pressed on to the back of the cavern, the pile of hair-covered bodies of all sizes beginning to come into view.

Elfheim

Corfus had been listening. To all of them, Barthow, Klement, Raileanu, and Monika. Time was becoming short, and he knew it. Industry was beginning; innovation and inspiration were creeping back into the world, as they had not since before the Calamity. Like a climbing vine, to someone as ageless as Corfus, he could see it. All over the world, it was growing an inch a day. While ordinary people can notice a few vines spreading a few inches a day in spring, Corfus and Elfkind could see billions of vines, all encroaching inches a day. This type of growth has no season. No pruning could contain it, as it was all springing from the same root - massing human consciousness. Every event, now, whether tragic or transformative, would all be fertilizer to this vine now. No intervention could tame it or control it. Slowing the progress to a crawl by preventing knowledge of and access to ancient technology was the best way the High Elves had calculated to help, and by removing all remnants of the past civilization and the mistakes they had made.

The High Elf Corfus had sent Kleet to help Raileanu in Texas the month before because the Orbs that lie hidden around the world were the most significant threat.

They just weren't a tool mankind could use to become more dangerous; they could move a few who found them into a godlike status. They can know everything about everyone, all at once. Responding to simple commands, their power could irreversibly scar all of God's creation in a day, split continents, harness the vast energies of gravity, magnetism, light, electricity, and even the vibrations of atoms, to carry out the desires of those in their possession. There were hundreds, maybe thousands of unstoppable metal soldiers locked away in the crevices and undercrofts of the earth's crust from the time before. If knowledge of those, in conjunction with the power of an Orb, were to fall into the hands of a single person, magical or ordinary, nothing ordinary could stop them.

The Orbs were crafted in the last two hundred years before the Calamity. They were assembled at the atomic scale from quartz crystal interlocking lattices and Bendra-17 by supercomputers, designed to supplant the machines that had made them. They were an indestructible artificial intelligence. Powered for all time by their structure, using an immeasurable force of energy that permeates the universe. They could connect to, control, communicate with, and even manipulate matter using that same energy field. Corfus knew immediately that what had plagued the people surrounding my father, the Diggers, Father Callious, was this force. What he could not see was where the source, the Orb, was until it was too late. Kleet died on that mission, and what no mortal could know, what I didn't know until many years later, is that the reason they were being so cautious was that there were only five of the High Elves left. Not the hundred they had spoken of. Not nearly as many as it would take to find and collect the remaining Orbs before it was too late. It was also the reason they determined it was time to ask us to join them. I understand their rationalizing, their caution, now. Having known it though, I think I would have abandoned any idea of returning to a normal life, my work at this moment in time was still something I was using to try and ease my suffering from having lost my mother and father. I wish they had told me sooner.

The High Elves, who still existed, resided in Elfheim. With around 200 subterranean levels, it was a domed city at the southernmost point on Earth. When the Calamity had been predicted by them and ignored, they retreated underground and stayed there for a long time. All their needs were met. Their physical and mental transformation enabled them to control all elemental forces and materials. They can easily rearrange substances at will. They can focus on a point in our universe, and 'pull' themselves through the empty spaces - the space between spaces- to that point in their mind. They had many technical terms over the few years I spent in their company that I never did understand. Learning that the bloodlines and forces we call magic were, in fact, physical alterations made intentionally before the fall of mankind was easy enough to grasp. It made some sense, hereditarily, I suppose one child is good at something, then it fades and reappears a generation or two later. The darkness that spread from the Orb in Texas to the Wormwell prison, infecting my father and several others, was particles of the same type, directed by simple instructions after making contact in the only way the Orb could.

In the hundred years after the Calamity, the landmass that Elfheim was on became shrouded in frost and ice. The very position of the planet was changed in that event, and the snow and ice just kept coming. The city they inhabited was flawless in its design and operation. Nothing ever wore out or broke down. Nothing decayed. Perpetually bright, white, and clean, it maintains and repairs itself constantly by design. They never want for food or water. Over the millennia, more and more were killed by humans, by sorcerers, each trying to use them for their own power, over a land that had reverted from the pinnacle of civilization and harmony to a hellscape of starvation, mass death, and brutality. They retreated from trying to help or rebuild for thousands of years and had not had any meaningful contact in so long; most, even in the magical world, considered them myth.

Corfus alone now watched the Americas and their related connections in Europe. There was too much to monitor and so few left to be Watchers. He could not risk intervention, even for the Professor, unless the opportunity to secure another Orb or other relic showed itself clearly. It was good that they were so different from the rest of us. A human with deep emotional connections could not stay that removed and focused on one thing. Fourteen thousand eight hundred years, and being emotionless, we must seem almost irrelevant to them, really.

Corfus had collected many musical performances that he could listen to at any time, over the last ten centuries. He liked listening to a thousand orchestras simultaneously and examining every note of every instrument in every concert hall at once. He compared it to their ability to watch so much of the world at once. Well, his part anyway. A few hundred years ago, there were ten watching the Americas; now there are so many more people to watch. If despair was something they could remember, I'm sure he would have it with the task they set themselves.

He had located the Professor and Dolphus Tangleweed's house. He knew that neither Dolphus nor Runetta had the codebooks to decipher *The Book*. He was trying hard to locate Runetta, or her copy of the book, which he was sure she had. However, each time she dislocated, he had to start listening to the thousand orchestras again to try to find her. The Professor, though being blinded and his torture beginning soon, would have to wait. To prevent rash action on the part of anyone else involved, Corfus sent word through his medallions to me, Monika, and Klement that he had found the Professor, and everything was alright for now, not to worry. It would have to be ok for now.

I only tell you this now because decades passed before I learned much of the work of the High Elves, and I held resentment against them that whole time. They could have acted faster to save my father, Father Callious, and all those who died in those first days of my involvement. My mother's killing would haunt me for years in nightmares, and I quietly held it against them. I don't want any reader of this to hold the same disappointment or anger towards them. In fact, their stoic acceptance of the events they faced alone benefited all. All their long watch ended up serving the course of events in ways none other could have, save the High Elves. The knowledge of their grasp on even the smallest particles of matter is relevant, and at the time of this writing, the world was first beginning to learn about things at the smallest scale. What the CIGI was, how they did what they did, and the effects on the world are relevant. Granted, none of this made sense to me when it was explained in 1836-37. Now, in 1891, only a bit more is understandable, but each passing year, the truths and warnings the High Elves gave me become more and more clear.

Corfus also told me there were far worse versions of the CIGI; they called them CISI, and he hoped we never had to deal with one of those. He said they were so powerful, so dangerous, that the nations of the earth at that time kept them secret, even from their own people. There was no way to know how many there were, only suspicions about their locations based on the nations that could have created them in the decade before the Calamity. He was right to warn us. What difficulties lie ahead in dealing with but a few of the Crystalline Integrated General Intelligence (CIGI) Orbs was bad enough.

Chapter Nine

Klement's Home, Vienna

Not reaching Corfus, Klement knew that there was no time to waste, and if he didn't have some resolution by the end of the day, Haizek would, rightly, return and express concern and want to contact the school immediately. Klement went immediately to his wife, who still possesses all her magical abilities. Advising her of the importance of the situation, she agreed to travel by dislocation to the headquarters of the Inquisitor General of Magical Forces and bring them a letter from him. The letter described the verified abduction of a celebrated professor and requested that an official come to his office immediately. When he finished writing the letter, Klement stood, handed it to his wife, and kissed her cheek. She left directly from his study, and Klement went to spend time with his children, anxiously waiting for her return.

Laverne Metternich was a well-known figure, and her arrival in the headquarters' main lobby drew immediate attention from the supervising captain behind the desk. He took her to the Director General's office, who was alone. He motioned to her to enter, and the captain closed the door behind her. She handed him the letter and waited patiently. He read over it for only a few seconds, then reached for his reading glasses and continued.

Laverne looked around the room, saw his many certificates and awards, and praise from kings and leaders around Europe. She looked straight down and saw his name on a long wooden plaque. Director General Kofingsburn. While he may not have recognized her immediately, she was glad to see the nameplate, as she did not know his name or how to address him appropriately. Behind him was an elaborately carved teak desk and cabinetry that reached to the ceiling. Books on history, both magical and ordinary, filled the cabinetry, with no small trinkets or knick-knacks. All business. She saw no pictures of anyone else and glanced at his hands.

He was a large man, with expansive shoulders, a massive barrel chest, and his tailored uniform fit just so. It was similar in design to what she recognized as Austrian and German, but was a deep maroon red, with black cordage and stitching, and woven silver amongst it. His hands and fingers were very thick, reminding her of sailors' hands. She could hear the coarse skin of his hands rustling on the paper of the letter, and she saw he was still wearing his wedding band, although his wife had passed more than a decade before. He had bushy eyebrows, and with his glasses and intense look, she couldn't make out his eyes. With his thick moustache and the angle of his head tilted down, she couldn't make out the rest of his face. He read the letter for only twenty seconds, and laid it down, removed his glasses, and looked up at her.

"Madam," his voice was deep and gravelly, almost hard to understand, "this will not stand. I have already heard of the events in Texas regarding Mr. Tellafrog and his family. We have hunters already tasked with searching out these fiends." He picked up the letter, and, shaking it parallel with the desk, he continued. He then reached under the desktop and pulled out a little drawer, which Laverne strained to see into. It was about ten inches wide, lined with black velvet, and had about a dozen compartments, each a few inches square. In each little spot was a clear crystal dome. General Kofingsburn picked one up from the middle of what she could see and held it to his right eye, closing his left.

"I have someone to handle this immediately. Your husband knows him. We will solve this today, madam, do not worry," the General said. He set the domed crystal in his hand and spoke. "Hartge, I see you are unoccupied at the moment. Come at once!" he said with such force and command that several passers by the office paused and looked in, then scurried off.

At the far corner of the desk from Laverne, a man appeared, standing at attention. He looked to Laverne to be no form of soldier, although his posture was exemplary, his clothing was far from remarkable. Before she could think of closer examination, by definition, judgment, the General cleared his throat. He had surely seen her side-eyeing his charge.

"This is Hartge. As I said, your husband is well aware of his work, and I will have him return with you to settle this matter once and for all. Oh, and tell Klement that I have reissued the arrest order for Runetta and Dolphus, effective in any location they are detected. Thank you for your visit." The General went right back to whatever official paperwork he was doing when Laverne came in.

"Shall we, madam?" Hartge looked at her, his stance relaxed and still a bit slight compared to the problem solver figure she had hoped would respond to this dire circumstance. Laverne gave him a polite nod, and they both dislocated back to the Metternich home.

In the years since, I had asked Laverne only once to describe the surely impressive office of General Inquisitor of Magical Forces, and in the company of her husband, she paused, looked to Klement, and he just shook his head, no. There must be a security reason I was not aware of, so I must leave that to later authors with access to things that I do not possess.

The pair of them arrived back in Klement Metternich's study, and not a moment later, Klement unlocked the door and came in, locking it behind him.

"Sir, Hartge at your service. Good to see you again. The General himself received your wife and recalled me straight to his office. I am here to find the Professor and detain anyone I deem involved in the affair."

Klement went straight to him, gripping his out-stretched hand with both his own, shaking it up and down. "Laverne, dear, there is no one better the General could have sent," he said, looking at her with an uncharacteristic smile, and she could tell his ease at the situation now.

"Happy to help, dear. Nice to meet you, Hartge." Laverne was happy to return to the children. With all the terrible events in the last month or so, she truly felt that a moment with them should never be unshared. She unlocked, opened, then shut the door behind her. She paused for a moment, waiting for Klement to lock it, and when he had, she went back downstairs.

"Can you already see the Professor?" Klement asked, returning and sitting on the edge of the desk.

Once Mrs. Metternich had left, Hartge set his hands against his head, middle fingers on his temples. "Yes, I can. He is with Dolphus Tangleweed. That diabolical man is trying to pry knowledge about some code from his mind. The professor is unhurt, for now." He lowered his hands, interlocking his fingers and letting his arms hang in front of him.

Klement put his hand on his chin and looked down, pressing his eyebrows together, thinking. Raileanu and Monika would be here any minute. Should he tell him? Would it matter? He decided not to tell either of them, just let Hartge get on with it. None had heard from Corfus, which could be good or bad, but no way of knowing which. He would go ahead and dispatch this talented hunter and let all of this play out. When all available information is assessed in a time-compressed emergency, inaction is usually far worse than the best plan available at the time.

"You already have all the information you need?" Klement asked, standing and walking around behind the desk, pulling out a drawer, reaching in, and pulling out a wooden box.

"Yes, and sir," Hartge pulled his long coat to the side with his right hand, revealing a holster with the butt of a revolver's handle easily seen. "I already have one. They issued them not three days ago."

"Good. I am glad it is you, and don't waste any time on me. I would very much like to save him and put this whole dirty tale to rest." He paused again, making the same concentrating face, and sat down. Runetta has been seen in several cities, from Portugal to Vienna, in the last few days alone. Dolphus's hideout is unknown. Would you..." He shuffled some papers, pulled out a map, turned it to Hartge, and handed him a pen.

"Of course. The General would need to know where that place is if something happens to me, you're right." Hartge said with a smirk. He looked around the map, closed his eyes for a second, and then indicated with an "X" where he was going. "Don't worry, sir, you know why he called me. I will be alright."

The location was on the eastern side of Mt. Schönberg, in a deep crevice that ran down that side of the mountain, with thick, ancient trees so dense that no road had ever been attempted there. It was in that family's holdings, and little was known of the interior of that region, other than the rare wood harvested there that grew in no other place known on earth.

Hartge waited until Klement was finished looking at the spot, and recalling what he could of it. Klement gave him a nod, and then Hartge dislocated. All Klement could do was hope for the best. Klement did not know, but Dolphus had been using his skill for viewing with his crystal balls to watch him. Luckily, consumed with his new guest, Dolphus had no idea what was coming.

Ute Territory

Barthow made his way to the back of the cave as cautiously as possible. He observed the ground precisely before each step. A single pebble, twig, or change in the surface of the floor that could cause him to lose balance, make a noise indicating movement, or alert any still-breathing monstrous animal to his presence could lead to his death. He stepped with his thick, yet supple leather boots, the soles modeled on moccasins, in the style he had learned from the natives. The outside front edge of one foot is set down, then the toes, making sure that the footing is secure, then loading the leading foot with half his weight, finally, transferring the balance of his weight to the forward foot, and lifting the trailing foot straight up, so as not to touch any straw, twigs, or anything else, and repeating the procedure. It was slow going, but it had never failed him.

When he was within fifteen feet, he could tell that the pile was in fact several of the adult giants, maybe sacrificing themselves, protecting the young ones he saw while remote viewing. He had counted at least eight full-grown adults and half-grown ones along the far wall on his approach to the rear of the cave. They had never made a sound or moved, so he figured he would double-check them on the way out, skirting that wall on the way back to the entrance. When he reached the pile, he observed it for two full minutes before proceeding. Not a breath, a movement, and with no air moving all the way at the back where he was, not a single hair on the bodies moved.

Barthow used his wand to levitate the first body off the top of the pile and move it to the left, laying it about ten feet away. Scanning the whole of the pile of bodies and seeing no change, nothing. Then the second body, this one a female, and he laid it next to the first. One after the other, he continued until he reached the bottom, where he did find the two small, young ones. They were crumpled together, slightly facing each other, with their arms across the other's back, their legs and feet a tangle he couldn't make out.

Regardless of the savage nature of these beasts, the killing of young creatures still bothered him. Sure, if you have a baby goat born and the mother rejects it, it's best to put it down. The mother always knows when it comes to animals. They can detect whether their insides are functioning properly from their breath, urine, and solid waste. Even though Barthow couldn't always see a problem with a cow, sheep, or goat, it always proved the mother right. Even a year on, coddling a sickly baby animal, sooner or later, they suffer and die.

Barthow lifted the one on the left, as it rose and its limbs went limp, untangling from the sibling, and as he set it down, he could tell that even these small ones were the same height as him. He shook his head at the size of it, the massive musculature, the complete lack of a neck structure that would allow full turns of the head. Red hair mingled with flat black; at least 90% of the surface of the skin was six to eight inches long on both of them. Paying close attention to his movement of the figure, he laid it gently on the pile of adults and turned back to the other. That is when he saw something that froze him, making his whole body run cold and his adrenaline surge. All he could do was stare at it. He took his left hand from the ground where he had been steadying his crouched position, and dug the medallion out of the neck of his shirt, and held it tight.

Dolphus' Home

After ensuring the Professor was indeed immobile and unable to know what was going on, Dolphus went back into his house and returned to the clearing with a split crystal ball, holding each half in a hand, flat side up. His footsteps were choppy and unsteady; this had been more walking in a hurry than Dolphus had done in years. He was pretty excited; however, the prisoner he had in his possession might help decode The Book's newest entries. He assumed that the changes were made to hide important notations, and he was anxious to discover them. Shuffling along, the wet leaves and twigs had built up on top of his feet as he moved closer, but his diabolical smile was proof of how little he cared for his appearance and near crippled gait.

He sidled up to the Professor, still in his ridiculous frozen pose, and raised his hands with the halves to his head, placing the flat center of each half on the temples of his prey. When he felt the jolt in his hands of the halves making a good connection through the professor's mind, he raised his gaze to the sky and closed his eyes. Dolphus had learned that it helped him concentrate, being less distracted by things and sounds, when the sky above was the only thing his senses were facing. Images of recent events flashed in the clear crystal halves, and Dolphus could see them in his mind. The professor was helpless and oblivious to what was happening to him. Dolphus dove deeper, looking for anything of value. What he did not know was that he was not alone in the Professor's mind. He could not feel or detect that his efforts were being redirected by someone else. Unfortunately, Corfus was busy with this dilemma, trying to protect the source of the new encoding for The Book, and knew that the hunter sent by the magical authorities was about to arrive. Corfus only had to protect the Professor's mind for a few more minutes. From the safety of Elfheim, he was doing all he could for the protection of the world. He could monitor the whole world under his purview in one state of mind, but entering one, controlling another in that mind, meant he was unable to answer Barthow's urgent call.

Dolphus was probing for any sign of The Book and the Professor's work with it. At last, he found a memory, not long ago, with writing in it by the Professor's hand. Concentrating on the writing, he could see it was in perfectly normal English. Damnit, he thought. Trying to peer into the future from that point, he saw a meeting in a well-appointed office. He recognized one person, Klement Metternich. Cursing, he moved from that image and tried to look around the room at who else might be there. The clown Metternich had no power, and the world of the ordinary he occupied was useless to Dolphus. Each time he tried to look around the room, it was as though the professor's gaze in his memory was preventing him from looking anywhere else. Now all he could see was the floor. Corfus was keeping him from looking around the room.

If that cursed Runetta had only done as he had asked from the beginning. The blasts of energy released during the battle back in Texas had prevented Dolphus from seeing very much of that event in his crystal ball. He had asked Runetta to go there, suspecting the spread of dark matter was connected to an Orb. She, in her vanity and disobedience, had sent one of her kerr minions, and whatever actually happened was lost with his demise. Damn that woman, he thought.

Dolphus then saw the Professor's gaze raise slightly, and could hear muffled sounds, talking, of someone, but the words and the speaker were blocked. The view rose until it rested on the desk in the room, where a large silver teapot was in view. Dolphus concentrated as hard as he ever had on it now. The teapot's rounded belly offered a panoramic view of the people in the room. One stood out, with unfamiliar clothing and a raw, rowdy appearance. He was sure he had seen glimpses of him in Texas; yes, it was clear now that it was the same person. Maybe this vagrant-looking dog knew something. There was no literature in Europe on the languages, much less the writing of those native peoples in the Americas; it would make sense to switch to one of those pictograph-style codes.

Removing the halves of the crystal ball from the Professor's head and laying them down on the ground, Dolphus held the image of the man in his mind. Now he placed his own hands on the sides of the Professor's head, with his thumbs on his closed eyes. Once they were positioned correctly, Dolphus raised his head again, entered the mind, and pushed the image into it. Then, he groaned under the strain; the veins in his neck, arms, and hands throbbed, the tendons protruding and straining. He didn't remember it being this difficult to force a subject to give him an answer, but he realized it may have been twenty years since he tried.

"I command you!" gritting his teeth now, releasing little gasps of breath under pressure. "Who is this man! Where is he!" His demands were shouted, not merely questions being asked.

The Professor's mouth fell open, animated by Dolphus's will, not his own motivation. It moved unnaturally, now as if both men were straining. Neither knew, but Corfus was doing all he could to prevent any of this.

Weak, jerking movements of the Professor's jaw began forming sounds. "Bar - Bart - Barth...ooo" Then he fell limp onto the ground. Dolphus broke his concentration and stared at the lump of a man there; this had never happened before. Why was this so hard? He knelt, picked up the halves of his ball, and put them back on the head of the Professor. Now he was going to look for this Bart-whatever man. If this man knew him, the whole image would help Dolphus find him now.

In place again, the halves began forming a clear image of Barthow. He was in a dark cave, approaching a pile of some large creatures, only a slight glow from his wand illuminating the area around him. That was fine. Dolphus pulled his own mind out away from this ruffian sneaking around some cave, and drew higher until he was inside a rock formation, then higher until he emerged into the night sky above a long rise of solid rock, above a high plains desert, somewhere. Proceeding even higher into the air, Dolphus could see the shape of the American continent, and finally, he had a precise fix on where he needed to find this man.

Hartge had come close to the home, in a small clearing, choosing to arrive at the back of the run-down house. He carefully listened and looked around, sure he was not being seen by anyone. He crept below the drip edge of the few windows, even though they were covered by climbing vines and thorny saplings. Surprise was his only tool when tracking and capturing villains, and this time, he would not fail. Reaching the corner, he peered around and saw a long row of split firewood stacked from the front edge of the house, about four feet high, and twenty feet or so long. Staying low and moving silently, he reached the stack and tried to peer through the gaps in the wood. He could make out two forms on the ground, but not with enough clarity to tell who either of them was. He drew his wand and moved all the way to the end of the stack, then peered around for a better look.

One was on the ground, dead or unconscious, based on the uncomfortable manner in which the body lay on its limbs. The other wore a filthy and burr covered woolen black cloak. Both were facing away from him, and he could not be sure which was the Professor. He had a gut feeling that the one in the black cloak was Dolphus. Just as he was pointing his wand, conjuring the confinement spell in his mind, the man in the cloak vanished in a sharp red flash of light. The one still on the ground was the Professor. What looked like a crystal ball that was split into two pieces fell into the leaves near the Professor's head, and was still settling as Hartge stood, making a crunching sound as they wobbled. He ran to the Professor and fell to his knees, checking him quickly for injuries. He felt his neck for a pulse and was relieved that the man was still alive.

He made good note of the surroundings, but not wanting Dolphus to return and surprise him, Hartge grabbed the professor's wrist and dislocated them back to the infirmary at headquarters.

Doctors ran to help, as Hartge lifted the professor from the ground with one arm over his shoulder, carrying him to a nearby bed.

"What has happened to him? Do you know?" the doctor pressed in a hurried tone, looking him over.

"He was paralyzed and being probed for information, that is all I know for sure." Hartge wiped his forearm across his head to get the beads of sweat from running into his eyes. It didn't matter how many times he was that close to killers or what the weather was like; he always built up immense heat internally, but the sweat never came until it was over. "Whatever it was, it involved some crystals the perpetrator was using to look in his head. I am sorry, doctor, I must speak with the General right away." The doctor nodded without looking back as he continued his diagnosis with his wand.

CHAPTER TEN

UTE TERRITORY

B arthow was sure the giants were all deceased. The last body lay on its right side, with the right arm straight up and the head resting on it. It was a young male, and what that animal and its sibling were huddled around when he first remote-viewed them was what made him lock up. Releasing a pent-up breath he had held since he saw it, and going fully forward on his knees to rest a moment, he leaned to his left and got a better look.

It was at least half of a giant Orb, broken, not cleanly severed. Golden flashes of light emanate from within it, interrupted by silvery-blue flashes that seem to chase the golden ones. It was about two feet in diameter, larger and different from the one he had seen in Texas. Daring to lean closer, and realizing he had been holding his breath again, not breathing naturally, he had a few deep calming breaths before scooting even closer. On his last breath, he could detect warmer air. Was it from his deep breathing?

Or was it, from that thing? He scooted closer, still on his knees, and extended his left hand towards it. He held his wand firm in his right hand, ready to dislocate or defend himself. What looked like small coppery-silver hairs were coming out of the sphere, just a minute amount. Blinking a few times and raising his bushy eyebrows to get as much resolution in his aging vision, the little hairs almost seemed to be moving. His left hand could feel warmth coming off it now. Pulsing, not steady like a fire or stove might feel.

This was what the little ones must have been huddled around when he first saw them; they were using it for heat. That thought helped him snap out of the awe he had been locked in with this one, different from the first one he saw. Swallowing a few times to clear his dry mouth, Barthow realized he hadn't heard from the elf. "Dang fool Elf, what good is it to give me this thing if'n you ain't gonna answer me!" He gripped the medallion again with his left hand, remembering what Corfus had said about the heat from his hand giving it power to work. Then he tried again to reach him. "High Elf, are you really there? I am inna pickle here, found one'a yer shiny ball things, you'd better git here snappy!" He stood fully up, knees cracking and popping so loud they made their own little echo in the cave. "Ow, dangit," he struggled to stand straight, stretching back a little and then turning around. At this point, he was sure he was alone there.

Just then, he saw a light coming down the slope at the entrance and felt relieved. It seemed odd. Why didn't that Elf just come here, where I am? Why's he walking the whole length of this cave? Hmm. Well, maybe he wanted a good look at the giants, after all, that's why he sent me in the first place, he thought. After all his crouched, careful movement around the cave, he was ready for a sit-down, and with the Elf here, he looked left and right until he found a large enough rock to suit him. He sat, squirmed a bit, got settled, and looked back at the light. It was bobbing and shaking more than it should have been for the Elf's stride. Barthow felt uneasy all of a sudden and raised his wand, just in case. Then he decided maybe it would be best if this mystery person didn't see him at all. He let himself slowly disappear, becoming indiscernible from the rock he sat on. A good wizard could spot invisibility if prepared to do so. Still, it is much harder to spot someone who is concealing themselves by camouflaging themselves with actual natural materials they are in contact with. In other words, Barthow's exterior was covered with actual rock, identical to the one he was sitting on, and the whole cave was made of it as well. Leaned flat against the wall, his wand, now in his left hand, tucked just inside the right breast of his jacket, he slowed his breathing to inaudible.

This mystery person was clearly hobbling as they walked and was a bit smaller than Barthow, so clearly not Corfus. A few moments more of feet shuffling through the rubble and loose material on the floor of the cave, and he could see it was an older man in a tatty black cloak. He was moving down the center of the space, not along the wall where Barthow was waiting to see what was going to happen, and if the Elf would show up in time, or if he would have to intervene. Barthow felt safe enough to wait; he was 25 feet or so from this person's path, and close enough to draw the broken sphere to him in an instant and dislocate if he had to. It lay to his right, and the tip of his wand could come out of his jacket in a fraction of a second, pointing right at the target. He stared at the area of the object, because even shifting his eyes would make a noise now, which could betray his ruse.

When this man was about 20 feet from the object, he paused, as if in shock, leaned forward, took a deep breath, straightened, and exhaled heavily. He extended a leathery, gaunt hand from the end of his cloak's sleeve; no wand was visible, so Barthow waited, wrongly. In a blinding crack of lightning and a deafening rip of thunder, the broken Orb and the old man were gone.

"Damnit!" Barthow exclaimed, he stood, releasing the camouflage charm, gravel and stones falling to the flat floor, clacking and scattering in front of him. "Where is the damn ELF!" lighting the wand again so he could see, and he ran - as best he could after years on horseback - to the ramp leading up and out of the cave. He dislocated to his horse's last location, and saw his old friend had been killed with a vicious ripping curse. His steed was dead, the cuts were deep to the bone, and he had been dead for maybe ten minutes. Steam still rose from the carcass. Whoever that ass of a man was, he also turned Barthow's belongings on the horse to dust. "Well, he's thorough. I'll give him that." Barthow's lip began to tremble, glancing back to what had been his horse for eight years. "Killing whoever that was is the only other thing I will give this bastard." He grasped the medallion again, this time with anger. "Some old man just came, nearly blinded and deafened me, took the Orb thing, and killed my horse. I'm going to bury him and get back to Texas. Don't call me again until you know where I can find this man. I mean it, Elf." He took the medallion from around his neck, stuck it in a pocket inside his waistcoat, and went to his knees next to his horse. After a few pats on the undamaged portion of the neck, he stood. He had been hardened in his years, and the thought of tears or long goodbyes was a childish memory now. He excavated a pit through solid rock about six feet deep, the same shape as his horse, placed it in the pit, and covered it with rubble, all in three waves of his wand. Turning to look away, he twisted his neck back to the cave for a second, then looked southeast towards home. He was going to stop by the Utes and his men on the way back, but decided to go straight to headquarters. They should at least make a report about the giants, and that they were handled. He closed his eyes and dislocated.

Corfus had only seen the last minute or so of the events in the cave with Barthow. There was no time for him to react in a way that would have satisfied Barthow. He heard what Barthow had said. He felt a slight kinship with Barthow, as he behaved with a sense of duty and purpose that the High Elves could relate to. His anger over being left alone, his horse passing, and no action when an artifact was encountered was a common trait amongst ordinary and magical mortals he didn't care for, or have time to deal with. The man was Dolphus, who had taken the artifact, and now Corfus would have to ask for the help of those he had confided in. If Dolphus knew what it was and where the other half was, it had to be stopped. Corfus had long suspected that the desire to find the Orbs in the family of Dolphus and Runetta was due to their knowledge of what they were, and maybe because they had a partial Orb already. Dolphus' reaction when he saw it might as well have been the proof. They had to act fast, find both of them, and extract the information Corfus needed to rectify the situation.

Corfus appeared in Klement's study, silently and without any indication. Klement alone was in there and had been going over files on his desk. Pausing in frustration, breathing out heavily, he flung his glasses on the pile of files and papers, grasping the bridge of his nose with his eyes closed. He wore them only for reading, and he massaged the place on his nose where they sat.

"Klement, do not be alarmed," Corfus said in his usual monotone way.

"Damnit!" Klement recoiled into his chair, grabbed the arms, and looked toward where the sound came from. "Where have you been? The Professor has been taken, and I called you, but no one has answered my call for help!" Frustration leaked through his polite speech, and recognizing it, Klement raised his hand briefly as if to wave off the implied disrespect.

"I know, the Professor is safe, taken to the Inquisitor General's Infirmary by a hunter. He is recovering safely. No harm befell him that we are aware of yet. But more has occurred. I need to have Raileanu and Monika brought here as soon as possible. We have work to do." Corfus stood, still looking with nervous intent at Klement.

Klement fell back into his chair with relief, sighing and letting his hands fall in his lap. "That is good news, I suppose." He looked around the room to see if any of the people in the portraits were there, who might not should see Corfus.

"Do not concern yourself. I am not visible through those unless I choose to be."

"Alright, Raileanu and Monika are downstairs. I held them here when the professor went missing. I did not want to alarm them without cause." Klement stood, walking around the desk, when Corfus turned to him and held up his hand.

"You want to take them and visit the professor, yes?" Corfus assumed.

"Yes, of course, they are good fri - " he was cut off by Corfus, indicating a pause again with his hand.

"I am concerned we do not have time. We must go to Dolphus Tangleweed's home immediately. I assure you the professor will be able to visit later; he is currently unconscious. Please. Can you bring them here to the study?"

"Yes, I will be right back." Corfus lowered his hand and stepped to the side, allowing him to pass by. Klement went out and turned to relock the door behind him, but it clicked into its locked state; presuming it was Corfus, he hurried downstairs.

It took me several years to piece together the exact order of events that happened during that two- or three-day period. Some of the participants were unwilling or unable to discuss those circumstances. Still, the end results made it clear that there were very few other possibilities than what I have written here. To some, it may seem excessive to record so many of these things in detail. The importance of the occurrences cannot be overstated, and in memory of so many who did their best on behalf of all life on earth. I spent several years visiting the locations of their parts in the stories to gain a better understanding and perspective to combine with their story. Paying homage to their work and sacrifices fell to me, and I will honor them in this telling.

Klement came more hurriedly than I had seen him move downstairs before. I couldn't tell if he was excited or upset, so I stood abruptly, leaving Monika mid-sentence, looking up at me, then Klement as he came around the lounge to where we were.

"I have word of the professor. He is safe, but I must ask you to come with me. Now." Klement said his piece and, without waiting for a response, turned and began walking quickly back up the stairs. Monika and I looked at each other briefly and then stood, took each other by the hand, and followed him.

We passed one of the maids on the wide staircase, and when we reached the third flight up to the third floor, I saw she was gone, out of sight. The carpeted stairs and the tapestries lining the walls made it relatively quiet, so I felt comfortable asking Klement something.

"Is there something that has happened? Will I need my sidearm?" Monika stopped on the stairs, her face shocked. Klement also stopped, two steps above us, and came down very close to us.

"Corfus is in my study. He said the professor is safe, but he needs our help immediately, so I would say, yes, something has happened. Retrieve whatever you feel you need." Klement was very intent, and the seriousness of the circumstances became clear. Monika and I, still holding hands, looked at each other, and I gave her a nod. Klement turned and climbed the stairs as quickly as he felt safe in doing, with us right behind him. He proceeded down the hall to the study, while Monika and I went to our rooms.

Our attire was befitting the Metternich home, but in no way would it suit confronting dark enemies of mankind. Klement had given us all the information he had, and knowing a couple of the High Elves now, it was probably all he knew as well. I went into my room, and Monika into hers. I stripped off the ridiculous tailored jacket with twelve buttons, adorned with woven gold braid embellishments and shoulder bars, and flung it across the bed. I unlatched the two straps on the belt that crossed my chest, holding the saber belt, which was part of the attire, even though I wasn't wearing the saber. I went to the trunk that had all my belongings from Texas and hastily put on the pistol belt, now with two pistols and my father's Damascus Bowie. I flung the satchel over my shoulder, holding more shot and powder, pulled the large neckerchief - still tied - over my head. I grabbed the

Patterson revolver carbine that was lying under that, and then the leather bag that held six pre-loaded cylinders. Those would work in my pistol or the carbine. I made sure they still had all their percussion caps in place and put that in the satchel. I took the long coat out of the trunk and swung it around as I put it on. I turned to leave the trunk at the end of the bed and saw the coat rack by the door. Hanging on it, just under my hand-formed greenish-gray mushroom stetson hat, was the saber. More than once, I had been outmatched by magic recently, and I decided that if I had to face enemies with powerful magic, I had better have every advantage possible. I reached back to the bed and grabbed the belt and over-the-shoulder strap for the saber, connecting it all together as I went to the rack. I clipped the saber to the two points on the belt it was designed for, put my hat on, and went out the door into the hallway.

Monika was already down by the study door, waiting for me. She had only changed her footwear to high charcoal-gray suede boots laced all the way up to her calves, and a long-sleeved, flowing light-gray fabric coat. She had her wand in her hand, and her hair tied back. What would have taken an ordinary lady half an hour, my magical fiancée had done with a wave of her wand in an instant. When I got close to her, she had a look of impatience for a split second, then a forgiving smile. I rapped the door with a knuckle, and it opened.

Corfus was there, hands behind his back, and Klement was facing us with his arms crossed, leaning back on the front of his desk. We entered with anticipation and concern written all over our faces. Corfus turned to us and said what I needed to hear.

"The man behind what happened to your family has been found, and has also found a part of an Orb. I would like your help in retrieving that artifact and stopping this man. He is the one who was involved in the kidnapping of the Professor. Magnus Templeton is safe now, unconscious, but safe."

"How do we get to him? That's all I care about." I could see Monika nodding in my periphery.

"He is hundreds of miles to the east. I can take you all there." Corfus checked each one of our faces, gauging our resolve. When he was satisfied, he came toward us and reached out his hands. He nodded to his outstretched arms. Klement went back behind his desk, took out a small nickel-plated pistol, and put it in his pocket, then reached under the desk and took out a short double-barreled shotgun. Then he came towards us.

"You know I cannot dislocate." I gave him a sour look because, for all their wisdom, my limitations were becoming more than an irritant; having to remind everyone was starting to rankle me past politeness.

"Raileanu, I do know. It is you who are unaware of all the forces on the earth that God has hidden from mankind. Please." Again, motioning to take his hand. I took Monika's hand, holding my carbine in the other; she held Corfus's hand, and he took Klement's free hand. He leaned forward and checked that we were all ready. He then stood straight again, raised his chin upwards, and closed his eyes. I looked only to Monika and saw a green glow spread from Corfus to her, then up my arm, enveloping me. Then we were surrounded by complete darkness.

CHAPTER ELEVEN

Hartge arrived right outside the Inquisitor General's office. Upon seeing him there, the General raised his left hand, looking back down to his desk, and waved him in with three fingers, the door opening on its own. Hartge shut the door behind him and stood at attention in front of the desk.

"Well, is the Professor safe?" the General asked.

"Yes, sir. Dolphus escaped before I could approach him safely, leaving the professor behind. I do not know where he dislocated to, but I feel as though I should go and inspect his home. The reports of this man and his associates have caused enough trouble, I think." Hartge relaxed his position a bit during his response.

"I agree. The ordinary authorities are inquiring about him and that detestable Runetta as well. Find out anything you can. Take a looking can with you." The General kept his focus down while pointing with a pen in his right hand to a wooden crate on a cabinet, containing four-inch-long, two-inch-diameter ruby tubes with ornate silver-wound exteriors. "Report back when you are finished."

Hartge looked down at the General's desk. He had a glass plaque with a painted black wooden frame. Red and green illuminated lines crisscrossed the glass's surface, ending in a blinking dot. He could see that there was engraving all over the glass, but couldn't make out what it was - writing or drawings. The General sensed Hartge standing there looking at it.

The General looked up. "Is there anything else?" He now looked over his brass-rimmed glasses at Hartge.

"No, sir. Thank you." He went and picked up a Looker from the rack and left the office. He checked the tool to make sure it was working. If he rotated the fittings on the outside, it would record whatever he pointed it at. He moved the fittings to another position, and it projected a moving image of what he saw on the floor. Good. Now, back to Dolphus's home.

Bexar

Barthow arrived in the adobe wall-enclosed backyard of the Texas Territorial Magical Rangers. It was nearly morning now, the pink in the sky beginning to creep higher than the tops of the pines of the town. It was still a couple of hours to daylight when he left the cave, he reckoned. When he took the first couple of steps towards the back porch, gravel and dust fell off him, probably still leftover from the folds in his clothing. Several chickens ran up from the tomato plants at the back wall, thinking he was spreading dried corn, which he frequently did for them.

"Whatcha doin' back here, ol' Bart?" the voice inside echoed out the sun-dried clay walls. It was his boss, leaning back in his chair at his desk. Ol' Bart is what he always called Barthow, you know the type, deciding on a nickname they made up instead of using their given name. The desk and his boss, facing the front of the small building, although he briefly let his head lean back, as if to broadcast his booming voice more. He looked back down to his front, hearing Barthow's boots on the wood floor planks approaching.

Barthow came around the front of the desk and saw Geoff whittling a little figure. He had gotten it in his mind that he would learn chess and was intent on making his own little figures for the game. This one was a pistoleer wearing a big sombrero and holding two pistols.

"You heard of anything peculiar outta Europe in the last day or so, bossman?" Barthow sat in the rocking chair across from Geoff.

"Naw, nuthin' important I can recall. Thar's some posters come in yesterday, but ain't heard nuthin' else." He motioned with his little whittling knife at the desk, then went back to his figure's detail work. Barthow reached up to the desk, noticing the sun had crested the horizon now, and his hat was casting a shadow on what he was trying to look at; he set it on the uncluttered corner of the desk. He sorted through them, looking only for someone who might look like the man he saw in the cave.

"You han'l them giants and whatnot up northways?" Geoff asked. The deputies must have sent word where they were going. He would have to have words with them about that. It was up to him to say which and when, not them.

"Yessir, all han'ld." He kept looking through the posters and notices without raising his head.

"Well, that's good. We don't want nun them hairy meat-eaters 'round these parts, no sir. Whatcha lookin fer?" Geoff stopped and looked at 'Ol Bart' now.

"There was a feller there, showed up right at the end of it all. He was a'lookin fer somethin. Didn't git a good feelin' 'bout him neither." Then he saw a name, and a likeness that might be a match, and held it up in the light better.

Still holding the wanted poster for Dolphus, he noticed the text beginning to change. Someone was adding or changing something. Keeping a close eye on it, he saw that a possible location of his whereabouts was written. Dolphus's home's location was pinpointed.

"I gotta go, boss. I'll catch you up later, alright?" Barthow looked at his boss, who just gave him a wave away with his knife and never stopped his carving. That's the best kind of boss.

*****

I don't know what type of travel Corfus was using. I had never heard of anything like it. It was not just dark; there was nothing. I couldn't feel the ground, Monika's hand, any sound, any air wafting across my face as had been in the study. My body did not detect any weight, almost as if I were floating on the surface of water, which is when I realized there was no way to know whether I was right side up or upside down, no sensation of direction or movement, nothing at all. It didn't concern me, though; it was actually comforting. Absent all these material influences, there was a sense that even time was suspended. I couldn't tell if we were moving, or had, or even how long this had been the case.

Free of the concerns of impending conflict, I felt like it was safe, for reasons I can't explain, to consider all the events of the last few months. The pace of things had let me evade the tugging from all the dead who littered the path that led me here. I had left my father's death with no unsaid things. He was loved, he was proud of me, and in his final days, he sat with Momma and me, holding his hands. Then, helpless at the hands of a magical assassin, I watched as my dear sweet mother was killed most brutally. I had learned in the midst of these events how ancient artifacts from an age unknown to me - or anyone else on earth - had been the cause of all of it. More deaths were to come as a result of it—that one single artifact. Now, based on the High Elf's demeanor, we all suspected another one had been located, but kept unfounded concerns to ourselves.

At this point, I didn't care about whether it was another Orb. All I wanted to do was face as a man, on as equal terms as I could gather, some of these villains who wrought havoc on my life, and took nearly everything of importance from me.

For fifteen years, I had pursued something I was adept at that paid my salary, such as it was. Before this began, Klement had given me a prestigious position, a promotion, and a guaranteed income for life. I was withholding pride for that until I had seen to my father. As events unfolded, I never even got to mention it to my father. The truth was, all of it felt a bit like charity, and I had held a quiet resentment against it from the beginning. I lost my magic as a child, and while there can be no doubt that some of the botanical discoveries made over these years have shown significant benefit and opened up new industries for magical potions and medicine, I never liked it. That was the truth of it. It was just something I could do to feel useful. Here, in the dark place outside space and time, I had decided to abandon the sham of it all. Monika, I always knew, could see right through me. She knew I existed in a place where the magical and ordinary worlds decided I fit in very well. I could feel in this strange point of suspended existence that if I pronounced at the end of this excursion, I was finished with all of it, she might weep in happiness. That is, if we all lived.

I would not be hesitant this time. There would be no concern for their eternal soul and their rightness with their Creator. Their poisoned tentacles had touched the wrong family; they were not dealing with a people who were satisfied with a caste-type existence, content with staying in the place the world assigned them. Retribution, justice, violence of action, and determination were the sensations I could feel growing in prominence inside myself now. The high, crooked, and overloaded shelves in my mind and heart, where all the stores of the facade my consciousness built of what my life was about, crumbled into pointless piles, then disintegrated into dust, then powder, then were gone entirely. Wherever we were going now, when I emerged, I would be a completely different animal. Walking away from the conflict awaiting us, I would LIVE. I would LOVE Monika in ways and with a depth she could not fathom yet. The dedication and intensity I would hold her would honor my mother and father. For a moment, I could almost see parts of that life materialize, made of pinpricks of light with dull color in a curved space around my mind. It gave me a flicker of hope that there was a life past whatever lay ahead.

Prague

Upon arrival at Dietrick Metternich's home, Jon Roqueford laid out what he knew. It was later the same day that he had spotted, then followed, what he thought was Runetta Lynchos. By this time, Dietrick had learned of the professor's kidnapping. In accordance with the government's agreement for the separation of magical and ordinary worlds, he did not mention that to Jon. He did, however, send him immediately, with personal orders to head to Prague, where Jon suspected Ruentta may be. The orders signed by Dietrick gave him unrestricted travel on the train systems in place at that time in Austria. It would be the following midday before he could reach the home under surveillance there. If he was unable to find her within twelve hours, he was ordered to go to Portugal and investigate the situation there.

There was but one delay on the trip at the border crossing, and, surprisingly, the officials there issued him a letter allowing him to continue his investigation there as well. Relations had not always been agreeable for official matters, but were usually cordial. He had to wait at the station for a second train to arrive and was given a back room with a cot by the border guards to rest while he waited.

He had lost people he was following before, and a couple of things bothered him. Not once did he lose sight of the hooded figure he was trailing in the hour he followed. He could not remember a time when another person in similar clothing had crossed his wide, attentive gaze. That was a trick often used by pickpocket gangs, when daylight or inclement weather made it easy for ordinary folk to mistake one person for another. It didn't happen this time, though. When what he thought was Runetta made a left turn, not twenty-five feet in front of him, into a shop, he could clearly remember the ringing of a doorbell and the clatter of glass panes when a door shut before he reached it. It was the same sound every door with nine panes of glass on a cold, dry day makes, with the bell hung on a thin, curved strip of steel designed to brush the doorframe when it is opened or closed, creating a jingle. This time, there was no door. The old arched single-wide doorway had been bricked up. In fact, there wasn't even room in that entrance, maybe two feet, to have walked into it at the speed he saw her go, without significant injury.

Moreover, when he returned to Haizek Moon's home, the doorway to the courtyard he had left from was also made of a solid stone block. Something was happening that he couldn't explain, and all of it was too ridiculous for him to mention to anyone. He was relaxing on the cot, considering all this, when he drifted to sleep.

The shaking of his shoulder woke him. He looked up and saw the ticketmaster, in his grey flannel uniform and matching cap, standing there.

"Sir, the train has arrived. If you would please," he motioned to the door.

Jon gathered his bag and coat off the cot and tipped his hat to the man as he hurried out the door and onto the platform. The ticketmaster passed him and went to the second car, extending his right arm, palm forward, toward the train car's steps. With a glance at the sky, he stepped up the three stairs and turned to the right, looking in the car. There was a seat available at the back right-hand side, and so he went to it and sat down. He checked his watch, seven thirty. Good. He should be in Prague by ten o'clock tonight. His man would meet him there and take him to their apartment. There were two of them who worked as pressmen at one of the newspapers in Prague, but were actually intelligence officers for the Austro-Hungarian Empire. They had been keeping an eye on that house where Runetta was spotted for more than a week now. Jon settled in for the last leg of his trip.

Jon woke as the hisses of steam and squealing of the wheels on the train slowed as it came into the station. He stood, took the long overcoat that he had been using as a pillow, and put it on. He had his small leather satchel with him, containing a change of underclothes, his Bible, and a bottle of port, which he rarely drank from but had used many times to clean cuts and scrapes. Tucked in an inner pocket, hard to find unless you knew it was there, was the wanted poster for Runetta, some paper money in different denominations and from various countries, and ten gold troy-ounce coins in a canvas sleeve he had made from an old shirt. Each coin had its own little pocket, and folded in half, it made no noise when jostled. He reached into his inner pocket on his waistcoat, where the letter he had been given gave him authority to seek this person of interest, in case he needed it.

He went to the closest exit and stepped into the clouds of steam, counting on the platform being where it should be, as he couldn't actually see it. He kept his eyes parallel with the horizon, scanning each face and shape for his contact, and anyone else that gave him a twinge of instinct. Along the far wall, through the people meandering around, he could see his contact. It was a slender, almost lanky, man dressed smartly in a brown suit, but as his assignment dictated, not tailored, nor new. He had a thin, wide mustache of sandy blond, matching his weekly-cut hair, which was short under his bowler hat. The hat, too, was as clean as it could be, but not new, and showed signs of wear anywhere he had to touch it, along with the collected darker patches consistent with the oils of a hand regularly adjusting it. A slight hint of white stretched up from the junction of brim to cap, salt from the summer that leeches from sweat into the fabric of the hat.

The crowd swelled and thinned as the train passengers embarked and disembarked, and Jon made his way around the thicker masses, to his left, to the wall of the station house. There were several beggars along that wall, either sitting on crates or right on the platform as he made his way to the contact. Pausing to let a young couple drop their bags and embrace, he looked at the man he was going towards, and he was still searching the crowds, so he had not noticed Jon yet.

Jon was experienced in protecting his belongings in crowds from thieves, and had relied on what he called -only to himself- his 'bubble'. He could sometimes feel when people with bad intent had entered his 'bubble', and he could stop and stare intently at them. Those unlucky enough to have tried this were immediately discouraged, and their response had encouraged Jon that the feeling was real and worked well. This time, either because there was no ill will to detect or because his skill wasn't as finely tuned as he had hoped, someone tugged several quick times at his left elbow's sleeve. Whipping his stern look at the subject, he saw an older woman who had been sitting on a weak-looking crate, but had stood hunchbacked and shaking just from the effort to touch him. She was no more than five feet tall, probably a hundred pounds soaking wet. It was such a bold thing to do, he stopped and turned to face her, suddenly curious about what she wanted. She sat back down on her crate. She had several kinds of single-layer clothing, frayed and decades old, he guessed. Underneath the outer garments was a cared-for paisley full-length dress. She had several bracelets with little charms dangling from them on each wrist, and rings of silver, mostly on every shriveled, wrinkled finger. Under the light red cloth hood, perched halfway on her head of gray hair, the gold dangle headband showed prominently. She was looking down after she sat, as if in contemplation.

"Ma'am. Is there something I can do for you? Why did you touch me?" Jon asked, almost amazed that he felt he should ask her anything, much less stop here.

She waited only a second before looking up. She was indeed old; the sun- and hard-winter-worn wrinkles started at her hairline, no doubt from her short stature, which had forced her to look up to converse with anyone her whole life. Her eyes were flat grey, no other color. The wrinkles went all the way to the edges of both her ears, which had four or five clasp earrings of varying styles and materials. She had smiled and cried thousands of times in her life, but nothing Jon could detect led him to think this woman was disingenuous in any way. Again, he marveled at why he felt he should speak with her at all.

"Jon. Your name is Jon. You hunt men, but not today. Mmm. Yes. Today, it is a woman. I had to tell you, Jon. She is not what you think, and you are in danger." She was determined and sincere, he could tell that. She reached into her robes and pulled out a small pouch. It had a big brass button and was made of heavy cowhide. She had to work hard, her hands shaking, to unbutton it, then she rummaged around until she had something in her hand. With her hand closed except for her index finger and thumb, she rebuttoned it and returned the pouch to her side under her clothing. She held the closed hand out and opened it palm up. There was a small silver cross, small but with wide members, quite sturdy, and a circle piercing the two beams of the cross. Jon had seen them before, but was not entirely sure of their significance. Beside it was a large, half-inch glass bead with flecks of copper, on a leather lace. She moved her hand closer to him, almost lunging twice. "Take it, for protection from this woman. It is all that can protect you from her devices, sir. I want nothing but to protect you."

"You're sure?" Jon asked. This was not the kind of behavior of a typical fortune teller or gypsy thief at all. She nodded and held her open hand even higher. So he held out his open hand under hers, and she turned her hand sideways, letting it fall into his.

"Pray, Jon. Pray for protection from the powers of this woman you seek. That is all I ask in return." She leaned back against the wall and closed her eyes.

"Sir, are you ready to depart?" It was his contact, standing next to him, so Jon quickly put the items in his coat pocket, opposite the man.

"Yes, yes, let's get on our way, son," Jon said, walking away towards the platform exit into town, with the young man behind him, but momentarily catching up beside Jon.

"Was that woman causing a problem, sir?" He asked

"No, she just said she wanted to tell me something, that's all," Jon said, walking through the streets with a purpose and sense of direction that surprised the young man. "Let's just get to the house. I want a full briefing and to see your logs as soon as I can."

CHAPTER TWELVE

DOLPHUS'S HOME

We arrived in a small clearing, all of us - Monika, Klement, Corfus, and I. We were all looking up, and I saw that all of us non-elven kind had our eyes closed, and I watched each slowly open their eyelids. I didn't remember beginning the trip with my eyes closed, strangely enough. It was night, and overcast. I also noticed that I had no discomfort of any kind. Only the silvery outline of heavy clouds overlapping each other was visible in the sky. We released each other's hands, and each in turn raised their tool of choice: a wand, a pistol, and a carbine, and began to evaluate our surroundings. Tall, twisted, thick-trunked trees surrounded the clearing, maybe a hundred and fifty feet across. Turning my head to the right, I saw a structure and made a full-body turn to see a large cottage. It had a very old wood-shingled roof; about half the height of the walls was stone, the rest wattle and daub that had once been whitewashed. Sections of the walls were suffering subsidence, and the roof dipped in accordance with those areas. Moss and lycan draped whole sections of the structure, and a wild thorn vine had completely covered the right side of the cottage and obscured at least two windows. A crumbling chimney was on the left side, barely higher than the roof line. In the center of the building was a relatively low doorway, and the top beam was lopsided. The door stood open, and the inside of the door was also covered in green-gray lycan, indicating to me at least, it had been open for a long time. Maybe it couldn't close because of the sagging top beam over the doorway. A wide oak table was to the left of the entrance, with what looked like a selection of crystal balls on it, each on a small ring-shaped wooden base. On the opposite side of the table from us was a high-backed chair that looked well-worn. Just to the right side of the table, from our view in the middle of the clearing, was a ring of rectangular stones with smoke rising from within it. There were no lights about, inside the home, or anywhere in the woods beyond we could see.

We were all in a line now, facing the home. Corfus turned his head side to side, seemed to me to be looking into the trees, so I looked at them as well. More eyes are better than fewer. Corfus then pointed to the sky with his right index finger, still focused on the tree line. At each point he aimed his finger at, a bright white ball appeared in the sky, three in total. Now the whole clearing was well lit. Still pointing at the center ball, he lowered his hand, and the ball followed his aim into the trees, maybe twenty feet behind the first row of them.

We can all see now that these trees are entirely covered in clumps of huge, black thorns: trunk, branches, all of it. Even the leaves were spiked, and reminded me of horse nettle. I knew what they were.

"Bloodthorn Trees," I said loud enough for only my group to hear. "We don't want to go anywhere near those; they will draw your blood with the slightest scrape, and the pain is very intense." Turning just enough to make sure everyone heard me, as they were all nodding a bit. Except Corfus. I checked what he was looking at again. It was the trunk, about five feet off the ground. I didn't see anything, but he must have. He then checked every tree in about the same place.

"Raileanu is correct," Corfus said. "Do NOT go near the trees." He then made a tiny twirling motion with his index finger, and the ball of light in the trees began moving around the perimeter, about chest high, in and out of the trees. "That light will sense any movement or presence, and illuminate it for you. I will be able to see what it finds regardless of where I am." He could tell we all heard and agreed. "Raileanu, could you and Monika stay here in front of the house, focus on the light, and watch for anyone. The pistol you have, that was made for your mother, will be effective against anything I feel we may encounter."

"Yes, we will do that." Before I even looked at her, Monika grabbed my free hand and gave me a squeeze of confirmation. She then let go and assumed a fighting stance, as did I.

"Klement, would you come with me, please, into the house?" in a statement, more than a question, as Corfus began his wide gait to the front door. Klement followed, with his scattergun at the ready. Stopping abruptly, Corfus turned his head to the left and looked at the crystal balls on the table. A flash of light on the table obscured them, and when it had faded, all the balls were reduced to a bright orange molten blob. Then he entered the house, ducking his seven-foot frame to pass through the short door frame, with Klement right behind him.

Klement reported later what he saw in the house, as neither Monika nor I entered. It was a disgusting mess. A long table stacked with small animals in varying states of decay was directly in front of them. The entire right side of the open area in the house was stacked floor to ceiling with burlap sacks, wooden crates, and the skeletons of animals Dolphus had been eating. Fur and dried flesh still hung to their bones in places. The stench was thick and pervasive. Only a small pallet of blankets and furs was in front of the fireplace to the right, with barely enough room between the stone hearth and the pallet to walk to and lie down. To the left was a small kitchen area, with a sink made of black granite, several bottles of wine scattered around the wooden bar, and, beyond that, shelves floor to ceiling, each compartment one foot by one foot. Each one had a crystal ball, or two smaller ones. There were probably three hundred of them. Most had long been covered by cobwebs, proof of their lack of value to Dolphus and what he had been seeking. At the back of the kitchen, opposite the front wall of the house, was a narrow gap between the shelving. Corfus, having taken in all the disarray and obsessive lifestyle that led to the layers of dirt and filth, walked quickly back to the gap.

He motioned his head in a sharp jerking motion around the corner to glance in. His long white hair swayed in a fluid motion, then settled. He pointed again, as he had outside, and the light from past the shelves fell out on the floor of the kitchen, and Corfus went in. Klement, not wanting to risk touching anything, was very careful in his movements and told me later that he was remembering the quickness and violence with which the assassin who killed my parents arrived and moved. He admitted that he had begun sweating and had to adjust his grip several times on the shotgun as he moved to follow Corfus.

"Do you hear anything?" I asked Monika. She didn't answer, so I turned to face her quietly. She had frozen her movements, all but her eyes. They were narrowing as she peered into the dark among the trees. The light Corfus had cast in the woods was a good fifty feet to our right, still weaving around trees, moving away from us. I crouched slightly and tried to gauge the pitiful light in the area where she was concentrating. For me, at least, when I try to focus my gaze on a specific spot, I find my mind begins to filter out the movements on either side of my focus. I didn't want us to miss something because we weren't looking at the big picture. Thunder rumbled then, and the wind picked up, swirling leaves around the clearing, making listening harder to do. I didn't notice a flash of lightning changing anything, so that it could have even been on the other side of the nearby mountain. Still, thunder and lightning don't cause gusts of wind. Rainfall can, or magic, I thought.

Lightning did throw a brilliant blue-white light across the little clearing for a split second this time, followed a second later by deep, rolling thunder, muffled on and off as the sound filtered through the clouds. A glint behind us, which I wouldn't have seen had I not turned to look at Monika, caught my attention in the flash. It was behind where we had arrived, and nearly covered with leaves.

"What's that?" I whispered. Then another strike of lightning, this time coming from the clouds to the ground somewhere out in the woods, and lighting everything up like daylight. There were two of whatever they were. As the light subsided and my eyes adjusted again to the dark, my mind processed what it might be. They looked like glass bowls, clear glass bowls.

"I can't look right now. I am watching something move out there. It's a shadow, but I can't find the thing making it, and it's not the same shape each time the lightning comes. I am not taking my eyes off it," she told me.

"Please don't. I bet your skills will be more important to protect us than mine in this place. It looks like two glass bowls or something, behind us in the leaves."

"Alright, just remember where they are, help me watch whatever this is," she whispered, more serious, and, for a moment, a bit funny to me. Whatever it might be, I thought, has already seen us standing here like in broad daylight twice now. We're not hiding from it. I turned and took a couple of steps to be slightly ahead of her and to her left. I raised the revolver carbine to my shoulder, and aimed it - best I could tell - where she was watching, mimicking her slightest movement. Three quick strikes this time of lightning, then a flicker of branches of light crawled through the clouds like bony fingers. When the thunder started this time, low and rumbling, it didn't stop the rest of the time we were there. A few sounds from the tops of the trees, like handfuls of sand thrown against leaves, filtered down to us. I made a glance in its direction without changing my aim. I didn't see anything, but then the wind began to come in, pushing gusts, and the sound became clear: rain started falling in great sheets, as curtains dragged across the clearing. Monika, never breaking gaze, gave her wand a quick flick, and the rain began falling around us, and we could hear the wind moving the leaves and branches of the trees, but the deafening sound of the rain was no more.

Inside, Corfus and Klement made their way down the narrow hallway, about ten feet long. Both sides of the passage held crystal balls and rare, natural specimens in glass cylinders. The hallway's ceiling was as low as the front door, and Corfus was nearly bent at the waist to make it through. Klement looked around him, as well as he could, and saw a large door with a lock on it. He recognized the symbol etched into the lock as a dangerous curse, but before he could say anything, Corfus had reduced it to a pile of rust and pushed the door open. A few more hunched steps, and he stood erect in a large room. Once they had both come into it, they could see several small tables piled with parchment, drawings, and writing on them. The walls were completely covered with paintings, not portraits. Some were of castles, some of great homes, some like painted schematics of fortresses, with hand-written descriptions of rooms and features so small one would need a magnifying glass.

"Corfus, I don't recognize any of these," Klement said, looking at the many pictures. Klement turned and looked at Corfus after he made the statement. Corfus held his hands, fingers spread wide, moving them over the stacks of documents.

"You wouldn't. All of those are structures from at least 10,000 to 15,000 years ago. Anything that remains of them is a ruin now." Corfus stopped and looked down at where his right hand was. He picked up a document case from under several inches of dust-covered papers. He opened the top flap and began sorting through the scrolls and papers inside, as if he knew the one he was looking for. He stopped on one with writing Klement had never seen before, and a depiction of a small castle. Squiggly lines with arrows went from the castle to lines of text below. Corfus, still holding the document, walked around the table to the far wall and looked at one of the drawings. He then held the document up next to the picture.

"Please, come with me. We must go to another location immediately." Corfus kept the paper, crouched over to go back through the hallway, and Klement jerked to quickly follow, refusing the urge to scour the room of secrets for anything of value to fight the will of darkness. Emerging from the front door, Corfus stood fully erect again, and Klement came out behind him.

"WAIT!" Monika yelled, holding her left hand up at Corfus and Klement. Lightning now struck not a quarter mile away, and that sound was deafening, leaving a ring in my ears. Everything I heard for the next few minutes was muffled and accompanied by an annoying ringing.

Corfus looked right where Monika was aiming her wand. Even through the rain, he knew what it was. He grabbed Klement and ran the dozen or so of his strides toward Monika and me, virtually flinging Klement against me, making himself and Monika with outstretched arms a barricade.

"You can fire at it, Monika, but that shadow will be unaffected by it," Corfus said in his usual unemotional way. "I know where we must go. That shadow is not of magic, nor the world I am from. That is evil, and we will be unable to stop it. It is Dolphus's Shadow. They can only come from a Dybbuk."

None of this made sense, then, in between more frequent cracks of thunder and fluttering lightning, Corfus pointed one hand at the cottage, while the other he kept trained, along with his sight, at the Shadow. A spire of white-hot fire spewed from Corfus's left hand into the front of the house, and one from his right hand into the woods where the shadow was. The house burst into flame, ripping out the windows and through the vines, exiting the roof in a dozen places. The plume that entered the woods turned into a wheel of fire, rolling at great speed around the perimeter. I watched as the Shadow began, well, dancing, for lack of a better term.

"No." Corfus had a hint of a disappointed tone. "The spaces I saw on the trees earlier were worse than I thought."

Creaking and cracking began to surround us. That sound was not isolated from the shell, keeping the rain off us. It was the sound of the bloodthorn trees breaking apart. Terrible shapes, malformed and with eerily long limbs, almost human-like. They had no faces, just wild splintered tops where a head would be, and legs and arms of branches, growths of clumped spikes all over the length of them. Every tree ringing the clearing had a form of life springing from it that was gruesome, and now on fire. The pelting of rain was beginning to put them out, hissing and steaming, as they stepped closer and closer, moving further from the ring of fire. All around us, these animated beings began to move towards us. The wet rending of living wood encircled us, and with each second, they slowly closed the distance, one creaking, disjoined movement at a time.

Monika let fly with her wand, casting an explosive spell at three in quick succession. The location where the strikes landed blew apart one foot holes in the bodies, but made no difference. Simultaneously, Klement fired one barrel of buckshot at two of them, again, knocking only shards of bark and wood and thorns off. I fired all six rounds from my Patterson Carbine at one of them, and it did stop moving towards us, frozen in place.

"The enchanted shot of wand cores seemed to stop this one!" I shouted. I looked to the Elf while I pulled the pin on the cylinder and let it fall to the ground, reaching into my satchel and grabbing another.

"Interesting. Save your shots, then Raileanu, we may need them still. Allow me." Corfus said.

Corfus held his hands together, as if in prayer, of all things, muttering something that I cannot recall even today. Several more stripes of lightning ripped the sky, with accompanying peals of thunder, and the rain seemed to shiver in the air with each one. Then Corfus held up a small trinket, again, that I could not see well enough to identify. Each of the tree creatures he held it to and said his words at, stopped in its tracks. It took some time, more than we had, as nearly a hundred of them were pressing on towards us now. Klement fired his shotgun at a couple more of them, this time at their 'legs'. That seemed to weaken their appendages, and the weight of their arms and torsos overpowered the remaining wooden structure, and they fell to the ground. It was then that I saw the front of the portion of the trunks that lay between the arms. There was no bark, in a perfect circle, and a strange symbol, with the gleam of firelight showing the symbol was in blood.

These had fallen not eight feet from us. It had encouraged Klement, who was now firing as fast as he could reload.

"Monika! Fire at their legs!" Klement shouted. By now, I had changed the magical wand core shot cylinders to standard lead ball ones, but I only had two, giving me twelve shots total. I put the wand core cylinder in my coat pocket. While doing this, Monika had begun firing her spells at their legs, and it was obliterating them. Some falling backwards from the force of her power. Those who had fallen face-first started crawling towards me.

"Monika, hit this one before he gets to me!" I had to shout over the shotgun, her blasts, the roaring wheel of fire still in the trees, and the thunder. She wheeled over to my side and stepped across to point her wand at it. The hole it created went four feet into the ground, turning the majority of it into splinters. Thorns and wooden shrapnel pelted my face, and I couldn't see. I reached up and felt several large chunks of wood had entered the skin of my face. Based on their oblique angle, they actually hit the skull between my nose and right eye and slid across it, lying flat against my face. I felt a large thorn sticking out of my right eye, and could feel the dull ache as I tried to move my eye. Sight returned to my left eye, and now I could feel the blood running off my face and onto my neck.

Seeing my blind clutching and reeling action, Monika put her hand on my shoulder and turned me toward her, and recoiled. I could hear her gasp.

"That bad, huh?" I let out, followed by me releasing several anguished sighs of my own. She relented from her fighting, and brought her wand to my face. A warm yellow glow began to curl off the tip of it and reached my face, which went numb. Two more explosions from Klement's shotgun, and he turned to look at why Monika had stopped fighting.

"Corfus!" Klement shouted, closing his shotgun breech again and firing both barrels. "Corfus, check Raileanu!"

Not realizing that I had reclined, I was looking almost straight up, and saw the tall Elf turn, his hair moving in slow motion to me, waving back and forth after he stopped turning his head, and then looking down at me. Just a wink from him and I could tell, numbed and all, that he had extracted the wood and thorns from my face. Monika kept the light of her wand on me for a moment longer. I was holding my head up level with the ground now, and saw one of the tree creatures stepping over the wreckage of another, almost on us. I pulled the pistol that my mother had been given and fired twice into it. Being right-eye dominant, I wanted to be sure I was seeing the target and hitting it. It stopped mid-stride, was off balance, and fell to the right.

Corfus had rotated his position now and was more or less facing the direction Monika and I had been. The creatures were no longer creaking and snapping wood behind us, so he must have been successful on his side. Monika released the light from her wand to my face, and as feeling returned, I could tell there wasn't fresh blood leaking from any of the wounds.

"I only have six more rounds!" Klement yelled, his head turned toward us, still facing away, letting two more shotshells go into the approaching danger. When he returned his head to its forward position, one of them was reaching for him. I could see the legs of it to the right of Klement, so I fired two shots quickly into it. It stopped, but then it fell right on him as he was closing the breech, knocking him down right next to me. The thorny beast wasn't moving, but he was impaled by twenty or thirty of the long, bloodsucking thorns, and let out an agonizing scream as they sank deep into him. It was lying from his thighs to his feet, and his instinct to try and wrench his legs back and forth to kick it off made the thorns break off in his body, forcing another bloodcurdling scream from him.

Monika stood on my side, twirling around and facing the hundred and eighty-degree arc not covered by Corfus, who was still systematically pointing and muttering at the creatures. There were probably only a dozen left from our collective barrage of gunfire, magic, and fire damage. It took about ten seconds apiece for Corfus to disable them, and strangely, something occurred to me then, and I'm not sure why it took that long. Why didn't Corfus have us all dislocate again, the same way he brought us here? Another thorny arm and twisted twig hand reached up from the pit Monika had created a few moments ago, and was much closer than any of the others. I stood as quickly as I could, a bit unsteady, and grabbed Monika's right arm, as she was facing away from this one, and I wanted her to not be in the way if it fell, as the one on Klement had. Then I fired the last two shots in that pistol's cylinder, both hitting it in the center. Holstering the empty pistol, I picked up the carbine, which I had dropped when I caught the splintering. It had a standard ball load, so I held my sightline on it and spun around to see if any others had broken free and closed the distance. None had.

I went to Klement, knelt, and looked him over. Each of the thorns was dripping blood from its broken ends, still drawing from their victim as they would have, if still on the tree. As many as there were, I decided to try and pull the largest, which were in the meatiest part of his thighs. I twisted and pulled on the first one, and Klement jerked, the agony written on his face. Cracks and ripping explosions continued to echo around me from Monika's savage attacks on these unfeeling perversions of nature as I worked. Focusing on the most prominent and most profusely leaking thorns, I removed two or three more. Then I saw a trunk and an arm that was really nothing more than a collection of sticks, but it was dragging closer. I snatched the double-barrel from Klement's grip and blew it apart. The angle of its approach was such that the blast pushed all the debris away from us, instead of into our midst. I laid it back across Klement's chest and went to work on the thorns.

I don't remember how many more explosions I heard while working on Klement, but not many. Then Monika fell to her knees alongside us, used her wand to deaden his legs, and began removing them as well, stopping the bleeding from each. After the last thorn, I looked at Corfus, who had also stopped, and then waved his hand over Klement, and even the blood from his clothes was gone, as were many of the smaller splinters I had skipped. I stood, still somewhat unsteady, having to learn balance and depth perception as I went along. Corfus looked at my eye now and held his hand sideways over it for a minute. I felt a warm bubbling sensation, similar to when the High Elf Kleet had healed my knife wound before.

"I am sorry, Raileanu, I am not sure I can repair that damage to your eye fully," Corfus said, reaching down to help Klement up.

"We can worry about that later. What were those things? Why did we stay and fight? Why didn't we just leave?" I needed to know.

"I will explain, I will have to, to all of you, but we are not finished. Dolphus is not here, but I know where he has gone. It may be worse than this was. Please reload your weapons and prepare to travel again. We have little time." Corfus scanned the entire edge of the clearing again. "I do not see it."

"What? What do you not see?" Monika asked.

"The Shadow. The one you saw in the trees before they came for us." Corfus's eyebrows came closer together, and his chin drew up, his mouth almost a frown. "He may know we can find him now."

A bright white flash with an orange center popped to our group's right, and when it faded, it was Barthow. With the fire all around, and Dolphus's home fully ablaze, it was easy to see him. He came over to us, stepping carefully around the dozens of thorny wooden corpses. He took off his hat and surveyed the scene.

"Well, this ain't no good. Y'all alright?"

"Yes, considering. We were about to pursue that villain. Would you please assist us?" Corfus asked. Barthow looked at him and shook his head, looking down.

"I gotta tell you first. This old feller..." he trailed off as he looked back at the house, squinting at the blaze, then looking back up at Corfus. "He was the one in the cave in Nevada territory. He took half uh Orb thing. Bigger than the other un, differn' colors in it too." He shook his head again. "The location he was 'a suppos'd to be at was, uh here."

"I see. We will have to go now. Barthow, do you have more wand core shot with you?" Corfus asked.

"Yeah, uh, six cylinders, but that's all," he began digging them out of his inner coat pockets. "Oh, and some buckshot as well. Got maybe fifty of em."

"Give them to Klement and Raileanu. You will be more effective with your wand. They will need them," so he handed them over to us, three each, and we tucked them away.

Corfus looked back to the cottage, and with a single downward glance, the remaining fiery timbers collapsed into a heap, spewing showers of sparks high into the night and surrounding canopies, crackling and popping. "Everyone ready?" Checking our faces, he took the hands closest to him, and we all did the same. Then silence and darkness again.

Chapter Thirteen

T his time, I was not alone in the dark place. I could
feel the others, then a resonant voice. Not the actual
sound of the High Elf, but as though my body could feel
the vibrations of the words as they were thought. Difficult
to describe, but I could tell the others could hear it, too.

"This is the Underneath, as we High Elves call it. It
exists at all times, in all places. It is the conduit that links
all minds, all thought, for all time. It allows us to search
for the artifacts. It is also the pathway I use to travel. It
requires singular concentration to bring matter into and
out of. Time as a linear function does not exist here, nor is
time here affected by objects or gravity. It is beyond light,
but it is not actually darkness either. Can you all hear me
well enough?"

"Yes," was the consensus answer from all four of us.

"Do we not have to hurry to the place where Dolphus
is?" I asked him. I could feel the vibrations in all my
connective tissue of each word as I thought it, and could

tell my mouth was not even moving. In fact, I couldn't feel any part of my body.

"No, not here. The bodies and our minds are separate right now, but when we finish here, we will arrive at our destination the same second we departed. That is too much for you to grasp; do not concern yourselves with the mechanics."

Again, we all agreed, and Corfus continued. "I saw a painting in Dolphus's home of a castle that I recognized. The features around the edges gave me a clue to its location. It showed a curved, dimly-lit ceiling and a domed rise the castle sat on, surrounded by mirror-smooth waters. The castle depicted showed no lines indicating where individual stones had been quarried to build it. The castle is identical in design and scale to one that sits atop a singular rocky hill with steep sides and is surrounded by a forest. The construction technique matches one known only to the High Elves and the Dwarves. Then I remembered that where the castle sits was once a wizardess who was about to be killed for witchcraft, but she vanished, and we could not see her. The castle in question was built several hundred years later on that spot. How it might relate to Runetta or Dolphus was calculated after I remembered the wizardess in question was a distant relative of the Glauer family. When I lowered my perception through the Underneath into the earth itself, I found a Dwarvish-built castle a thousand feet below in a spherical cavern. The knowledge of it must have come from that wizardess, and after discovering its location, she could dislocate to it at will. Mirroring its design above is something all people do after a traumatic event, honoring the memory of what saved them. Runetta has been using it for many years. She must have thought Dolphus was unaware of it."

"Corfus, if it is a thousand feet below ground, are there any other ways in?" I asked.

"No, the Dwarves abandoned it some ten thousand years ago." He answered.

"Well, forgive my concern, but if something happens to you, Klement and I will not be able to leave."

"Oh, you're right." Monika thought to us all.

"Then let us all keep that in mind. I do not think the challenge ahead is more perilous than what we just did." Corfus explained.

"Speaking of what just happened, what happened with those Bloodthorn trees? Were they animated by magic, or what?" Klement asked.

"No, that did concern me," Corfus said.

"The Shadow. That was not magic, was it?" Monika asked nervously.

"No. That was a Dybbuk. They are evil spirits that cling to a person, driving a hunger for things that override all natural restraint. They are from the spirit world, soldiers of the Fallen One, who exist only to corrupt God's creation and lead people away from Him. They are bound at the smallest level to the physical form of a person, to the body. Trying to remove them is extremely painful. Their connection to a person's flesh drives needs that seek to override moral judgment. Dolphus has perhaps been coexisting with one so long that their relationship is symbiotic now. He had the dark matter of the Dybbuk stay behind when he left, to activate the trees to attack us. Our suffering was the bait he used to lure the Dybbuk into temporarily separating from him. Dolphus had clearly already enchanted the trees, with an ancient symbol carved in the wood, awaiting only a command to force a golem to rip forth from the living wood of the trees." Corfus paused for a long time, as if recalling the cost of lessons learned from his vast experience. "We could not leave those bloodthirsty creatures. They would have descended on the nearest village in the deep of night without sound or mercy, and no mortals could stop them. No, we could not leave them."

Almost all of us simultaneously asked the same question at that point. "If that is what he left behind, what could be waiting for us at this castle?"

"I do not see any trees, if that helps." Corfus was never reassuring. "There are at least two werewolves there, outside the castle. But I wouldn't worry about them."

"Werewolves! Don't worry!?! Have you ever tussled with werewolves, Elf?!" Barthow demanded.

"Again, all of you. There are many things you do not know. What we are trying to stop is far worse than werewolves. I will not ask you to face them; in fact, there is no reason to harm them. I assure you." The Elf was always monotone and unemotional, and even the resonance of his thoughts was in this place as well.

"Well, shoot, that's just fine then. Those lightning-fast meat-eatin' ten-foot-tall varmints are all yours then."

Barthow was pleased with this arrangement, as were we all.

"You can't see anything else we should know about?" Monika and all of us wondered.

"No, this place, it seems, was a solitary refuge for Runetta to hide from the abuses of Dolphus over the years. The construction of the place means I cannot see inside it at all. I have seen an image of a large chamber in the dungeon of the castle, deep below."

"The rest is what, just empty?" I asked Corfus.

"I cannot see, and that is not uncommon for some places built by the Dwarves. Some of their early constructions and power sources required specialized techniques that prevented any observations. They were designed to keep energies in, but that design works both ways."

"I would ask all of you to withhold deliberately destroying things, however, until we have a chance to examine the castle thoroughly. We may learn of other things related to our duties in this place."

"You mean like back at Dolphus' house? Like when you burnt everythin' up?" Barthow barked. "I certainly didn't git to look at nun of it. I did what ya wanted out in that cave with them giants, what if sumethin in thar was gonna help me?"

"I know everything that was in there, Barthow. All of it, his whole life, was pointed at the object you found, which he has now, and where we are going. I would be more than capable of detailing all of it later if you would like. I will not withhold anything from you." Corfus never seemed to be upset when any of us were. He was always calm and direct, and it was actually irritating to all of us over the years.

"I expect you would." That was all Barthow could come up with to reply. He knew it was pointless, but also, I think looking back, once he realized it didn't bother the Elf, Barthow amused himself by doing it from time to time.

"Where are we going to arrive, and what should we be looking for?" Monika was a bit more contemplative regarding our trip, and her pointedness when engaged was always impressive to me.

"I will have us arrive on the platform outside the back of the castle, opposite where the werewolves are. All of you stay behind me, and I will take care of them. For no reason will any of you hurt them. You must trust me."

"Oh, we will. We are counting on you for that," we all thought.

"From there, we will proceed inside, and you are welcome to fight and protect yourselves as you see fit. We will try to find the way into the lower levels, where I suspect Dolphus is with the partial CIGI. When we first arrive, I will pause and see if I can detect any other things we must know about, then I will take us to the main narrow path that leads to the entrance, where the werewolves are."

With that, we could all sense that we understood and were in agreement. We could feel a draw, or suction, almost on our minds back towards unity with our mortal bodies. The next sensation we had was gently re-seating into our nervous systems.

The cavern was enormous, and if some blue-green luminous material had not lighted the perfectly domed ceiling, I would not have been able to see the other side. It looked to be a half mile across. The 'cavern' was not a great descriptor, as it was perfectly circular. It was manufactured, obviously. Not a single seam, block, or crack was visible from where we were. A body of black still water, forty feet across, separated us from the center mound, which was easily seven hundred feet high. It was shaped like an upright boot, with the castle at the very top. Corfus was right; in terms of design, it looked exactly like the Hohocherwitz Castle on the surface. The whole cave, the mound, and the castle were made of diorite. It is a very dark rock with large amounts of white quartz. The surfaces were as smooth as glass, and, while very dark in color, they reflected all the artificial light, and the glittering quartz was quite beautiful. This was obviously the back side of the structure; the only openings were narrow arrow slit style loopholes.

As Corfus had said, he raised his hands, indicating for us to all wait a moment. He closed his eyes and drew in a deep breath. I spotted one eyebrow raise ever so slightly, which was interesting, almost like a reaction of some kind. I recall nearly letting a laugh out. But I didn't. He held his breath for a while, then exhaled heavily through his nose. We all saw, and reacted by pointing and looking at each other, silver sparkling dust in his exhaled breath. It immediately split into four streams, circling the edges of the gigantic cavern and then into the castle.

"What the heck was that?" Barthow asked, pointing to it, but speaking quietly.

Corfus opened his eyes and looked at Barthow. "Those are some of the particles that keep my body working properly. I control them. They are going to see what they can find inside the structure I cannot see into. I will see what they see."

"That would be handy, I can't git none of them?"

"No, they are bound to me. There is no way to make more of them. Without them, I will die. It is part of the basis for what you all know as magic."

"Oh. Naw then, never mind, I kinna like you around, Elf." Barthow winked at him and gave him a click of his cheek.

"I will need a moment to process the ten thousand images I am getting. I will collect them as we pass through the castle, but we may be able to pinpoint where the sphere is." Corfus then closed his eyes and stayed silent for a moment. Every few seconds, he seemed to look up or down or to one side, like mapping the whole structure in his mind.

Corfus suddenly winced, bent at the waist, and an inexplicably bright flash beamed out of the castle, lighting the entire interior of the space. Corfus let out a sigh and stood again, opening his eyes and looking at us.

"Dolphus has united the sphere halves. I have not found where he is; it is in a secret part of the castle." He then looked at the cavern wall near us, a spot with no discernible features. His head straightened up, as he was still kneeling from wincing at the Orb becoming complete. He kept his eyes trained on the wall.

A fire-orange-colored ring was forming on the wall, about 4 feet in diameter. Once the edges of the fire met, the center of the ring filled in top to bottom with the same molten rock color, then it went black. The rock, hissing and still steaming, gave way to the sound of boots running towards the opening. We all turned with purpose towards it, drawing our weapons and wands.

"No, all of you, wait. They are coming to help." Corfus stated, throwing his large hand up to us.

"Who! Who is coming?" Barthow bellowed. "I don't think I can take any more surprises today!"

"The Pale Dwarves. They have detected the sphere being reactivated."

Monika took my arm with her free hand, but not to shield herself, to steady herself against whatever was about to come. To face it with me side by side. No greater love for a woman has existed that I am aware of. I certainly couldn't love her more right then. Time, as I have found, consistently adds volume to the heart, the more of it that passes.

Ten stout, thick-limbed Dwarves emerged from the hole and stopped in front of us. All of them were wide-faced, large-eyed, tough-skinned, and wearing some armor and clothing I had never seen before. It was very angular, with many facets and joints that seemed impossible to craft by means I understood. They held what looked like blued-steel and brass short rifles, but were dotted with small red lights, silver pipes running along their sides, and a tube on top like a jeweler's loupe. Their boots went nearly to their knees, and were made of a black, spongy material on the soles, the rest plated with the same type of armor as the rest of them. They wore helmets that surrounded their faces, with a bluish lens of some kind of glass covering their entire faces. Their skin was indeed so pale it had no color at all, like marble. Some had green eyes, some had yellow. They all had thick beards and woolly eyebrows, which extended out the bottom of their helmets and across most of their frontal armor. All of their noses were very wide and crinkly up the bridge. The leader's beard and wild eyebrows had once been red, but most now were grey. The others' beards were brown, pure white, and red. From what I had learned of the Dwarves in school, myth really, their beards were of great pride, fireproof, and were never cut. Their length symbolized their long life, victories, and successes.

One stepped forward of the others, marked by a prominent white axe symbol on the front of his helmet, above the faceguard. He reached up and touched the side of the helmet, and the glass disappeared. He pointed to the castle with his right hand and shouted in a language none of us had ever heard. Corfus raised his hand and waved it a bit, and the volume of the dwarf lowered – but only by a little. Corfus spoke in the same tongue back to him and seemed to calm the leader a bit. The others nodded to each other at whatever Corfus had told them. A few more back and forth, and then their leader gathered them together in a small circle, their backs to us.

Corfus turned to us. "They are here to help. If, in fact, we are correct, and the sphere's halves are connected, we will need their help. I explained that we are here to stop them and that there may be a Hoplite present as well."

"A what-lite?" Barthow asked quietly, far more quietly than he ever spoke around me anyway.

"You mean one of the soldiers you were worried about, right?" I said.

Monika and Klement looked at me.

"Ones Kleet had spoken about before he died, right?" I looked at them sternly. Kleet had died specifically to prevent everything before us, and I became very nervous. Fighting an old wizard and retrieving a broken Orb was one thing. This was something more.

"Yes. One of those soldiers is in there; they were called Hoplites." Corfus said. The leader Dwarf came over beside him and spoke to him, waving his finger at all of us. Corfus nodded to the dwarf. "This is Tinfer, he is their commander. He is going to armor all of you for the battle to come. Hold very still."

"Armor, what armor?" Klement asked.

"If that Hoplite is active, or any technologies controlled by that sphere, you will need it. That is a CISI, not like the Orb that you encountered at home, Raileanu." Corfus said. Tinfer listened to Corfus, with his hand on the side of the helmet, then looked to us and nodded. "I told Tinfer you are all my associates in the search for the spheres. He knows you will die without the armor they can provide, and he is right."

Looking earnestly at Tinfer, then to Klement, Monika, and Barthow, and nodding, I said, "Please, we would be honored to be armored by you."

Tinfer moved his hand from his ear and closed his face shield. I could see him speaking, and then a voice emitted from the front of his helmet, like someone speaking through a metal tube. "Hold still, people. This will take only a moment. Oh, you magical people, put your wands on the ground for a moment, and your weapons. You will need them on the outside of your armor."

We all did as instructed and laid the wands, rifles, pistols, belts, and my hat on the ground. Tinfer reached his right hand over his back and retrieved a small rod. He held it pointed at me first, and a line of white light came out in a flat triangle, the tip of it from his rod and the widest part at my shoulders. It moved up and down over me several times, and he moved around behind me. Monika released my arm and stepped to one side, letting Tinfer do his work. When he returned to the front, he rotated the base of the small rod, and the light switched from white to black, and I could actually feel pressure as particles smaller than dust struck and adhered to themselves. In less than half a minute, the plates and cloth of their style armor began locking together and covering me. When it reached my head, I could feel it very close to everything, but it barely moved a single hair. When the rigid plates were all locked in place on the helmet, the face shield appeared. Inside the helmet, I could hear and understand Tinfer as he spoke.

"Does that feel comfortable?" he said.

I moved my arms up and looked down at the armor. It was identical to the Dwarves, only for my size. "How do I..." I was about to ask how to raise the face shield when it did on its own.

"Like that, son. Think it, and it will do what you need." Tinfer explained.

"Thank you so much, sir."

"Think 'full shield', and the shield will become reflective from the outside. You will need this, as the CISI and the Hoplite will try to identify you by your face, and you will not escape its wrath."

"What did he say?" Monika asked.

"Yeah, we can't understand them at all." Barthow joined in.

"The armor does what we think. And it will protect our identity, if we but ask."

"Oh, that's how the glass turned into a mirror?" Monika asked.

"Yes. Who's next?" Tinfer asked.

"Oh, and I can understand the Dwarves when they speak. The helmet translates for us. Monika, are you ready?" I asked.

"Oh yes, I want armor like that, definitely," she said, smiling and adjusting her stance towards Tinfer.

I motioned to him towards Monika, and he began using his light rod tool on her. "It tickles a little!" she said. I bent down, picked up the pistol belt, strapped it on, then picked up the carbine and my hat, looking at it disappointingly.

"Here, Raileanu." Corfus held out his hand, palm up, and the hat leaped to his hand, then vanished in a ball of light. "It is at Klement's home, in your room."

"That is thoughtful. I really didn't want to lose it." I nodded thanks to him. Monika's armor was beginning to assemble itself, and, turning towards her to watch, I noticed that the soles of the boots were like cushions, very soft and silent. As the plates and fabric beneath climbed above her waist, she raised her arms a bit and watched it, with a little giggle at how amazing it was. She was right, magic, regardless of the type or source, is awe-inspiring. As it climbed to the helmet sections, I was suddenly awash with emotion for the form God had graced her with; even here in Dwarven armor, she was beautiful. She could tell what I was thinking, and the smile grew wider, and she batted her eyes at me and blushed a little. She liked the armor, who wouldn't?

"Oh yeah, buddy boy, me next, me next, alright?" Barthow set his hat down and took off the duster coat he was still wearing, with the burn damage from his first encounter on our journey against these villains. "Don't you worry none about that dern coat, Elf, I'll be gitttin me a new'un when we finish here." He turned to face Tinfer, closed his eyes, lifted his chin, and held his arms out to the sides. I noticed his belly sticking out front, and that struck me as funny just then. I considered how these few moments behind this castle, marked by warmth between friends and my fiancée, stood in stark contrast to the dire events to come. None of us had dared question the arrival of the Dwarves, as we were all frightened about the prospect of fighting whatever she had hidden in that fortress. Surely it was worse than the diabolical bloodthorn trees, especially if this was her secret refuge and repository. I was glad for the few minutes there. As Tinfer worked on Barthow, I thought of something maybe worth asking.

"Tinfer, sir, your people built the castle before us. Can you see inside and tell where they may have the sphere?" I shot my eyes over to Corfus, and he was pushing his bottom lip up and giving a confirming nod.

"Yes, my boy. We can. Torsten, Cristos, scan that and compare it to our original designs. See what's different, and spot that power surge that brought us here!" he said into his helmet as he continued to finish up Barthow's armor. Two of the other Dwarves walked to the edge of the rim and began moving their sightlines back and forth across the castle and the mound. "There we are, you big man. All done." Tinfer walked to Klement and began his work again. Barthow was looking over all his armor, flexing his hands, squatting, and jumping, which went well.

"Whoa!" Barthow jumped probably five feet straight up into the air and landed with hardly any sound. "That's incredible!" he shouted into the helmet, which the Dwarves, Monika, and I could hear, but no one else.

"Yes, the armor is self-powered; you can jump, climb, grab, and punch, all of it with ease. It will tell you where you are looking and apply the correct energy to get you there. It is limited to about twenty feet." Tinfer said as the armor began creating Klement's helmet, and he heard the instructions as well.

"Now all of you, if that is a..." Tinfer stopped and cocked his head as if listening to the other two scanning the castle. "Yes, it is a Hoplite. It is not activated yet, but the sphere is. They found it in the very bottom chamber of the dungeon. That's not all, it's behind an enchanted door she's installed; we know where it is, but Corfus, you might have to get us through that. Also, eleven oubliettes are surrounding that chamber. They were for fuel storage when we built it, but she has put some truly diabolical creatures in them. Whatever you do, don't open those doors. That Hoplite is built of materials that are a thousand times denser and thicker than your armor. Do not let it get a hold of you; it will crush you easily. For all other attacks, the suit of armor I have given you should protect you well. Corfus, you can handle the Orb if you get within a few feet, right?"

"Yes, Tinfer. I will take care of it. I need only see it to remove it from the earth forever."

Chapter Fourteen

Prague

Jon Roqueford waited at the bottom of the three steps to his contact's modest, unremarkable house, going through the three keys that locked the front door. It was diagonally across the street from the barber shop that the contact had used to monitor Runetta's home. Once the door was unlocked and forced open with a shoulder impact, they both entered and closed it, locking only one of the three behind them.

"What has happened since you last wrote?" Jon said, throwing his bag on the floor next to the sofa, then turning to face his contact, Irvin.

"She arrived last night. Again, none of us ever saw her enter; she was just inside, walking around at about ten o'clock. We wouldn't have even seen that had we not gone out to speak with the men at the train station. We saw it when we returned." Irvin then went to a room down the hall, brought back a blanket and pillow, and returned to the front room.

"Where is the other man assigned here? I have not met him yet." Jon asked as he walked to the small kitchen in the back of the first floor of the three-story house.

"Hartge! Get down here and report to the boss!" Irvin yelled with his head angled up the stairs. A squeaky hinge set sound rattled down the stairway, echoing off the hardwood paneled walls. With no decorations or portraits, no rugs or carpeting throughout, the house facilitated the sounds of Hartge coming downstairs, quicker than Irvin had ever heard him move in their time working here.

A man smaller in stature than Jon expected came down the stairs, using the bannister as an anchor to keep his speed up, cornering into the front room to meet his employer. He was dressed in well-maintained dark grey tweed with a subliminal green thread. He wore a small flat cap and had clean, but well-worn, brown leather shoes. Jon felt it was a good appearance for his duties, as he might have difficulty tracking him in a crowd of the public he had just witnessed on the trip from the train station to here. He had thick black hair in need of a cut, and a thick moustache that covered his upper lip completely, and did not extend past the edges of his mouth. Stubble betrayed his surveillance duties and had not been maintained in the last few days, and although it fell below expected grooming standards, Jon decided it was worth it.

"Sir, Hartge, reporting as ordered!" He quite unnecessarily snapped to attention behind Jon, who was getting a pot of water ready and preparing the match for the coal in the stove. Irvin had a chill of tension run through him, not knowing if Jon might take this as a ridiculous mockery of the importance of the duty, or if Jon could tell Hartge was sincere.

"None of that, son, not here." Jon never stopped what he was doing; he had taken a single glance at him before he knelt to light the stove. Irvin was still in the front room and was looking around the corner to see how it would go, because he really wasn't sure. Hearing Jon's calm and understanding statement, he went back to preparing the room for his boss's stay. Hartge relaxed and just waited until Jon had finished.

Dusting his hands off from the coal dust, Jon stood and turned to Hartge. "So, anything of interest, or is she just in her house acting normally?" When he finished speaking, he put his hands on his waist and lowered his gaze at him.

"Sir, she..." Jon held up his hand.

"Son, just call me Jon in the field. You have to recognize that we are all just friends here, because if we are actively observing someone, it is possible that, at any time, you too are under observation. Please, continue." He lowered his hand when he finished and returned it to his waist.

"She doesn't seem to be doing anything. It is quite peculiar; we haven't seen her enter or leave the house. We have not seen anyone delivering foodstuffs to the home either." He stopped and looked at Irvin, who had walked into the little kitchen with them. "We can't even figure out if anyone in town has spoken to her before, worked there, or how she even enters the city." Irvin was nodding and pursing his mouth, showing confusion at all of it.

"Well, boys, come morning, we will be speaking with her. In fact, I want both of you to be ready even to arrest her if I signal for it." Jon then turned to the boiling water and set to making a pot of tea.

"What signal is that, si-, uh, Jon?" Hartge asked.

"I will say, where might I find you if I need to ask anything further, ma'am?" He turned to face them, cup to mouth, checking the heat, steam swirling around his face. "Understand?"

"Yes, sir."

"Yes, sir."

"Now, let's get some rest. Which of you is set to be up tonight to be on watch?" Jon finally took a sip, and by the face he made, it was still too hot.

"Hartge is on watch tonight, Jon," Irvin said.

"Alright, son, you come get me if there is anything unusual, or if you see her on the street. I would rather approach her on the street, where she wouldn't be able to stay locked in her house, and we cannot enter by force," Jon said.

"I understand. I will head back upstairs if that is alright?" Hartge asked.

"Yes, I will write up my reports first, then I will turn in. Where is the office?" Jon said, fighting through another hot sip.

"Second floor, end of the hall," Irvin said.

All three set to their areas then, Jon to the second floor, Irvin to the other end of the second floor where his room was, and Hartge, after making himself a cup of tea, to the third floor.

There were a dozen panes of glass in the shops across the street that reflected the front of Runetta's home. This house had a wide-knit type of drapery so that the spyglass the team used could sit invisibly, but they could easily observe any goings-on in her home. Hartge set his cup down on the little table by the window, bent over to check the view, and, seeing nothing, set about his actual work.

Hartge had been using an illusion of himself sleeping the last few days to report to his actual job with the Magical Inquisitor's office with General Kofingsburn. He was prepared to allow Runetta to be taken into custody by the ordinary authorities, as ordered. Best he could determine, the top-level magical personnel would acquire her if needed after her acquisition. For now, he was following orders. Stay on her, stay in cover, and be ready to intervene without displaying magic. He had done it before and felt confident in this responsibility. He always carried two wands. One was very small, and held in place on his left wrist by a leather grieve with three small brass buckles. It was completely obscured, even when his coat was off and sleeves rolled up. His favorite and most powerful wand, a twisted white oak with an electrum handle, was in the right sleeve of his coat. It would stay in the sleeve and be unseen even when the coat was removed, unless the sleeve were turned inside out, and you looked for it.

He could use either in the blink of an eye, and as many years as he had spent in the ordinary world, most of the criminal wizards he had taken part in arresting had taken him for a helpless, terrified peasant, to their dismay.

Most of the Inquisitors' offices around the world practiced very secretive spellcasting in private enclaves. Through repetition and little-known mind broadcasting charms, many had individualized spells that none knew the counter for, which these experts could cast with only a thought. The range of spells depended greatly on the skill of the wizard or sorceress. Some were gifted at casting containment spells, some at confinement. A few could cast a memory charm in a way that anyone observing an event would not know about events for up to a minute, while simultaneously forcing dislocation on the target. The target, too, would have no memory of how they got to the secure cell they found themselves in. This was extremely effective, as the targeting agent was never known to the offender. Sadly, after much effort and time, only a few dozen in the world at any one time were capable of these types of discharges.

Hartge wished now, with the attention of both worlds on this lady, that he was one of them, but he was not. What he could do was cast a confusing blanket of darkness into a subject's mind, while remaining invisible, and, once in contact with a disoriented target, dislocate to a waiting holding cell. Worst case, this is what he would do. Hoping for a smoother event tomorrow, he waited until Jon had gone to sleep and retrieved his bag. When the information about Runetta first began, he had cast some protection charms on Irvin's clothing, hoping to protect him, but also woven an invisible layer of enchanted silver thread into his wrist irons, his pistol's barrel, and his hat. If the wrist irons were closed on a magical person, it would prevent spellcasting. The clothing would be resistant to most common criminal attack spells, such as fire, lightning, and the like. Lacing the pistol's barrel with it would, well, should allow the rounds fired through it to be unaffected by magic. That was his hope, anyway. He took his time, and after over fifteen minutes, was able to apply all the same enchantments to Jon Roqueford's clothing and equipment. When they approached Runetta, she would be in custody tomorrow, one way or the other.

Hartge, after verifying that both coworkers were still asleep, opened the window at the back of the third-floor room, which, with an angled roof, was just one big room used for storage before they rented it, and let his owl in. He penned a quick note to his boss and attached it for travel in early fall weather. As he went to the window again to release the owl, he heard a strange, low coo, almost a growl, emanating from deep in his friend. The owl was looking up into the clouds. Hartge could hear a leathery flapping now, from the direction the owl was watching. It was a bat, by the sound, but quite a bit larger-sounding than anything he had heard before. He stuck his head out and sent the owl off. Looking to his left, he could see an open window on the house Runetta was in, with candlelight reflecting off its panes. A giant bat, with a wingspan of probably three feet or more, lit on the ledge under the window and closed its wings. It stood two feet tall. Then it walked in, clearly intentionally, and seemed familiar with the place and the process. Then the window closed.

Hartge had heard of bats being used as couriers by some magical people before, but that was regular bats; this was an indigenous Indonesian species, known locally as the 'flying fox', and had no business in this part of the world. Just thinking of the diet that it would take to maintain such a creature made him shiver. Whole-house cats were at risk from a bat of this size. For a minute, Hartge considered going in through the same window and ending this now. Suppose things went wrong, though, the exposure to the ordinary world of his disappearance, or worse, the murder of a foreign spy. He was aware of the danger this woman posed, and she had recently performed acts of magic almost in plain view deliberately.

He shut the window as quietly as he could, and returned to his tea and his observation post. Runetta was reported to have had connections to recent violent deaths, maybe even directly, of up to eight people. Some mercenary types are also rumored to be in her employ, and there could be some in that house. It might be prudent to wait until he has help.

While thinking this through, he went to the kitchen and was pouring the last of the warm tea into his cup. When he set the kettle on the pad on the counter, it caught the end of the teaspoon, knocking it to the aforementioned bare wood floor. With people sleeping in the house, his polite duties were to keep as quiet as possible. When the kettle hit the floor, the loud sound it made sent an icy shockwave of adrenaline through his whole body. Hartge just froze. The same spike of electric energy he first felt as a child playing hide-and-seek, when he was found and ran like a scared rabbit. The feeling wasn't from fear of waking his companions, but perhaps Runetta could hear it. After a whole long minute with his eyes wide and ears stretched out listening to the still night air for any sound, he finally exhaled. As loud as that had been, not even his housemates were affected by it.

Maybe he could wake Jon and Irvin now, and tell them that he spotted an open window out back that he could enter while they knocked on the door at the front. That might work. He could easily assume any magical means necessary while out of their sight, and in the middle of the night, fewer defenseless citizens would be at risk of witnessing the event, or worse, hurt by an outraged criminal sorceress. He could spend a few minutes before he woke them, casting a spell of concealment over Runetta's home, impenetrable for any sound or light to leave past its barrier. He could do that from here. He figured that if he placed the boundaries about three feet away from the structure on all sides, no protections or alerting sentry spells or charmed devices of any kind would be triggered that would alert her to their presence. Spending a few minutes out a front third-floor window, and the same rear window he was at earlier, he also decided to pen a letter for the General Inquisitor, which would be picked up by his owl and delivered if something went wrong. When he was finished, he went to attach it to the outside of the rear window, which he did with a furniture tack and the handle of his small revolver. Rain began no sooner than the window was closed again. There was a steady tapping, muffled by the roof and then the ceiling of the room, but the clouds meant there would be no moon; even darker outside, better for them to move quickly. Holding umbrellas, Jon and Irvin would be unrecognizable to anyone who might see them on the streets. Besides, with the rainstorm beginning, it would be much easier for Jon to request entrance to her home politely.

When he was ready with all the preparations, Hartge took the candle tray and went to both men, waking them, and explaining that she was home, awake, and moving around. With everyone in the neighborhood asleep, it might be a good idea for them to at least ask her questions. They agreed and were ready within 5 minutes.

Jon verified that he had his notebook and pencil, checked his pistol, and put on his overcoat. Turning toward Irvin and Hartge, holding his hat, he stood and waited until they were paying attention to him. "Gentlemen, as suggested, Irvin and I will knock on the front door and do everything we can to enter the home. I will ask her the questions I need to. Both of you stay alert, and I need you to try to look at and remember every detail inside that house. Be professional; whether she has engaged in criminal activity is for me to determine. This Runetta Lynchos is part of a very old, very wealthy family, and we must provide her with every courtesy." Jon looked sternly at both of them, impressing the attitude he wanted them to display. "Understand?"

"Yes, sir," Hartge risked the 'sir' because of how seriously Jon was looking at them. Irvin just nodded and fidgeted some, more nervous than Hartge had seen him before. Jon walked to him and put his hand on Irvin's shoulder, with his face calmer and more relaxed.

"Don't worry, son, you just do a good survey of the home, try and notice anything strange. I will do all the talking," Jon patted his shoulder a couple of times, then he looked at Hartge. "You go ahead out back, and we will wait half a minute before we go out front, alright?"

Hartge gave him a nod and walked out of the front room, through the kitchen, and to the back door. He set the candle on the counter and opened the door, closing it as quietly as he could.

Jon and Irvin took their umbrellas and opened the front door to the house. Looking both ways, Jon was relieved that the rain had started; at this hour, no one would be on the streets, but any who might have been would stop and find a dry place in the dark. Intense, cold gusts began blowing the rain into sheets, their imprint on the brick roadway moving along like little rows of soldiers on parade.

Once he was sure the front door had been closed, Hartge went out the back and immediately shielded himself with a concealment spell. Anything other than direct observation, even by magical peoples, would appear as no more than a slight distortion. The same distortion one might expect in the dark or rain when vision is not at its zenith. He then let his wand lift him to the third-floor window. Hovering for just a moment, his eyes barely over the lip of the ledge so he could get a good look at the room.

It was a bedroom, with a huge four-post bed, fluted oak pillars, and an arched roof inlaid with mirrored panels. The whole room was very dark in its decoration. Dark red sheets of silk, thrown up to the head of the bed, and on the many pillows spread around the bed. Tall silver candlesticks in the form of long rose stems held red candles whose wax had dripped into long stalactites. Dark wood paneling lined the walls, with but two portraits. One was a beautiful, dark-haired lady who Hartge guessed was Runetta. The other was a man he did not recognize, but who was young and handsome. He saw that the door on the far side of the room was open, and then he could hear the knocking at the front door from Jon and Irvin. Footsteps were leading away, downstairs. Glancing around the room again, he was not sure where the giant bat was that he had seen going in earlier. Rising an inch at a time, he scanned all around again. He saw clothes scattered all over the room, an open bottle of champagne, and TWO glasses on the table. He whipped his eyes back to the bed just in time to see movement squirming around under the sheets and pillows. Someone else was here. It was the bat, but no bat at all. Hartge could take no chances; very few people choose the form of a flying fox. It is one of the few forms that require the diet of the creature to be maintained to conjure the change. That means several pounds of insects and whole small birds every day, and few can tolerate it.

He rose enough to get his wand in the window, pointed at the form in the bed, and pushed a shell of silence around it. Hoping this person was asleep, the silence would pass unnoticed, and ensure this person could not call for help. Then he rose, slid through the window without touching a thing, and rotated himself to land on the thick oriental rug that covered the whole floor of the room. Then, aiming carefully, Hartge bound the form in the bed with impenetrable iron bars, resembling a medieval iron maiden. It prevents any movement, even of a finger. Held securely in the bed, the bars piercing the exquisite red silk sheets in the casting of the spell, he could still not tell who it was there, but he needed to move on, and hopefully surprise Runetta from behind, and bind her. Surely without suspecting any magical interference, he could overpower her enough to get the enchanted irons on her wrist. Just to be sure, as soon as he could see even her head, he could hit her with an inebriating spell, flooding the brain with alcohol-laden blood. That was his plan.

Walking delicately as he could, Hartge went to the far side of the room and then out the open door onto the landing at the top of the stairs. Inching forward until he could see the front door, where she was indeed talking to his associates just inside. Hartge aimed very carefully, as he didn't need his own people suddenly drunk. Then he let the spell fly. Her head immediately began to wobble, and her knees became unsure of their duties, locking and then popping forward, making her long dark hair swing side to side across the back of the red silken sheet she had wrapped herself in to answer the door. Her arms that had been crossed in front of her fell to her sides, and then Hartge felt safe enough to proceed into full sight of his colleagues. Quickly stepping down the two flights of stairs, he pulled the enchanted wrist irons out at the last two steps and opened them. Then he went to the room behind the entrance, released himself from the spell concealing him from view. Now visible, he walked slightly crouched with the wrist irons out in front of him.

Hartge heard Jon asking her about her movements of late. He noticed Jon's glance, so subtle, seeing him without alerting her to his location. Runetta was now slurring her speech, and despite her impeccable accent and attempt to limit her sudden impairment, she began to sound silly. It was comical to listen to her trying, mid-word, to repair the sounds already uttered. Hopefully, Jon and Irvin either thought she was drunk already or, if they had heard her speak well to begin with, thought she was perhaps trying to feign drunkenness. Hartge used his left hand to clamp her left wrist, and his right hand to her right wrist, bringing the two together and closing the right one. She was secure. Runetta, perhaps four or five inches taller than Hartge, let her head roll around to see who had her wrists.

"Well, hannsomme. Whass your name?" she smiled, now amused at herself for being uninhibited and slurring her words. Hartge thought to himself that he might have to make a note of how long this effect lasts, because it had worked out quite well.

"Jailer, ma'am," was all Hartge said.

"Good work, everyone. Let us take her to our house. Irvin, please check the schedules and see when the next train to Vienna is, and take this." Jon handed him a large billfold. "There is enough in there to buy an entire carriage for us to transport her to Vienna. I want you to go straight to the station and wake up the ticketmaster, and show him the letter of authority I was given to operate here." Jon took firm hold of the chain between her wrist irons and turned her back to him. "Hartge, get that rain cloak over there on the coat rack. Put it over her head, and then I want you to look through the rest of the house." Hartge did as asked and adjusted it so she would be dry and unidentifiable to any prying eyes. Hartge tied the waist belt of the overcoat to hold her sheet - and the coat - tightly closed.

"Hartge, do not touch anything. This woman is a suspect that we must interrogate. But given her family status, I don't want anything in her home interfered with. Just look," Jon gave Hartge a stern look, wide-eyed, waiting for a response.

"Yes, sir. I understand."

"No more than fifteen minutes. Get right back to the house, understand?"

"Yes, sir. Fifteen minutes." Hartge looked at Runetta, who was smiling, her eyes even seeming to wander a bit at times. Maybe it was a bit strong, but it was working well, he thought.

"Hannnsomme, I could give you a tour, alrighty -" she even tried to walk towards Hartge, but got her legs tangled together and almost fell over. Her legs broke through the layers of sheet and coat, then, in a very unflattering way, and it was evident to all three of the men that she was nude under the sheet. After straightening up and laughing out loud again at herself, Jon opened the front door, turned her, and went out into the rain. Irvin tucked the billfold into his overcoat, gave Hartge a little smile and nod, then went out also and closed the door behind him.

"Fifteen minutes. Alright." Hartge set to his quick work, planning on ending in the third-floor bedroom where his other prisoner was still confined. He would dislocate with that person straight to the cells at the Inquisitor General's office, then return as instructed.

First, he checked the ground floor, looking for any passages or entrances to any basement levels, but every-thing was strangely ordinary. He couldn't even see any signs of magic work in the kitchen, which seemed odd, since he knew she had been here for days sometimes without leaving. Regardless, he proceeded to the second floor.

Here, there were several charms and systems of con-cealment, but he was able to penetrate those with ease. They were books, journals, some maps, things of that nature. He found a large satchel of stout leather, almost in the style of a saddlebag, and began loading anything of interest into it. Several small address books, a few very small books of poems, and a bottle of absinthe, in which he could detect some magical ingredients by the color dispersion through the bottle when he used his wand to produce differing variations of the light spectrum on the backside of the bottle. He could sort that out later. These were all in a long, high library that took up half the home's second floor. There was a painting of a castle that he didn't recognize, but something seemed wrong about it. He had to hurry.

Hundreds of correspondence and business records for the family lay about unsorted. Stacks of books lay open on top of each other, and a glance at the pages that they were opened to all had spells, reports, or writings concerning crystal balls, and some suits of enchanted armor, or something. He came across some hand-drawn designs for ring-wands. That was new; he hadn't seen any of those before. He straightened himself, looked upwards, eyes going side to side for a moment, thinking. Runetta had a spot on her right index finger that was paler than the skin around it, a mark from wearing a ring, but she wasn't wearing it...

He went straight upstairs to the third floor, and, gripping the doorframe to the bedroom to look in, he saw that the other prisoner was still held. Running out of time, he went to the only other door on that floor, and it was a cleaning closet. He went right back to the bedroom and looked on Runetta's vanity chest, all around the top, looking for the ring he saw in the drawing. There were dozens of beautiful rings, incredibly expensive, he was sure, but ah- there it is. The only one made of wood. He put it in his pants pocket and looked around the room again. The portrait he saw earlier was definitely Runetta, now that he had seen her up close. She was beautiful, no doubt. Now he studied one of the young men. He saw some initials in the corner of the painting and made a note of them. There was no other identifying information on the painting or the frame. The clothing scattered about did not indicate anything he could use, either, except that he now noted it was all women's clothing. Whoever that other person was, the foxbat, either transforms nude, which is impractical for a person with magical ability, or was, in fact, a woman.

None of that matters; he had to get to headquarters with this prisoner and the information he had collected, drop it off, and return in time. The General could decide how to proceed. Slinging the satchel over his shoulder and head, Hartge went and grabbed a bar of the cage on the bed, and dislocated to headquarters.

There was a room at headquarters, especially made to be devoid of any identifying features. A single oil lamp lit it on a single table. The floors, walls, and ceiling were perfectly smooth white marble with no doors or windows. It was used when nonmagical people had to be brought there for one reason or another, or criminals had to be questioned with no hope of knowing their location. There was but one crack on the back side of the leg of the wooden chair at the table that was left unprotected by enchantment, and that is how they entered. Once inside, the subject was still in suspended animation, so Hartge dislocated into the general's office to explain the situation.

"Good work, Hartge. I see you found the woman!" the old general said through his huge mustache, his wiry salt and pepper - mostly salty - hair unkempt, like his eyebrows.

"No, sir, that is an accomplice or acquaintance of Runetta. Runetta is in the custody of the ordinary investigator. How would you like me to proceed? I am supposed to return to them in just a few minutes."

He sat, his gaze downcast at the immense stacks of paperwork, stroking his long, pointed beard. Then he glanced up at a large map on the wall. This map showed both the active agents in Europe and tiny blinking red sparks where crimes of magic were being committed. He leaned back in his chair, over to the right, grabbed his glasses off the desk with his left hand, and then stood to get a better look at the map.

"Yes, that will do. Return immediately, freeze your compatriots at the safe house, and return with Runetta here. I will dispatch a Clearing Team to release them and remove any memory of the event." Nodding, he turned to Hartge with a look of approval of his plan.

"Sir, don't forget Mr. Metternich is the one who sent the investigator," Hartge said, hoping the Clearing Team wouldn't remove too much of their memory.

"They will not remember that they captured her. They will stay in surveillance, assuming they haven't seen her yet," the General said reassuringly.

"Ah, good plan, sir." The General gave him a nod and waved him out the door. "Here is a satchel of the things I saw in her house. I will do a full report when I return." Hartge set the satchel in a chair against the wall near the door. He did as he was instructed and returned to the safe house in the blink of an eye, right on the doorstep.

He gave a quick knock, as it was still pouring rain. The deadbolts and crossbar were undone, and Irvin stood behind the door as he opened it, letting Hartge dash in out of the rain. He looked around, and Runetta was sitting on the sofa, slumped over, appearing passed out. Irvin shut and relocked the door, then, rubbing his hands together, shuffled past Hartge to the kitchen at the back. Jon was stoking the small fire in the stove, probably preparing some hot tea. The fall night and the rain did make it quite cold, and when both of them were in the kitchen with their backs to him, standing near the warmth of the stove, Hartge pulled his wand and locked them in place. The few sticks in the fire would keep them warm for an hour or so, until the Clearing Team came. He walked to Runetta, snoring unladylike now, and took hold of her by the wrist, dislocated with her to another secret cell back at headquarters. This cell had a small cot with a mattress and blanket. He laid her down and covered her up, then exited the room through a crack in the chair leg.

Chapter Fifteen

Runetta's Castle

P repared, informed, and now arrayed for battle, Corfus walked to the edge, near the still water, looking
down into it. Standing in a semicircle facing him, we waited for him to tell us what we must do. He turned back, still
looking down, and let out a sigh. His distinctively Elvish
clothing became, faster than an instant, heavy plate armor, the same as one might expect to see on display in
any European castle. It was a medium gray color, with a
pattern that appeared to be woven fabric. He extended
his right hand, and a helmet appeared in it. It was not
medieval in design; instead, it was ovoid, shaped to fit a
human head, with a wide glass panel at the front.

"Tinfer, you and your men shall accompany me to the
dungeon where we know the Orb and the Hoplite are.
There are some questions I must ask that man there,
so do not destroy him on sight, please." The Dwarven
company all nodded in understanding and agreement.

Now able to hear and understand the Dwarves, we all paid close attention, as this was originally their castle, and they knew it well.

"Corfus, we will focus on destroying that Hoplite. You do whatever you want with that Orb and the man. I might ask that one of my men go with these humans, as there is no telling what they will find in the rest of that place." Tinfer waved his left hand at us while speaking dismissively. None of us questioned that we four were surely out of our element, and we thought it was a good idea to have help.

"Agreed, my wise friend," Corfus put his helmet on. "I will transport all of us to the assigned places. Your equipment will store a record of everything you see, so do not linger. If there is no prisoner or danger to yourselves, view the rooms and move on." We could hear his voice clearly in our helmets. A diagram of the castle before us appeared on the glass, drawn in thin red lines. I turned my head a little side to side, and it stayed right on the castle. In a moment, I realized the other lines inside the outline were a three-dimensional representation of the rooms that must be inside. "I will go first and deal with the werewolves. Then you all will be taken where you must go. Remember, Barthow, Klement, Raileanu, and Monika, do not harm the men you find at the entrance. They will be the healed werewolves, asleep. We will need to speak with them when we are finished." We four responded with "Yes, sir," quietly.

Corfus turned to face the castle and was gone. Whatever means the High Elves use for travel is as amazing to me each time I see it as an ordinary person would be to see dislocation. Not twenty seconds later, and all the Pale Dwarves except Torsten were gone as well. He turned his head slightly towards us, but not directly, "Don't worry, *humans*, everything is going to be all right." Even through the translation, the derision in his voice came through. We all detected it and glanced at each other briefly.

Then we, too, were taken to the bridge leading to the castle's entrance gate. I looked behind us, down the bridge to the road that circled the castle, leading down and away. A high wall with turrets every hundred feet or so, wide enough to walk comfortably amongst the crenellations, wound along the outer side of the road. Torsten began running inside almost before we were fully materialized, shouting in our helmets, "Follow me!" I took Monika by the hand, and when Klement began running, we followed behind him. The bridge was only ten feet wide and almost three hundred feet long. We had been set at about the midpoint to begin, and Torsten went all the way to the gate before he slowed, running faster than any of us could, despite his legs being only two feet long! Reaching the gate, Torsten threw his left hand up in the air, and the whole massive rusted gate slid up its grooves into the turret above the entrance. He glanced slightly to the right as he entered through the now open portcullis, and looking there, I saw two nude men, motionless. Those must be the ones Corfus told us to look for. It would have been impressive to see a real werewolf, but I was actually glad they were not something I had to face in a violent format. We passed them, and Torsten was waiting for us, moving his head around, looking up and down, and it was obvious that things in our immediate space were not what he was looking at. I, too, looked up and down, and to the right, at a wall, and, in fact, the red outlines showed the castle's interior structural features that matched perfectly.

This was the gatehouse, the passageway into the interior of the castle. One portcullis was in place at the very entrance, but it was lowered only a foot. Just a glance showed it was of a metal I did not know, and it was one solid piece - there were no rivets, bolts, or bars making it up; even the points were cylindrical, not pyramidal like others I had seen. Beyond that, on each side, there was a curved hemispherical wall with what we would call arrow loops, three on each side. Again, and now up close, it was incredible how this structure was so solid and so smooth, a single piece of stone. Above us in the ceiling, I could see another slot, the width of the passageway, through which another portcullis would typically be. This one was fully retracted to the tower room above us, with only the pointed tips visible. We moved slowly and could sense that Torsten was being cautious.

"What can you see, sir?" I whispered.

He turned and looked at me, "I can see everything, can you not?"

"I don't know what you mean by everything," I said.

He approached me and motioned for me to lean my head down towards him, reaching up with both hands. His rifle stayed touching the front plate of his armor, like a magnet holds a nail. I complied, and he turned or tapped something on the right side, and then I saw blue lines appear on the glass, outlining the items stored in the adjacent room. "I can see everything now. Thank you."

"You do not have to speak quietly. No sound leaves these helmets." Torsten replied. He gripped his rifle again, singularly and violently, aiming it right beside my hip, pointing behind us. Before I could turn and look, he had fired - whatever it was they used - a white-hot stream to the wall at the left side of the entrance we had already passed. "Gravotor! They know we are here!"

"What! What was it?" Klement and Monika asked at the same time.

"There was a seam on that wall that would have looked like a crack to you. There are no cracks in Dwarven constructions. It was concealed by its angle on the rounded tower edges and was full of spider eyes. They could have only been placed there as a warning tool."

I heard in my helmet then that Torsten was calling to Tinfer and Corfus, telling them they might know we are here. Corfus and Tinfer said at the same time, "Keep us on a separate channel," whatever that meant. Tinfer then continued alone in my ear, "You concentrate on cataloguing the contents of the castle." I didn't hear from either of them again until the events in the castle had concluded. "Let us proceed into the interior, keep your eyes open, there's no telling what the Glauers have for us here to deal with."

"Will do, sir," I said, with similar confirmations by my colleagues following. We all five went past the second, raised portcullis into a large open room with staircases beginning on both sides of us, escalating to a landing on the second floor directly ahead of us. The stairs and the railing staves were simply cylindrical, with no other defining features, and the handrail was again a solid, contiguous, smooth stone. It was so beautiful in its construction, but it also seemed utilitarian, designed more for function than aesthetics. The atrium was three stories high, and the ceiling was a single domed crystal that let light from the cavern's ceiling in. I could see that the second floor had an identical staircase leading to the third floor.

"I can make some fancy stonework, son, but this is sumethin special," Barthow remarked. I looked back at him, as he and Klement were behind Monika and me, and we were behind Torsten. Both were looking all around.

"Indeed. Your craft is magnificent," Klement agreed, still panning his view to everything, surely marveling at the technical abilities of his suit of Dwarvish armor, and the helmet's functions.

The staircase to our right had a doorway at the top of the first four steps, as the flight turned towards the wall opposite the entrance. To the left, there was a doorway about two-thirds of the way down the wall, under the stairs. Torsten then began speaking to all of us, "Raileanu and Monika will follow me to the doorway on the right. Klement and Barthow go to the room on the left. Do NOT go up or down any of the stairs without my word. Survey the room, then come back here, and we will meet before going upstairs. Protect yourselves." He then motioned with his left hand for Monika and me to follow him, and we did, my carbine ready, and her wand in her right hand. After our first step, Torsten made a wide chopping motion with his hand flat to the left.

"Oh, I reckon that means fer us to go," Barthow said. He had his wand in his left hand and his pistol in his right hand. It struck me as humorous that, as he moved away from us, he hunched a bit, like a child playing hide-and-seek.

We were much closer to our door than they were, and once at it, Torsten stopped. He moved something - a small button or lever- on the side of his rifle, and then pointed it at the lock housing on the door. It was solid stone, like the rest of the structure, with no handle, latch, or lock. The hair-thin line in the outline of a round-topped door was the only indication it was there at all, really. Our helmet's glass visor did have it outlined in a thin red line, so to us it was apparent. A distinct bubble of force, only noticeable by a blue shimmering halo, exited the barrel of the rifle, striking the location one would expect a handle to be, and the door whipped open. Torsten nearly ran into the door as it opened. He was so fast entering the room, whipping his rifle side to side, then up to the ceiling. He had lowered it even before I, then Monika, could enter. It was only then that I could hear how quick her breathing had become. She was extremely nervous, and, honestly, so was I. We saw nothing in this room of note; it was wall-to-wall racks of medieval weapons from spears and poleaxes to shields and daggers. All of it was draped with centuries of cobwebs and dust.

"Nothin here but gold and silver, uh, Torsten." Barthow's voice announced from the room they were in.

"Yes. Tons of it. But no sign of Dolphus or anything dangerous. We are coming back." Klement said.

Coming back together in the entrance to the atrium, Torsten stopped and looked around with his helmet again, adjusting a knob with his right hand. It seemed he had a plan after a moment or two, as he had finished turning in little short steps to survey the rooms around us. "Alright, laddies and ladies. There is little of interest in these rooms, save one. We will all go there together, then continue to the back half of the castle, behind the central courtyard. Agreed?" He again began sprinting away towards the staircase and up its steps before anyone could answer. So, letting our heads sway in frustrated agreement, we followed him. Running up those steps was one moment I recall where I had to think about anything else. The sense of fearing the unknown had been settling in the back of my mind, and I took this chance to let the spectral dog that had haunted and taunted me all my life loose on it. I didn't want to hold a leash and force unwanted concerns away from the fore at the same time. I could not afford it for either Monika or me. No sooner than I went through that process, the concern for what Corfus, Tinfer, and the rest of the Dwarves were dealing with entered my mind.

I can tell you now what I learned only after we had finished this ordeal. It provides continuity to the story, but be sure, I was quite concerned about the events unfolding in the dungeon below as we kept moving through the castle. It would not have helped calm me.

Corfus, Tinfer, and the Pale Dwarves did indeed appear, quite unexpectedly, in the circular chamber where Dolphus was working to reassemble the CISI Orb. Assuming he was in a secret place and untouchable, he had not bothered to cast any protections or defenses before his work. However, his years of gazing into crystal balls and forcing his mind abroad in search of the artifacts did give him enhanced perceptual powers. He sensed immediately that there were intruders in this sanctum, and without a glance at them, he and his work were shielded by an illusion that even Corfus could barely detect.

The Dwarves arrived in an outward-facing ring around Corfus and immediately darted out in the direction each was facing. They proceeded to the thirteen iron doors that Runetta had installed. When this was a Dwarven outpost, they had used the small oubliettes that ringed the center as fuel storage for their power source, which I still don't understand. They each scanned what they had found, using their helmets to peer behind the doors. None of it was good. They spoke to Tinfer via their helmets, and by the time they had completed that survey, Corfus had detected the slightest shimmer of the illusion in the center of the room. This all happened very quickly, and at the exact moment Corfus ripped a wide slash through the fabric of the illusion to see inside, Dolphus wound his wand in the air, opening each of the thirteen doors, and simultaneously tried to weave the gash back together. Corfus knew this meant it was not only an illusion but also a rare field of power that would stop his kind of magic from penetrating. The Dwarves' weapons could have disabled or killed Dolphus, but they were busy now themselves. So busy in fact, even Tinfer engaged the monstrous troubles emerging from those deep pits, and had no concern for what lay in the center of the room, veiled, and engaged by Corfus.

The first creature to show itself was a Giant Peacock Tarantula. Nearly six feet across and eight feet high, the exoskeleton of this venomous predator was mirrored green. The sensory hairs that grew from each gap in the plates were the same as the sword and eye feathers that peacocks have. Beautiful, but only on display after taxidermy. It clicked and tapped its way up the narrow path leading out of its pit, pausing at the door only for a second. The Dwarf nearest the creature, Lank, shouted to the others what he was facing, but they, too, were quite engaged. He fired the same kind of white hot stream of energy at the spider, but missed as it scuttered away up the wall toward the ceiling, so he continued firing, each good hit knocking a portion of a leg, or segment of the abdomen off. Puss-like green ooze then flung about as the spider headed toward one of the other Dwarves, named Dages. Dages had been tracking another doorway, seeing an undefined form moving towards his line of sight, waiting for where he could fire upon it. He had his back to the massive arachnid. Lank led his target just a little and landed a hit on the spider's brainpan, causing a gush of yellow-green brains and internal fluids to splash over Dages from behind.

Luckily, Dages's view was not impaired because the emergent foe was a ganglemorph. It gripped the edge of the doorway with eleven fingers on each of its four arms, each with long, sharp, blued steel claws sunk deep into the writhing flesh. Its colors were constantly changing, from fuchsia to gray to light purple. The beast was a mish-mash of creatures it had subsumed, and could take the outer form of any or all of them to suit its needs. The grotesque eyeballs on two-foot-long stalks dripping ooze poked around the corner where Dages was aiming. He knew that any single strike on it, even the eyes, was not sufficient to cause severe damage to it. Able to change shape and form, even growing armored shells and plates, it resembles a dinosaur, belied by its ancient lineage. They had but one weakness, the nerve bundle that always resided in the very center of its mass, regardless of exterior shape. If Dages fired too soon, it could adapt and armor the vulnerable area. He had to wait until the entire form was presented. So wait, he did, and while doing so, he saw another arachnid emerge from the same doorway as the first one. He pulled out a pistol, and a violent pulsing blast of fire and molten metal went off, like a hundred pistol shots in a couple of seconds, without even turning his head to look. It ripped the second eight-legged troublemaker in half, and it fell back into the pit it had come from. Then, Dages made a change on his rifle and fired a shot into the opening, and it erupted with a deafening crack, and collapsed that opening onto itself, sealing any more of the spiders inside. The ganglemorph then slid in a putty-like blob shape around the edge of the doorframe onto the wall - it had retracted its eyestalks. It flattened itself with only the talons tick-tacking along the wall at its edges, but when the center was obvious, Dages fired a cone of brilliant red light at the brainmass, and the beast fell with the hole where its brain had been still visible, with a plop to the floor. Dages and Lank gave each other a nod and then went to check the other entrances into the room...

Corfus and Tinfer were still facing the center of the vast room, where Dolphus had cast a protection shell spell over his prize, the Hoplite. Corfus was still trying to rip a hole in the shell large enough for him to affect the events unfolding behind it. Tinfer was trying every mode of firepower he had to do the same. Green seams of light were torn into the shielding, but closed as soon as they opened. Tinfer glanced at Corfus, and while the whole exercise was becoming irritating to him, Corfus was still unfazed by the battle. That changed in a moment, when, behind where they were standing, a call came from the two Dwarves guarding the doorways to their rear. "ANIMECARNE! VESPERTIO DEMONIC!" All in the battle heard in their headsets. Corfus raised his left hand palm up, then drew it to him, closing his hand into a fist as he did. Tinfer glanced for only a moment, then continued on his attack on Dolphus's dome.

"You'd better have a way to handle that, Elf! We aren't equipped to deal with ungodly demons." Tinfer relayed in his gruff tone. "I do indeed," Corfus said, attention back to the task of unsealing the actual threat.

Six individual pockets of white light, each the size of a man, appeared amongst the ring of Dwarves. As the light faded, it was clear that six magical clergy had come to the aid of the battle. Two immediately went to the rear of Corfus and Tinfer, where the alarm had been raised from, and began working their holy magic on the two unnatural threats.

From one of the doorways, where the cry of Vespertio Demonic had originated, a huge bipedal, heavily muscled, nine-foot-tall batlike creature burst forth. Its wingspan was at least twelve feet, visible as it immediately jumped and flew into the air, its claws gouging into the chamber's wall. It bared its dagger-like yellow teeth and then dove off the wall towards a Dwarf that was looking away to the other side of the room.

"Trinew! Watch out!" a Dwarf named Hambre yelled into the helmets so all could hear. Without stopping or looking, Trinew, one of the two Lady Dwarves, ducked and rolled away to her left just in time. The hairy bat-beast landed, arched its back much like a cat, and let a gargling scream of fury out. Trinew, now crouched from her roll, shot at the creature and hit it clearly in the center of the chest. Simultaneously, Hambre hit it from behind. As it writhed in pain, one of the six Priests had moved close enough to throw a silver chain around its neck with two loops. About every foot of this chain had a cross. This terrifying nightmare then fell limp on the ground in a heap. From the gunfire or the Priest's work, we didn't know. Hambre and Trinew went and bumped their helmets together in a sort of gesture of congratulations. I found out, in the process of piecing all this together, that they were engaged to be wed, with the date not a month later. That fact is relevant, as an event not seen in ten thousand years is related to it.

The other named beast that was called out was not a beast; it was many. What looked like corpses, years dead by the look and odor, began shuffling out of the opening, three at a time, and they just kept coming. Porto, Donager, and Kam were the three Dwarves watching that side, and they began firing into the horde of them moving forth from the door. "Aim for their legs!" Kam said calmly. That change in direction of fire obliterated their mode of movement, and the corpses began piling up. The rotting meat and old bones of them being torn apart, splintering and spattering the walls. As the heap grew, they started climbing over it. The height grew until the force of them pushing from behind laid the pile over towards the Dwarves, the mindless clawing of those still able to scrape the stone floor. Ripping the rancid meat of their fellow mindless, tearing their moldy clothing as they did, inching closer. Now that the movement had been degraded, the three stood shoulder to shoulder, firing into the skulls of the undead, halting their motor functions and giving them a discernible purpose. Then a Priest of the six came over and began shouting rites and commands specific to dealing with revenants and possessed bodies. His wand beamed light like the yellow glow of the sun, firing it deep into the pile and down the shaft from whence they had climbed. In just a few minutes, the entire mound of writhing, rotted flesh stopped moving.

Kam then fired a projectile into the doorway, and it exploded, collapsing that doorway shut as well. The Priest who had bound and stopped the first bat creature with his wand forced it back into the cell it had come from and shut the door, sealing it. Reforming their defensive circle and checking on each other, the Priests and Dwarves were able to concentrate on the other side of the large chamber they were in. There were doors equally spaced around this room, and whatever was in the oubliettes on the other side of the room would have to come around the center, where Dolphus had set up his defenses. Or so they thought.

Dages's quick finish of the first ganglemorph had given pause to the second target of the ganglemorph. There were three in there, according to the readout he had. It had stopped and not moved any further, its eyes just looking at all the activity and the number of people moving about. Tiring of waiting for this creature, which all Dwarves know too well, he repositioned and was sure he had a better angle. He could not just collapse this doorway as with the other creatures, because a ganglemorph could squeeze through a hole the size of his thumb. He would have to kill it, risk it replacing any one of them before this was over, or have it retreat to a place none of them would detect. None of the array of technologies had been built to deal with these maligned forms of corrupted life. Just before seeing the creature, pressed tight to the wall, a buzzing, humming cacophony began to echo in the room. They were ancient cicadas. A foot long, their shells made of carbon-chrome, even capable of mimicking human voices, they only care to feed on meat, then lay their thousand eggs in the remains. And they were coming straight over the top of the domed chamber, and would be falling on their prey in mere seconds.

Tinfer relented on his attacks at the center of the room, looking straight up, and said only one word. "No." This creature had not been dealt with in thirty centuries, and he could not think of a way they could be defeated. There were literally a thousand or more of them.

Wolly, the only other Lady Dwarf in this company, spoke calmly into the helmets. "This one, we might need help with, Elf." She was right. No tool in their arsenal could pierce the carbon chrome shells; they were not equipped to dispense poisonous chemicals that might help, and their mandibles could easily break into the Dwarves' armor in a few seconds. Having not shown a split second of fear or concern up to this point at the terrifying foes, the comment did make Corfus break his focus on Dolphus for an instant. He looked up to the leading edge of the cicadas, and then back to the center of the room. One by one, the giant insects began turning to ash, in a bright orange line moving through the swarm, much like a line of fire might through a stoked stack of coal. Their empty shells then rained down around them in a clatter of ringing and clanging throughout the entire cavern. In less than ten seconds, the whole column of them had been wiped out. The assembled Dwarves looked at each other, shrugged, and smiled. Wolly was the one who said what they were all thinking, "Guess it's good to have an Elf now and again!" and they all gave hearty laughs.

"Dages, Porto, Donager, Kam, you all circle the center and make certain the threats from the perimeter of this room are dead, or covered!" Tinfer directed. They set off at a sprint around the edges to the opposite side, Dages and Porto to the left, the other two to the right. "Thanks, Elf," Tinfer said. Then he could hear the Elf speaking in his mind, not the helmet. "I am going to have the Priests try to pull back this shielding. I want you and the remaining four Dwarves to move to the edges of the room - at oblique angles, and fire on anything or anyone you see from those sides, please." Corfus instructed.

"You four, with me!" Tinfer spoke into the helmet. Once he had their attention, he directed them with hand signals to the far edges of the room, two a side, and they knelt, aiming their rifles right at the distortion field in the center where Dolphus was. Four of the Priests made a semi-circle around Tinfer and Corfus, and they pointed their wands at the tear in the bubble, and began straining to pull back the edges of it. Tinfer laid his rifle over, changed its function, and then a violet beam emerged from the barrel at the bottom of the tear. It began to widen, and Tinfer slowly directed the beam up, and the gap widened as he did. When it was perhaps a foot wide and three feet high, fire began pouring in from the Dwarves on each far side, criss-crossing into the shell. Occasionally, the orange blasts from them could be seen ricocheting around inside the shell.

"I don't think my rifle has much power left, Corfus." Tinfer thought, hoping Corfus could hear it. After a couple of seconds, and not detecting a response, he turned his head slightly to look at him, and actually saw the Elf's eyes had narrowed, and a tiny drip of sweat was making its way down his face between his ear and eye. He had never seen an Elf sweat; he didn't know if he should be worried or not. "I am alright, we almost have it open. Your rifle should last, sir," Corfus stated.

He was right. Ten seconds later, the entire volume of the great cavern was filled with white flashes and golden sparks as the enveloping shell was rendered helpless by the onslaught, peeling it apart like a flower opening. Dolphus stood before a great horizontal stone slab, facing Corfus. He was not the same withered, crippled old man he had been an hour before. He stood fully erect, in his physical prime, and covered head to toe in glittering quartz armor.

CHAPTER SIXTEEN

The Priests had joined the Dwarves around the opposite side and were trying to detect what was down the last two doors. Preoccupied with this, they did not break focus to the foe now revealed behind them, noticing, but not reacting to the shower of sparks that fell among them. A low, but frighteningly long and reverberating growl, unmistakable from a large cat of some kind, emanated from one of the tunnels leading down from the exposed doorway. All the Dwarves and Priests were concerned by this; now they pointed their wands and rifles towards the sound, leaving the last doorway unguarded. Taking advantage of this, the last, terrifying force emerged from its tunnel in a powerful stream of particles about a foot in diameter.

"It is a Dust Demon! Join me to contain it!" the older Priest of the group shouted, and the rest of them ran, wands out front, to his aid. They all made the appropriate motion with their powerful wands, and it was captured in a force resembling a large glass tube filled with green light. It required much focus and force to drag it from the edge of the stairwell, where it undoubtedly was planning to escape, and onto the ground. "We can hold it," looking at the other Priest closest to him, "begin exorcism, NOW!" The four others all held their wands in one hand, and their book for Rites of Exorcism floated in front of them, ensuring the correct procedure and the proper order of language. Their perfect synchronization of speech and pronunciation echoed throughout the room. A second Dust Demon, moving along the wall, a single particle thick, shot past them unnoticed. With all being preoccupied, it went straight upstairs, no doubt to seek out the five of us, or escape, as we were still working to clear the above-ground rooms of the castle.

Unnoticed by the assembled forces of Elves and Dwarves battling the Dust Demon and Dolphus, ever watchful of the Hoplite being activated, a huge, over-muscled, Chromataphor Panther slipped out of the last doorway and up the stairs leading out of the room. Even Corfus and the enhanced equipment of the Dwarves did not, nor could they have, detected it.

The skin of the Chromataphor Panther generates pigments in swift and accurate quality to match its surroundings, which is displayed through the hair of the beast. Each hair is clear and 'funnels' light from the pigmentation down its length. Simply put, it can look exactly like the surrounding area. The physical action of this is so quick that it can occur at any speed of movement short of a full sprint. When they choose, it is impossible to see them at all, except their eyes, which are completely gloss black. There is no pupil, no whites, and, save their blackness breaking up whatever pattern the body produces, there is little hope of seeing them. Moreover, their bodies had been designed in such a way that their muscle mass was double that of a natural panther of the same size. Over time, their bones doubled in density, making this one of the most feared predators to survive the Calamity. It was no wonder that Runetta kept one. It was truly one thing I wished they had seen coming towards us further up in the castle, and had been able to warn us of.

Corfus spoke to Tinfer and the rest of the Dwarves, who had rejoined them all facing Dolphus, "We may be fortunate, he has chosen to repair himself, and not to activate the Hoplite. The quartz armor is impervious to our weapons and magic, but I must learn what other damage this vile warlock has done to the world. I wish not to destroy him until I can see into his mind."

Tinfer responded in the helmets so his team could hear and knew Corfus would as well, "We are here to eliminate that CISI, and that Hoplite, do what you want with that fool. We will help disable him, but then we are attacking the Hoplite!" Tinfer barely finished speaking before the Dwarves began firing at Dolphus, each with a different spectrum of light-based weapons. The quartz armor absorbed all, each area struck glowing the same color as the type of fire used before the light dissipated into the armor's structure. The Priests were still working to disempower the Dust Demon, and it was taking all their collective energy to control and strip the dust of the possessing evil.

"You hapless fools! Ha ha ha ha!" Dolphus, drunk with his new physical prowess and sheathing of impenetrable armor. "The events across the world I have begun will result in the fall of all your pointless structures!" Dolphus looked, smiling a diabolical, hate-filled grin, at his arms and his legs fully working as they hadn't in fifty years. He held up an arm to see his reflection in the smooth quartz. "Oh, I am the ruler this world will need...What I have begun does not die with me, DO YOUR WORST, ELF!" He became so full of hubris that he even pointed at the assembled force while he was laughing at them. Corfus ignored him, now looking at the CISI Orb and noticing the sparkling lights within it beginning to increase in activity.

Again, with thought only, Corfus spoke to the Dwarves and the Priests, "If you would, please focus on the Orb and Hoplite - break the bonds between them. I will indeed handle this troublemaker." And with that, the Dwarves split into two groups, sprinting to the left and right, then leaping with their powered suits onto the great slab, and began laying streams of invisible energy across both the Orb and Hoplite, so intense that the mirror-smooth granite slab began cooking. Great clouds of smoke and pops of cracking diorite and metal leapt off the machine-man and the Orb. Corfus again - "Tinfer, you may not be able to damage that Orb. Can you sever the connection it has made to the Hoplite? If so, then seal it away in a canister, as you use for your fuel ore." Tinfer looked at Corfus, nodded, and changed his position on the table to direct his fire onto the cable that had grown to connect the two. Another, Trinew, then Wolly joined in the work.

Dolphus looked down and to the left, and, unconcerned with what the diminutive fighters were doing, looked back to Corfus, who was gone when he looked back. Appearing behind Dolphus, the High Elf grasped the sides of Dolphus's helmet and, with a quick wrenching side to side, using a specific high frequency vibration, his power and assistance of his own unique armor, shattered the joining, interlocking rings between the helmet and torso. All before Dolphus could react. Shards entered his neck, and he could feel the repair work on his body being performed by the newfound power of the CISI particles, and barely let a sound of discomfort out. It was enough time for Corfus to rip the helmet clear of him and grasp the whole of Dolphus's head in his large hands. The High Elf leaned his head back a bit and closed his eyes, ever so briefly. Dolphus was unaware of what was happening, but his entire mind was being absorbed into the Elf's mind. Frozen and unable to react to the power of the Elf, Dolphus's expression was blank, and his mouth hung open. The whole process took less than five seconds. Then, Corfus let go with his left hand and raised it high in the air. With a motion resembling pulling a thick rope, Corfus drew a bolt of lightning a foot wide from the atmosphere in the room down into the top of Dolphus's head. The Elf stepped back, and the lightning burned through the warlock's skull - causing it to glow yellow through his skin - and it blew out the ankles of the armor and into the ground. When the bolt of electricity stopped, the joints and boots of the armor had been seared solid, with the reeking and smoking corpse still steaming inside it. The lightning destroyed the CISI particles Dolphus had spent his conceited time absorbing, along with their power to heal him. The mass of his now-useless armor and cooked flesh, seared into a standing position, then fell forward and clanked as a bronze bell dropped on a wooden floor, that dull, short ring echoing in the cavernous room.

Stepping towards the slab where the Hoplite lay, Corfus could tell the Dwarves were making progress on the mechanical menace. Looking at Tinfer, he saw that the outer shell of the bundle of transparent glass-like fibers was broken through. Tinfer released his rifle and pulled a short rod from his belt with his right hand. Flinging it downward, a three-foot shaft with a diamond-shaped axe head extended to full form with a 'ting'. He raised it high up over his head and brought it down on the bundle of blinking cords with immense force. The fibrous connection was severed, and the flashes and blinks in the Orb slowed. He made a similar, yet reverse, motion with the axe, and it collapsed back to its original size and returned to his belt. Then he pulled a pair of rings out of a pocket on his chest and stretched them apart until they were just larger than the diameter of the Orb. He set the pair on top of it, and the lower ring fell to the surface, while the top one stayed put. Touching a few times on the left forearm of his armor with his right hand, the rings let out a hum, and a criss-crossed brown material joined the rings to encase the Orb.

Once the Orb was safely contained, Tinfer ordered his fighters to cease firing on the Hoplite. He knew that without the Orb, the Hoplite would not be useful to anyone. The damage inflicted by the Dwarves' weapons was extensive. Jagged rips bore down into the joints of its arms and legs and neck. The plain faceplate, which bore no distinguishing features, was burned only a few fingernail depths, revealing a microscopic honeycomb pattern of exotic metallic threads. The team of Dwarves each set one hand on the platform and jumped down to the ground, looking to Tinfer for more instructions.

"All of you," Tinfer motioned towards the group of Priests and the staircase leading up and out of the room, "Go destroy that dust the Priests are fighting, and pursue the one that escaped. Make sure the group upstairs can finish their work unmolested by the creatures that were bound here. Once this place is cleared, we will meet back at the dimensional gate and destroy this cavern and everything in it." The team of fighters went straight to the dust demon being contained, and made necessary adjustments to their weapons to fire into the magical jar holding it, raised them to their shoulders, and then blue-white flame began to fill the jar, although no visible light emitted from the barrels of their rifles. The heat from that process was felt throughout the cavern's interior. In under a minute, the fire had cleansed the dust particles of any possessing forces, and they fell to the bottom of the cylinder in which the Priests had imprisoned them. The Dwarves relinquished their fire, then the

Priests stopped their exorcism, and the others ceased the form of the jar.

"We must clear the remainder of the castle of evils!" The older Priest among them shouted, motioning with a wide wave of his arm, as the rosary beads he had clutched in his upraised hand clattered against one another. They all nodded and ran up the stairs close behind the detachment of Dwarves sent ahead.

"Tinfer, please let me hold the Orb, and assist your team in clearing the castle, if you would." Corfus politely asked. He was surveying the destruction and all the dead and destroyed forms of life that Runetta had been holding prisoner, for God knows what reason.

"What will you do?" The Dwarf commander asked.

"The things Dolphus has been doing for decades are clear to me now. I must speak with, and derive from, Runetta Lynchos what her part is in his plans, and what she knows." Corfus looked now at Tinfer. "It may take me some time, but it is important for all of us and the future, sir. Is that acceptable?"

"Aye, we are together in this, Elf. Those damn Orbs have never belonged to this world. This has gone fairly well, if I am honest." Tinfer, now, was also surveying the carnage strewn about, one hand on his hip. "Indeed, we are fortunate the guardian of this Orb has not arrived, if one is still bound to it." Corfus looked at him, "You are right about that." Tinfer nodded and headed to the group that had already proceeded upstairs.

Our group entered and surveyed each of the rooms in the castle's front stronghold. Most were never used, occupied only by old cobwebs and meaningless stacks of crates, or by ancient, unused weapons rusting and rotting. There were three levels, each with a six-foot-wide passage about fifty feet long to the rear, and a larger, more formidable keep built on the highest ground of the central dome of the cavern.

The Dwarf led the way, and when we had determined there was nothing of concern in the forward keep, he suggested we begin at the third level passage and proceed to work down each floor. He knew there was a passage at the back of this structure, on the first floor, that led to the 'reactor room' as he called it. We could go down and meet the rest there, if we hadn't come across them before that. He was at the front of our column, then Klement, Barthow, with Monika and me side by side at the rear. I marveled at how this armor, given to us by the Dwarves, was so incredibly silent as it moved, especially on the mirror-smooth stone floors. Whoever it was in the distant past who had locked these brilliant people below ground, they were utter fools. Granted, it was their initial isolation and poor treatment that led shortly to their own abandonment of their overlords, who perished not long afterwards, in the Calamity. The world is much better for them having kept to themselves, and I was glad they were in it.

The pathway opened into an expansive rectangular room, with a half-circle wall to our left. That wall was the sheathing of a spiral staircase leading downstairs. To our right was a door, and near it, right across from where we entered, was another doorway. From there, we could see that the doors were the same layout on the other side of the room.

"You three go to our left, I will take Klement, and go down the hall to the right," Torsten said. He took off immediately at a quick step. Klement shrugged his shoulders, holding his open hand out, then turned and followed.

We did as instructed and went through the left door-way. It was another long hallway leading to the back of the castle, and we could see all the way to the end. On the left side, halfway down the hall, was one door leading to the stone balcony that lined the perimeter of the open courtyard below. Directly in front of us was a stairway leading down in an open alcove, with arrow loops on the exterior wall. Behind us was a room built into the corner of the keep, whose door was open. Three loops were on its walls as well. Metal shelves covered the far walls and loops. Many strange, confusing items were there.

"Those are old tools for technology. Keep moving." Corfus's voice said in our helmets. He was obviously keeping an eye on us; however, he does that. So we did. Moving down the hallway, we came to a door that was not locked. Barthow turned the ring handle, and the door opened inwards. It was a dark closet, so Barthow lit it up with his wand. Rack after rack of brooms. Their handles and brushes were stained with blood. Some had their shafts broken. I had read in school that one thing that had been common for over a thousand years was taking the broom of a defeated foe as a trophy, especially for battles between witches. I was not in the magical world as much as Monika, Barthow, or Klement, but it wasn't something that I had not heard of happening in my lifetime. They were not dusty or unkempt; it felt more like a trophy room. But the number of them and some of their styles made me think this had been a family collection spanning generations. Seeing it in that light was macabre. There had to be several hundred of them, each representing a life taken by another.

"I have catalogued all of the brooms in that room. I can note from which person each had been taken at a later time. Please proceed." Corfus's voice said plainly in our ears.

Mirroring the hallway that Monika and I were down, Torsten and Klement had a large open area on the other side of the half-round stairs, then a long, narrow passage towards the back of the castle. Mounted to three wooden pedestals were were-jaguars in half-metamorphosis. Each had a name, a date of capture, and a location wanded into the base. Wanding into wood was similar to carving, save that it was performed magically, was controlled mentally, and had the carven-in writing burnt to black carbon. This quality was the work of a master, as anyone can do it, but the perfection of the script was a professional taxidermist's hand. Frozen in the agony of changing bone, skin, tendon, and growth of fur, it was not something that a moral wizard would do. They peeked into the diagonal corner of the area, nothing more than a firing slit cupola that hung out over the first and second floor exterior walls.

The first room Torsten and Klement came to had no door. This long, narrow room was filled with floor-to-ceiling racks for wands, as one would see in a shop window. Hundreds of little metal 'J' hooks were affixed to vertical planks of wood secured to the stone walls. Dozens of broken wands were carefully placed horizontally on the hooks. All of these were also, obviously, from fallen enemies. Ensuring that his helmet had seen everything, Torsten turned and went back into the hall to the next room. This one was nothing more than a bedroom, perhaps for a visitor, as the accommodations were very Spartan. So was the next room on that side. The last area was another alcove with stairs leading down. They proceeded to the end of the hall and went right to the back of the floor to wait for the rest of us to arrive.

There were only two rooms left on our side of the castle, both of which were libraries. For a brief moment, Monika lowered her wand and approached the rows of tomes, running her fingers across the books. Taking one down that caught her eye, she closely examined the covers and spine before bringing the bottom edge of the large book to her face. It was twelve by eighteen inches, and four inches thick. I was still at the doorway and could see from there that the paper was unusually thick.

"What is it? What can you tell?" I asked. She seemed mesmerized by the whole book. She didn't respond or react at all. "Monika?"

She set the book back in its slot on the shelf. Turning slowly to me, she looked at many of the others on every wall of the room. "Most of these are bound in and written on human skin."

"That ain't sumethin folks do anymore. Right?" Barthow asked, looking sharply at each of us. Monika just kept looking around. Barthow then looked at me, "Raileanu, is it??"

"She would know, book binding and preservation is her expertise. I believe her." I said, waving my hand toward her. "Are these old books, or newer. Um, I mean, has Runetta done this, or is it her family's collection?"

"Most are older than a hundred years. It has been against our laws for much longer than that. I am at a loss for what to do. They cannot be allowed to leave in their bindings, but what is written here may have led to their knowledge of the Orbs. We will have to take these with us to a safe place." She was adamant in her statements, and we all agreed with her.

"You see now why we have little to do with any of you, magical or not. You are savages." Torsten said with disdain in his voice. None could disagree.

We proceeded to the back of the castle, to the last opening of the hallway. It had shelves carved into the stone itself, packed with hundreds of jars, each different from the next, yet all with very wide mouths. It seemed like a great deal of work for empty jars, so I went to the back of the room, where I saw a door. It was locked. Torsten went to one of the walls with the jars and appeared confused.

"What is it, lil buddy?" Barthow asked.

"I am not your buddy, fat human." This caused Barthow to stop, and even through the visor, I could see him stick out his bottom lip; then he looked down at the bulging arc of the armor over his gut. Until then, I suspect he imagined himself quite dashing in the armor. He dismissed the comment with a shrug. Torsten continued, "There was a door here, leading to a set of stairs, but I see no sign of it now. Perhaps it had been closed off. Should be one here on each floor; the set of stairs leads to the 'reactor room'. The Dwarf stood puzzling over it for a few moments, so the three of us proceeded to try to get through the locked door and the room behind.

"Lemme see if'n I can just bust that dern door down." Barthow puffed up and marched right up to the door and gave it a mighty blow with his shoulder. It did indeed unlock; it fell off the hinges, splintering and cracking, ending with Barthow on the remains of the door, face-first on the floor. It would have been humorous, if not for the room he had fallen into. It was a large, wide rectangular room with a high arched ceiling of black stone. Across from us, where Barthow was still grumbling as he struggled to stand up with dignity, was another array of inset stone shelves holding glass jars. Floor to ceiling, sixteen feet, and perhaps thirty feet long, curving to our left around the whole wall. These jars were not empty.

CHAPTER SEVENTEEN

"I thought the style of jars out there had a familiar look to them," Monika said, her voice shaking. She was right. I remembered what she had told me of her meeting with Runetta in the Imperial Gardens, of what was in the jar that night. These were the same. Some three hundred jars, each with a tiny spark of light illuminating the contents - beating human hearts. The one I had seen with my only encounter with her had no light; that heart was still and lifeless. None of us could look away from the display. Now inside the room, close to them, we could hear the faint sound of them, a discordant mess of low thumps, some even moving the jars as they pulsed. It was sickening.

Now to his feet, and marveling in revulsion at the sight, Barthow exclaimed, "What in tha Sam Hill is that?" He looked back at Monika and me. "These are Runetta's.

She showed one to Monika in Vienna." I looked at her. "Yes. She said she had one for each person in her service. This is frightening, if these all serve her, or Dolphus." Barthow turned back to the wall, "Well, I never." I looked to the left, at the rest of the room. Torsten was already inventorying everything he could. Rifling through things on the vanity table, books, and clothing, he was showing no concern for preserving evidence. I took a good look around the room to see what else might be of interest here.

It was a lavish bedroom, at its center a huge half-circle bed atop a platform about a foot high that extended three feet around the bed. The canopy above it was quite obviously grown over a long period of time from bloodthorn. The trunks that make up the four posts, and the flat head-end of the bed, were twisted and wound artfully. The horrendous thorns that gave the trees their name had all been removed, further proof of their diabolical nature in the human-like scars that formed where the thorns had been pulled. Their bases were set in the platform, or rather came through it from below, and rose eight or nine feet in height before their branches arched across the expanse of the bed. Woven as a hedger would, carefully and with purposeful intent, it made a tight-barred prison for hundreds of lightning bugs who lived inside. Their green glow pulsed and flickered, illuminating the bed and the ceiling. The bed had a raised, cushioned headboard of red velvet. The pillows were cast carelessly about, their silken covers half on, the sheets also blood red silk. A heavy black canvas blanket, which seemed odd, hung from one post, most of it on the floor.

Several paintings of locations none of us recognized were scattered around the walls, with little planning or purpose; a couple leaned against the far wall to the right of the bed. All seemed unkempt, dusty, and even had a few cobwebs across their corners. One, above the small vanity table to the right of the mirror arrangement, seemed well cared for and also perfectly straight. It was of a young man who didn't strike a chord with any of us. When I looked right at it, I did hear a very slight, "I see," from Torsten.

"Told you. You are all savages." He continued pulling drawers out onto the floor and flinging wardrobes open. "You do know that she can influence every person with her magic, that she has a heart jar for." We all looked at him now, waiting to hear whether he had anything to recommend. Monika walked to the wall and inspected each jar and its shelf. "What are you looking for?" I asked, stepping up beside her to help, if I could. "To see if there are any indications as to who these all belong to. We should record that, if we can, before..."

"Yes, we must destroy them," Torsten announced, done with his search. "Come on, humans, I am going to go to the second floor now. I can burn that filth later."

"He is right. These cannot continue to exist." Monika said, looking over to me. "No, of course not." I turned my head up in disgust and saw the ceiling. The highly reflective surface of all the stone that made up this castle had been set in my vision so long, I didn't notice until just then that the ceiling wasn't the same glass-smooth rock. It had a frame, almost like one around a painting. Very ornate and beautifully carved, coated in emeralds, rubies, and gold leaf. The frame followed the contours of the arched ceiling, and within its borders was a shimmering sea of, maybe mercury. It undulated and moved like water on a millpond in a light breeze. From where I was standing, it looked like there was a wooden door on the wall opposite us, where the stairway Torsten was looking for would be. Glancing at that spot on the wall, I saw nothing but stone.

Torsten had already left the room, so I called to him, "Torsten, does this mean there is a door here?" He walked back into the room, looking at me. I pointed to the ceiling, and looking up, he saw the image of the door. He went to that section of the wall, and touched the side of his helmet, then that section of his forearm, and looked back at the wall. Cautiously approaching it, he extended his fingers and arm toward it. Perhaps an inch off the surface of the stone, the air in front of it shimmered. I looked back at the ceiling for a second, and the image there shimmered identically. Torsten reached through it with purpose, found a door handle, and opened it. "Yes, this is the stairwell. Cleverly concealed." He looked back at me.

"That thar is magic I dunno," Barthow said, dramatically putting his hands on his hips, which looked ridiculous in armor. Monika giggled. "You *call* it magic," Torsten said. The Dwarf left the door open and proceeded out of the room the way we came in. "Let's go. There is a lot more castle to clear." We all followed him. The spiral stairs in the part of the castle we were in led to the second floor.

Halfway down, Torsten stopped and cocked his head as though listening intently. Fearful of impending danger, we all stood perfectly still and waited for him to inform us of what he had heard.

"There is at least one peacock tarantula, and maybe even a ganglemorph loose from the lower level. That ganglemorph can dissolve this armor if it gets on you, so don't give it the chance. And that filthy spider, it, too, can pierce this armor. The ganglemorph is silent, but you will hear the claws on the ends of the legs of that spider." He turned back to the front and kept right on going down the stairs.

"What the heck is a gangle-e-morffey?" Barthow asked. I looked at Monika, who just shuddered at the thought. "And how big'un is that, uh, peacock spider thing?"

"Just shoot at anything that isn't us, alright. Let's focus on staying alive. I can explain what they are if we make it out of here, alright?" I said to him. "Alright, shoot anythin' that ain't us. Got it," he said, looking around with a bit of a crouched stance now.

We made it to the second floor, and Torsten said we should check that room behind us, where Runetta's room and the staircase were hidden on the third floor. This time, there were no shelves, no bedroom, just storage. Barrels of ale, casks of wine and port, racks of cheese wheels. A few bins of milled grains - barley, wheat, rye. Two small barrels of honey mead, and a hundred square glass bottles, maybe a gallon each, of honey. Paper labels were affixed to each of them, with a date and the location where the honey was collected. I had learned of the variations of the honey based on the weather and flora from which the bees had collected pollen, but had never seen so many together from such varied places. They all had different hues and even colors. Some were very light in color, and some were very, very dark. One label said 760 AD. It was over a thousand years old. It would be a shame to destroy these, I thought, and might attempt to save them, if the circumstances allowed.

"Be prepared! Several of the beasts that were held prisoner below have escaped and are heading up into the castle!" we all heard in the helmets. It was Tinfer shouting, and the noises in the background made it clear they were having much more trouble than we were. Torsten did not hesitate; he knew that the only path the creatures could take was the staircase we had discovered. He positioned himself in the opening of that secret stair, his rifle pointed down the descending steps.

"Get out of that room, humans, get behind me!" Torsten shouted angrily, "We must head down there immediately before it gets out of the stairwell into the first floor and we lose it!" We all filed past, and behind him, Barthow first, then Monika, myself, and Klement at the rear. As soon as Klement had made it past Torsten, the Dwarf began running down the stairs, and we followed close behind.

"Whatcha reckon these beasts are?" Barthow asked. "What er we lookin' fer?" Torsten, winding down the steps, asked for us. Tinfer answered, still with commotion in the background from where he was, below with Corfus and the Priests. "A Dust Demon, and we heard a large cat-like animal briefly, but there is nothing in the cells where it came from. It may have escaped unnoticed! We have been busy!" "KAFAR!" Torsten said under his breath. He paused, laid his rifle over on its right side, and fiddled with something. One of the tubes running along the side of the rifle's frame lit up with an orange flickering light running back and forth inside it. He then grabbed a small cylinder off his belt, maybe four inches long and an inch in diameter. He flicked one end off, perhaps a cap, and held it in his left hand, alongside the barrel section of his rifle, and kept moving down. It was a small-diameter staircase, perhaps thirty steps between floors, and wound so tightly that it made me, and I am sure others, a bit dizzy, essentially walking briskly in a small circle.

When we exited onto the first floor, it was a larger room with no distinct opening to the floor below. There was room for all of us to exit the stairwell and collect at the opening. Torsten went out first and stood right by the door, eyeing the stairs coming up to our level as we moved beside him into the small chamber.

"You all stay here, do not let anything come up. Woman, you have magic. Stand a few steps back up the stairs, where a beast cannot see you, and be ready to cast a containment cage on a Dust Demon. Big man," looking at Barthow, "come with me. You will have to do the same thing, as we will have to hold that filthy demon and hope I can burn it out." He looked at the other three of us. "You have no tools against the Dust Demon at all. If anything else gets past us, kill it however you can." He didn't even

315

pause before running back into the stairwell. Barthow paused, looking at us, and we shooed him off because he was integral to the plan. I touched Monika on her right shoulder, and she followed Barthow, but turning right, going up around the corner in the stairs, and poking just her head and wand around enough to see. Klement and I stood at an oblique angle outside the spiral shape of the stairs, aiming our firearms at the point where anything rounding the corner coming up at us would be first visible. I stood right at the edge of the stonework, thinking I would basically fall into the stairs if I had to force an enemy out of the stairs into our little room. That is all I could think of to protect Monika if I had to.

"It's coming!" Tinfer said. "I don't see anything!" Barthow shouted in return. "Cast your cage, fool!" A floor-to-ceiling blade of sand, only a few grains wide, came tearing up the winding stairway along the outside wall and got past Torsten before Barthow threw up basically a wall with his wand that bowed out all the way to Torsten; the force of the sand collecting in it knocked Torsten down. As Barthow closed the net at the back of the wave of sand and dust, he looked down and behind himself at Torsten on the steps. His left arm had been cleaved off, through the armor and all, his blood pumping out where it had been. His left kneecap and its plate armor were also cleanly shorn off. Torsten sat up, his right arm still gripping his rifle's grip, groaning through his gritted teeth, and fired a steady beam of fire into the container. Inside, the debris and dirt shot around, bouncing off the walls in a display indicative of the pain it was experiencing. Barthow turned from the fiery mass and looked at Torsten, whose armor had begun to close the wound with a fibrous mass of its own, stopping the bleeding, and then built a shell of armor plating over it. When it finished, in less than a minute, a hemispherical cap bulged out where the shoulder had been. Then Torsten stood, still laying fire into the beast, holding his rifle with one hand.

Monika heard and understood what had happened from the cries and sounds, and also built a magical netting that filled the expanse of the stairs before it came to the opening where we were. It captured the dust that had injured Torsten and held it in a small ball in the center of the passageway. "Come here!" she said nervously, "I am going to take this and add it to the mass that Barthow is holding!"

"Alright, we are right behind you!" I said, grateful for her skills and poise in this event. No one is ready for facing terrible events, and no one knows for sure how they will react when the time comes. Some freeze, regardless of skill or training. Some run away. Some wait for others to lead them. Some have all rationality fail them and cannot function at all. Monika had none of these perils hidden in her character and was illuminated by a brilliant golden light from her cage spell in that dark spiral stairwell. The heart and bravery I saw in her face through the helmet's special glass still visit me in my dreams.

I was so close behind her descending the stairs that several times the metal of our armor clanked and tinked as it bumped together. Klement followed a few steps further up and behind, checking after finding solid footing with each step behind us to make sure there were no more surprises. In just a minute, we had joined the two fighting the larger mass of filth, and Monika let her little ball of light and dirt merge into the fiery crucible that was burning away the evils inhabiting it. I looked and saw Torsten's arm lying there, and the accompanying puddle of Dwarvish blood, noticing how much darker, almost maroon, it looked than human blood. The armor on the arm had closed its open end as well, which seemed strange at first.

"Don't just look at it, pick it up and put it on my back!" Torsten shouted. "NOW!" I didn't understand what purpose that would serve, but I did as asked. When I brought it, hand down, along the left side of his back, it was drawn to it and snapped out of my hand, landing on the metal plates and mechanical workings of the suit, as if a magnet had grabbed a nail. The fire in the shell continued for another moment, then, when Torsten could no longer detect sentient movement inside, he stopped the stream of fire. The dust and dirt lay on the bottom of the spell-jar, holding it motionless. "Alright, big fella, you can release it. It is just dirt now." So Barthow let go of it, and the dirt fell across the stairs. That was the instant we heard it. A growl that was so low, so deep, that even the air inside our armor reverberated. It came from further down this narrow, now confining spiral stairway. It must have been behind the fiery field that just ceased, and was coming closer. A slight, very faint scraping sound moved like padded paws across the eons of dust between us and it.

"The stairs from here to the dungeon room below, where everyone else is, are eighty feet." Torsten was speaking very quietly and deliberately. "Big man, you stand beside me, and the rest of you up and behind us one turn. That will give you room to react if it gets past us. We will go one step at a time until we find it, or those below catch up to it. Did you get that, Tinfer?"

"Agreed. On our way." Tinfer's gravelly voice came through in the helmets.

Monika stayed at the back this time, and Klement and I were in front as we went down one step at a time. Torsten took only a few steps, then stopped and attached his rifle to the front of his armor. He made changes on the side of his helmet a few times, looking up and around, then down and actually into the center. "Ah. There it is. I cannot change what you all see because it was damaged on my left arm. It is a Chromataphor Panther. It is enormous, with four tails that it can use to grab and hold you. Its fangs can pierce your armor. Sadly, it is like a chameleon, and it will be tough for you to see. Direct your attacks wherever I fire first, understand?"

Our response was unanimous and instantaneous, "Okay..." followed by an audible gulp. Torsten just shook his head in disgust at us and began to step down slowly, one after the other.

"KAFA-!"He said quietly, which I found blood-chilling, since I had derived that word as a Dwarvish curse word of some kind from his use of it earlier. "I cannot see it anymore...Hmmm." He moved his head around, then just went back to stepping slowly downward. There was a strange sound then, like the end of a large dangling rope bumping into an empty pail.

"Wait!" Barthow said, at almost a whisper. "I see a dis..."

Chapter Eighteen

The three of us looked around Torsten to try to see what he was talking about ahead of us, and we all stopped dead in our tracks. Torsten slowly raised his head to look almost straight up. It was then we saw a shimmer above his head, and as I followed the wavy lines of the distortion to the ceiling, a wall-shaking roar burst out, and then Torsten's head was just...gone. The distortion had enveloped his head, and then a wrenching, metallic ripping sound echoed out, mingled with his screams of pain, followed by gurgling and straining for a brief moment, then both sounds disappeared. We still couldn't tell what was happening, especially from the back, almost around the corner in the spiral staircase. Blood streams of dark, deep red shot out of the stump where Torsten's head had been, nearly to the top of the ceiling, but it stopped short. It was spraying onto something that became quite obvious after a few splashes. The face of a giant cat, the Chromataphor Panther was now mostly coated, and it couldn't hide with its unique natural camouflage. It dropped the scheme altogether when it saw we all knew it was there. The beast was hanging from the ceiling by the use of blue-steel claws. The cat's eyes were pure black, no color, no pupil, no reflection of any kind, like empty holes in its head. The fur was so black it appeared dark blue, rippling across the massive muscles of the animal's frame. Furious at its ruse failing, the mouth opened, and Torsten's head, helmet and all, crushed and broken, fell to the floor and rolled down the steps. It stretched its face wide open, screaming a horrendous cry at us, the purple tongue retracted to the back of the mouth. Its teeth were also like blued steel, gleaming from its watering snout, set in the only part of it that had any distinct color. The interior of the mouth was bright red, like the blood you would find inside a beef liver.

We were petrified with fear, well, Monika, Klement, and I were. Barthow, closest, and also now splattered with the blood of Torsten, raised his wand, and it began to vibrate with the imparted power he was about to unleash. One of the tails of the panther whipped toward his wand hand, but Barthow let fly fast enough to strike the tail first. "AAERGH! Bastard!" He screamed as a ripping spell tore the tail off the beast and flung it forward and down the stairs. The cat crouched closer to the ceiling and used another tail, which Barthow could now see had been holding Torsten's right arm and rifle, preventing him from moving it, probably simultaneously to the attack on his head. That tail flung Torsten's remains down the stairs with a single motion, clanging and clattering as it rolled away.

Klement and I raised our rifles and began firing at the monster, striking it with every shot. Other than a flinch locally in the vast, tightly bound muscles where we hit it, it barely reacted. The bullets were penetrating, but maybe not enough through the flesh to strike a bone and limit movement. Monika, from behind us, fired a spell that attempted to lash it with iron bars to the ceiling. Klement and I took the chance to switch to our pistols and emptied those, this time, with a bit more careful aim, into its head and neck area. One shot, I believe from Klement, hit the right eye and bloodied it, knocking a chunk of meat and bone off from the edge of the eye socket. Barthow began using his wand in a jabbing motion, up, up, up, up, with each one making a long slit that looked to me like a stabbing wound from a double-edged European sword. Those must have made deep entries into critical areas, because the beast got *really mad* then.

Two of the three remaining tails grabbed at the flat iron bars, trying to bend them away from its head, to make enough room to get out, it hoped. The third tail was having a hard time reaching Barthow's wand, as he was about two feet further away than Torsten had been. The cat growled and writhed in pain, as Monika strained to tighten the bars around the creature. Klement and I had reloaded when this was happening, and Klement fired first with his shotgun, destroying the whole eye socket of the remaining eye. Debris from the impact hit the wall, falling in chunks to the steps below, followed by long, thick streams of its blood.

The bars of the front began to move after it lost the second eye, and it scrunched all the way to the back of the imprisoning bars, as if it were thinking of pouncing out, by the looks of it. A cacophony of stomping, metal scraping on stone, and cries of Dwarves we heard in the helmets was approaching up the steps towards us. Their yelling as they approached turned to all-out warcries when they saw Torsten lying in their path.

Not knowing our plan or current circumstances, they began firing at the caged animal from behind as soon as they rounded the corner. Four of them were shooting powerful bursts of blue-white light that filled the tight space we were in with a massive barrage of popping sparks. It hit the caging and burst it open at their side, the back of it from where we were. The rear of the up-side-down cat fell, hind legs swung straight at Barthow, knocking him down, and his wand went rolling down the steps towards the Dwarves. He fell on Klement and me, and we fell back as well. Monika avoided our clumsiness with a quick step back. She switched from her cage maintenance to the same spell Barthow had been using, stabbing at the underbelly of the cat. That motion made the cat's tails and front massive paws release, and it fell, essentially on Barthow, sprawled across his chest with its head and front legs. It began biting wildly at his face and chest, blood from the several head injuries splashing all over his facemask. With no wand, he was trying to wipe it off with his left hand and grab his pistol with his right.

Now the Dwarves were holding their fire, not wanting to hit us in a comingled pile on the floor. They flung their rifles up and over their shoulders and grabbed a tube off their waists or chests. Those tools opened into swords, axes, or battlehammers, according to their preference. They began attacking the rear of the massive cat, which stood and, with its muscular girth, took up three-quarters of the whole passageway. The panther just turned back for a second towards the Dwarves, to scream its cat-cry at them, then it went over Barthow and lunged towards the three of us at the back of the group. Klement and I had stood just in time to be leaning on the sides of the walls, and it was almost past us, when we looked at each other, and each grabbed a tail to keep it from Monika. The armor gave us incredible strength, and we were able to hold it. The Dwarves stepped past Barthow, who went downstairs to retrieve his wand. They began attacking it with their weapons, inflicting massive wounds, but aside from thrashing around, it kept trying to get Monika.

One of the strikes from the Dwarf with the axe sheared the tail off that Klement was holding. It turned and ripped across the front of his armor, exposing his clothing beneath, which was ripped, and he had a foot-long gouge beneath that. It bit his right arm, and the rear of the animal had his left arm pinned down by his waist. Klement screamed in agony as the steely teeth pierced his arm armor and sank into his muscles, and all easily heard a crack from one of the bones in his forearm. On instinct alone, I began striking it around the head with a fist. I at least had the foresight not to fire my pistol towards my friend. In the midst of this, I found a tiny split-second to thank my father for his instruction in firearms, which didn't need to be done, as I was in a magical family. This had the effect, however, of having the cornered, injured, blinded, dangerous animal turn its attention to me. As it released Klement, who fell slumped to the floor, one tail and one hind leg snapped backwards, throwing two of the Dwarves into the other two, and they all rolled back into Barthow, who was returning from retrieving his wand.

Almost in slow motion, the creature turned its broad, powerful, and blood-soaked head to my left thigh and bit cleanly through the armor. Afterwards, I saw where all four of its dagger-sized teeth pierced cleanly top-to-bottom, and vice versa, through the not-unsubstantial meat of my leg. Simultaneously, with the front left paw and a now free tail, it grabbed Monika, threw her against the wall next to me, and began snapping at her midsection with its teeth and claws. I turned to look, and it was more of a motion that was instinct than an attack, as it was finally dying. The attack from the swiping paw had broken off the plates at her belly, and she was bleeding from the injury, lying back against the wall. The cat's mouth kept snapping open, then slowly closing a few more times before stopping, and the whole mound of terrible predator went limp.

****

Far down below, in the chamber where Dolphus was put down, Corfus considered the knowledge he had collected from that wizard's depraved mind while verifying each of the oubliettes surrounding the main chamber was empty, safe, or sealed off forever. The Priests, who were convinced the space was clear of any lingering spiritual influences, came together with Corfus back at the large slab where the Hoplite lay broken and nearly dismembered.

"There are more of these in the world, aren't there?" The eldest asked.

"Yes. We are not sure where they all are, as the records of how many and where were not complete, even in my time." He stared blankly at the machine before them. "Do you feel sure it is safe from any more devilry here?" He leveled his eyes at the elder, then the others. They all nodded to him and each other in agreement, drawing closer to see the machine warrior of old.

"I must leave for a short time. There are things Dolphus knew, and others that only his niece, Runetta Lynchos, knows. I must get her and bring her here for further questioning." Corfus walked around the table towards the group of Priests, extending his hand to them in thanks.

"Thank you all, thank you," he shook each hand in turn and locked his stalwart, serious eyes with every one of them as he did. "There are two rooms in the castle above that you should go to now. One has books that you need to secure and take to the fortress of your order beneath the Vatican. Learn what you can." He took a step back from the group and looked upward briefly, then continued. "The other is the antechamber to Runetta's bedroom: heart jars, several hundred. Please see if there is anything other than standard dark magic associated with them. Tell the Dwarves I will return here, and please help the others; several are wounded. I must interrogate Runetta here before they seal this cavern for all time." He waited until the group had agreed on which task each couple would undertake. Corfus then disappeared, as only High Elves can.

The Priests arrived in the stairs' entrance cupola on the first floor, just as the Dwarves and Barthow were helping the other three of us down the last few steps, and set us up against the wall. When the Dwarves saw the Priests coming, Tinfer said, "Stand back, you lot. Let them work. We are going to that room at the front half of the castle to destroy that ancient technology." They proceeded back up the spiral stairs and left us with the Priests. Two stayed with us, and the rest ran up after the Dwarves.

"Where are them other Priests a'goin'?" Barthow asked, kneeling beside Klement, examining his wounds with his wand already glowing warm yellow at the tip. Barthow had already healed the more minor wounds on his own arm, but the buildup of blood inside the plates of his armor was still dripping out, depending on how he moved his arm, landing in the dust of the floor with a tap each time.

"They are all attending to things that Corfus and Tinfer saw through your helmets. The beasts are all gone, but knowledge is sometimes far more dangerous than any monster." The elder monk said, checking Monika's mid-section lacerations. Being familiar with Dwarvish equipment, he tapped a few times on the armband around her left forearm, and the armor began disassembling itself, just as it had formed on us, only in reverse.

"There, there, now I can get a look at those cuts." He said with calm surety in his voice. "Oooh, tssk, tssk. There is a foul festering from the mouth of that cat setting in here already." His wand moved, casting a blue light that was hard to look at. Monika smacked her mouth a couple of times, "Oh my, that, whatever you're doing is very odd, I have a taste in my mouth like a copper coin."

"That is actually a good sign, my dear. Don't worry yourself," and he continued his work. Monika, to this point at least, had not made a single murmur of disquiet over her injuries.

"I have to say, dear, you are managing the pain of that terrible wound with immense grace!" I said, leaning toward her and trying to speak privately. I am glad it isn't worse for you."

"Oh, it was terrible! I could feel the tearing of my skin as the teeth, then the broken shards of armor, broke into it! I don't understand this armor at all, but I did feel a pinprick in my side after the attack, and the pain seemed to fade very quickly. I think that may have had something to do with it, dear." She smiled, then grimaced as the monk worked to repair what he could.

"There, there. Monika, is it?" He looked up at her, who was still wincing with her eyes shut, but did nod in reply. "The Dwarves welcome their ladyfolk into the ranks of warriors. Precautions are made so that they can tolerate immense pain and continue fighting. You received some of the medicine that comes in all female warrior suits. Their whole culture venerates the mother and their supreme importance to the world."

The one monk attending to my wounds had also begun the process of my armor disappearing, and was quite a bit more expressive in his face at his prognosis of my injuries. It must have been bad, worse than I thought, as when the armor left my leg, the pulsing in my head got unbearable, and I passed out for a moment.

My head was wobbling around as I came to, the pain in my leg was searing hot now, and the monk had the end of his wand inside my leg, maybe three inches deep. I didn't know if he was cleaning it, healing, or what. I grasped the thigh above the wounds with both hands and gritted my teeth, trying to tolerate the pain and blood loss. As I clamped down, I felt the lightheadedness subside a bit. "Is that helping?" the monk asked, glancing briefly at me. "Seems to be, yes." So he retracted his wand from inside my leg and pointed it at the spot I was gripping. A notched belt with a buckle appeared and tightened up around my leg. I let go, and it threaded itself and latched, so I put both hands flat on the ground. "Okay, son, I will need you to roll over, flat on your stomach, so that I can clean and seal the ones on the back of your leg." I did as instructed, and he went to work on those four, or six, or however many holes were back there.

Another of the monks then came to us, from below, and stopped to help Barthow and Klement. He began by having their armor disassembled so that all injuries could be inspected.

"Work on Klement first, buddy. I've got mine," Barthow said, checking his arm and wiping blood away with a handkerchief.

Shifting his weight in his robe on his knees, the monk grabbed Klement's arm and wiped his blood away on the sleeve of his robe. "My name is Rufus. This doesn't look too bad." He rotated his forearm to check underneath, seeing it was alright, and went back to the top. Rufus laid his wand flat across the scratches, and the same intense blue light began sizzling, and Klement gave the same smacking sound, commenting on the strange taste of copper.

The elder monk working on my thigh had a look of un-settled desperation for a fleeting minute, then he decided to tell me what was concerning him. "I can not make these wounds clean properly. Are any of you having success?" he directed at the other clergymen.

"Honestly, sir, no. I can close the penetrations, but the torn or crushed areas that came in contact with the teeth and gums of that cat are not returning to normal, healthy tissue." Rufus said, and all of them looked back to their elder, nodding.

"Where is Corfus?" Monika asked. "He healed Raileanu before; maybe he can."

"He had to leave to try and find Runetta, as there may be other factors besides the horrors of this castle that must be stopped, or our battles here could be for naught. He said he will return as soon as he can." The elder stated, still focused on cleaning and healing my injuries. "I think we have stopped any bleeding. Does everyone feel as though we could move down to the room in the dungeon, that is where Corfus will return to?"

"I think so," Monika said. "That is a good idea, we should be ready when he does return. "Yeah, I feel as though I could," I said, and Klement agreed with a nod. That seemed like a good plan, but when we each tried to stand without the armor's assistance, we all gave up halfway and slumped back to the floor.

"No worries, we will levitate you there." The elder monk stood up, followed by the others, and Monika, Klement, and I were lifted by magic into our sitting positions, and we began the dizzying flight down the very tight spiral stairs to the lowest level. Between the floating, the blood loss, and still leaking, gory wounds, both Klement and I let our stomach's contents go on the wall, right before we made it to the room where the battle had taken place. There was a horrible stench lingering in the whole of that space. The smell of burning insects, the bile of creatures unknown until now, spread thick on the walls and floors, the bone-chilling stench of rotten earth that held decaying human and animal flesh alike, the distinct spike of electrical discharge from so much conjured lightning. On the huge stone slab in the center of the room was what looked like a broken suit of armor. Only later would the details of what all happened in this chamber be made clear to me.

****

Arriving on the train where everyone in the car was asleep, Corfus went to Hartge and touched his head ever so gently. Removing the memory of Runetta and replacing it with the knowledge of her secret chamber in the library in Portugal, and the plight of the twins enslaved there, he made the shackles on Runetta vanish. After contact with his mind, Corfus could also remove the knowledge of Runetta's capture from his boss and his colleague. Then he transported Hartge onto a train headed for Portugal, about 200 miles to the west. Corfus then disappeared with her to the room in Portugal where the twins were. Runetta hung limp in the air, behind and just to the right of Corfus. He immediately caused the one twin Looker who was awake to lie his head on the desktop and begin snoring gently. He acquired the Book from the space between the twins, and it disappeared somewhere into his person, as magical people often do to store things safely. Then, a cask with clean water and a tap appeared on the large table, along with a basket full of bread, apples, salted meats, dried beef, walnuts, and raisins. The slumber he cast on them would last for two days in waves, allowing them to eat and sleep in peace and comfort until Hartge could arrive to rescue them. A glance at the copy the twins were working on for the whole of the Glauer clan turned to ash, along with the twins' memories of the book.

The suffering of these two, their plight, and the truth of what they had been doing would be fine for Hartge and the Inspector General to learn of. Them having any of those materials the twins had been working on would not be. It should satisfy both to know Runetta was discovered, and this atrocity would shame them into obscurity for some time. Satisfied with the actions and decisions, Corfus returned to the room where Dolphus died with Runetta in tow.

The row of us wounded and being tended to by the Priests was directly across from where Corfus and Runetta arrived. We saw him appear, as he does, right in the middle of the array of destruction we were still coming to grips with. The pain in my leg was worsening, and I was starting to be concerned that even the work of the magic wasn't going to be enough. I let out a groan, gripping my leg again.

"What is it, Raileanu?" Corfus started towards us and leaned up against the wall.

"There was a Chromataphor Panther. It nearly killed all of us." I said through my teeth. Corfus actually knelt in front of me and looked at the injury. Looking to his left and right at all of us, then around further to his right and left, his long white hair swooshing to keep up.

"Where is Torsten?" Corfus said, looking for Tinfer.

Chapter Nineteen

T infer came down the stairs with what was left of Torsten. Corfus stood and lowered his head in reverence. A scream from the far side of the cavernous room echoed out, the cry of a female Dwarf. It was Wolly, and she ran at a full sprint towards Tinfer as he lay Torsten down. He stood, holding what was left of Torsten's helmet. Wolly fell to her knees before she even slowed, and slid next to his body. She went to wrap her arms around him, but recoiled when she saw Tinfer lay the remnants of his helmet on the ground by his shoulders. She let out a primal scream of loss and pain, the likes of which I had never heard before or since, then went silent. She drew in a deep breath, leaning back on her heels, hands in shaking fists, then threw her braided blonde hair back and cried "TORSTEN, NO!" before falling across him, going silent in grief, but for the staggered breaths and weeping.

Tinfer came over to where we were and looked up at Corfus before shaking his head, then looking down and adjusting his weight on his feet. "Next week would have been their hundred and fiftieth anniversary, Elf." he stood shaking his head, unable to speak at all. After a few minutes, he said, "I sent him because knowing what these evil witches and wizards were doing was vital to us all. Kafar, kafar all."

Corfus put his hand on Tinfer's shoulder, and after a moment, Tinfer looked up at him. "Torsten, my friend, your son, was quite honestly one of the greatest Dwarves I have ever known. Will you welcome me to his remembrance and stone-setting?" Tinfer nodded and returned to the side of his son and daughter-in-law. He knelt and held her.

"Raileanu, Barthow, Monika, and Klement. These wounds are different from normal mortal wounds. There are forces, tiny particles at work from the mouth of that creature that I cannot repair. I can stop the bleeding and heal the bones, but the deep penetrating wounds may not close." He looked to Monika then. "Yours are not from its teeth, here, those I can repair completely." Then, reaching to her with his large hand to cover the whole of her exposed stomach, the skin began to glow yellow, then red. When he pulled his hand away, it was as if nothing had happened to her at all. I let out a sigh of relief, a larger mass of air that I had been holding onto, fearing for her, that I didn't know I had. Corfus then went to work on the other three of us.

Dwarves and Priests were wandering around back and forth, Dwarves kicking corpses and parts of giant spiders and taking trophies. The Priests were performing rites and wandwork I knew nothing of on remains, door-frames, and around Dolphus's broken body. Runetta was still suspended in midair, five or six feet off the ground, completely limp, wrapped in a red silk sheet, as if asleep.

"Excuse me, Father, I didn't get your name," I said as the elder Priest walked by. "I did not give it. We have no names, we are just Priests from the magical order that serve God," He said, turning to walk to us. He had been at Dolphus before the others arrived there. "Yes, but that other Priest gave us his name," I said, pointing to him. He looked and smiled back. "Yes, he is a Priest from Mexico who has just joined our order. He is not fully initiated yet and, as such, retains his name. We are recruiting from outside the order to try and contain the rise in events such as this one," he went on about his business, then, inspecting the entrances to the oubliettes.

Klement looked at the elder Priest, "Forgive me, Father, the more I learn, the longer I live, the more I wonder about the nature of God. How can he allow this kind of darkness and danger to spread, or even exist at all?" Klement waved his hand at the whole room, then at us, and our injuries. The Priest gave a little smile, then looked at Corfus, who stood straight up, and almost appeared upset with the question. Klement looked back and forth at the two of them, concerned he had irritated a four-teen-thousand-year-old High Elf.

"Sir, do you not understand yet that the Creator has but one way to measure the hearts of men? There is only one truth, and no device, no knowledge, no machine can discern the truth in the hearts of men and women.

Only God can see into the heart, and mark my words of experience, before the end comes, none of you will be able to trust your eyes, ears, or hands. In those days, only God will know if you love, fear, and serve Him. He can only ascertain that if you are given free will to choose to follow Him, or worship yourselves and your creations." After Corfus had seen that Klement and the rest of us were content to consider his words, he turned and walked back to the slab in the center, beside which Runetta was still floating. As he neared it, Runetta's limp form turned to face him.

"What has Dolphus had you doing?" Corfus interlocked his fingers in front of himself, waiting for the response. Runetta's mouth was hanging slightly open, head tilted to the right just a bit. Her eyes were shut, and her face and limbs hung almost lifelessly.

Then, a weak, warbly groan began to emit from her, building in intensity, until her mouth jerked to form words. The speech was slurred and undefined. Monotone.

"*Watching*"

"Watching who?"

"*Whoever he thinks will be useful to him.*"

"I have seen all in Dolphus's mind. You cannot lie to me about what he is doing. I want to know what YOU have been doing in his service. You have not been fully honest with him.

"No."

The elder Priest turned to Corfus and asked, "Wouldn't it be faster just to read all of her mind as you did for Dolphus?"

"Faster, yes. Possible, no. I cannot absorb another entire human mind for some time. Only ten percent of the information I collected has any use to us, and I will have to purge the other ninety percent at a later time."

The Priest shook his head in understanding, turning back to the task of clearing this huge room of evil and witchcraft.

"Who is the man in the paintings, in your Vienna home, in Prague, and here?" Corfus went back to his line of questioning.

A long pause, before she tried to speak. Her lip quivered a moment, then a tear fell from the corner of her eye, which never moved or twitched.

"Bru...Brunell."

"Why do you have his image? Was Dolphus using him somehow?"

"He wanted to. He forced me to give him something—a piece of wood."

"Why, what kind of wood was it? I cannot see the memory of this in him?"

"I do not know. It had a worm in it, but..."

"But what?" Corfus now leaned slightly against the slab of stone, I figured, as slow as Runetta's words were coming, he knew this might take a while.

"When I began to watch him, I fell in love with him. In three days of watching, I was overcome with the brightness of life and hope he had for the world. I could not disobey

Dolphus, so I spent but ten minutes with him and gave him the piece of wood. I chose not to let him see anything in his crystal balls that would allow him to use this man further, especially involving me. To save him, to love him, all I could do was never go near him again."

"Is she serious? She was responsible for the death of Raileanu's mother! For so many in Texas! She has a room full of jars with human hearts in them!" Monika said to Corfus, furious at what she felt was a ruse.

"She cannot lie in this state. Whatever she says here is true." Corfus never looked in acknowledgment of us.

"How did she even learn of the illness my father had?" I asked. "Her interest in Monika in Austria, or my family at all, is what led to their deaths."

Corfus was silent, but looking at Runetta, I suspect asking her the question, maybe agreeing it was worth asking. So much slow talking, with weak control over her face; she now had a long stream of drool running from the lower corners of her mouth onto her blanket or bedsheet, which she arrived wrapped in. It looked like a long black streak on the blood-red silk.

"Dark wizards and witches always watch the Tellafrog family. Many ancient plans have been thwarted by those who can speak with frogs. Black masses in hidden places at night almost always have a frog or toad as a witness. That's how Dolphus saw the illness and how it spread. He told me to send someone to look for an Orb. They say it can do many things and is no mere crystal ball. So I sent one."

"Who is the changeling foxbat who was in your house in Prague?" Corfus moved on, seeing that I was satisfied with her answer.

"She is my half sister. When her mother revealed her as his child, Dolphus cursed her to be a huge bat anytime she is outside at night. I am the only one who cares for her at all. Please don't hurt her. She eats only fruit and insects; she is nineteen years old, just a child. She has never hurt anyone."

Corfus closed his eyes, and - I later learned - released the girl from the custody of the Magical Inquisitor. She was returned to her mother, and the curse was removed. What these Elves can do, and honestly what they cannot, is still amazing and baffling to me.

"I need a list of every person Dolphus told you to interact with and what you did when interacting with them. He does not have any memories of viewing the crystal balls for each job he sent you on. I have seen what he has done to you, child. Would you help me, now that he is gone?"

Without delay, her weak, low, and slow voice responded.

"He is dead?"

"Open your eyes, child. He lies right there." Corfus slowly pointed to the heap of quartz armor and his lifeless form.

She did open her eyes, one at a time and very slowly. Almost as if the organ of the eye was allowed to absorb the sight, without reaction, then they closed. Now tears fell from both closed eyes, rolling over the surface of her blushing, round cheeks and onto the silken wrap again.

"*Yes, I can help, unless I am your prisoner like I was to him.*"

"No, no prisoners, we just want to undo what he has tried to do. Who else knows of this place, Runetta?"

"*No one since my mother passed. Not even my half sister Kora.*"

"What is the family name of the two men you have held as werewolves at the entrance to this castle? Why did you keep them and not heal them?"

"*Carinfor. They are the Carinfor twins. Dolphus was afraid of them. He had been hurt by a werewolf before and almost died. It was all he feared; when they were brought to me to heal, I wanted to keep Dolphus away more than help them. I took much more care of them than he did of me. I never hurt them.*"

Again, Corfus lifted his head and transported them back to their family home, into the upstairs bedroom of the Carinfor family estate, he told me later. At that time, they occupied Rustoy Manor in England, keepers of the tunnels and chambers that led to the contact point with the Norse Dwarves. That domain stretched from almost Gibraltar to Northern Finland of today's maps, their most recent collaboration with humans being the Norse, in the 200s AD. No other groups, save the Irish in 200BC, had dealt with them in as many years.

Tinfer walked into the midst of Corfus and us then, with clear intent to interrupt with what he thought was a more important line of questioning, hand held high. "Just get to the point, Elf. Where did she get that Orb? Where did she get the Hoplite? Are there more?"

"You are right." He looked back at Runetta, who had stopped crying. "Where did this metal soldier come from?"

"*A false crystal ball sold to me by Mason Stringfellow had hidden magical text within it, describing it and its location. Deep in a great canyon of the New World. In a long, deep cave. Off the side of the canyon. At an arch near a large carved-stone chamber, inscriptions told me I needed the whole Orb, but it had only half, locked away in its tunnels. Something had broken it intentionally. I don't know where the other half is.*"

"Dolphus found the other half watching Barthow. It was in a cave six hundred miles north of where you found yours, protected by wild giants, who just used it for warmth." Corfus turned to us to explain. "I saw the giants that were attacking the Ute Indians of the region." Barthow spoke up then, "Them's the ones I went after, huh?" Corfus gave him a nod and looked back at us. "I sent Barthow to find them. This Orb is different from the ones I have seen before, and I cannot destroy it or break it, as this one was. I don't know what can."

"Do you know the guardian of the Orb?" Tinfer asked Corfus.

"No. I know nothing of this one." He raised his gaze back to Runetta. "Did the cave you found indicate the origin or Guardian of this Orb?"

"*Yes. Sealed there in its broken half by its creators, after catastrophe eighteen thousand eight hundred years before.*

343

When the Earth was cracking from the mistakes of sound, the Orb was broken by its Guardian. The first Glass Hydra. That is all I know."

"Show me in your mind the location." Corfus concentrated for a moment, then asked, "Give me the names and influence of the people alive today that Dolphus had you interact with, Runetta."

"Uuh. I remember a few. He began erasing my mind periodically from what he had me doing, after Brunell, and he suspected my betrayal. Pasteur. I told him how fascinating it was that milk grew curds not a year ago. I gave him a broad smile and told him how handsome he was."

"A man named Faraday. Dolphus asked me to give him an amber rod wrapped in a rabbit pelt as a gift, remarking on how the sparks they made made me tingle. That was around ten years ago."

"Last year, in Belfast, I anonymously gave a book as a gift to a boy on his birthday in June. It was a book on mathematics, if I remember. That is all. I can remember no more."

"Do you know them?" Klement asked Corfus.

"No, but I can learn about them. I think they are bound for the sciences. Dolphus intends to accelerate the world's technology, using ordinary people as pawns. God only knows what further influences he may have intended if they excel in those areas."

"What about the Glass Hydra, do you know anything of that?" Monika asked. She was right to, there is no recorded existence of Hydras, and any writing is truly considered fantastical. All of us were hoping none of

THOSE stories were true. They were massive, incredibly intelligent, and single-minded.

"There are no instances of them being real in the fourteen thousand years that I have witnessed. She did say the Orb and reference to the hydra were at a time of collapse, even before the time of the High Elves, and the Calamity we lived through, which was the beginning of your age." Corfus paused then, as though listening, cocked his head to the left a little, his eyes darting around. "Oh no."

The remaining Priests and Dwarves came down from upstairs, then the Dwarves went to Tinfer. Trinew stopped and stood tall, at attention in front of Tinfer. "We destroyed all the heart jars and old technology. We found the ganglemorph that tried to hide, and obliterated it, not a speck left of it," she said.

"Good work. Corfus, can we destroy this place now, seal it up with stone forever?" Tinfer asked over his shoulder.

"May we wait a while? I may need to refer back to these things again soon. I can give you my word that I will seal it if you like." He said, still attentive to something else.

"No, we will do it, Elf. My son has died here; I demand the right to do it. It will be a monumental tomb for him." Tinfer didn't even tilt his head to deliver this ultimatum.

"Understood, my friend. We may have another problem. I have just learned that the Glass Hydra isn't a myth; it is on its way to the mountain above us. I will take the Orb to it and attempt to reason with it. I can stop it on my own if it is unreasonable. Please, may I take it?" Tinfer had set it down at the head of the slab and brought it to him, thrusting the handle at him. "You swear on your life, Elf, that thing never finds its way to the world of men, magical or not." He stared at Corfus, and the fury and certitude in his eyes projected authority to everyone in the room watching. "Of course, my life is yours if that were to happen." The Dwarf released the handle and walked into his group of fighters. He turned back to all of us, pointing his stumpy yet mighty index finger at all of us, the Elf and Priests included, "Get out of here. Do not return to this place." Then, he turned, and together, they began carrying Torsten up and out of the room.

"Raileanu, Monika, Barthow - I am sending you straight to your home in Texas. Remain there until I come to you. Klement - I will send you back to the Metternich home in Vienna. You will not be seen. Monika, would you please invite Haizek Moon and Mason Stringfellow to visit you in Texas, and ensure they know it is urgent and imperative. I must speak with them as soon as possible, and will come when I see they have arrived at the privacy and safety of Raileanu's home."

"Alright, sir, yes," Monika said. The Priests were all finished with what they could do for us, and even the work of Elf magic hadn't solved the injuries. She looked at me, and I nodded in agreement that we were ready to move if that was what we needed to do. I certainly didn't want to see a Hydra of any kind. I was okay with taking the Elf's generosity to get us home, since runeshifting was actually very exhausting, and I was in no shape to do it now.

Corfus had been watching us as we all conferred with looks and nods. Then he picked up the canister containing the Orb. When he saw we were ready, concerned about the impending arrival of a powerful creature none of us could fight, he delivered all of us to the predetermined locals.

Monika and I were deposited on the sofa in the living room of my family home in Central Texas before either of us could blink. Alone now, we both exhaled and sank into the thick cushions. Barthow was behind me and to the right, in my father's chair, with his wounds elevated. He too relaxed into it after the long period of high stress and battle.

"Oohf, y'all. I am glad to be back in Texas, dunno about y'all." Barthow said while taking deep breaths. He threw his head back on the chair. "I do hope that thar Elf hann'ls whatever a hydro thing is. Ain't nun of us able to much fer a few days." The heat of September, and the humidity in contrast to the cold, still dry air of the giant cavern that housed the castle, and Austria before that, lay heavy on us, but for a change felt good. Our voices must have made it outside, as the bleating of Momma's goats came in through a back window. Glancing around the room, even my hat was delivered with us, sitting on the coatrack at the front door.

CHAPTER TWENTY

What follows is the account Corfus explained to me after he came to visit us later.

He appeared at the peak of Hochosterwitz Castle's highest tower. It was three o'clock in the morning, overcast, with barely any light coming through the fast-moving clouds that night. He cast everyone inside into a deep sleep, then turned his attention to the small hamlets in the whole of the valley, ensuring all of the people, and for that matter, the animals as well, fell into a deep slumber. The arrival of a gigantic, six-headed transparent dragon - for all intents and purposes - would be challenging to conceal otherwise. He waited only five or six minutes, precise time is hard to garner from an Elf's telling, before the sound of its wings became audible. Like the thick hemp sheeting of a massive galleon ship in changing winds, they whooped and snapped as it came and lit on the wall opposite Corfus.

It was enormous, a hundred feet tall, and its dual tails with pointed barbs wrapped around the turret on the side of the castle. It kept the massive wings spread wide, intimidation or stretching, Corfus did not know. He knew nothing of this beast. The outer four of the six heads had four long, twisted horns facing forward like a Jacob's Sheep, were ten feet long each, and glistened in the passing moonlight like fearsome icicles. The two heads in the center each had one horn, like a single spike, also ten feet long. Observing each other for a moment, Corfus noticed the two center heads seemed to move in perfect unison. Sparkling scales, lit from the moonlight passing through its body, covered the ancient serpent. He could see the internal organs also in this light. Their outlines at least. Undulating heart and lungs. The intestines and stomach are churning like a giant cauldron of pythons. The two center heads seemed to gaze at a tiny red dot in the deep blue blanket of night, different from the sparkling white specs of other stars in the sky. Then, in perfect unison, the two center heads looked right at Corfus, measuring him. The feet, built more like five-fingered hands, gripped and reset themselves constantly, grinding stones and grit off the structure as it did. The booming, drawn-out speech, perfect in dialect and pronunciation, began as a rumble from deep within the creature.

"You came after me, Elf. I am older than you." The gaze of the Glass Hydra fell from Corfus's eyes to the container at his side, which held the Orb. "You have what is mine."

"You broke this Orb?" Corfus asked, hoping for a helpful answer.

"Yes. It poisoned the world once." The slender, crystalline forked tongue flicked out after each word now, testing the air.

"How long have you been here?" Corfus hoped polite conversation would increase his understanding of this ancient serpent. He noticed slivers of light moving all up and down the length of the creature, from eyes to the huge claws at the end of each toe, like the tiniest representation of lightning possible to witness, bound up in the nervous system of the Hydra.

"Half a million times I have circled the sun, Elf. Grrrmmmrrar! I see now you crave only knowledge, Elf." The four heads sprang from the ringing center pair and flailed discordantly, angry, and more rocks broke under the shifting weight of the action, falling to the courtyard below with complex, cracking sounds. Two fist-sized areas of golden light appeared in the translucent beast, near where Corfus calculated the Hydra's heart might be, then a pulse of energy burst forth from the creature, the shockwave nearly knocked Corfus off balance, which is not easily achieved against the footing of a High Elf, I assure you. "You know nothing. You offer nothing. I cannot let you have that. I must break it again. I can do this while you hold it; it makes no difference to me."

Immediately, and after he had regained his footing, Corfus threw up his hand to the beast, offering what he hoped would be seen as a peaceful gesture. "I *need* you to break it again. I do not want it. I am trying to protect the world from all things like this."

"Give it to me. Or I will take it and end your time here."

"I will, but I can offer you something in return for breaking it."

"I have walked the dark side of the moon for a thousand years, my twelve eyes scanning the vast expanse of space for reason, for another like myself. I watched your kind rise and leave this world. It gave me hope for a moment. Then you, as the others before you, fell. I have walked the surface of the earth in three formations of its crust, oceans, and ice. I watched from afar as each one called the Son of Man taught, and felt hope again for you all. I stood in dismay when he fell, observing as the Creator flashed his body into light, and marveled at the beauty of His design. I watched the humans crush every light that came among them, in every nation. So, what can you offer me, puny creature? You are barely more than those humans."

"I can take you to another world. A world where you can continue your search. Where these despicable affronts to the Creator can remain outside the reach of man."

"What world? I see your *emites*, they cannot do that. I have seen older and more sophisticated *emites* than yours. They cannot move me to The Red World, I see your mind, Elf." Corfus explained later to me that emites, he gathered, were what the Glass Hydra called the particles he had tried to explain to me that allow the use of magic.

"Yes. Indeed, they can. I know how you travel. You must have seen it, been there, to travel there, yes?"

"Yes." The expression of the Hydra's central heads changed to, well, almost a curious stare. The scaled brow above each of the center heads relaxed from their fierce gaze just a moment before. Even the four outer heads stopped their flailing and turned intently towards Corfus. "How is that possible, your *emites* are so primitive?"

"I cannot see your, *emites* as you call them. I can only assume that yours are so special, so precise, that the abilities are far beyond what I can imagine. While mine are primitive compared to yours, their power is far less specific, but designed for maximum focus on whatever I choose. I can travel through the tunnel behind the wake of light and choose my time to exit, allowing me to approach a place before choosing the exact spot where my form appears. This tunnel is outside the confines of time, or beneath it, so this is not difficult for me." The Hydra's central heads raised as he spoke, eyes twitching a bit but never leaving Corfus, as if considering what had been said, and the viability of this procedure.

"Take me there, teach me that, as I can alter my *emites* at will, and I agree to the terms." The central heads said in perfect, thunder-like, resounding unison.

"Break this for the sake of the world, and you alone can guard its collected remains on the Red World for all time. That, I can offer."

"Agreed, Elf." The Glass Hydra leapt into the courtyard, the outer four heads wisping around the interior as cobras move, scanning the darker corners of the space, while the central heads looked up at Corfus. It then lifted its front right foot, indicating that is where it wanted the Orb placed. The center of this courtyard was not cut stone placed by men. It was solid, shaped granite of the spire upon which the castle was built. "This rock is solid for over two thousand feet, Elf. Place it here under my foot, then take me as promised so that I may explore the New World."

Corfus dislocated from the tower directly in front of the building-sized animal, and gently set the canister in the appropriate spot, then walked backwards to the edge of the courtyard. He then called up a sphere of protection for himself that glimmered like thin sapphire, and waited. Raising its foot another ten feet, the arm bulging with translucent muscles as big around as a stone footbridge, it then stomped down, shaking the entire mountain. It ground the fist onto the granite, the two central heads still locked in simultaneous motions, looked down, grimacing at the task. The deafening cracks and squeaks of grinding glass echoed in the walls of the fortress, streams of fiery-orange sparks began pouring out across the ground, bouncing like smooth stones thrown across a pond, until, at once, a crack like the loudest thunder rippled up and out of the walls and into the clouds. The Hydra lifted its foot and looked. Two halves, ragged and uneven, lay there, with a small pile of glass dust between them.

"Forth. My name is Forth, Elf. Take me there now as agreed." It rumbled at Corfus.

"Corfus, my friend, my name is Corfus. Let us go then." He stepped forward to the Hydra. Forth used the head to the left of the center two to gingerly pick up the halves, handing one to the next head over, to keep them apart. The head to the right of center then came in directly over the pile of ground glass, slowly opening its jaws to ninety degrees, then let out a column of blue-white energy, like pure white light, for only a few seconds. When the fire stopped, the pile of glass was gone. "I will have to touch you to take you there. Is that alright?"

The Hydra's center heads looked at Corfus, then one of the tails came around the side of the legs and stopped midair beside Corfus. Looking at each other, Corfus took his right hand and set it on the spike of the tail, and they were both gone.

****

Klement arrived at home, and his wife immediately came to assess the events and his injuries. To no avail, the wounds suffered by the Chromataphor Panther never healed properly and caused him trouble the rest of his days. As the story goes, his wonderful children may have been told of his battle with a huge, mythical beast, but to most it was attributed to old battle wounds or to falling off a horse, depending on the company. I remained close with Klement and his children throughout the rest of my life. Duties and the injuries meant he only visited my home in Texas twice the rest of his life, one being my wedding with Monika the following spring. We moved it there, since all those in attendance would be magical, except for Klement, and my wounds and difficulty travelling were far worse than his. He insisted, in fact, that we do it in Texas. Agreeing to retain my salary and title, although I could not teach, allowed us to stay and raise a family in Texas as long as we could produce one book of instruction-worthy material every two years. That was as much as either of us could hope for, and we were much satisfied with it.

Monika did as Corfus asked and wrote to both Mason Stringfellow and Haizek Moon, asking them to come to Texas at their earliest convenience. They replied within two weeks. Both agreed that the earliest they could promise any time would be at our wedding, for which both promised a month's stay. Corfus did not return for two whole weeks after sending us home. We hoped and prayed each day that he was alright and that the meeting with the Glass Hydra would be profitable and not dangerous.

The Inquisitor General, Hartge, and his group did exactly as Corfus hoped: they freed the twins in Portugal and found nothing out of the ordinary beyond their detention and conditions. Corfus and the Priests had secreted away the tomes of specific interest. Supposedly, word reached the Order that there were several secret compartments in that library containing works forbidden by the magical world that Corfus didn't detect. We learned ten years later that Corfus had put Runetta on the steps of St Paul's Church in Zurich, Switzerland. We weren't sure why. That was just before he went to face the Glass Hydra, and she was the one who told the Order about the secret places. It was not the last time we dealt with her, but for the time being, she had honestly changed her ways. She abandoned influence, drunken high-society balls and parties altogether, and was seen in cathedrals in prayer more than once by Priests who report to the Order.

While convalescing at home, Monika and I spent the first week together without any incidents since everything began. By the time work on the wedding started, we had held each other a dozen times in tear-drenched silence at our fortune to be alive, and together. A dozen more times, at the prevalence of death and injury that had enveloped us in the past couple of months. Each time we hoped the wave of uncontrollable weeping would be the last, but it was difficult to digest all the events in such a short time, and the profound changes to one's life, ideas of existence, and plans for the future. I know that God did not design us to trudge through the mire of life alone, and these events had only made it so apparent that I couldn't imagine having gone through all this alone. The next chapter was upon us, our visitors, wedding guests, and the merry month of it all fast approached...

The vicious spectral wolf that has followed me, that has tempted me to run into the wild, to attack those who irritate me, came to me the first night home, in my dreams. At first, I jerked away from it, prowling at the end of my bed towards me - it was not on my mental leash as it should be. It paced back and forth. The yellow eyes that had always pulsed with their own light were now a pale, unlit yellow. It never took its gaze off me, but now it wasn't intimidating, nor inviting me to run with it. Once my demeanor had settled into the new arrangement, and it sensed it, the animal walked to the side of the bed, coming closer to me. It rested its chin on my leg, and I could tell it understood the injuries I had sustained and wanted to be my companion, not the feral associate that any family or friends would despise as it had been. It was very comforting, and was one more thing I could set aside that I had been dragging along behind me my whole life.

Each morning, for twenty-four years at that point, I would wake and remind myself that I had been born magical and had lost it as a child, seemingly by chance. Henceforth, I had determined that all of it, loss of magic included, was part of a plan that we can only see the beauty and brilliance of the older we get. So, proceed as an ordinary person, who was granted access - albeit limited - to the magical world as long as I could supply things of value to that world. Decide each day what I can work on to provide value, thereby securing my place in that world. I would begin going through all the plant and animal discoveries that may lie just outside the door in my mind, and how I would exploit them to those ends. Then, I would feel the growl of this spectral dog, hot and vibrating against my skin. It would grab my ankle and grind its long canines into my bones and tendons, reminding me that I am truly unredeemable, unremarkable, and unworthy of such a life. Trying to lure me into the wild, never to return. Even at thirty-five years old, taking that animal by the scruff, collaring it, and putting my imaginary bootheel on its head was something I had to do every day. The desire to continually strive to be a wild animal was passing. I knew now, after this unusual visit in my dreams, that it would not require that of me any longer, that it would be a calming, protective force of my spirit for the rest of my days.

About the author

A fourth-generation Texan and U.S. Army veteran, Torin lives with his wife on a small hobby farm in East Texas. A devoted Christian, he is the proud father of four and grandfather of two. His historical fantasy fiction series blends rich settings with imaginative storytelling, using science-based explanations to ground fantastical elements in realism. Drawing on his faith, heritage, and life experiences, he writes with a passion for exploring the intersection of science, history, and the unseen.

The Tellafrog Series:
- Tellafrog: Part One (Released July 2025)

- Tellafrog: Two (Released January 2026)

- Tellafrog: Stringfellow-Moon (Expected Summer 2026)

- Tellafrog: The Last Elf (Expected Winter 2026)

- Tellafrog: (yet to be named – Expected Summer 2027)